TIME
MANIFOLD 1

Voyager

STEPHEN BAXTER

TIME

MANIFOLD I

HarperCollins*Publishers*

Voyager
HarperCollins*Publishers*
77–85 Fulham Palace Road,
Hammersmith, London W6 8JB
http//www.voyager-books.com

Published by *Voyager* 1999
3 5 7 9 10 8 6 4 2

A catalogue record for this book
is available from the British Library

ISBN 0 00 225768 8

Typeset in Sabon and Gill Sans by
Palimpsest Book Production Limited,
Polmont, Stirlingshire

Printed and bound in Great Britain by
Clays Ltd, St Ives plc

To two space cadets:
My nephew, James Baxter
Kent Joosten, NASA

Reid Malenfant:

You know me. And you know I'm a space cadet.

You know I've campaigned for, among other things, private mining expeditions to the asteroids. In fact, in the past I've tried to get you to pay for such things. I've bored you with that often enough already, right?

So tonight I want to look a little further out. Tonight I want to tell you why I care so much about this issue that I devoted my life to it.

The world isn't big enough any more. You don't need me to stand here and tell you that. We could all choke to death, be extinct in a hundred years.

Or we could be on our way to populating the Galaxy.

Yes: the Galaxy. Want me to tell you how?

Turns out it's all a question of economics.

Let's say we set out to the stars. We might use ion rockets, solar sails, gravity assists. It doesn't matter.

We'll probably start as we have in the Solar System, with automated probes. Humans may follow. One per cent of the helium-3 fusion fuel available from the planet Uranus, for example, would be enough to send a giant interstellar ark, *each ark containing a billion people*, to *every* star in the Galaxy. But it may be cheaper for the probes to manufacture humans in situ, using cell synthesis and artificial womb technology.

The first wave will be slow, no faster than we can afford. *It doesn't matter*. Not in the long term.

When the probe reaches a new system, it phones home, and starts to build.

Here is the heart of the strategy. A target system, we assume, is uninhabited. We can therefore anticipate massive exploitation of the system's resources, without restraint, by the probe. Such resources are useless for any other purpose, *and are therefore economically free to us.*

I thought you'd enjoy that line. There's nothing an entrepreneur likes more than the sound of the word 'free'.

More probes will be built and launched from each of the first wave of target stars. The probes will reach new targets; and again, more probes will be spawned, and fired onward. The volume covered by the probes will grow rapidly, like the expansion of gas into a vacuum.

Our ships will spread along the spiral arm, along lanes rich with stars, farming the Galaxy for humankind.

Once started, the process will be self-directing, self-financing. It would take, the double-domes think, ten to a hundred million years for the colonization of the Galaxy to be completed in this manner. *But we must invest merely in the cost of the initial generation of probes.*

Thus the cost of colonizing the Galaxy will be less, in real terms, than that of our Apollo program of fifty years ago.

This vision isn't mine alone. It isn't original. The rocket pioneer Robert Goddard wrote an essay in 1918 – *ninety-two years ago* – called 'The Ultimate Migration', in which he imagined space arks built from asteroid materials carrying our far-future descendants away for the death of the sun. The engineering detail has changed; the essence of the vision hasn't.

We can do this. If we succeed, we will live forever.

The alternative is extinction.

And, people, when we're gone, we're *gone*.

As far as we can see we're alone, in an indifferent universe. We see no sign of intelligence *anywhere* away from Earth. We may be the first. Perhaps we're the last. It took so long for the Solar System to evolve intelligence it seems unlikely there will be others, *ever*.

If we fail, then the failure is for all time. If we die, mind and consciousness and soul die with us: hope and dreams and love, everything that makes us human. There will be nobody even to mourn us.

To be the first is an awesome responsibility. It's a responsibility we must grasp.

I am offering you a practical route to an *infinite* future for mankind, a future of *unlimited* potential. Some day, you know it, I'll come back to you again for money: seedcorn money, that's all, so we can take a first step – *self-financing even in the medium*

2

term – beyond the bounds of Earth. But I want you to see why I'll be doing that. Why I must.

We can do this. We *will* do this. We're on our own. It's up to us.

This is just the beginning. Join me.

Thank you.

Michael:

This is what I have learned, Malenfant. This is how it is, how it was, how it came to be.

In the afterglow of the Big Bang, humans spread in waves across the universe, sprawling and brawling and breeding and dying and evolving. There were wars, there was love, there was life and death. Minds flowed together in great rivers of consciousness, or shattered in sparkling droplets. There was immortality to be had, of a sort, a continuity of identity through replication and confluence across billions upon billions of years.

Everywhere they found life.

Nowhere did they find mind – save what they brought with them or created – no *other* against which human advancement could be tested.

With time, the stars died like candles. But humans fed on bloated gravitational fat, and achieved a power undreamed of in earlier ages.

They learned of other universes from which theirs had evolved. Those earlier, simpler realities too were empty of mind, a branching tree of emptiness reaching deep into the hyperpast.

It is impossible to understand what minds of that age – the peak of the species, a race hundreds of billions of times older than your mankind, Malenfant – were *like*. They did not seek to acquire, not to breed, not even to learn. They had nothing in common with us, their ancestors of the afterglow.

Nothing but the will to survive. And even that was to be denied them by time.

The universe aged: indifferent, harsh, hostile and ultimately lethal.

There was despair and loneliness.

There was an age of war, an obliteration of trillion-year memories, a bonfire of identity. There was an age of suicide, as the finest of

3

humanity chose self-destruction against further purposeless time and struggle.

The great rivers of mind guttered and dried.

But some persisted: just a tributary, the stubborn, still unwilling to yield to the darkness, to accept the increasing confines of a universe growing inexorably old.

And, at last, they realized that *this was wrong*. It wasn't supposed to have been like this.

Burning the last of the universe's resources, the final down-streamers – dogged, all but insane – reached to the deepest past. And – oh.

Watch the Moon, Malenfant. Watch the Moon. It's starting –

I
—

BOOTSTRAP

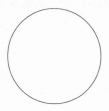

What seest thou else
In the dark backward and abysm of time?
WILLIAM SHAKESPEARE

Emma Stoney:

Of course Emma had known that Reid Malenfant – failed astronaut, her ex-husband, her current boss – had been buying up Space Shuttle rocket engines and static-firing them in the California desert. She'd thought it was all part of an elaborate waste-disposal plan.

She hadn't known he was planning to use the rockets to reach the asteroids.

Not until Cornelius Taine told her about it.

About that, and a lot more besides.

'. . . Ms Stoney.'

The voice was soft, dry, and it startled her. Emma straightened up from her softscreen.

There was a man standing before her, here in the pastel light of her Las Vegas office: a thin Caucasian, 1980s pinstripe suit, neatly cropped hair. 'I surprised you. I'm sorry. My name's Cornelius,' he said. 'Cornelius Taine.'

Neutral accent. Boston? He looked about forty. She saw no sign of cosmetic enhancement. High cheekbones. Stress muscles around his eyes.

How the hell had he gotten in here?

She reached for the security touchpad under her desk. 'I didn't notice you come in.'

He smiled. He seemed calm, rational, business-like. She lifted her finger off the button.

He stretched out his hand and she shook it; his palm was dry and soft, as if even his perspiration was under control. But she didn't enjoy the touch. Like handling a lizard, she thought. She let go of the hand quickly.

She said, 'Have we met before?'

'No. But I know of you. Your picture is in the company reports.

Not to mention the gossip sites, from time to time. Your complicated personal history with Reid Malenfant –'

He was making her uncomfortable. 'Malenfant is kind of high profile,' she conceded.

'You call him *Malenfant*.' He nodded, as if storing away the fact.

'You're with the corporation, Mr Taine?'

'Actually it's *Doctor*. But please, call me Cornelius.'

'Medical doctor?'

'The other sort.' He waved a hand. 'Academic. Mathematics, actually. A long time ago. Yes, in a manner of speaking, I am with Bootstrap. I represent one of your major shareholder groups. That's what got me past your very conscientious secretary in the outer office.'

'Shareholders? Which group?'

'We work through a number of dummies.' He looked at her desk. 'No doubt when you get back to your softscreen you'll soon be able to determine which, and the extent of our holdings. Ultimately, I work for Eschatology, Inc.'

Oh, shit. Eschatology, as far as she knew, was one of those UFO-hunting nut groups which were attracted to Malenfant's enterprises like flies.

He watched her, apparently knowing what she was thinking.

'Why are you here, Dr Taine?'

'Cornelius, please. Naturally we wish to check on how your husband is using our money.'

'Ex-husband. You can do that through the company reports or the press.'

He leaned forward. 'But I don't recall any news releases about this waste-reduction enterprise in the Mojave.'

'You're talking about the rocket plant. It's a new project,' she said vaguely. 'Speculative.'

He smiled. 'Your loyalty is admirable. But you've no need to defend Malenfant, Ms Stoney. I'm not here to criticize or obstruct. Divert, perhaps.'

'Divert what?'

'The trajectory of Reid Malenfant's covert activities. I'm talking about his true purpose, beneath all the misdirection.'

'True purpose?'

'Come now. You don't think anyone believes an entrepreneur with Malenfant's track record is reconditioning man-rated rocket

8

engines *just* to burn industrial waste, do you? . . .' He studied her. 'Or perhaps you truly don't know the truth. How remarkable. In that case we both have much to learn.' He smiled easily. 'We believe Malenfant's motives are sound – that's why we invest in him – although his objectives are too narrow. I saw his speech in Delaware the other night. Impressive stuff: colonizing the Galaxy, immortality for mankind. Of course, he hasn't thought it through.'

'Would you believe me if I said I don't know what the hell you're talking about?'

'Oh, yes.' He eyed her. His eyes were a pale blue, the colour of the skies of her California childhood, long gone. 'Yes, now that I've met you, I believe you. Perhaps we understand your ex-husband better than you do.'

'And what is it you understand about him?'

'That he's the only man who can save the human race from the coming catastrophe.' He said it without inflection.

She had absolutely no idea how to reply. The moment stretched.

Once more she wondered if this man was dangerous.

On impulse, she decided to cancel the rest of her day and drive out to Malenfant's desert operation. Maybe, all things considered, it was time to see it for herself. And she invited Cornelius along for the ride.

She called ahead to let Malenfant know she was on the way. But, working on the principle that she should never miss a chance to make Malenfant's life more difficult, she didn't warn him about Cornelius Taine.

Out of Vegas she took the I-15, the main route to LA three hundred miles away. Out of town she was able to cut in the SmartDrive. The car's limiter, controlled by the invisible web of satellites far above, switched out as the automatic control took over, and her speed rose smoothly through a hundred and fifty miles per hour.

As the sun climbed, the air grew hotter. She rolled up her window, felt the air conditioning cool and moisten the air.

Without warning Cornelius said, as if resuming an interrupted conversation, 'Yes, the Delaware speech was interesting. But something of a throwback for Malenfant. He's usually much more discreet about his true ambitions . . .'

When Malenfant had first started making money, as a small-scale aerospace consultant, he had spread himself over the media arguing for an expansion of American effort in space: a new generation of

9

heavy launchers, new manned vehicles, a return to the Moon. He talked about the riches waiting in space, escape from Malthusian limits to growth, the ability to save the species from such calamities as an asteroid collision with the Earth, and so forth. The usual space-buff propaganda.

Cornelius said, 'The image Malenfant built of himself was clear. Here was a man who was rich and was destined to get richer, and who was clearly prepared to throw some of his money at the old dreams of space. But then his businesses started to struggle. Isn't that true? . . .'

It was true. Investors had grown wary of this talk-show visionary. Space was important for business, but business only cared about the constellations of utilitarian satellites in low Earth orbit, for communications and weather and surveillance. Thus far and no further.

And Malenfant attracted no support from serious agencies – particularly from NASA. NASA had long grown wary of frightening away its political backers by thinking too big, and was focused on doing sexy science with small, cheap unmanned probes, while sustaining the careers and empires associated with the giant bureaucracy which ran the manned space programme, with its ageing Shuttle fleet and a half-built and much-delayed Space Station.

In fact Malenfant himself started to attract unwelcome personal attention. There were bar-room psychoanalysts all over the media who found a common pattern in his failure to have kids, his frustrated ambition to fly in space, and his lofty ambitions for the future of man. And then there were the kooks – the conspiracy theorists, the UFO nuts, the post-New Age synthesists, the dreaming obsessives – none of whom had anything to offer Malenfant but bad PR.

Then along had come the yellow babies in Florida, and even NASA space launches were suspended, and that seemed to be that.

As Cornelius talked, she discreetly booted up the car's softscreen and referenced Cornelius Taine.

Thirty-eight years old. Born in Texas, not that you'd know it from the accent. Once a professional mathematician, an academic. *Brilliant* was the word used in the brief biog she found.

A full professor at Princeton at twenty-seven. Washed out at thirty.

She couldn't find out why, or what he'd been doing since then. She set off a couple of data miners to answer those questions for her.

After the yellow babies, Malenfant had regrouped.

He disappeared from the TV screens. He continued to fund educational efforts – books, TV shows, movies. Emma, working within the Bootstrap corporation, saw no harm in that, nothing but positive PR, and tax-efficient besides. But in public Malenfant largely withdrew from his propagandizing, and withheld any investment from what he started to call the 'pie-in-the-sky stuff'.

And, quietly, he began to build a seriously large business empire. For instance, he had pioneered the mining of methane as a fuel source from the big high-pressure hydrate deposits on the sea bed off North Carolina. He had leased the technology to other fields, off Norway and Indonesia and Japan and New Zealand, and bought up shares judiciously. Soon methane production was supplying a significant percentage of global energy output.

The giant tents Malenfant's companies had erected over the sea floor, to decompose the hydrates and trap the gases, had become a symbol of his flair and ambition.

And Malenfant was on his way to becoming remarkably rich.

Space, it seemed, was the place Reid Malenfant had started from, not where he was going.

. . . Until – Emma thought, if Taine is right – *this*.

'Of course,' Cornelius said, 'Malenfant's ambition is to be applauded. I mean his real ambition, beyond this – umm, diversionary froth. I hope you understand this is my basic position. What grander goal is there to work for than the destiny of the species?' He spread thin fingers. 'Man is an expansive, exploring animal. We conquered Earth with Stone Age technology. Now we need new resources, new skills to fund our further growth, space to express our differing philosophies . . .' He smiled. 'I have the feeling you don't necessarily share these views.'

She shrugged. This was an argument she'd rehearsed with Malenfant many times. 'It's such a gigantic, mechanistic, depressing vision. Maybe we should all just learn to get along with each other. Then we wouldn't have to go to all the trouble of conquering the Galaxy. What do you think?'

He laughed. 'Your marriage must have been full of fire.' And he continued to ask her questions, trying to draw her out.

Enough. She wasn't prepared to be pumped by this faintly sinister man about her boss, let alone her ex-husband. She buried herself in e-mails, shutting him out.

Cornelius sat in silence, as still as a basking lizard.

* * *

After an hour they reached the Californian border.

There was a border post here. An unsmiling guard scanned Emma's wrist bar-code, her eyes hidden by insectile camera-laden sun-glasses. Since Emma and Cornelius proved to be neither black nor Latino nor Asian, and did not intend to take up permanent occupancy in the Golden State nor seek employment there, they were allowed through.

California, Emma thought sourly, is not what it used to be.

Highway 58, heading towards Mojave, took them through the desert. The sun climbed higher, and hard light fell from a hot, ozone-leached sky. The ground was baked, bleached, flat and hard as a paving slab, with only gnarled and blackened Joshua trees to challenge the endless horizontals. Somewhere to her right was Death Valley, which had, in 2004, logged the world's all-time highest temperature at 139 degrees.

They reached Edwards Air & Space Force Base – or rather they began to drive alongside its chain-link fence, forty miles of it running alongside the highway. Edwards, with its endless expanse of dry salt lakes – natural runways – was the legendary home of the test pilot. But from the highway she could see nothing at all, no planes or hangars or patrolling men-in-black guards. Nothing but miles of link fence. The accountant in her began, involuntarily, to compute the cost of all that wire.

Still, the closeness of Edwards, with its connotation of 1960s astronaut glamour, was, she was sure, the reason Malenfant had chosen this area for his newest project. Malenfant's methods with people were coarse, but he knew the power of symbols.

And it was, indeed, only a little way beyond Edwards that she came to the site of Malenfant's project.

The main gate was little more than a hole in the fence, barred by a crash barrier that carried a small, almost unobtrusive, Bootstrap corporate logo. The guard was a hefty woman with a small, dazzling-bright pistol at her hip. Emma's company credentials, appended to the u-v barcode i-d she wore on her left wrist, were enough to get her and Cornelius through the gate.

Inside the gate there was a Portakabin, once more displaying the corporate logo. Beyond that there was more desert. There was no metalled road surface, just tracks snaking to the dusty horizon.

Emma pulled the car over and climbed out. She blinked in the sudden light, felt perspiration start out of her flesh after a few seconds of the desert's dry, sucking warmth. The shade of the cabin, even badly air-conditioned, was a relief.

She took in the cabin's contents with a glance. Malenfant's joky company mission statement was repeated several times: *Bootstrap: Making Money in a Closed Economy – Until Something Better Comes Along* . . . There were display stands showing the usual corporate PR, much of it approved by herself, about the methane extraction fields, and Bootstrap's clean-up activities at Hanford and the Ukraine nuke plants and Alaska, and so forth.

Bootstrap had tied up a recent youth-oriented sponsorship with Shit Cola, and so there was a lot of bright pink Shit livery about the stands. Cornea gumbo, Emma thought: too cluttered and bright. But it defrayed the costs. And the Shit audience – sub-age-25, generally sub-literate consumers of the planet's trendiest soft drink – were showing themselves amenable to subtle Bootstrap persuasion, mixed in with their diet of endless softsoaps and thongathons.

No evidence here of giant rocket plants in the desert, of course.

Cornelius was looking around in silence, an amused half-smile on his lips. She was finding his quiet know-all attitude intensely irritating, his silences disturbing.

She heard the whine of an electric engine, a car of some kind pulling up outside. With relief she stepped out the door.

The car was a late-model jeep, a bare frame mounted on big fat tyres, with a giant solar-cell carapace glistening like beetle chitin. It carried two people, talking animatedly. The passenger was a woman, unknown to Emma: sixty, perhaps, slim and smart, wearing some kind of trouser suit. Practical but a little hot, Emma thought.

And the driver was, of course, Reid Malenfant.

Malenfant got out of the car like a whip uncoiling. He bounded up to Emma, grabbed her arms, and kissed her cheek; his lips were rough, sun-cracked. He was ruinously tall, thin as a snake, bald as a coot. He was wearing a blue NASA-type jump-suit and heavy black boots. As usual, he looked somehow larger than those around him, as if too big for the landscape. She could smell desert dust on him, hot and dry as a sauna. He said, 'What kept you?'

She hissed, 'You've a hell of a nerve, Malenfant. What are you up to now?'

'Later,' he whispered. The woman with him was climbing out of the car with caution, but she seemed limber enough. Malenfant said to Emma, 'Do you know Maura Della?'

'Representative Della? By reputation.'

Maura Della stepped forward, a thin smile on her lips. 'Ms Stoney. He's told me all about you.'

'I bet he has.' Emma shook her hand; Della's grip was surprisingly strong, stronger than Cornelius Taine's, in fact.

Malenfant said, 'I'm trying to win the Representative's support for the project here. But I suspect I've a little way to go yet.'

Della said, 'Damn right. Frankly it seems incredible to me that you can attempt to build an eco-friendly project around rocket engines . . .'

Malenfant pulled a face at Emma. 'You can tell we're in the middle of an argument here.'

'We sure are,' said Della.

Malenfant fetched plastic water bottles from the car and handed them out while Maura Della kept on talking.

'. . . Look, the Space Shuttle actually dumps more exhaust products into the atmosphere than any other current launcher. Water, hydrogen, hydrogen chloride and nitrogen oxides. The chloride can damage the ozone layer –'

'If it got into the stratosphere,' Malenfant said amiably, 'which it doesn't, because it rains out first.'

'65% of it does. The rest escapes. Anyhow there are other effects. Ozone depletion because of the deposition of frozen water and aluminium oxide. Global warming contributions from carbon dioxide and particulates. Acid rain from the hydrogen chloride and the NOX products –'

'Limited to a half-mile around the launch site.'

'But *there*. Anyhow there are also the toxins associated with rocket launches, which only need to be present in small amounts. Nitrogen tet can cause acute pulmonary oedemas, hydrazine is carcinogenic – and there are old studies linking aluminium with Alzheimer's.'

Malenfant barked laughter. 'The aluminium in rocket motors is one hundredth of one per cent of the total US annual production. We'd have to be launching like Buck Rogers to do any real damage.'

'Tell that to the mothers of the Florida yellow babies,' Della said grimly.

It had been a massive scandal. Medical studies had revealed a series of birth abnormalities showing up in Daytona, Orlando and other communities close to Cape Canaveral, in Florida. Abnormal livers, faulty hearts, some external defects; a plague of jaundice, sometimes associated with serious neurological diseases. *Yellow babies.*

Naturally Malenfant was prepared for this. 'First of all,' he said evenly, 'the medicos are split over whether the cluster exists at all. And even if it does, who the hell knows what the cause is?'

Della shook her head. 'Heptyl has been detected in soil and plants. Along the east coast of Florida it reaches as much as point three milligrams per kilogram –'

Emma asked, 'Heptyl?'

'Dimethyl hydrazine. Unburned rocket fuel. Highly toxic; hydrazine compounds are notorious liver and central nervous system poisons. Furthermore we know it can linger for years in bodies of water, rivers and marshes . . .' Della smiled thinly. 'I'm sorry. I guess we got a little worked up, driving around out here. As you probably know, Malenfant has been kibitzing Congress for some time. Me specifically. I thought I should come see if this rocket shop of his is just another hobby-club tax write-off, or something serious.'

Emma nodded. Right now she didn't see why she should make life easy for Malenfant. 'He calls you Bill Proxmire in a skirt.' Proxmire had been a notorious NASA-opposing Senator of the late twentieth century.

Maura Della smiled. 'Well, I don't wear skirts much. But I'll take it as a compliment.'

'Damn right,' said Malenfant easily, utterly unfazed. 'Proxmire was an unthinking opponent of progress –'

'While I,' said Della dryly to Emma, 'am a *thinking* opponent of progress. And therefore, Malenfant is calculating, amenable to persuasion.'

'I told you it was a compliment,' Malenfant said.

As the two of them fenced, Cornelius Taine had been all but invisible, standing in the shadows of the Portakabin's doorway. Now he stepped forward, as if materializing, and smiled at Malenfant. Cornelius didn't blink in the harsh sunlight, Emma noticed. Maybe he was wearing image-processing cornea implants.

Malenfant frowned at him, startled. 'And who the hell are you?'

Cornelius introduced himself and his company.

Malenfant growled. 'Eschatology. I thought I told the guards to keep you kooks out of the compound.'

Emma tugged his sleeve. 'I brought him in.' She murmured about the shareholding Cornelius represented. 'Take him seriously, Malenfant.'

15

Cornelius said, 'I'm here to support you, Colonel Malenfant. Really. I don't represent any threat to you.'

'Malenfant. Just call me Malenfant.' He turned to Della. 'I apologize for this. I get these bullshit artists all the time.'

Della murmured, 'I suspect you only have yourself to blame for that.'

Cornelius Taine was holding up manicured hands. 'You have me wrong, Malenfant. We're not psychics. We are scientists, engineers, economists, statisticians. Thinkers, not dreamers. I myself was formerly a mathematician, for instance.

'Eschatology has built on the pioneering work of thinkers like Freeman Dyson who, in the 1970s, began to consider the future scientifically. Since then we, and others, have worked hard to compile, umm, a road map of the future. In fact, Colonel Malenfant, we already have proof that our studies of the future are generally successful.'

'What proof?'

'We've become rich out of them. Rich enough to invest in *you*.' He smiled.

'Why have you come here today?'

'To emphasize we support you. That is, we support your true objectives. We know about Key Largo,' said Cornelius.

Della looked confused. 'Key Largo? In Florida?'

The name meant nothing to Emma. But she saw it had caught Malenfant off balance.

'This is too complicated for me,' Malenfant said at last. 'Get in the jeep. Please. We've got some hardware to see. Now that I *do* understand.'

Meekly, harbouring their own thoughts, they obeyed.

It was a three-mile drive to the test stand, further than Emma had expected. Bootstrap owned a big piece of desert, it seemed.

Malenfant's base here was like a miniaturized version of Edwards: miles of chain-link fence cutting out a hole in the desert, a hole within which exotic technology lurked, the scent of other worlds.

But there was a *lot* of plant here: fuel tanks and hangar-like buildings and skeletal test stands. Malenfant just drove past it all without comment or explanation. *Was* there a secret purpose here, more equipment than could be explained away by the waste-disposal cover story?

Malenfant and Maura Della continued to argue about space and rockets. Cornelius Taine was oddly detached. He sat apparently relaxed, hands neatly folded before him, gaze sweeping over the desert, as the babble of chemical names and statistics went on. There was something repellent about his surface of self-containment.

Emma was financial controller of Bootstrap – not to mention Malenfant's ex-wife – but that meant little to Malenfant in terms of openness and sharing of information with her. She knew he did rely on her to keep the company within the fiscal regulations, though. And that meant that, in a bizarre way, he trusted her to break through his elaborate webs of deceit and concealment in time to comply with the reporting rules. It was a kind of dance between them, a game of mutual dependence played to unspoken conventions.

In a way, she admitted to herself, she enjoyed it.

But she did wonder – if Cornelius turned out to be right – if Malenfant had gone too far this time. Secret rocket ships in the desert? So 1950s, Malenfant . . .

Still, here in this desert, just a few score miles from Edwards itself, Reid Malenfant – supple, tanned, vigorous, cheerful – seemed at home. Much more than in a boardroom in Vegas or Manhattan or DC. He looked like what he was, she thought – or rather what he had always wanted to be – a Right Stuff pilot of the old school, maybe somebody who could have gotten all the way into space himself.

But, of course, it hadn't worked out that way.

They reached the engine test facility. It was a big open box of scaffolding and girders, with zigzag walkways scribbled across the structure, and a giant crane peering over the top of everything. Lights sparkled over the rig, bright despite the intensity of the afternoon sun. It looked like a piece of a chemical factory, unaccountably shipped out here to the dull California desert. But on a boxy structure at the centre of the ugly conglomerate Emma could see, crudely painted over, a NASA roundel.

And there, as if trapped at the heart of the clumsy industrial metalwork, she saw the slim, snub-nosed form of a Space Shuttle external tank: a shape familiar from images of more than a hundred successful Cape Canaveral launches, and one memory-searing failure. White vapour was venting from somewhere in the stack and it wreathed around the girders and tubing, softening the sun's glare.

Oddly, she felt cooler; perhaps the heat capacity of this giant mass of liquid fuel was sufficient to chill the desert air, her own body.

Malenfant pulled up the jeep, and they stepped out. Malenfant waved at hard-hatted engineers, who waved or shouted back, and he guided his party around the facility.

'What we have in there is a kind of mock-up of a Space Shuttle. We have the external fuel tank, of course, and a complete aft section, with three main engines in place. Where the rest of the orbiter would go we have a boilerplate truss section. The Shuttle engines we use are obsolete: they've all flown in space several times, and have been decommissioned. We got the test hardware from NASA's old Shuttle main engine test facility in Mississippi, the Stennis Space Center.' He pointed to a fleet of tankers parked alongside the facility. They were giant eighteen-wheelers, but against the rig they looked like beetles at the foot of an elephant. 'At Stennis they bring in the fuel, lox and liquid hydrogen, by barge. We don't have that luxury . . .'

They reached a flame pit, a mighty concrete conduit dug into the desert alongside the test rig. Malenfant said, 'We've already achieved 520-second burns here, equivalent to a full Shuttle flight demonstration test, at one hundred per cent thrust.' He smiled at Maura Della. 'This is the only place in the world anybody is firing Shuttle main engines right now, still the most advanced rocket engines in the world. We have a nineteen-storey-high fuel tank in there, eight hundred tons of liquid fuel chilled through three hundred degrees or below. When the engines fire up the turbo-pumps work at forty thousand revs per minute, a thousand gallons of fuel are consumed every second –'

'All very impressive, Malenfant,' said Della, 'but I'm hardly likely to be overwhelmed by engineering gosh-wow numbers. This isn't the 1960s. You really think you need to assemble all this space hardware just to lose a little waste?'

'Surely. What we plan is to use rocket combustion chambers as high-temperature, high-volume incinerators.' He led them to a show board, a giant flow diagram showing mass streams, little rockets with animated yellow flames glowing in their hearts. 'We reach two to three thousand Centigrade in there, twice as high as in most commercial incinerators, which are based on rotary kiln or electric plasma technology. We feed the waste material through at high speed, first to break it down and then to oxidize it. Any toxic products are removed by a multistage cleansing process that includes scrubbers to get acidic gases out of the exhaust.

'We think we can process most poisonous industrial by-products, and also nerve gas and biological weapons, at a much greater speed and a fraction the cost of conventional incinerators. We think we'll be able to process tons of waste every *second*. We could probably tackle massive ecological problems, like cleaning out poisoned lakes.'

'Getting rich by cleaning the planet,' Della said.

Malenfant grinned, and Emma knew he had worked his way onto home ground. 'Representative, that's the philosophy of my corporation. We live in a closed economy. We've girdled the Earth, and we have to be aware that we're going to have to live with whatever we produce, useful goods or waste . . . *But*, if you can spot the flows of goods and materials and economic value, it's still possible to get rich.'

Cornelius Taine had walked away from the others. Now he was clapping, slowly and softly. Gradually he caught the attention of Malenfant and Della.

'Captain Future. I forgot you were here,' Malenfant said sourly.

'Oh, I'm still here. And I have to admire the way you're handling this. The plausibility. I believe you're even sincere, on the level of this cover-up.'

Maura Della said, 'Cover-up? What are you talking about?'

'*Key Largo*,' said Cornelius. 'That's what this is really all about. Isn't it, Malenfant?'

Malenfant glowered at him, calculating.

Here we go, Emma thought bleakly. Not for the first time in her life with Malenfant she had absolutely no idea what was going to come next, as if she was poised over a roller-coaster drop.

Cornelius said, 'I watched your Delaware speech the other night.'

Malenfant looked even more uncomfortable. 'Expanding across the Galaxy, all of that? I've given that talk a dozen times.'

'I know,' said Cornelius. 'And it's admirable. As far as it goes.'

'What do you mean?'

'That you haven't thought it through. You say you're planning a way for mankind to live forever. Getting off the Earth is the first step, et cetera. Fine. But what then? What is *forever*? Do you want eternity? If not, what will you settle for? A billion years, a trillion?' He waved a hand at the sun-drenched sky. 'The universe won't always be as hospitable as this warm bath of energy and light. Far downstream –'

'Downstream?'

'I mean, in the far future – the stars will die. It is going to be cold and dark, a universe of shadows. Do you hope that humans, or human descendants, will survive even then? . . . You haven't thought about this, have you? And yet it's the logical consequence of everything you're striving for.

'And there is more,' Cornelius said. 'Perhaps you are right that we are alone in this universe, the first minds of all. Since the universe is believed to have evolved from others, we may be the first minds to have emerged in a whole string of cosmoses. That is an astounding thought. And if it is true – *what is our purpose?* That, you see, is perhaps the most fundamental question facing mankind, and ought to shape everything you do, Malenfant. Yet I see no sign in any of your public statements that you have given any consideration to all this . . .'

The meaning of life? Was this guy for real? But Emma shivered, as if in this hot desert light the wind of a billion years was sweeping over her.

'We understand, you see,' said Cornelius.

'Understand what?'

'That you are trying to initiate a clandestine return to space here.'

Malenfant barked, 'Bull hockey.'

Emma and Maura Della spoke together,

'Malenfant, he alleged this earlier –'

'If this is true –'

'Oh, it's true,' Cornelius said. 'Come clean, Malenfant. The truth is he wants to do more than fire off rockets to burn waste. *He wants to build a rocket ship* – in fact a fleet of rocket ships – and launch them from here, the heart of the desert, and send them all the way to the asteroids.'

Malenfant said nothing.

Della was visibly angry. 'This is *not* what I came here for.'

Cornelius said, 'Malenfant, we back you. A mission to a NEO, a near-Earth object, makes obvious economic and technical sense: the first step in any expansion off-planet, in the short to medium term. And in the long term, it could make the difference.'

Della said, 'What difference?'

'The difference,' Cornelius said easily, 'between the survival of the human species, and its extinction.'

'So is that what you came to tell me, you swivel-eyed freak?' snapped Malenfant. 'That I get to save the world?'

'Actually we think it's possible,' said Cornelius evenly.

Della frowned, eyebrows arched sceptically. 'Really. So tell us how the world will end.'

'We don't know *how*. We think we know *when*, however. Two hundred years from now.'

The number – its blunt precision – startled them to silence.

Malenfant looked from one to the other – the suspicious ex-wife, the frowning Congressman, the mysterious prophet – and Emma saw he was, rarely for him, hemmed in.

Malenfant drove them back to the Portakabin. They travelled in silence, sunk in their respective moods, wary of each other. Only Cornelius, self-absorbed, seemed in any way content.

At the cabin Malenfant served them drinks, beer and soda and water, and they stood in the Californian desert.

Voices drifted over the baked ground, amplified and distorted, as a slow countdown proceeded.

Malenfant kept checking his watch. It was a fat, clunky Rolex. No implants or active tattoos for Reid Malenfant, no sir. For a man with his eye on the future, Emma thought, he often seemed wedded to the past.

The firing started.

Emma saw a spark of light, an almost invisible flame at the base of the stand, billowing white smoke. And then the noise came, a nonlinear crackle tearing at the air. The ground shook, as if she was witnessing some massive natural phenomenon, a waterfall or an earthquake, perhaps. But this was nothing natural.

Malenfant had once taken her to see a Shuttle launch. She'd had tears in her eyes then, from sheer exhilaration at the man-made *power* of the thing. And there were tears now, she found to her reluctant surprise, even at the sight of this pathetic, cut-down half-ship, trapped in its steel cage and bolted to the Earth.

She said, 'Cornelius is right. Isn't he, Malenfant? You've been lying to me for months. Years, maybe.'

Malenfant touched her arm. 'It's a long story.'

'I know. I've lived it. Damn you,' she whispered. 'There's a lot of unfinished business here, Malenfant.'

'We'll handle it,' Malenfant said. 'We can handle this guy Cornelius and his band of airheads. We can handle anybody. This is just the beginning.'

Cornelius Taine watched, eyes opaque.

Bill Tybee:

My name is Bill Tybee.

. . . Is this thing working? Oh, shit. Start again.

Hi. My name is Bill Tybee, and this is my diary.

Well, kind of. It's really a letter for you, June. It's a shame they won't let us talk directly, but I hope this makes up for your not being home for your birthday, a little ways anyhow. You know Tom and little Billie are missing you. I'll send you another at Christmas if you aren't here, and I'll keep a copy at home so we can all watch it together.

Come see the house.

Here's the living room. Sorry, I folded up the cam. There. Can you see now? You notice I got the video wall replaced, finally. Although I hate to think what the down payments are going to do to our bank balance. Maybe we could have got by with the old one, just the hundred channels, what do you think? Oh, I got the solar-cell roof replaced too. That storm was a bitch.

Here's Billie's bedroom. I'm whispering because she's asleep. She loves the hologram mobile you sent her. Everybody says how smart she is. Same as her brother. I mean it. Even the doctors agree about Billie; they're both off the, what did they say, the percentile charts, way off. You managed to give birth to two geniuses here, June. I know they don't get it from their father!

I'll kiss her for you. There you go, sweet pea. One from me too.

Here we are in the bathroom. Now, June, I know it's not much as part of the guided tour. But I just want to show you this stuff because you're not to worry about it. Here's my med-alert ribbon, this cute silver thing. See? I have to wear it every time I leave the house, and I ought to wear it indoors too. And here are the pills I have to take every day, in this bubble packet. The specialist says they're not just drugs but also little miniature machines, tumour-busters that go prowling around my bloodstream looking for the defective cells before breaking themselves up and flushing them out of, well, I won't show you out of where. Here I am taking my pill for today. See? Gone. Nothing to worry about.

The Big C just ain't what it used to be. Something you have to live with, to manage, like diabetes, right?

22

Come on. Let's go see if Tom will let us into his room. He loves those star pictures you sent him. He's been pinning them up on his wall . . .

Emma Stoney:

Emma was still furious when she drove into work, the morning after her trip to the plant.

Even this early on an August morning, the Vegas streets were thronged. People in gaudy artificial fabrics strolled past the giant casinos: the venerable Caesar's Palace and Luxor and Sands, the new TwenCen Park with its cartoon reconstructions of 30s gangster-land Chicago and 60s Space Age Florida and 80s yuppie-era Wall Street. The endless lights and laser displays made a storm of colour and motion that was dazzling even against the morning sunlight, like glimpses into another, brighter universe. But the landscape of casinos and malls didn't stay static; there were a number of vacant or redeveloping lots, like missing teeth in a smiling jaw.

And whatever the façade, the scene within was always the same: square miles of lush, ugly carpet, rows of gaming machines fed by joyless punters, blackjack tables kept open twenty-four hours a day by the virtual dealers.

Still, the people seemed to be changing, slowly. Not so fat, for one thing; no doubt the fatbuster pills were to thank for that. And she was sure there were fewer children, fewer young families than there used to be. Demography in action: the greying of America, the concentration of buying power in the hands of the elderly.

Not that it was so easy to tell *how* old people were any more. There were fewer visible signs of age: faces were smoothed to seamlessness by routine cosmetic surgery, hair was restored to the vigour and colour of a five-year-old's.

Emma herself was approaching forty now, ten years or so younger than Malenfant. Strands of her hair were already white and broken. She wore them with a defiant pride.

Malenfant had moved his corporation here, out of New York, five years ago. *A good place for business,* he said. *God bless Nevada. Distract the marks with gambling toys and virtual titties*

23

while you pick their pockets ... But Emma hated Vegas's tacky joylessness. It had taken a lot of soul-searching for her to follow Malenfant.

Especially after the divorce.

He'd said, *So we aren't married any more. That doesn't mean I have to fire you, does it?* Of course she had given in, come with him. Why, though?

He wasn't her responsibility, as the e-therapists continually emphasized. He wasn't even open with her. This latest business with the Shuttle engines – if true – was yet another piece of evidence for that. And he had, after all, broken up their marriage and pushed her away.

Yet, in his own complex, confused way, he still cared about her. She knew that. And so she had a motive for working with him. Maybe if she was still in his life, he might give more thought to his grandiose plans than otherwise.

Maybe he would keep from strip-mining the planet, in order to spare her feelings. Or maybe not.

Her e-therapists warned that this was a wound that would never close, as long as she stayed with Malenfant, worked with him. But then, maybe it was a wound that wasn't meant to close. Not yet, anyhow. Not when she still didn't even understand *why*.

When Emma walked into Malenfant's office, she found him sitting with his feet on his desk, crushed beer cans strewn over the surface. He was talking to a man she didn't know: an upright military type of about seventy, dressed in a sports shirt and slacks straight out of *Cheers* circa 1987, with a bare frosting of white hair on a scalp burned nutmeg brown. The stranger got up on Emma's entrance, but she ignored him.

She faced Malenfant. 'Company business.'

Malenfant sighed. 'It's all company business. Emma, meet George Hench. An old buddy of mine from Air & Space Force days –'

George nodded. 'When it used to be just plain Air Force,' he growled.

'Malenfant, why is he here?'

'To take us into space,' said Reid Malenfant. He smiled, a smile she'd seen too often before. *Look what I did. Isn't it neat?*

'So it's true. You're just incredible, Malenfant. Does the word *accountability* mean anything to you? This isn't a cookie jar you're raiding. This is a business. And we can't win with this. A lot of people have looked at commercial space ventures. The existing launcher capacity is going to be sufficient to cover the demand for the next several years. There is no market.'

Malenfant nodded. 'You're talking about LEO stuff. Communications, Earth resources, meteorology, navigation –'

'Yes.'

'Well, you're right, although demand patterns have a way of changing. You can't sell cruises until you build a cruise liner. But I'm not talking about low Earth orbit. We will build a heavy-lift booster, a direct ascent single-throw out of Earth orbit . . .'

And now she knew that everything Cornelius Taine had told her had been true. 'You really are talking about going to the asteroids, aren't you? *Why*, for God's sake?'

George Hench said, 'Because asteroids are flying mountains of stainless steel and precious metals, such as gold and platinum. Or they are balls of carbon and water and complex organics. A single metallic-type near-Earth object would be worth, conservatively, trillions in today's market. It would be so valuable, in fact, that it would change the market itself. And if you reach a C-type, a carbonaceous chondrite, full of water and organic compounds, you can do what the hell you like.'

'Such as?'

Malenfant grinned. 'You can throw bags of water and food and plastics back to Earth orbit, where they would be worth billions in saved launch costs. Or you could let a hundred thousand people go live in the rock. Or you can refuel, and go anywhere. Bootstrapping, like it says on the letterhead. The truth is I don't *know* what we're going to find. But I know that everything will be different. It will be like Cecil Rhodes discovering diamonds in southern Africa.'

'He didn't discover the mine,' she said. 'He just made the most money.'

'I could live with that.'

Hench said earnestly, 'The key to making money out of space is getting the costs of reaching Earth orbit down by a couple of magnitudes. If you fly on Shuttle, you're looking at thirty-five thousand bucks per pound to orbit –'

'And,' said Malenfant, 'because of NASA's safety controls and qual standards it takes years and millions of dollars to prepare your payload for flight. The other launch systems available are cheaper but still too expensive, unreliable and booked up anyhow. We can't hire, Emma, and we can't buy. *That's why we have to build our own.*'

Emma shook her head. 'But it's impossible. People have been trying to come up with cheap launchers for years.'

'Yes,' said Hench. 'And every time they are killed by the Gun Club.'

She eyed him. 'The "Gun Club"?'

'NASA,' Hench growled. 'Bureaucrat lifers with turf to defend. And the space lobby in the USASF, which anyhow has always been overruled by the fighter pilots who run that service –'

She turned back to Malenfant. 'And the permissions we'll need? The legal obstacles, the safety rules? Have you thought about any of that stuff? Malenfant, this is such a leap in the dark. Not even NASA are launching space ships right now.'

Hench cackled. 'But that's the beauty of it. The excitement. Ms Stoney, we are historically a capitalistic frontier people. We've known space is the new frontier since 1950. Now's the time to wriggle out from under the Gun Club federal guys and do it the way we always should have.'

Malenfant shrugged. 'Emma, I've got the business plans lined up if you want to see them, and potential investors coming out of my ass – bankers, investment brokers, merchant bankers, financiers, venture capitalists from Citibank, Prudential Bache, Morgan Trust –'

'All of which you've kept from me. For God's sake, Malenfant. Forget your drinking buddies and after-dinner audiences. How the hell do we persuade real investors to risk real money?'

Hench said, 'By building incrementally. By cutting tin fast. By building a little, flying a little, getting off the ground as fast as we can. That's how we built the Thor . . .' In the 1950s, with the Atlas and Titan intercontinental ballistic missiles already under development, the US defined a need for a smaller, simpler weapon for intermediate range missions, to be based in Britain and Turkey. The Thor, built from Atlas parts, would be the answer. '. . . You'd call it a Skunk Works operation today,' Hench said. 'We had that damn bird on the pad a year after the contract was signed. And we did it within budget, too. Not only that, McDonnell took it over and upgraded it to the Delta, and that baby is still flying and making money today. And that's why I'm confident I'm going to be able to deliver . . .'

Hench's eyes were a washed-out, watery brown, and flecked by damaged blood vessels. Malenfant was listening, rapt, to this old man's reminiscences.

Emma realized that, of course, his decision was already made, the new program under this man implemented and running, a done deal; Malenfant would implicitly trust Hench, his personal Wernher von Braun, to deliver as he promised, and he would take a personal interest again only when there was hardware ready to fly on some launch pad.

But even if the technology worked, even if the costs worked out as Malenfant seemed to believe, there was the Gun Club and all the other opposing forces which had killed earlier turf-threatening new initiatives – forces which had pushed Malenfant himself into this covert scheme, obviously concocted over years, in absolute secrecy even from her.

But now it's out in the open, what, she thought uneasily, is to stop the bad guys from killing us too? And if they do, where will that leave Malenfant? Where, in fact, will it leave me?

For she knew, of course, that she was already involved: that she would follow Malenfant wherever his latest dream took him, for better or worse. What a schmuck I am, she thought. She resolved to make more time for her e-therapists.

Hench talked on, urgently, meaninglessly, about rockets and engineering projects. For some reason she thought of Cornelius Taine, his cold eyes, his bleak, crazy warnings of the future.

'. . . Malenfant.'

'Yeah?'

'What *are* you doing at Key Largo?'

Spaiz Kadette:

> Copy this and pass it on.
> The news is just incredible. After all that coverage over the weekend there can't be a soul on the planet who isn't aware of Reid Malenfant and what he's trying to do out in the Mojave.
> Naturally the usual nay-sayers are hovering, moaning that Colonel Malenfant is acting outside the law, or is screwing up the environment, or is in some other way irresponsible.
> And there is the usual stench of hypocrisy and decay from the bloated corpse that is NASA, our space agency, the agency that should have done all this for us decades ago anyhow.

> Here's the pitch.
> Following a hastily-convened gathering in Hollywood, CA, a new society tentatively called the Flying Mountain Society has been formed. If you want to join, it will cost 500 dollars US or equivalent.
> For that investment you won't get any information or brochures or member services. We will not print glossy magazines or feed a giant staff. In fact we will have no full-time employees. As we are not another NASA booster club you won't get glossy pictures of spacecraft that will never be built. All you will get is a guarantee that we won't waste your money.
> FMS isn't the only space organization, but it does exist *solely* to get us into space.
> Here's the catch. Don't join unless you are a hard-working person. Don't join unless you support Colonel Malenfant's goal of developing a space industry in our lifetimes, and are prepared to work for it.
> In fact we'd prefer you didn't join at all. We'd prefer you started up your own local chapter, affiliated to the Society, which we hope will evolve into a global umbrella organization of pressure groups and activists.
> You can start with a bake sale. You can start by bombarding the schools with images of asteroids. You can start by hiking out to the Mojave, rolling up your sleeves and helping Colonel Malenfant any way he can use you.
> There is incidentally no truth in the rumours propagated in some sections of the press that the Flying Mountain Society is in any way affiliated with or funded by Bootstrap Inc. or any of its subsidiaries or affiliates as, quote, 'a propaganda exercise'. This is in fact counterfactual malice spread by Colonel Malenfant's turf-warrior enemies.
> If you want to get involved, reply to this mail. Better yet just get to work . . .

Maura Della:

Open journal. September 3 2010.

It was soon after my visit to Malenfant's experimental site in the Mojave that the news broke about Bootstrap's true purpose – that is, to assemble a private heavy-lift vehicle with Space Shuttle technology, to send some kind of mining mission to an asteroid.

I don't know if Cornelius Taine had anything to do with that. Presumably yes, if it served his shadowy organization's purposes. But it wasn't impossible the leak had come from elsewhere; Bootstrap is surely as porous as any large organization.

Anyhow, I find myself being sucked into the project. Somehow, through the leak and my covert involvement – the fact that I didn't blow the whistle immediately I got back from the Mojave – I'm becoming seduced into considering not just rocket engine firings, not just a private launch system, but the NEO mission itself.

This seems to be Malenfant's modus operandi: to build up an unstoppable momentum, to launch first and answer questions later.

The usual forces of darkness are already gathering in Congress to oppose this. It's going to be a struggle.

But I already know I'm not going to walk away from Malenfant, despite his outlandish, covert scheming.

You see, I happen to think Reid Malenfant is right. For the cost of one more space launch – which is undisputed, financial and environmental – it might be possible to reach a near-Earth object, actually to start exploiting one of those sun-orbiting gold mines, and so, just as Malenfant's corporate title suggests, bootstrap a new human expansion into space.

I think we've all become desensitized to the state of our world.

We live in a closed economy, an economy of limits. Grain yields globally have been falling since 1984, fishing yields since 1990. And yet the human population continues to grow. This is the stark reality of the years to come.

It seems to me our best hope for getting through the next century or so is to reach some kind of steady state: recycle as much as possible, try to minimize the impact of industry on the planet, try to stabilize the population numbers. For the last five to ten years I have, in my small way, been working towards exactly that goal, that new order. I don't see that any responsible politician has a choice.

I must say I entered politics with rather higher hopes of the future than I enjoy now.

But even the steady state, our best-hope future, may not be achievable without space.

Without power and materials from space we are doomed to shuffle a known – in fact diminishing – stockpile of resources around the planet. Some players get rich, others get poor. But it's not even a zero sum game; in the long term we're all losers.

It isn't just a question of economics. It's what this does to our spirit.

We are frightened of the future. We exclude strangers, try to hold on to what we have, rather than risk the search for something better. We spend more energy seeking someone to blame for our present woes than building for a better future. We've become a planet-ful of old people – old in spirit, anyhow. Speaking as a sexagenarian I know what I'm talking about.

The point is that if we could open up the limits to growth, then we can all be winners. It's as simple as that.

That is why I'm prepared to back Malenfant. Not, you'll note, because I like his methods. But the ends, I suspect, in this case justify the means.

However all this is going to take some extremely delicate opinion management. Especially over what Malenfant is doing at Key Largo . . .

Sheena 5:

. . . And, in the warm, shallow waters of the continental shelf off Key Largo:

The night was over. The sun, a fat ball of light, was already glimmering above the water surface, which rippled with flat-light. Sheena 5 had spent the night alone, foraging for food among the sea bed grasses. She had eaten well, of small fish, prawns, larvae; she had been particularly successful using her arms to flush out hiding shrimp from the sand.

But now, in the brightness of day, the squid emerged from the grasses and corals, and rose in the water. The shoals formed in small groups and clusters, eventually combining into a community a hundred strong that soared in arcs and rows through the water. Their jets made the rich water sing as they chattered to each other, simple sentences picked out by complex skin patterns, body posture, texture:

Court me. Court me.
See my weapons!
I am strong and fierce.
Stay away! Stay away! She is mine! . . .

It was the ancient cephalopod language, Sheena knew, a language of light and shadow and posture, the 'words' shivering one into the other, words of sex and danger and food. It was a language as old as the squid – millions of years old, much older than humans – and it was rich and beautiful, and she shoaled and chattered with joy.

. . . But there was a shadow on the water. And Sheena's deep gravity sense told her of an approaching infrasonic rumble, quite characteristic: it was a barracuda, a vicious predator of the squid. This one was young and small, but no less dangerous for that.

The sentinels, scattered around the fringes of the shoal, immediately adopted concealment or bluff postures. Their simple words blared lies at the approaching predator, and warned the rest of the shoal.

Black bands on the mantle, arms limp, swimming rapidly backwards: *Look at me. I am a parrotfish. I am no squid.*

Clear body, dark arms in a downward V: *Look at us. We are sea grass, sargassum, drifting in the current. We are no squid.*

A pseudomorph, a squid-shaped blob of ink, hastily emitted and bound together by mucus: *Look at us. We are squid. We are all squid.*

Turn to predator, spread arms, white spots and false eyes to increase apparent size: *Look at me. I am strong and fierce. Flee!*

The dark shape lingered close, just as a true barracuda would, before diving into the shoal, seeking to break it up.

Sheena knew that there would be no true predators here, in this garden-like reserve. Sheena recognized the glimmer of steel, the camera lenses pockmarking the too-smooth hide of the beast, the regular churn of the propellers in back. She understood that the shadow could only be a watching Bootstrap machine.

But she sensed a dull recognition of this fact in the glittering animal minds of her cousins, all around her; they were smart too, smart enough to know they were safe here. Besides, so sophisticated were their defences that the squid were rarely troubled by predators. So there was an element of play in the darting concealment and watchfulness of the shoal.

And then came the hunt.

The slim cylinder cruised through the posturing, half-concealed squid. Recognition pulsed through the shoal. Some of them spread their arms, covered their mantles with patterns of bars and streaks. *Look at me. I have seen you. I will flee. It is futile to chase me.*

Now one of the squid shoal, a strong male, broke free and jetted in front of the barracuda. A pattern began to move over his skin in steady waves, a patchwork of light and dark brown that radiated from his streamlined body to the tip of his tentacles. It was the pattern Dan called the passing cloud. *Stop and watch me.*

The barracuda cruised to a stop.

The male spread his eight arms, raised his two long tentacles, and his green binocular eyes fixed on the barracuda. Confusing patterns of light and shade pulsed across his hide. *Look at me. I am large and fierce. I can kill you.*

The metal barracuda hung in the water, apparently mesmerized by the pattern, just as a predator should have been if it had been real.

Slowly, cautiously, the male drifted towards the barracuda, coming to within a mantle length, gaze fixed on the fish.

At the last moment the barracuda turned, sluggishly, and started to slide away through the water.

But it was too late for that.

The male lunged. His two long tentacles whipped out – too fast even for Sheena to see – and their club-like pads of suckers pounded against the barracuda hide, sticking there.

The barracuda surged forward. It was unable to escape. The male pulled himself towards the barracuda and wrapped his eight strong arms around its body, his body pattern changing to an exultant uniform darkening, careless now of detection.

But when the male tried to jet backwards, hauling at the prey, the barracuda was too massive and strong.

The male broke the stand-off by rocketing forward until his body slammed into the barracuda's metal hide – he seemed shocked by the hardness of the 'flesh' – and he wrapped his two long, powerful tentacles around the slim grey body.

Then he opened his mouth and stabbed at the hull with his beak. The hull broke through easily, Sheena saw; evidently it was designed for this. The male injected poison to stun his victim, and then dug deeper into the hide to extract the warm meat beneath. And meat there was, what looked like fish fragments to Sheena, booty planted there by Dan.

The squid descended, chattering their ancient songs, diving through the cloud of rich, cold meat, lashing their tentacles around the stricken prey. Sheena joined in, her hide flashing in triumph, cool water surging through her mantle, relishing the primordial power of this kill despite its artifice.

. . . That was when it happened.

Maura Della:

'Ms Della, welcome to Oceanlab,' Dan Ystebo said.

As she clambered stiffly down through the airlock into the habitat, the smell of air freshener overwhelmed Maura. The two men here, biologist Dan Ystebo and a professional diver, watched her sheepishly.

She sniffed. 'Woodland fragrance. Correct?'

The diver laughed. He was a burly fifty-year-old, but the dense air mixture here, hydreliox, turned his voice into a Donald Duck squeak. 'Better than the alternative, Ms Della.'

Maura found a seat between the two men before a bank of controls. The seat was just a canvas frame, much repaired with duct tape. The working area of this hab was a small, cramped sphere, its walls encrusted with equipment. It featured two small, tough-looking windows, and its switches and dials were shiny and worn with use. The lights were dim, the instruments and screens glowing. A sonar beacon pinged softly, like a pulse.

The sense of confinement, the *feel* of the weight of water above her head, was overwhelming.

Dan Ystebo was fat, breathy, intense, thirtyish, with Coke-bottle glasses and a mop of unlikely red hair, a typical geek scientist type. Igor to Malenfant's Doctor Frankenstein, she thought. His face was underlit by the orange glow of his instrument panel. 'So,' he said awkwardly. 'What do you think?'

'I think it feels like one of those old Soviet-era space stations. The Mir, maybe.'

'That's not so far off,' Dan said, evidently nervous, talking too fast. 'This is an old Navy installation. Built in the 1960s, nearly fifty years ago. It used to be in deep water out by Puerto Rico, but when a hab diver got himself killed the Navy abandoned it and towed it here, to Key Largo.'

'Another Cold War relic,' she said. 'Just like NASA.'

Dan smiled. 'Swords into ploughshares, ma'am.'

She leaned forward, peering into the windows. Sunlight shafted through dusty grey water, but she saw no signs of life, not a fish or frond of seaweed. 'So where is she?'

Dan pointed to a monitor, a modern softscreen pasted over a scuffed hull section. It showed a school of squid, jetting through the water in complex patterns. The image was evidently enhanced; the water had been turned sky blue. 'We don't rely on naked eye so much,' Dan said.

'Which one is Sheena 5?'

Dan touched the softscreen image, picking out one of the squid, and the virtual camera zoomed in.

The streamlined, torpedo-shaped body was a rich burnt-orange, mottled black. Wing-like fins rippled elegantly alongside the body.

'*Sepioteuthis sepioidea*,' Dan said. 'The Caribbean reef squid. About as long as your arm. See her countershading? The light is downwelling, coming from above; she has shaded her mantle – brighter below – to eliminate the effect of shadow. Making herself disappear . . . Squid, all cephalopods in fact, belong to the phylum Mollusca.'

'Molluscs? I thought molluscs had feet.'

'They do.' Dan pointed. 'But in the squid the foot has evolved into the funnel, *here*, leading into the mantle, and the arms and tentacles *here*. The mantle cavity contains the viscera – the circulatory, excretory, digestive, reproductive systems. But the gills also lie in there; the squid "breathes" by extracting oxygen from the air that passes over the gills. And Sheena can use the water passing through the mantle cavity for jet propulsion; she has big ring muscles which –'

'How do you know that's her?'

Dan pointed again. 'See the swelling between the eyes, around the oesophagus?'

'That's her enhanced brain?'

'A squid's neural layout isn't like ours. Sheena has two nerve cords running like rail tracks the length of her body, studded with pairs of ganglia. The forward ganglia pair is expanded into a mass of lobes. We gen-enged Sheena and her grandmothers to –'

'To make a smart squid.'

'Ms Della, squid are smart anyway. They are molluscs, invertebrates, but they are functionally equivalent to fish. In fact they seem to have evolved – a long time ago, during the Jurassic – in competition with the fish. They have senses based on light, scent, taste, touch, sound – including infrasound – gravity, acceleration, perhaps even an electric sense. See the patterns on Sheena's hide?'

'Yes.'

'They're made by chromatophores, sacs of pigment granules surrounded by muscles. The chromatophores are under conscious control; Sheena can open or close them as she chooses. The pigments are black, orange and yellow. The underlying colours, blues and violets, are created by passive cells we call reflecting . . . Ms Della, Sheena can control her skin patterns consciously. She can make bands, bars, circles, annuli, dots. She can even animate the display. The mantle skin is like a reverse retina, where neural signals are converted to patches of shade, rather than the other way around.'

'And these patterns are signals?'

'Not just the skin patterns. A given signal seems to be made up of a number of components: the patterns, skin texture – rough or smooth, posture – the attitude of the limbs, head, body, fins – and locomotor components – whether Sheena is resting, jetting, hovering, grabbing, ink-jetting. There may be electric or sonic components too; we can't be sure.'

The diver growled, 'Ms Della, we've barely scratched the surface with these animals. Not to mention their deep water cousins. Until the last few decades all we did was lower nets and see what we could catch. We used to say it was like trying to understand the animals of the land by working with a butterfly net from a balloon in the clouds.'

Maura said, 'And what do they use this marvellous signalling for?'

Dan sighed. 'Again we aren't sure. They don't hunt cooperatively. They forage alone by night, and shoal by day. The shoaling seems to be to provide protection while they rest. The squid don't hide on the bottom like octopuses; they shoal over seagrass beds where there are few predators. They have elaborate courtship rituals. And the young seem to learn from the old. They post sentinels. Very effectively too; though they may have six or seven predator encounters per hour – with yellow jacks and mutton snappers, barracuda and houndfish, coming at them from anywhere – the squid kill rate is very low.

'But a squid shoal is not a community like ours. They don't play or groom. There are no leaders among them. The squid don't show much loyalty to each other; they don't care for their young, and individuals move between shoals every few days.

'And they live only a couple of years, mating only once or twice. The squid live fast and die young; it's not clear to us why such short-lived animals need such complex behaviour, communication systems and breeding rituals . . . Yet they have them. Ms Della, these are *not* like the animals you may be familiar with. Perhaps they are more like birds.'

'And you claim that these *communication systems* are actually a language.'

Dan scratched his beard. 'We've been able to isolate a number of primal linguistic components which combine in a primitive grammar. *Even in unenhanced squid.* But the language seems to be closed. It's about nothing but food, sex and danger, as far as we can see. It's like the dance of the bee.'

'Unlike human languages.'

'Yes. What we have done is open up the language of the squid. We built on the basic patterns and grammar the squid already employ. The number of signals Sheena can produce is not unlimited, of course, but even unenhanced squid have a very wide "vocabulary" taking into account the range of intensity, duration and so forth they can employ. We think they express, for example, moods and intentions with these factors. And some of this stuff is extremely ancient. Some of the simpler signals – the deimatic displays designed to drive off predators, for example – can be observed among the octopuses. And the squid diverged from *them* back in the early Mesozoic, some two hundred million years ago. Anyhow, building on this, we believe Sheena – or at any rate her descendants – should be able to express an *infinite* number of messages. Just as you or I can, Ms Della. Squid are clever molluscs. Giving them language was *easy*.'

'How do you train them?'

'With positive reinforcement. Mostly.'

'Mostly?'

He sighed. 'I know what you're asking. Yes, cephalopods can feel pain. They have free nerve endings in the skin. We use low-voltage electric currents to deliver mild shocks during discrimination training. They react as if – well, as you would if I touched you with a stinging nettle. It's no big deal. Ms Della, I hope you aren't going to get hung up on this. I cherish Sheena – above and beyond her mission. I wouldn't damage her. I have no interest in hurting her.'

Studying him, she realized she believed him. But she sensed a certain lack in him, a lack of a moral centre. Perhaps that was a prerequisite in any sentient creature who would inflict pain on another.

Dan was still talking. '. . . Designing the Sheena series of enhancements, we were able to prove that the areas of the brain responsible for learning are the vertical and superior frontal lobes that lie above the oesophagus.'

'How did you prove that?'

Dan blinked. 'By cutting away parts of squid brains.'

Maura sighed. Memo, she thought. Do not let Igor here repeat this Nazi doctor stuff in front of the cameras.

She felt uneasy on a deeper level, too. Here was Dan Ystebo hijacking the squid's evidently remarkable communications senses for his own purposes: for capturing banal commands transmitted by humans. But Dan had admitted he didn't know what all this rich speech was really *for*. What if we are damaging Sheena, Maura thought, by excluding her from the songs of her shoals?

Does a squid have a *soul*?

They studied Sheena. Her head was crowned by a beak surrounded by flipper-like arms, and two forward-looking eyes, blue-green rimmed with orange, peered briefly into the camera.

Alien eyes. Intelligent.

How did it *feel*, to be Sheena?

And could Sheena possibly understand that humans – Reid Malenfant and his associates, in fact – were planning to have her fly a rocket ship to an asteroid?

The squid school on the softscreen seemed to be hunting now. They were moving in formation around an unmanned camera buoy. The images were spectacular, Jacques Cousteau stuff.

'They swim awful fast,' she said.

'They're not swimming,' Dan said patiently. 'When they swim, they use their fins. Right now they are squirting water out of vents. Jet propulsion.'

'You understand why I'm here. Malenfant is asking me to go into bat for you on the Hill Monday. I have to put my reputation on the line, to enable this project.'

'I know that.'

'Tell me this, Dr Ystebo. You're sure, absolutely sure, this is going to work?'

'Absolutely.' He spoke with a calm conviction. 'Ms Della, you have to see the power of Malenfant's conception. I'm convinced Sheena will be able to function in space and at the NEO. She is smart, obviously adapted to gravity-free conditions – there'll be no calcium depletion or body fluid redistribution or any of that crap for her – almost as if she has been evolved for the conditions of space travel, as we self-evidently haven't. And she can manipulate her environment. We have a variety of waldo-driven instruments which will enable her to carry out her functions on the NEO.'

'I'm told the squid are social creatures. And they're very mobile, obviously. Whereas Sheena will be alone, and the can we're going to cram her into –'

'She'll have a lot of facilities, Ms Della. Including comms, of course. We'll do everything we can to keep her functioning.'

Functioning. 'Why not an octopus? Squid are social creatures – in fact, isn't it true that their consciousness arises from their social structures? Whereas octopuses, I'm told, are solitary, sedentary creatures anyhow who could stand the isolation and confinement.'

'But not so smart,' Dan said. 'They work alone. They don't need to communicate. And they rely on smell, not sight, to hunt. Thanks to those squid eyes – forward-placed for binocular vision – Sheena will be able to *navigate through space* for us. It had to be a squid, Ms Della. If she's a little uncomfortable en route, that's a price we'll have to pay.'

'And what about the return trip? The stresses of re-entry, re-habilitation . . .'

'In hand,' Dan said vaguely. He blinked like an owl.

In hand. Sure. You're not the one going to the asteroid, you charmless nerd.

Maura found herself convinced. Malenfant knows what he's doing, right down the line. I have to force the approvals through, on Monday. Sheena – smart, flexible and a lot cheaper than an equivalent robot, even when you took into account the launch costs for her life support environment – was the item that had closed Reid Malenfant's interplanetary design.

There were some things working in her favour. Behind the scenes Malenfant had already begun to assemble promises of the technical support he was going to need. His old buddies at NASA had started to find ways to free up deep space communications, and provide support for detailed mission design and other support facilities. And it would help, she thought, that this wouldn't be solely a NASA-related project; cooperation from Woods Hole in Massachusetts and the research institute at Monterey Bay Aquarium in California diluted the hostility NASA always attracted on the Hill.

. . . But, she thought, if I succeed I will be forever associated with this. And if the news about the brave little squid turns sour enough I may not survive myself.

Dan said, 'I've been working with Sheena for months now. I know her. She knows me. And I know she's committed to the mission.'

'You think she understands the risks?'

Dan looked uncomfortable. 'We're counselling her. And we're planning to have Sheena make some kind of statement of her own. Something we can broadcast, of course with a translation. If something does go wrong we hope the public will accept it as a justified sacrifice.'

Maura grunted, unconvinced. 'Tell me this,' she said. 'If you were her – would you go?'

'Hell, no,' he said. 'But I'm *not* her. Ms Della, every moment of her life, from the moment she was hatched, Sheena has been oriented to the goal. It's what she lives for. The mission.'

Sombrely Maura watched the squid, Sheena, as she flipped and jetted in formation with her fellows.

I need to pee, she realized.

She turned to Dan. 'How do I, uh . . .'

The old diver type handed her a steel jar with a yellow label that had her name on it. 'Your Personal Micturition Vessel. Welcome to the space program, Ms Della.'

Perhaps reacting to some out-of-shot predator threat, the squid shoal collapsed to a tight school and jetted away with startling speed, their motion three-dimensional and complex, rushing out of the virtual camera's field of view.

Sheena 5:

The courting began.

The squid swam around each other, subtly adopting new positions in time and space: each female surrounded by two, three, four males. Sheena enjoyed the dance, the ancient, rich choreography – even

39

though she knew courting was not for her: it never could be, after she had been selected by Bootstrap.

Dan had explained it all.

. . . But now, regardless of Dan's strictures, regardless of the clamouring mind she carried, he came for her: the killer male, one tentacle torn on some loose fragment of metal, bearing his wound proudly.

She should swim away. But here he was next to her, swimming back and forth with her. She fled, a short distance, but he pursued her, swimming with her, his every movement matching hers.

She knew this was wrong. And yet it was irresistible.

She felt a skin pattern flush over her body, a pied mottling of black and clear, speckled with white spots. It was a simple, ancient message. *Court me.*

He swam closer.

But the other males, still orbiting her, began to encroach, their eyes hard and intent. The hunter, *her* male, swam up to meet the most bold, his arms flaring, head dark, bright bands on his mantle. *Get away. She is mine!* The male refused to back off, his body pattern flaring to match the hunter's. But the hunter raised his body until his fins bumped the intruder's, who backed away.

Now he came back to her. She could see his far side was a bright uniform silver, a message to the other males: *Keep away, now. Keep away. She is mine!* But the side closest to her was a soothing uniform grey-black, a smooth texture into which she longed to immerse herself, to shut off the clattering analysis of the brain the humans had given her. As he rolled the colours tracked around his body, and she could see the tiny muscles working the pigment sacs on his hide.

Now he faced her, open arms starfished around his mouth. His eyes were on her: green and unblinking, avid, mindless, without calculation. Utterly irresistible. And already he was holding out his hectocotylus towards her, the modified arm bearing the clutch of spermatophores at its tip.

For a last instant she remembered Dan, his rigid human face peering out of glass windows at her, the little panels he sent into the water flashing their signs. *Mission Sheena mission. Bootstrap! Mission! Dan!*

She knew she must not do this.

But then the animal within her rose, urgent.

She opened her mantle to the male. He pumped water into her, seeking to flush out the sperm of any other mate. And then his hectocotylus reached for her, striking swiftly, and lodged his needle-like spermatophore among the roots of her arms.

Already, it was over.

And yet it was not. She could choose whether or not to embrace the spermatophore and place it in her seminal receptacle.

The male was withdrawing. All around her, the squid's flashing songs pulsed with life.

She knew, compared to a human's, her life was short: flashing, bright, lasting one summer, two at most, a handful of matings. And she was alone: she did not know her parents, would never know her young, might never see this mate of hers again.

And yet it did not matter. For there was consolation in the shoal, and the shoal of shoals: the ancient songs that reached back to a time before humans, before whales, before even the fish. The songs, poetry of light and dance, made every squid aware she was part of a continuum that stretched back to those ancient seas, and on to the incomprehensible future; and that her own brief, vibrant life was as insignificant, yet as vital, as a single silver scale on the hide of a fish.

Sheena, with her human-built mind, was the first of all squid to be able to understand this. And yet every squid *knew* it, on some level that transcended the mind.

But Sheena was no longer part of that continuum. Dan understood nothing of the shoal – not really – but he had stressed that much to her. Sheena was *different*, with different goals: human goals.

Even as the male receded, she felt overwhelmed with sadness, loneliness, isolation.

Flaring anger at the humans who had done this to her, she closed her arms over the spermatophore, and drew it inside her.

e-CNN:

. . . Following the revelation that a genetically enhanced squid is to be the effective control centre of Reid Malenfant's quixotic mission to an asteroid <detail>, there has been a predictable outcry from conservation and wildlife rights groups.

But there was an unexpected reaction on Wall Street today where stocks in information technology companies took a beating. Prices <full listing> quoted for the traditional giants like IBM <link> and

Microsoft <link> tumbled, but so did the prices for companies like Qbit <link> and Biocom <link>, recent stars of the markets with their stream of successes in the burgeoning fields of quantum-technology computing and bio-computing <backgrounder>.

The reason for all this action is Bootstrap's rejection of traditional IT solutions in favour of the apparently exotic choice of an enhanced animal. Now, analysts are questioning whether the industry's reputation for overpriced, unreliable and bug-ridden products is finally taking its toll.

Most of the firms we contacted refused to comment. But an e-spokesperson for IBM said today <animation> that . . .

Ocean Child:

Thank you, your honour. I only want to say this.

I want everybody to know what we in the Eden League are attempting.

We are developing an internal technology which will selectively suppress the so-called 'higher' brain functions in humans. It is clear to us that our 'intelligence' has been of no real evolutionary advantage and therefore we intend to discard it. That is why I have no regrets about the mine we attempted to drop onto the laboratory at Key Largo. Frankly I wish it had worked, and I know that statement will affect my sentencing. I don't care; in fact I welcome it.

And I can announce from this platform that we have already started researching a counter-technology that will similarly restore the squid to their innocence.

What those fascist scientists are doing is cruel.

I don't mean the experiments where they scoop out the brains of a sentient, intelligent creature. I don't mean the way they plan to put them to work, farming the oceans for us and even shooting them off into space, where once they were free.

I mean the fact that these animals have been given minds at all.

For centuries we have dragged these beautiful creatures from the Ocean for our food. Now, for our own convenience, we have committed a much greater crime. We have inflicted on these squid an awareness of mortality. And for that, may the Mother Ocean forgive us.

Thank you. That's all.

Emma Stoney:

Cornelius Taine said, 'We are invoking deep principles of scientific thinking. Copernicus pointed out that the Earth moves around the sun, not the other way around, and so we were displaced from the centre of the universe. The Copernican principle has guided us ever since. Now we see Earth as just one star, unexceptional, among billions in the Galaxy.

'We don't expect to find ourselves in a special place in *space*. Why should we expect to be in a special place in *time*? But that is what you have to accept, you see, if you believe mankind has a future with very distant limits. Because in that case we must be among the very first humans who ever lived . . .'

'Get to the point,' Malenfant said softly.

'. . . All right. Based on arguments like this, we think a catastrophe is awaiting mankind. A universal extinction, a little way ahead.

'We call this the Carter catastrophe.'

Emma shivered, despite the warmth of the day.

Malenfant had suggested they follow up Cornelius Taine's sudden intrusion into their lives by accepting his invitation to come to the New York head offices of Eschatology, Inc. Emma resisted – in her view they had *far* more important things to talk about than the end of the world – but Malenfant insisted.

Cornelius, it seemed, had gotten under his skin.

So here they were: the three of them sitting at a polished table big enough for twelve, with small inlaid softscreens, and on the wall a grey-glowing monitor screen.

Malenfant sucked aggressively at a beer. 'Eschatology,' he snapped. 'The study of the end of things. Right? So tell me about the end of the world, Cornelius. What? How?'

'That we don't know,' said Cornelius evenly. 'There are many possibilities. Impact by an asteroid or a comet, another dinosaur killer? A giant volcanic event? A global nuclear war is still possible. Or perhaps we will destroy the marginal, bio-maintained stability of the Earth's climate . . . As we go on, we find more ways for the universe to destroy us – not to mention new ways in which we can destroy ourselves. This is what Eschatology, Inc. was set up

43

to consider. But there's really nothing new in this kind of thinking. We've suspected that humanity was doomed to ultimate extinction since the middle of the nineteenth century.'

'The Heat Death,' said Malenfant.

'Yes. Even if we survive the various short-term hazards, entropy must increase to a maximum. In the end the stars must die, the universe will cool to a global uniformity a fraction above absolute zero, and there will be no usable energy, anywhere.'

'I thought there were ways out of that,' said Malenfant. 'Something to do with manipulating the Big Crunch. Using the energy of a collapsing universe to live forever.'

Cornelius laughed. 'There have been ingenious models of how we might escape the Death, survive a Big Crunch. But they are all based on pushing our best theories of physics, quantum mechanics and relativity, into areas where they break down – such as the singularity at the end of a collapsing universe. Anyway we already know, from cosmological data, that there *is* no Big Crunch ahead of us. The universe is doomed to expand forever, without limit. The Heat Death, in one form or another, seems inevitable.'

'But that would give us billions of years,' said Malenfant.

'In fact more,' said Cornelius. 'Orders of magnitude more.'

'Well, perhaps we should settle for that,' Malenfant said dryly.

'Perhaps. Still, the final extinction must come at last. And the fact of that extinction is appalling, no matter how far downstream it is.'

'But,' said Emma sceptically, 'if you're right about what you said in the desert, we don't have trillions of years. Just a couple of centuries.'

Cornelius was watching Malenfant, evidently hoping for a reaction. 'Extinction is extinction; if the future must have a terminus, does it matter when it comes?'

'Hell, yes,' said Malenfant. 'I know I'm going to die someday. That doesn't mean I want you to blow my brains out right now.'

Cornelius smiled. 'Exactly our philosophy, Malenfant. The game itself is worth the playing.'

Emma knew Cornelius felt he had won this phase of the argument. And, gradually, step by step, he was drawing Malenfant into his lunacy.

She sat impatiently, wishing she wasn't here.

She looked around this small, oak-panelled conference room. There was a smell of polished leather and clean carpets: impeccable taste, corporate lushness, anonymity. The only real sign of unusual wealth and power, in fact, was the enviable view – from a sealed, tinted window – of Central Park. They were high enough here to be above the Park's main u-v dome. She saw people strolling in the Park, children playing on the glowing green grass, the floating sparks of police drones everywhere.

Emma wasn't sure what she had expected of Eschatology. Maybe a trailer home in Nevada, the walls coated with tabloid newspaper cuttings, the interior crammed with cameras and listening gear. Or perhaps the opposite extreme: an ultramodern facility with a giant virtual representation of the organization's Mister Big beamed down from orbit, no doubt stroking his white cat.

But this office, here in the heart of Manhattan, was none of that. It was essentially ordinary. That made it all the more scary, of course.

Malenfant said now, 'So tell me how you know we only have two hundred years.'

Cornelius smiled. 'We're going to play a game.'

Malenfant glared.

Cornelius reached under the table and produced a wooden box, sealed up. It had a single grooved outlet, with a wooden lever alongside. 'In this box there are a number of balls. One of them has your name on it, Malenfant; the rest are blank. If you press the lever you will retrieve the balls one at a time, and you may inspect them. The retrieval will be truly random.

'I won't tell you how many balls the box contains. I won't give you the opportunity to inspect the box, save to draw out the balls with the lever. But I promise you there are either ten balls in here – or a thousand. Now. Would you hazard which is the true number, ten or a thousand?'

'Nope. Not without evidence.'

'Very wise. Please, pull the lever.'

Malenfant drummed his fingers on the table top. Then he pressed the lever.

A small black marble popped into the slot. Malenfant inspected it; it was blank. Emma could see there was easily room for a thousand such balls in the box, if need be.

Malenfant scowled and pressed the lever again.

His name was on the third ball he produced.

'There are ten balls in the box,' said Malenfant immediately.

'Why do you say that?'

'Because if there was a thousand in there it's not likely I'd reach myself so quickly.'

Cornelius nodded. 'Your intuition is sound. This is an example of Bayes's rule, which is a technique for assigning probabilities to competing hypotheses with only limited information. In fact –' he hesitated, calculating '– the probability that you're right is now two-thirds, on the basis of your ball being third out.'

Emma tried to figure that for herself. But, like most probability problems, the answer was counter-intuitive.

'What's your point, Cornelius?'

'Let's think about the future.' Cornelius tapped the softscreen embedded in the tabletop before him. The small monitor before Emma lit up, and a schematic graph drew itself elegantly on the screen. It was a simple exponential curve, she recognized, a growth rising slowly at first, steepening up to a point labelled 'now'. Cornelius said, 'Here is a picture of the growth of the human population over time. You can see the steep rise in recent centuries. It is a remarkable fact that ten per cent of *all* the humans who have ever existed are alive now. More than five per cent of all humans, Malenfant, were born after you were . . .

'But that is the past. Let's imagine how the future might develop. Here are three possibilities.' The curve continued to climb, steepening as it did so, climbing out of Emma's frame. 'This,' said Cornelius, 'is the scenario most of us would like to see. A continued expansion of human numbers. Presumably this would require a move off-planet.

'Another possibility is this.' A second curve extrapolated itself from the 'now' point, a smooth tip over to a flat horizontal line. 'Perhaps our numbers will stabilize. We may settle for the resources of the Earth, find a way to manage our numbers and our planet indefinitely. A bucolic and unexciting picture, but perhaps it is acceptable.

'But there is a third possibility.' A third curve climbed a little way past the 'now' marker – then fell spectacularly to zero.

'Jesus,' said Malenfant. 'A crash.'

'Yes. Studies of the population numbers of other creatures, lower animals and insects, often show this sort of shape. Plague, famine, that sort of thing. For us, the end of the world, soon.

'Now. You can see that in the first two cases, *the vast majority of humans are yet to be born*. Even if we stay on Earth, we estimate we have a billion years ahead of us before changes in the sun will render Earth's biosphere unviable. Even in this restricted case we would have far more *future* than *past*.

'And if we expand off-planet, if we achieve the kind of future you're working for, Malenfant, the possibilities are much greater. Suppose we – or our engineered descendants – colonize the Galaxy. There are four hundred billion stars in the Galaxy, many of which will provide habitable environments for far longer than a mere billion years. Then the total human population, over time, might reach trillions of times its present number.'

'. . . Oh. And that's the problem,' Malenfant said heavily.

'You're starting to see the argument,' Cornelius said, approving.

'I'm not,' said Emma.

Malenfant said, 'Remember his game with the balls and the box. *Why are we here now?* If we really are going on to the stars, you have to believe that you were born in the first one-billionth part of the total human population. And how likely is that? Don't you get it, Emma? It's as if I drew out my ball third out of a thousand –'

'Far more unlikely than that, in fact,' said Cornelius.

Malenfant got up and began to pace the room, excited. 'Emma, I don't know statistics from my elbow. But I used to think like this as a kid. Why am I alive *now*? Suppose we do go on to colonize the Galaxy. Then most of the humans who ever live will be vacuum-sucking cyborgs in some huge interstellar empire. And it's far more likely that I'd be one of *them* than what I am. In fact the only pop curve where it's reasonably likely that we'd find ourselves *here*, *now*, is –'

'The crash,' said Emma.

'Yes,' Cornelius said sombrely. 'If there *is* a near-future extinction, it is overwhelmingly likely that we find ourselves alive within a few centuries of the present day. Simply because that is the period when most humans who ever lived, *or who will ever live*, will have been alive. Ourselves among them.'

'I don't believe this for a second,' Emma said flatly.

'It is impossible to prove, but hard to refute,' said Cornelius. 'Put it this way. Suppose I tell you the world will end tomorrow. You might think yourself unlucky that your natural life span has been cut short. But in fact, *one in ten of all humans* – that is, the people alive now – would be in the same boat as you.' He smiled. 'You work in Las Vegas. Ask around. Losing out to one in ten odds is unlucky, but not drastically so.'

Emma said, 'You can't argue from analogy like this. There are a fixed number of balls in that box. But the total number of possible humans depends on the undetermined and open-ended future – it might even be infinite. And how can you possibly make predictions about people who don't even exist yet – whose nature and powers and choices we know absolutely nothing about? You're reducing the most profound mysteries of human existence to a shell game.'

Cornelius said patiently, 'You're right to be sceptical. Nevertheless we have thirty years of these studies behind us now. The methodology was first proposed by a physicist called Brandon Carter in a lecture to the Royal Society in London in the 1980s. And we have built up estimates based on a range of approaches, calling on data from many disciplines –'

Malenfant said hoarsely, 'When?'

'Not earlier than 150 years from now. Not later than 240.'

Malenfant cleared his throat. 'Cornelius, what's this all about? Is this an extension of the old eggs-in-one-basket argument? Are you going to push for an off-planet expansion?'

Cornelius was shaking his head. 'I'm afraid that's not going to help.'

Malenfant looked surprised. 'Why not? We have centuries. We could spread over the Solar System –'

'But that's the point,' said Cornelius. 'Think about it. My argument wasn't based on any one threat, or any assumptions about where humans might be located, or what level of technology we might reach. *It was an argument about the continued existence of humanity*, come what may. Perhaps we could even reach the stars, Malenfant. But it will do us no good. The Carter catastrophe will reach us anyhow.'

'Jesus,' said Malenfant. 'What possible catastrophe could obliterate star systems – reach across light years?'

'We don't know.'

There was a heavy silence in the wood-laden room.

Malenfant said gruffly: 'So tell me what you want from me.'

Cornelius said evenly, 'I'm coming to that.' He stood up. 'May I bring you more drinks?'

Emma got out of her chair and walked to the window. She looked out over Central Park, the children playing. They were engaged in some odd, complex game of shifting patterns. She watched for a while; it looked almost mathematical, like a geometric form of communication. Kids were strange these days. Getting brighter, according to the news media. Maybe they needed to be.

But some things never changed. Here came a buggy, she saw, crossing through the Park, drawn by a horse, tireless and steady. The world, bathed in smoky, smog-laden sunlight, looked rich, ancient yet renewed, full of life and possibilities.

. . . Was it possible Cornelius was right? That all this could end, so soon?

Two hundred more years was nothing. There were hominid tools on the planet two *million* years old.

And, she thought, will there be a last day? Will there still be a New York, a Central Park – the last children of all playing here on that day? Will they know they have no future?

Or is all this simple craziness?

Malenfant touched her arm. 'This is one hell of a thing, isn't it?' She recognized the tone, the look. All the scepticism and hostility he had shown to Cornelius out in the desert had evaporated. Here was another Big Idea, and Reid Malenfant was distracted, like a kid by a new shiny toy.

Shit, she thought. I can't afford for Malenfant to take his eye off the ball. Not now. And it's my fault. I could have dumped Cornelius in Vegas, found a way to block his approach . . . Too late, too late.

She tried, anyhow. 'Malenfant, listen. I've been digging up Cornelius's past.'

Malenfant turned, attentive.

Some of it was on the record. She hadn't even recognized the terms mathematicians used to describe Cornelius's academic achievement – evidently it covered games of strategy, economic analysis, computer architecture, the shape of the universe, the distribution of prime numbers – anyhow he had been on his way, it seemed, to becoming one of the most influential minds of his generation.

But he had always been – well, odd.

His gift seemed non-rational: he would leap to a new vision, somehow knowing its rightness instinctively, and construct laborious proofs later. Cornelius had remained solitary: he attracted awe, envy, resentment.

As he approached thirty he drove himself through a couple of years of feverish brilliance.

Maybe this was because the well of mathematical genius traditionally dries up at around that age, a prospect which must have terrified Taine, so that he thought he was working against time.

Or maybe there was a darker explanation, Emma's e-therapists speculated. It wasn't unknown for creativity to derive from a depressive or schizoid personality. And creative capacities could be used in a defensive way, to fend off mental illness.

Maybe Cornelius was working hard in order to stay sane. If he was, it didn't seem to have worked.

The anecdotes of Cornelius's breakdown were fragmentary.

At first he was just highly aware, watchful, insomniac. Then he began to see patterns in the world around him – the cracks in the sidewalk, telephone numbers, the static of dead television screens. He said he was on the verge of deep cosmic insights, available only to him –

'Who says all this?'

'His colleagues. His doctors' case notes, later. You see the pattern, Malenfant? Everything got twisted around. It was as if his faith in the rationality and order of the universe had turned against him, becoming twisted and dysfunctional.'

'Yeah. Right. And envy and peer pressure and all that good stuff had nothing to do with it.'

'Malenfant, on his last day at Princeton they found him in the canteen, slamming his head against a wall, over and over.'

After that Cornelius had disappeared for two years. Emma's data miners had been unable to trace how he spent that time. When he re-emerged, it wasn't to go back to Princeton but to become a founding board member of Eschatology, Inc.

And here was Emma now, with Malenfant, in the orderly office of this apparently calm, rational, highly intelligent man. Talking about the end of the world.

She whispered urgently, 'Don't you get it, Malenfant? Here's a guy who tells us he sees patterns in the universe nobody else can make out – a guy who believes he can predict the end of humanity.' A guy who seemed on the point of inducing Malenfant to turn aside his own gigantic projects to follow his insanity. 'Are you listening?'

Malenfant touched her arm. 'I hear what you say,' he said. 'But –'

'But what?'

'*What if it's true?* Whether Cornelius is insane or not, what if he's right? What then?' His eyes were alive, excited.

Emma watched the children in the Park.

Cornelius returned and invited them to sit once more. He had brought a fresh chilled beer for Malenfant and a coffee for Emma: a decent latte in a china cup, smelling as if it had been freshly brewed and poured by a human hand. She was impressed, as was, no doubt, the intention.

Cornelius sat down. He coughed. 'Now comes the part you may find hard to believe.'

Malenfant barked laughter. 'Harder than the death of mankind in two hundred years? Are you for real?'

Cornelius said, with a nod to Emma, 'Here's a little more dubious logic for you. Suppose, in the next few decades, humans – our descendants – *do* find a way to avoid the catastrophe. A way for us to continue, into the indefinite future.'

'That's impossible, if your arguments are correct.'

'No. Merely highly unlikely. But in that case – and knowing the hugeness of the catastrophe to come – if they *did* find a way, what might our descendants try to do?'

Malenfant frowned. 'You're losing me.'

Cornelius smiled. 'They would surely try to send us a message.'

Emma closed her eyes. The madness deepens, she thought.

'Woah.' Malenfant held up his hands. 'You're talking about sending a message *back in time*?'

Cornelius went on, 'And the most logical thing for us to do would be to make every effort to detect that message. Wouldn't it? Because it would be the most important message ever received. The future of the species would depend on it.'

'Time paradoxes,' whispered Emma. 'I always hated stories about time paradoxes.'

Malenfant sat back. Suddenly, to Emma, he looked much older than his fifty years. 'Jesus. What a day. And this is what you want me for? To build you a radio that will pick up the future?'

'Perhaps the future is already calling. All we have to do is try, any which way. They're *our* descendants. They know we are trying. They even know *how* we are trying. And so they can target us. Or *will*. Our language is a little limited here . . . You are unique, Malenfant. You have the resources and the vision to carry this through. Destiny awaits you.'

Malenfant turned to Emma. She shook her head at him. *We ought to get out of here.* He looked bemused.

He turned back to Cornelius. 'Tell me one thing,' he said. 'How many balls were there in that damn box?'

But Cornelius would only smile.

Reid Malenfant:

Afterwards, they shared a cab to the airport.

'. . . Remember those arguments we used to have?'

He smiled. 'Which arguments in particular?'

'About whether to have kids.'

'Yeah. We agreed our position, didn't we? If you have kids you're a slave to your genes. Just a conduit from past to future, from the primeval ocean to galactic empire.'

'Right now,' she said, 'that doesn't seem such a bad ambition. And if we *did* have kids, we might be able to figure it out better.'

'Figure out what?'

She waved a hand at the New York afternoon. 'The future. Time and space. Doom soon. I think I'm in some kind of shock, Malenfant.'

'Me too –'

'But I think if I had kids I'd understand better. Because those future people who will never exist, except as Cornelius's statistical phantoms, would have been my children. As it is, they have nothing to do with me. To them I'm just a – a bubble that burst, utterly irrelevant, far upstream. So their struggles don't mean anything. *We* don't mean anything. All our struggles, the way we loved each other and fell out with each other and fought like hell. Our atom of love. None of it matters. Because we're transient. We'll vanish, like bubbles, like shadows, like ripples on a pond.'

'We do matter. *You* do. Our relationship does, even if it is –'

'Self-contained? Sealed off?'

'You aren't irrelevant to me, Emma. And *my* life, what I've achieved, means a lot to me . . . But that's me sublimating. That's what you diagnosed years ago, isn't it?'

'I can't diagnose anything about you, Malenfant. You're just a mass of contradictions.'

He said, 'If you could change history, like Cornelius says the future people are trying to – if you could go back and fix things between us – would you?'

She thought about that. 'The past has made us what we are. If we changed it we'd lose ourselves. Wouldn't we? . . . No, Malenfant. I wouldn't change a damn thing. But –'

'Yeah?'

She was watching him, her eyes as black as deep lunar craters. 'That doesn't mean I understand you. And I don't love you.'

'I know that,' he said, and he felt his heart tear.

Bill Tybee:

. . . June, I know you want me to tell you everything, good and bad, so here goes.

The good is that Tom loves the Heart you sent him for his birthday. He carries it around everywhere, and he tells it everything that happens to him, though to tell you the truth I don't understand the half of what he says to it myself.

Here's the bad. I had to take Tom out of school yesterday.

Some kids picked on him.

I know we've had this shit before, and we want him to learn to tough it out. But this time it went beyond the usual bully-the-Brainiac routine. The kids got a little rough, and it sounds as if there was a teacher there who should have intervened but didn't. By the time the Principal was called, it had gotten pretty serious.

Tom spent a night in hospital. It was only one night, just bruising and cuts and one broken bone, in his little finger. But he's home now.

If I turn this screen around . . . wait . . . You can see him. Fine, isn't he?

He's a little withdrawn. I know we discourage that rocking thing he does, but today's not the day.

You can see he's reading. I have to admit I still find it a little scary the way he flips over the pages like that, one after the other, a page a second. But he's fine, just our Tom.

So you aren't to worry. But I'll want assurances from that damn school before I let Tom go back there again.

Anyway, enough. I want to show you Billie's painting.

Emma Stoney:

When she heard Malenfant had hauled Dan Ystebo out from Florida, Emma stormed down to Malenfant's office.

'. . . Here's the question, Dan,' Malenfant was saying. 'How would you detect a signal from the future?'

Behind his beard, Dan Ystebo's mouth was gaping. His face and crimson hair shone, greasy, and there were two neat half-moons of dampness under his armpits: souvenirs, Emma thought, of his flight from Florida, the first available, and his Yellow SmartCab ride from the airport. 'What are you talking about, Malenfant?'

'A signal from the future. What would you do? How would you build a receiver?'

Dan looked, confused, from Malenfant to Emma. 'Malenfant, for Christ's sake, I've got work to do. Sheena 5 –'

'You've got a good team down there,' said Malenfant. 'Cut them a little slack. This is more important.' He pulled out a chair and pushed at Dan's shoulders, almost forcing him down. He had a half-drunk can of Shit; now he shoved it to Dan. 'Thirsty? Drink. Hungry? Eat. Meantime, *think*.'

'Yo,' Dan said uncertainly.

'You're my Mr Science, Dan. Signals from the future. What, how? Wait until you hear the stuff I'm onto here. It's incredible. If it pans out it will be the most important thing we've ever done – Christ, it will change the world. I want an answer in twenty-four hours.'

Dan looked bewildered. Then a broad smile spread over his face. 'God, I love this job. Okay. You got connections in here?'

Malenfant stood over him, and showed him how to log on from the softscreen built into the desk.

When Dan was up and running, Emma pulled at Malenfant's sleeve and took him to one side. 'So once again you're ripping up the car park.'

Malenfant grinned and ran his big hand over his bare scalp. 'I'm impulsive. You used to like that in me.'

'Don't bullshit, Malenfant. First I find we've invested millions in Key Largo. Then I learn that Dan, the key to that operation, is reassigned to this la-la Eschatology bullshit –'

54

'But he's done his job at Largo. His juniors can run with the ball a while . . .'

'Malenfant, Dan isn't some general purpose boffin like in the movies. He's a specialist, a marine biologist. If you want someone to work on time travel signals you need a physicist, or an engineer. Better yet a sci fi writer.'

He just snorted at that. 'People are what counts. Dan is my alpha geek, Emma.'

'I don't know why I stay with you, Malenfant.'

He grinned. 'For the ride, girl. For the ride.'

'All right. But now we're going to sit down and do some real work. We have three days before your stakeholder presentation and the private polls do *not* look good for us . . . Are you listening to me, Malenfant?'

'Yeah.' But Malenfant was watching Dan. 'Yeah. Sorry. Come on. We'll use your office.'

Reid Malenfant:

Malenfant had called the stakeholder presentation to head off a flight of capital after the exposure of his off-Earth projects.

He hired a meeting room at the old McDonnell Douglas Huntingdon Beach complex in California. McDonnell had been responsible for the Mercury and Gemini spacecraft back in spaceflight's Stone Age – or Golden Age, depending on your point of view. Mercury and Gemini, 'little ships that could', had been highly popular with the astronaut corps. Also he had the room lined with displays of pieces of hardware taken from his Mojave development shops: hydraulic actuators and auto-pilots and vernier motors, real, scorch-marked rocket engineering.

To the smart operator, Malenfant liked to say, everything is a symbol.

Emma nudged him. It was time.

He stood up and climbed onto the stage. The audience buzz dropped, and the lights dimmed.

Once again, a turning point, he thought, another make or break crisis. If I succeed today, then the Big Dumb Booster flies. If I fail – then, hell, I find another way.

He was confident, in command. He began.

*   *   *

'. . . We at Bootstrap believe it is possible that America can dominate space in the twenty-first century – making money doing it – just as we dominated commercial aviation in the twentieth century. In fact, as I will try to explain, I believe we have a duty to the nation, indeed the human species, at least to try.

'But the first thing we have to do is to bring down Earth-to-orbit costs,' he said. 'And there are two ways to achieve that. One way is to build a new generation of reusable spacecraft.'

The first challenge came, a voice floating from the back of the room. *We already have a reusable spacecraft. We've been flying it for thirty years.*

Malenfant held his hands up. 'Much as I admire NASA's achievements, to call the Space Shuttle *reusable* is to stretch the word to yield point. After each Shuttle flight the Orbiter has to be stripped down, reassembled and re-certified from component level up. It would actually be cheaper to build a whole new Orbiter every time.'

So you're proposing a new reusable craft? Lockheed have spent gigabucks and years developing –

'I'm not aiming for reusability at all, if you'll forgive me. Because the *other* approach to cutting launch costs is to use expendables that are so damn cheap that you don't *care* if you throw them away. Hence, the Big Dumb Booster.'

Using the giant softscreen behind him he let them look at a software-graphic image of George Hench's BDB on the pad. It looked something like the lower half of a Space Shuttle – two solid rocket boosters strapped to a fat, rust-brown external fuel tank – but there was no moth-shaped Shuttle Orbiter clinging to the tank. Instead the tank was topped by a blunt-nosed payload cover almost as fat and wide as the tank itself. And there were no NASA logos: just the Bootstrap insignia, and a boldly displayed Stars and Stripes.

There were some murmurs from his audience, one or two snickers. Somebody said, *It looks more Soviet than anything American.*

So it did, Malenfant realized, surprised. He made a note to discuss that with Hench, to take out the tractor-factory tinge. Symbolism was everything.

Malenfant pulled up more images, including cutaways giving some construction details. 'The stack is over 300 feet tall. You have a boat-tail of four Space Shuttle main engines here, attached to the bottom of a modified Shuttle external tank, so the lower stage is powered by liquid oxygen and hydrogen. You'll immediately see one benefit over the standard Shuttle design, which is in-line propulsion; we have a much more robust stack here. The upper stage is built on one Shuttle main engine. Our performance to low Earth orbit will be 135 tons – *twice* what the Shuttle can achieve.

'But LEO performance is secondary. This is primarily an inter-planetary launcher. We can throw fifty tons directly onto an inter-planetary trajectory. That makes the avionics simple, incidentally. We don't need to accommodate Earth orbit or re-entry or landing. Just point and shoot . . .'

It may be Big and Dumb but it's scarcely cheap.

'Oh, but it is. What you have here is a bird built from technology about as proven and basic as we can find. We only use Shuttle engines and other components at the end of their design lifetimes. And as I've assured you before I am investing not one thin dime in R&D. I'm interested in reaching an asteroid, not in reinventing the known art. We believe we could be ready for launch in six months.'

What about testing?

'We will test by flying, and each time we fly we will take up a usable payload.'

That's ridiculous. Not to say irresponsible.

'Maybe. But NASA used that approach to accelerate the Saturn V development schedule. Back then they called it all-up testing. We're walking in mighty footsteps.'

There was some laughter at that.

You have the necessary clearance for all this?

'We're working on it.'

More laughter, a little more sympathetic.

'As for our own financial soundness in the short term, you have the business plans, downloaded in the softscreens in front of you. Capital equipment costs, operating costs, competitive return on equity and cost of debt, the capital structure including the debt to equity ratio, other performance data such as expected flight rate, tax rates and payback periods. Even the first flight is partially funded by scientists who have paid to put experiments aboard, from private corporations, the Japanese and European space agencies, even NASA.'

You must realize your whole cost analysis here is based on flawed assumptions. The only reason you can pick up Shuttle engines cheap is because the Shuttle program exists in the first place. So it's a false saving.

'Only somebody funded by federal money would call any saving "false",' said Malenfant. 'But it doesn't matter. This is a bootstrap project, remember. All we need is to achieve the first few flights. After that we'll be using the resources we find out there to bootstrap ourselves further out. Not to mention make ourselves so rich we'll be able to *buy* the damn Shuttle program.

'I know this isn't easy to assess for any investor who isn't a technologist. Exercising due diligence, how would I check out such a business plan? Who else but by giving it to my brother-in-law at NASA? After all, NASA has the only rocket experts available. Right?

'But NASA will give you the same answer every time. *It won't work. If it did, NASA would be doing it, and we aren't.* All I can ask of you is that you don't just go to NASA. Seek out as many opinions as you can. And research the history of NASA's use of bureaucratic and political machinery to stifle similar initiatives in the past.'

There was some stirring at that, even a couple of boos, but he let it stand.

'Let me show you where I want to go.' He pulled up a blurred radar image of an asteroid, a lumpy rock. 'This piece of real estate is called Reinmuth. It is a near-Earth asteroid, discovered in 2005. It is what the astronomers call an M-type, solid nickel-iron with the composition of a natural stainless steel.

'One cubic kilometre of it ought to contain seven billion tons of iron, a billion tons of nickel, and enough cobalt to last three thousand years, conservatively worth six *trillion* bucks. If we were to extract it all we would transform the national economy, in fact, the *planet's* economy.'

How can you expect government to support an expansionist space colonization program?

'I don't. I just want government to get out of the way. Oh, maybe government could invest in some fast-track experimental work to lower the technical risk.' Nodding heads at that. 'And there may be kick-starts the government can provide – like the Kelly Act of 1925, when the government gave mail contracts to the new airlines. But that's just seedcorn stuff. This program isn't called Bootstrap for nothing.

'We have a model from history. The British Empire worked to a profit. How? The British operated a system of charter companies to develop potential colonies. The companies themselves had to bear the costs of administration and infrastructure: running the local government, levying taxes, maintaining a police force, administering justice. Only when a territory proved itself profitable would the British government step in and raise the flag.

'The French and Germans, by contrast, worked the other way around: government followed by exploitation and trade. By 1900 colonial occupation had *cost* the French government the equivalent of billions of dollars. We don't want to make the same mistake.

'We believe the treaties governing outer space resources are anti-quated, inappropriate and probably unenforceable. We believe it is up to the US government to revoke those treaties and begin to offer development charters along the lines I've described. What we're offering here is the colonization of the Solar System, and the appropriation of its resources as appropriate, on behalf of the United States – at virtually zero cost to the US taxpayer. And we all get rich as Croesus in the process.'

There was a smattering of applause at that.

He stepped forward to the front of the stage. Before him there was a sea of faces – mostly men, of course, most of them over fifty and therefore as conservative as hell. There were representatives of his corporate partners here – Aerojet and Honeywell and Deutsche Aerospace and Scaled Composites, Inc. and Martin Marietta and others – as well as representatives of the major investors he still needed to attract, and four or five NASA managers, even a couple of uniformed USASF officers. Movers and shakers, the makers of the future, and a few entrenched opponents.

He marshalled his words.

'This isn't a game we're playing here. In a very real sense we have no choice.

'I cut my teeth on the writings of the space colony visionaries of the '60s and '70s. O'Neill, for instance. Remember him? All those cities in space. Those guys argued, convincingly, that the limits to economic growth could be overcome by expansion into space. They made the assumption that the proposed space programs of the time would provide the capability to maintain the economic growth required by our civilization.

'None of it happened.

'Today, if we want to start to build a space infrastructure, we've lost maybe forty years, *and* a significant downgrade of our capability to achieve heavy lift into orbit. And the human population has kept right on growing. Not only that, there is a continuing growth in

59

wealth per person. Even a pessimistic extrapolation says we need total growth of a factor of *sixty* over the rest of this century to keep up.

'But right now we ain't growing at all. We're shrinking.

'We lose twenty-five billion tons of topsoil a year. That's equivalent to six 1930s dustbowls. Aquifers – such as those beneath our own grain belt – are becoming exhausted. Our genetically uniform modern crops aren't proving too resistant to disease. And so on. We are facing problems which are spiralling out of control, exponentially.

'Let me put this another way. Suppose you have a lily, doubling in size every day. In thirty days it will cover the pond. Right now it looks harmless. You might think you need to act when it covers half the pond. But when will that be? *On the twenty-ninth day.*

'People, this is the twenty-ninth day.

'Here's the timetable I'm working to.

'We need to be able to use power from space to respond to the global energy shortage by 2020. That's just ten years from now.

'By 2050 we need a working economy in space, returning power, microgravity industrial products and scarce resources to the Earth. We might even be feeding the world from space by then. We'll surely need tens of thousands of people in space to achieve this, an infrastructure extending maybe as far as Jupiter. That's just forty years away.

'By 2100 we probably need to aim for economic equivalence between Earth and space. I can't hazard what size of economy this implies. Some say we may need as many as a billion people out there. We can figure it out later.

'These are targets, not prophecy. We may not achieve them; if we don't try, we certainly won't. My point is that we've sat around with our thumbs up our butts for too long. If we start *now*, we may just make it. If we leave it any longer, we may not have a planet to launch our spaceships from . . .

'And,' he said, 'in the end, have faith.'

In who? You?

Malenfant smiled.

His speech was well rehearsed, and it almost convinced *him*. But Cornelius's Carter stuff nagged away at the back of his head. Was all this stuff, the exploitation of the Solar System for profit, really to be his destiny? Or – something else, something he couldn't yet glimpse?

He felt his pulse race at the prospect.

Behind him, the softscreen's software-generated images gently morphed into a shot of a Big Dumb Booster, real hardware sitting on the pad, a pillar of heavy engineering wreathed in vapour under a burning blue sky, a spaceship ready for launch.

Damn if he couldn't see some glistening eyes out there, shining in the transmitted desert light. 'This is a live image,' he said. 'We're ramping up for our first smoke test. People, this is just the beginning. I'm going places. Come aboard.'

He waited for the applause. It came.

Emma Stoney:

It only took a week before Dan had designed and set up his first message-from-the-future experiment, at a place called the National Radio Astronomy Observatory in West Virginia. Emma was relieved that the funding required was modest, comparatively anyhow, and Malenfant was able to pull strings to get his way without, as far as she could tell, any visible damage to the company.

Translation: nobody had found out yet what the hell they were doing.

Weeks went by and the experiment produced nothing useful. Malenfant shuttled between Vegas, the Mojave and West Virginia.

After a month of trying to convince Malenfant to come back to work, Emma cleared her diary and caught a flight to West Virginia.

She had a Bootstrap driver take her out to the radio observatory. She arrived at midnight.

The National Radio Astronomy Observatory proved to be set in a leafy valley surrounded by forest-clad hills. In the cloudless October sky a sliver of Moon floated among the stars.

As her eyes dark-adapted Emma made out a cluster of upturned dishes, each cluttered with spidery receiving equipment. The dishes seemed to glow, silver and white, as they peered up hopefully into an impenetrable, infinite sky. Occasionally one of the dishes would move on its fragile-looking stand, with a grind of heavy equipment, at the obscure command of one of the observers in the low, cheap-looking buildings. She wondered how many of the researchers here were now working for Bootstrap or for Eschatology – in either case, presumably, funded by Malenfant's money.

She was taken to a grassy area where half a dozen folding lawn chairs had been set up. Malenfant, Dan Ystebo and Cornelius Taine were working their way through a couple of six-packs. All of them were bundled up against the chill.

Dan, crumpled and slightly drunk, looked as if he hadn't changed his T-shirt since Florida. Cornelius wasn't drinking. He was wearing his customary designer suit, neat and seamless; somehow he seemed sealed off from this environment, green hills and silence and stately nature.

Malenfant was pacing, restless, his footprints dark against the dew on the grass.

She sighed. Malenfant, in this obsessive mood, took some management. Well, she'd expected this to take some time.

She sat down gingerly on a spare chair, and accepted a beer. 'I should have brought a heavier coat.'

Dan said sleepily, 'After the first six-pack you don't notice the cold.'

'So what have you picked up from our silver-suited descendants?'

Cornelius shook his head. 'We didn't expect success so easily. We just had to eliminate the most obvious possibility.'

She glanced around. 'These are radio telescopes. Right? You're expecting to pick up back-to-the-future messages by radio waves?'

Dan said, 'We're trying to build a Feynman radio here, Emma.'

'Feynman? As in Richard Feynman?'

Malenfant was smiling. 'Turns out,' he said, 'there's a loophole in the laws of physics.'

Cornelius held up his hands. 'Look, suppose you jiggle an atom to produce a radio wave. We have equations which tell us how the wave travels. But the equations always have two solutions.'

'Two?'

Dan scratched his belly and yawned. 'Like taking a square root. Suppose you have a square lawn, nine square yards in area. How long is the side?'

'Three yards,' she said promptly. 'Because three is root nine.'

'Okay. But nine has another square root.'

'Minus three,' she said. 'I know. But that doesn't count. You can't have a lawn with a side of minus three yards. It makes no physical sense.'

Dan nodded. 'In the same way the electromagnetism equations always have two solutions. One, like the positive root, describes the waves we're familiar with, travelling into the future, that arrive at a receiver *after* they left the transmitter. We call those retarded waves. But there's also another solution, like the negative root –'

'Describing waves arriving from the future, I suppose.'

'Well, yes. What we call advanced waves.'

Cornelius said, 'It's perfectly good physics, Ms Stoney. Many physical laws are time-symmetric. Run them forward, and you see an atom emitting a photon. Run them backward, and you see the photon hitting the atom . . .'

'Which is where Feynman comes in,' Dan said. 'Feynman supposed the outgoing radiation is absorbed by matter, gas clouds, out there in the universe. The gas is disturbed, and gives off advanced waves of its own. The energy of all those little sources travels *back in time* to the receiver. And you get interference. One wave cancelling another. All the secondary advanced waves cancel out the original advanced wave at the transmitter. And all their energy goes into the retarded wave.'

'It's kind of beautiful,' Malenfant said. 'You have to imagine all these ghostly wave echoes travelling backward and forward in time, perfectly synchronized, all working together to mimic an ordinary radio wave.'

Emma had an unwelcome image of atoms sparsely spread through some dark, dismal future, somehow emitting photons in a mysterious choreography, and those photons converging on Earth, gathering in strength, until they fell to the ground here and now, around her . . .

'The problem is,' Cornelius said gently, 'Feynman's argument, if you think about it, rests on assumptions about the distribution of matter in the future of the universe. You have to suppose that *every* photon leaving our transmitters will be absorbed by matter somewhere – maybe in billions of years from now. But what if that isn't true? The universe isn't some cloud of gas. It's lumpy, and it's expanding. And it seems to be getting more transparent.'

Dan said, 'We thought it was possible that not *all* the advanced waves cancel out perfectly. Hence all this. We use the radio dishes here to send millisecond-pulse microwave radiation into space. Then we vary the rig: we send out pulses into a dead-end absorber. And we monitor the power output. Remember the advanced waves are supposed to contribute to the energy of the retarded wave, by Feynman's theory. If the universe *isn't* a perfect absorber –'

'Then there would be a difference in the two cases,' Emma said.

'Yeah. We ought to see a variation, a millisecond wiggle, when we beam into space, because the echo effect isn't perfect. And we hope to detect any message in those returning advanced echoes – if somebody downstream has figured out a way to modify them.

'We pick cloudless nights, and we aim out of the plane of the Galaxy, so we miss everything we can see. We figure that only one per cent of the power will be absorbed by the atmosphere, and only three per cent by the Galaxy environment. The rest ought to make it – spreading out, ever more thinly – to intergalactic space.'

Cornelius said, 'Of course we can be sure that whatever message we do receive will be meaningful to us.' He looked around; his skin seemed to glow in the starlight. 'I mean, to the four of us, personally. For *they* know we are sitting here, planning this.'

Emma shivered again. 'And did you find anything?'

'Not to a part in a billion,' said Cornelius.

There was silence, save for a distant wind rustling ink-black trees.

Emma found she had been holding her breath. She let it out gently. Of course not, Emma. What did you expect?

'Crying shame,' said Dan Ystebo, and he reached for another beer. 'Of course experiments like this have been run before. You can find them in the literature. Schmidt in 1980. Partridge, Newman a few years earlier. Always negative . . . Which is why,' he said slowly, 'we're considering other options.'

Emma said, '*What* other options?'

Cornelius said, 'We must use something else – something that isn't absorbed so easily as photons. A long mean free path length. Neutrinos.'

'The spinning ghosts.' Dan belched, and took a pull at his beer. '*Nothing* absorbs neutrinos.'

Emma frowned, only vaguely aware what a neutrino was. 'So how do you make a neutrino transmitter? Is it expensive?'

Cornelius laughed. 'You could say that.' He counted the ways on his hands. 'You set off a new Big Bang. You spark a supernova explosion. You turn a massive nuclear power plant on and off. You create a high-energy collision in a particle accelerator . . .'

Malenfant nodded. 'Emma, I was going to tell you. I need you to find me an accelerator.'

Enough, she thought.

Emma stood and drew Malenfant aside. 'Malenfant, face it. You're being spun a line by Cornelius here, who has *nothing* to show you, nothing but shithead arguments based on weird statistics and games with techno toys. He's spinning some kind of schizoid web, and he's drawing you into it. It has to stop here before –'

He snapped, 'If something goes wrong in the cockpit you don't give up. You try something else. And then another thing. Again and again until you find something that works. Have a little faith, Emma.' Emma opened her mouth, but he had already turned back to Dan Ystebo. 'Now tell me how we detect these damn neutrons.'

'*Neutrinos*, Malenfant . . .'

Cornelius leaned over to Emma. 'The Wheeler-Feynman stuff may seem spooky to you. It seems spooky to me: the idea of radio waves passing back and forth through time . . . But it's actually fundamental to our reality.

'Why is there a direction to time at all? Why does the future *feel* different from the past? Some of us believe it's because the universe is not symmetrical. At one end there is the Big Bang, a point of infinite compression. And at the other there is the endless expansion, infinite dilution. They couldn't be more different.

'*We* can figure out the structure to the universe by making observations, expressing it in such terms. But what difference does it make to an electron? How does it "know" that the forward-in-time radio waves are the "correct" ones to emit?

'Maybe it's because of those back-in-time echoes. Perhaps an electron can tell where it is in time – and which way it's facing. And *that's* how come the forward-in-time waves are the ones that make sense.

'All this is analogy and anthropomorphism. Of course electrons don't "know" anything. I could say, more formally, that the Wheeler-Feynman theory provides a way for the boundary conditions of the universe to impose a selection effect on retarded waves. But that would just be blinding you with science; and we wouldn't want that, would we?' He was smiling, his teeth white. He was toying with her, she realized.

Malenfant and Ystebo talked on, slightly drunk, eager. It seemed to Emma that their voices rose up into the sky, small and meaningless, and far above the stars wheeled, unconcerned.

Bill Tybee:

Tuesday.

Well, June, I had my meeting with Principal Bradfield. She's still determined she won't take Tom back.

At least I found out a little more.

Tom, well, he isn't the only one. The only supersmart kid, I mean. There are three others they've identified at the school, and a couple more they're suspicious about. That makes it a couple per thousand, and that's about right.

It seems this is some kind of nationwide phenomenon. Maybe global.

But the numbers are uncertain. The kids are usually identified only when they get to school.

The Principal says they are disruptive. If you have one of them in a class they get bored and impatient and distract everybody else. If there is more than one, they kind of hook up together and start doing their own projects, even using their own private language, the Principal says, until you can't control them anyhow.

And then there's the violence. The Principal wasn't about to say so but I got the impression some of the teachers aren't prepared to protect the kids properly.

I asked the Principal, *why us?* But she didn't have an answer.

Nobody knows why these kids are emerging anyhow. Maybe some environmental thing, or something in the food, or some radiation effect that hit them in the womb. It's just chance it happened to be us.

Anyhow the school board are looking at some other solution for Tom. Maybe he'll have a teacher at home. We might even get an e-teacher, but I don't know how good they are. I did read in the paper there have been proposals for some kind of special schools just for the smart kids, but that wouldn't be local; Tom would have to board.

Anyhow I don't want Tom to be taken off to some special school, and I know you feel the same.

I want him to be smart. I'm proud that he's smart. But I want him to be normal, just like other kids. I don't want him to be different.

Tom wants me to download some of the stuff from his Heart for you. Just a second . . .

Emma Stoney:

Back in her Vegas office, Emma sat back and read through her latest submission to Maura Della.

. . . The antique treaties that govern space activities are examples of academic lawmaking. They were set down far in advance of any activity they were supposed to regulate. They certainly fail to address the legitimate needs of private corporations and individuals who might own space-related resources and/or exploit them for profit. In fact they are more political statements by the former Soviet Union and Third World nations than a workable set of legal rules.

We believe the most appropriate action is therefore to get our ratification of the Treaties revoked. There are precedents for this, notably when President Carter revoked the Panama Canal Treaty by an executive order. And to put it bluntly, since the US signed these Treaties with a single main competitor in mind – the Soviet Union, a competitor which no longer even exists – there is no reason to be morally bound by them . . .

Malenfant was picking a fight by *building* his damn spaceship, out in the desert, exposing it to the cameras, and daring the bureaucrats and turf warriors and special-interest groups to shut him down. That boldness had carried him a long way. But Emma suspected that Malenfant had had an easy ride so far; the bureaucratic infighting had barely begun.

Emma – with a team of specialist lawyers mostly based in New York, and with backing from Maura and other friends in Washington – was trying to clear away the regulatory issues which could ground Malenfant's BDBs just as surely as a blow-up on the pad.

Space activities were regulated, internationally, by various treaties which dated back to the Stone Age of spaceflight: days when only governments operated spacecraft, treaties drafted in the shadow of the Cold War. But the mass of badly drafted legislation and treaties gave rise to anomalies and contradictions.

Consider tort liabilities, for instance. If Malenfant had been operating an airline, and one of his planes crashed on Mexico, then he would be responsible and his insurance would have to soak up the damages and lawsuits. But under the terms of a 1972 space liability convention, if Malenfant's BDB crashed, the US government itself would be liable.

Another problem area was the issue of certification of airworthiness – or maybe spaceworthiness – of Malenfant's BDBs. Every aircraft that crossed an international border was supposed to carry a certificate of airworthiness from its country of registry, a certificate of manufacture and a cargo manifest. So was a BDB an air vehicle? Federal aviation regulations actually contained no provisions for certificating a space vehicle. When she'd dug into the records she'd found that the FAA – the Federal Aviation Administration – had dodged the issue regarding the Space Shuttle when, in 1977, it had ruled that the Shuttle Orbiter was *not* an aircraft, despite being a winged vehicle that glided home.

It was a mess of conflicting and unreasonable regulations, at national and international levels. Maybe it was going to take a bull-headed operator like Malenfant to break through this thicket.

And all that just concerned the operation of a private spacecraft. When Malenfant reached his asteroid, there would be a whole different set of problems to tackle.

Malenfant didn't want to own the asteroid; he just wanted to make money out of it. But it wasn't clear how he could do even that.

Malenfant was arguing for a system that could enforce private property rights on the asteroid. The patent and property registry of a powerful nation – specifically the US – would be sufficient. The claims would be enforceable internationally by having the US Customs Office penalize any import that was made to the US in defiance of such a claim. This mechanism wouldn't depend on the US, or anybody else, actually claiming sovereignty over the rock. There was actually a precedent: the opening-up of trans-Appalachian America in the 17th century, long before any settler got there, under a system of British Crown land patents.

But the issue was complex, disputatious, drowned in ambiguous and conflicting laws and treaties.

Unutterably wearying.

She got up from her desk and poured herself a shot of tequila, a particular weakness since her college days. The harsh liquid seemed to explode at the back of her throat.

. . . Did she actually *believe* all this? Did she think it was *right*? Did the US have the moral authority unilaterally to hand out off-world exploitation charters to people like Malenfant?

The precedents weren't encouraging – for instance, the British Empire's authorization of brutal capitalists like Cecil Rhodes had led to such twentieth-century horrors as apartheid. And there was of course the uncomfortable fact that the upkeep and defence of the British Empire, though admirably profitable for some decades, had ultimately bankrupted its home country, a detail Malenfant generally omitted to mention in his pep talks to investors and politicians.

Meanwhile – like a hobby for her spare time – she was, somewhat more reluctantly, pursuing Malenfant's other current obsession. *Find me an accelerator* . . . With glass in hand she tapped at her soft-screen, searching for updates from her assistants and data miners.

A candidate particle physics laboratory had quickly emerged: Fermilab, outside Chicago, where Malenfant had a drinking-buddy relationship with the director. So Emma started to assemble applications for experiment time.

Immediately she had found herself coming up against powerful resistance from the researchers already working at Fermilab, who saw the well-spring of their careers being diverted by outsiders. She tried to make progress through the Universities Research Association, a consortium of universities in the US and overseas. But she met more obstruction and resistance. She had to fly to Washington to testify before a sub-panel of something called the High Energy Physics Advisory Panel of the Department of Energy, which had links into the President's science adviser.

The problem was that the facilities and experiments required giant sums of money. The physicists were still smarting from the cancellation by Congress in the 1990s of the Superconducting Supercollider, a fifty-three mile tunnel of magnets and particle beams which would have been built under a cotton field in Ellis County, Texas, and would have cost as much as a small space station. And in spite of all the megabucks spent there didn't seem to have been a fundamental breakthrough in the field for some decades.

Well, the news today, she learned now, was that the approval for the Fermilab runs had come through.

It wasn't a surprise. She had found the physicists intelligent, prone to outrage – but also politically naive and easily outmanoeuvred.

She sat back, thinking. The question was, what she should do with this news.

She decided to sit on it for now, trying to squeeze a little more productivity out of Malenfant. Because when she told Malenfant they'd won, he would take the first plane to Chicago. And she had a *lot* of issues to discuss with him.

Such as the pressure Cornelius was applying for Bootstrap to get involved with another of Eschatology's pet projects: the Milton Foundation.

The Foundation was a reaction to the supersmart children who seemed to be sprouting like weeds across the planet. The Foundation was proposing to contact these kids to make sure their special needs were met, and to try to ensure they got the opportunities they needed to exercise their abilities. No potential Einsteins doomed to waste their brief lives toiling in fields, no putative Picassos blown apart in mindless wars – no more 'mute inglorious Miltons'. Everyone would benefit: the kids themselves, their families, and the human race as a whole, with this bright new intellectual resource to call on.

That was the prospectus, and it had sold easily to Malenfant; it fit in with his view of a future that needed to be managed, ideally by Reid Malenfant.

But it was worrying for Emma, on a number of levels.

Here was a report, for example, on some kid who'd turned up in Zambia, southern Africa. He seemed the brightest of all, according to some globally applied assessment rating. But did that make it right to take him out and dump him in some school, maybe on another continent? What could a kid like that, or even his parents, possibly know about getting involved with a powerful, amorphous Western entity like Eschatology?

And besides, what *really* lay behind this strange phenomenon of supersmart children? Could it really be some kind of unusually benign environmental-change effect, as the experts seemed to be saying?

Her instinct, if she felt she wasn't in control of some aspect of the business, was always to go see for herself. She had to get out there and see for herself how all this worked, just once. This Zambia case, the first in Africa, might be just the excuse.

Of course it could be the tequila doing her thinking for her.

Africa. Jesus.

She poured another shot.

The journey was gruelling, a hop over the Atlantic to England and then an interminable overnighter south across Europe, the Mediterranean and the dense heart of Africa.

She flew into Harare, Zimbabwe. Then she had to take a short internal flight to Victoria Falls, the small tourist-choked town on the Zimbabwe side of the Falls themselves.

At her hotel, she slept for twelve hours.

The next morning a Bootstrap driver took her across the Falls, through a comic-opera immigration checkpoint, and into Zambia.

The man she had come to meet was waiting at the checkpoint. He was the teacher who had reported the boy to the Milton Foundation. He came forward hesitantly, holding out his hand. 'Ms Stoney. I'm Stef Younger . . .' He was small, portly, dressed in a kind of loose safari style, baggy shirt and shorts fitted with deep, bulging pockets. He couldn't have been older than thirty; he was prematurely balding, and his scalp, burned pink by the winter sun, was speckled with sweat.

He was obviously southern African, probably from Zimbabwe or South Africa itself. His elaborate accent, forever linked to a nightmare past, made her skin prickle. But there were blue chalk-dust stains on his shirt, she noticed, the badge of the teacher since time immemorial, and she warmed to him, just a little.

They got back in the car, and drove away from the Falls.

Africa was flat and still and dusty, eroded smooth by time, apparently untouched by the twenty-first century. The only verticals were the trees and the skinny people, moving slowly through the harsh light.

They reached the town of Livingstone. She could discern the remnants of Art Deco style in the closed-up banks and factories and even a cinema, now sun-bleached and washed out to a uniform sand colour, all of it marred by ubiquitous Shit Cola ads.

Younger gave her a little tourist grounding.

This remained a place of grinding poverty. Misguided aid efforts had flooded the area with cheap Western clothes, and local crooks had used them to undercut and wipe out the textile factories that had once kept everybody employed.

Now the unemployment here ran at 80% of adults. And there was no kind of welfare safety net. If you didn't have a relative who worked somewhere, you found some other way to live . . .

Younger pointed. 'Look at that.'

At the side of the road, there was a baboon squatting on the rim of a rusty trash can. He held himself there effortlessly with his back feet, while he dug with his forearms into the trash.

Emma was stunned. She'd never been so close to a non-human primate before, outside a zoo, anyhow. The baboon was the size of a ten-year-old boy, lean and grey and obviously ferociously strong, eyes sharp and intelligent. So much more human than she might have thought.

Younger grinned. 'He's looking for plastic bags. He knows that's where he will find food. Tourists think he's cute. But give him food and he'll be back tomorrow. Smart, see. Smart as a human. But he doesn't think.'

'What does that mean?'

'He doesn't understand death. You see the females carrying round dead infants, sometimes for days, trying to feed them.'

'Maybe they're grieving.'

'Nah.' Younger wound down his window and raised his fist.

The baboon's head snapped around, sizing up Younger with a sharp tense glance. Then he leapt off the trash can rim and loped away.

Away from the town the road stretched, black and unmarked, across a flat, dry landscape. The trees were sparse, and in many instances smashed over, as if by some great storm. There was little scrub growing between the trees. But everywhere the land was shaped by tracks, the footsteps of animals and birds overlaid in the white Kalahari sands. The tracks of elephants were great craters bigger than dinner plates, and where the ground was firm she could see the print left by the tough, cracked skin of an elephant's sole, a spidery map as distinctive as a fingerprint.

Emma was a city girl, and she was struck by the self-evident organization of the landscape here, the way the various species – in some cases separated genetically by hundreds of millions of years – worked together to maintain a stable environment for them all. Control, stability, organization, all without an organizing human mind, without a proboscidean Reid Malenfant to plan the future for them.

But this, she thought, was the past, for better or worse. Now mind was here, and had taken control; it was mind which would shape this landscape in future, and the whole of the planet, not blind evolution.

Maybe there is a lesson here for us all, she thought. Damned if I know what it is.

At length, driving through the bush, she saw elephants.

They moved through the trees, liquid graceful and silent, like dark clouds gliding over the Earth, shapers of this landscape. With untrained eyes she saw only impressionistic flashes: a gleam of

72

tusks, a curling trunk, an unmistakable morphology. The elephants were myths of childhood and picture books and zoo visits, miraculously preserved in a world growing over with concrete and plastic and waste.

They came, at last, to a village.

The car stopped, and they climbed out. Younger spread his hands. 'Welcome to Nakatindi.' Huts of dirt and grass clustered to either side of the road and spread away to the flat distance.

Nervous – and embarrassed at herself for feeling so – Emma glanced back at the car. The driver had wound up and opaqued the windows. She could see him lying back, insulated from Africa in his air-conditioned bubble, his eyes closed, synth music playing.

As soon as she walked off the dusty hardtop road she was surrounded by kids, stick thin and bright as buttons. They were dressed in ancient Western clothes – T-shirts and shorts, mostly too big, indescribably worn and dirty, evidently handed down through grubby generations. The kids pushed at each other, tangles of flashing limbs, competing for her attention, miming cameras. 'Snap me. Snap me alone.' They thought she was a tourist.

The dominant colour, as she walked into the village, was a kind of golden brown. The village was constructed on the flat Kalahari sand that covered the area for a hundred miles around. But the sand here was marked only by human footprints, and pitted with debris, scraps of metal and wood.

The sky was a washed-out blue dome, huge and empty, and the sun was directly overhead, beating at her scalp. There were no shadows here, little contrast. She had a renewed sense of age, of everything worn flat by time.

There were pieces of car, scattered everywhere. She saw busted-off car doors used like garden gates, hub caps beaten crudely into bowls. Two of the kids were playing with a kind of skateboard, just a strip of wood towed along by a wire loop. The 'wheels' of the board were, she recognized with a shock, sawn-off lengths of car exhaust. Younger explained that a few years ago some wrecks had been abandoned a mile or so away. The villagers had towed them into town and scavenged them until there was nothing left.

'. . . You'll mostly see men here today, men and boys. It's Sunday so some of the men will be drunk. The women and girls are off in the bush. They gather wild fruit, nuts, berries, that kind of stuff.'

There was no sanitation here, no sewage system. The people –

women and girls – carried their water from a communal stand-pipe in yellowed plastic bowls and bottles. For their toilet they went into the bush. There was nothing made of metal, as far as she could see, save for the scavenged automobile parts and a few tools.

Not even any education, save for the underfunded efforts of gone-tomorrow volunteers like Younger.

Younger eyed her. 'These people are basically hunter-gatherers. 150 years ago they were living Late Stone Age lives in the bush. Now, hunting is illegal. And so, this.'

'Why don't they return to the bush?'

'Would you?'

They reached Younger's hut. He grinned, self-deprecating. 'Home sweet home.'

The hut was built to the same standard as the rest, but Emma could see within an inflatable mattress, what looked like a water-purifier, a softscreen with a modem and an inflatable satellite dish, a few toiletries. 'I allow myself a few luxuries,' Younger said. 'It's not indulgence. It's a question of status.'

She frowned. 'I'm not here to judge you.'

'No. Fine.' Younger's mood seemed complex: part apologetic for the conditions here, part a certain pride, as if of ownership. *Look at the good I'm doing here.*

Depressed, Emma wondered whether, even if places of poverty and deprivation did not exist, it would be necessary to invent them, to give mixed-up people like Younger a purpose to their limited lives. Or maybe that was too cynical; he was, after all, *here.*

A girl came out of the hut's shadows. She looked no more than ten, shoulder-high, thin as a rake in her grubby brown dress. She was carrying a bowl of dirty water. She seemed scared by Emma and she shrank back. Emma forced herself to smile.

Younger beckoned, and spoke to the girl softly. 'This is Mindi,' he told Emma. 'My little helper. Thirteen years of age; older than she looks, as you can see. She keeps me from being a complete slob.' He laid his soft hand on the girl's thin shoulder; she didn't react. When he let her go she hurried away, carrying the bowl on her head.

'Come see the star of the show.' Younger beckoned, and she followed him into the shadows of the little hut. Out of the glaring flat sunlight, it took a few seconds for her eyes to adjust to the dark.

She heard the boy before she saw him: soft breathing, slow, dusty movements, the rustle of cloth on skin.

He seemed to be lying on his belly on the floor. His face was illuminated by a dim yellow glow that came from a small flashlight, propped up in the dust. His eyes were huge; they seemed to drink in the flashlight light, unblinking.

Younger said, 'He's called Michael.'

'How old is he?'

'Eight, nine.'

Emma found herself whispering. 'What's he doing?'

Younger shrugged. 'Trying to see photons.'

'I noticed him when he was very young, five or six. He would stand in the dust and whirl around, watching his arms and clothes being pulled outwards. I'd seen kids with habits like that before. You see them focusing on the swish of a piece of cloth, or the flicker of light in the trees. Mildly autistic, probably: unable to make sense of the world, and so finding comfort in small, predictable details. Michael seemed a bit like that. But he said something strange. He said he liked to feel the stars pulling him around.'

She frowned. 'I don't understand.'

'I had to look it up. It's called Mach's principle. How does Michael know if he is spinning around, or if the universe is all spinning around him?'

She thought about it. 'Because he can feel the centripetal forces?'

'Ah. But you can prove that a rotating universe, a huge matter current flowing around him, would exert exactly the same force. It's actually a deep result of general relativity.'

'My God. And he was figuring this out when he was five?'

'He couldn't express it. But, yes, he was figuring it out. He seems to have in his head, as intuition, some of the great principles the physicists have battled to express for centuries . . .'

'And now he's trying to see a photon?'

Younger smiled. 'He asked me what would happen if he shone his flashlight up in the air. Would the beam just keep on spreading, thinner and thinner, all the way to the Moon? But he already knew the answer, or rather, he somehow intuited it.'

'The beam fragments into photons.'

'Yes. He called them *light bits*, until I taught him the physics term. He seems to have a sense of the discreteness of things. If you could see photons one at a time you'd see a kind of irregular flickering, all the same brightness: photons, particles of light, arriving at your eye one after another. That's what he hopes to see.'

'And will he?'

'Unlikely.' Younger smiled. 'He'd need to be a few thousand miles away. And he'd need a photomultiplier to pick up those photons. At least, I think he would . . .' He looked at her uneasily. 'I have some trouble keeping up with him. He's absorbed the simple math and physics I've been able to give him and taken them to places I never dreamed of. For instance he seems to have deduced special relativity too. From first principles.'

'How?'

Younger shrugged. 'If you have the physical insight, all you need is Pythagoras's theorem. And Michael figured out his own proof of *that* two years ago.'

The boy played with his flashlight, obsessive, unspeaking, ignoring the adults.

She walked out into the sunshine, which was dazzling. Michael followed her out. In the bright light she noticed that Michael had a mark on his forehead. A perfect blue circle.

'What's that? A tribe mark?'

'No.' Younger shrugged. 'It's only chalk. He does it himself. He renews it every day.'

'What does it mean?'

But Younger had no answer.

She told Younger she would return the following day with tests, and maybe she should meet Michael's parents, discuss release forms and the compensation and conditions the Foundation offered.

But Younger said the boy's parents were dead. 'It ought to make the release easier,' he said cheerfully.

She held up her hand to the boy, in farewell. His eyes widened as he stared at her hand. Then he started to babble excitedly to Younger, plucking his sleeve.

'What is it?' she asked. 'What's wrong?'

'It's the gold. The gold ring on your hand. He's never seen gold before. *Heavy atoms,* he says.'

She had an impulse to give the boy the ring – after all, it was only a token of her failed marriage to Malenfant, and meant little to her.

Younger noticed her dilemma. 'Don't offer them anything. Gifts, money. A lot of people come here and try to give the shirt off their backs.'

'Guilt.'

'I guess. But you give one money, they all want it. They have no ambition, these fellows. They sit around with their beer and their four wives. They're happy, in their way.'

She remembered that Younger had talked about the baboon in the trash in exactly the same tone of voice.

Mindi, the slim girl-child, now returned, carrying a plastic bowl of fresh water. She looked anxiously to Younger, and would not meet Emma's eyes.

If she was thirteen, Emma thought, the girl was of marriageable age here. Maybe Stef Younger was finding more compensation in his life here than mere altruism.

It was a relief to climb into the car, to sip cool water and brush ten-million-year-old Kalahari dust out of her hair.

That night, she had trouble sleeping. She couldn't get the image of those bright-button village kids out of her head. Mute inglorious Miltons, indeed.

On the way here Emma had done some more digging into the Milton Foundation.

Milton turned out to be a shadowy coalition of commercial, philanthropic and religious groups, particularly Christian. The Foundation was international, and its Schools had been set up in many countries, including the US. The children were in general separated from their families and homes, and spirited away to a School perhaps half a world away. In fact – so some journalists alleged – children were being moved from School to School, even between countries, making monitoring even more difficult.

Not everybody welcomed the arrival of a School full of children labelled as geniuses. *Nobody likes a smart ass.* In some places the Schools and children had actually come under physical attack, and there were rumours of one murder; the Foundation, she had learned, spent a remarkable amount of its money on security, and almost as much on public relations.

And there were darker stories still of what went on inside the Schools.

Emma's doubts about associating Bootstrap with the initiative continued to grow. But she knew that until she came up with a stronger case for pulling back she was going to be overruled by Malenfant himself.

She wished she understood Cornelius and his shadowy associates better. She didn't yet grasp how this program fitted in with Eschatology's wider agenda: the end of the world, messages from the future

. . . She had the intuition that what they were seeking wasn't just smart children, but something much more strange.

And she wondered if that was exactly what she had found here in Africa.

She stepped onto her balcony.

Looking up at the stars, Michael's stars, she could tell she was far from home. She recognized Ursa Major. But the familiar childhood panhandle shape was upside down, and its pointer stars were pointing below the horizon. And when the Moon rose, it climbed straight up into the sky, heading for a point somewhere over her head. Not only that, it was tipped up sideways; the Man in the Moon's forehead was pointing north.

But it wasn't the Moon that was tipped; it was herself; for she had flown around the belly of the planet, which was thereby proven to be round. It was a startling thought.

I should travel more, she thought.

How was it possible for a kid on the fringe of the African bush to figure out so much fundamental physics?

If she and Malenfant had had kids, she supposed, she might have a better instinct on how to handle this situation. But she didn't, and the whole world of children, damaged or super-intelligent or otherwise, was a mystery to her.

. . . On a whim, she unfolded her softscreen and looked up the properties of gold.

She learned that relativistic effects, the strange and subtle effects of very high speeds and energies, determined the colour of gold.

In light elements, electrons orbited the nuclei of atoms at a few hundred miles per second – fast, but only a few per cent of the speed of light. But in elements with massive nuclei – like uranium, lead or gold – the electrons were dragged around at a large fraction of the speed of light, and relativity effects became important.

Most metals had a silvery lustre. But not gold. And that was because of the strange high-speed phenomena Michael seemed intuitively to understand, relativity time dilation effects operating deep within the gold atoms themselves.

She took off her ring and put it on the balcony before her. The stars were reflected in its scuffed surface. She wondered what Michael had seen as he stared into her ring.

When she got back to the States she found Malenfant had found out about the accelerator project clearances, and had holed himself up at Fermilab . . . where Dan Ystebo claimed, almost immediately, to have results.

She flew straight on to Illinois.

New York Times:

From an unpromising grade school in a run-down neighbourhood at the heart of New York City has come what may prove to be the most striking example yet of the recent wave of brilliant children <backgrounder>.

A group of children here – average age just eight – seem to have come up with a proof of the mathematical statement called the Riemann hypothesis. This is concerned with the distribution of prime numbers <click for detail>. The hypothesis is something which generations of professional mathematicians have failed to crack – and yet it has opened up to a bunch of children, in a few weeks of their working together at the school in their lunch breaks.

The result has electrified, terrified, astonished, according to temperament. The children at this New York school are the first to attract serious attention as a potential national resource from the academic and business communities and the federal government.

And it has also become the first to require round-the-clock armed guards.

The news of this obscure mathematical result has crystallized the fear some people seem to be forming over these super-kids. Police were forced to head off a mob that marched out to the school: angry, scared, evidently with ugly intent, a mob that had even included some of the parents and older brothers and sisters of the children themselves . . .

Emma Stoney:

Fermilab turned out to be thirty-five miles west of Chicago, close to a town called Batavia. From the air Illinois was a vast emptiness, studded by lost-looking little towns. Disoriented, jetlagged, she glimpsed Fermilab itself, the perfect circle of the collider ring set amid green tallgrass prairie, presumably replanted.

79

She wasn't sure what she had expected of a super-science lab like this. Something futuristic, maybe, a city of glass and platinum where steely-eyed men in white suits made careful notes on super-advanced softscreens. What she found was an oddly park-like campus littered by giant constructions, like the abandoned toys of some monster child.

This artificial landscape, the huge constructions, made a startling contrast with the bare bleakness of Africa. But the concrete was cracked and streaked with rust and mould. This was an ageing, underfunded place, she thought, a lingering dream of a more expansive age.

But here and there she saw the sleek, cool curves of the Tevatron itself, a three-mile-wide torus within which subatomic particles were accelerated to a substantial fraction of the speed of light.

The main hall was called Wilson Hall, a surreal sixteen-storey sculpture of two towers connected by criss-crossing bridges. Inside there was a gigantic atrium stocked with trees and shrubs. Malenfant was waiting for her there. There were black stress rings around his eyes, but he was agitated, excited. 'What do you think? Quite a place –'

'It's a technocrat's wet dream.'

'They rebuilt the prairie afterwards, you know. They even have a herd of buffalo here.'

'We're not here for the buffalo, Malenfant. Shall we get this over?'

He grinned. 'Wait until you see what we got here, babe.'

He led her deeper into the complex, and into the cramped and jumbled technical areas. She found herself squirming past gigantic, unrecognizable pieces of apparatus. There were steel racks everywhere, crammed with badly-packed electronic instrumentation, and cable bunches over the floor, walls and ceilings; in some places they were bridged by little wooden ladders. There was a smell of oil, shaved metal, cut wood, cleaning solvents and insulation, all overlaid by a constant clamouring metallic noise. There was none of the controlled cool and order she'd expected.

Malenfant brought her to what he called the muon laboratory. This was some way away from the accelerator ring itself; it seemed that beams of high-speed protons were drawn off from the ring and impacted into targets here.

And here they found Dan Ystebo, wearing a smeared white coat over a disreputable T-shirt, hunched over softscreens spread out on a trestle-table. The screens were covered with particle-decay images and charts of counts, none of which Emma could understand.

Dan's broad face split into a grin. 'Yo, Emma. Have you heard? . . .'

Malenfant said, 'One step at a time. Tell her what you're doing here, Dan.'

Dan took a breath. 'Making neutrinos. We're slamming the Tevatron's protons into a target to make pions.'

'Pions?'

'A pion is a particle, a combination of a quark and its anti-quark, and it is unstable. Pions decay into, among other things, neutrinos. So we have our neutrino source. But it should also be a source of *advanced* neutrinos, neutrinos coming from the future, arriving in time to make our pions decay . . .'

'Backward ripples,' Emma said.

'Exactly – hopefully modified, and containing some signal.'

'How do you detect a neutrino?'

Malenfant grunted. 'It isn't easy. Neutrinos are useful to us in the first place because matter is all but transparent to them. But we have a full-scale neutrino detector: a ton of dense photographic emulsion, the stuff you use on a camera film. When charged particles travel through this shit they leave a trail, like a jet contrail.'

'I thought neutrinos had no charge.'

'They don't,' said Dan patiently. 'So what you have to look for is a place where tracks come out but none go in. That's where a Tevatron neutrino has hit some particle in our emulsion. You get it? You have a mass of counters and magnets downstream of the emulsion, and you measure the photons with a twenty-ton lead-glass detector array, and the results are stored on laser discs and analysed by the data acquisition software –'

He talked on, lapsing continually into jargon she couldn't follow.

But then they started talking about the neutrinos themselves.

Neutrinos, it seemed, barely existed: no charge, no mass, just a scrap of energy with some kind of spooky quantum-mechanical spin, fleeing at the speed of light. Spinning ghosts indeed. Most of them had come out of the Big Bang – or the time just after, when the whole universe was a soup of hot subatomic particles. But neutrinos didn't decay into anything else. And so there were neutrinos *everywhere*. All her life she would be immersed in a sea of neutrinos, a billion of them for every particle of ordinary matter, relics of that first millisecond.

81

At that thought she felt an odd tingle, as if she could feel the ancient, invisible fluid that poured through her.

Now humans had sent waves rippling over the surface of that transparent ocean. And the waves, it seemed, had come reflecting back.

Dan talked fast, as excited as she'd ever seen him. Malenfant watched, rigid with interest. 'Essentially we've been producing millisecond neutrino pulses,' Dan said. He produced a bar chart, a scrappy series of pillars, uneven in height. 'Anyhow, up until yesterday, we were just picking up our own pulses, unmodified. Then – this.'

A new bar chart, showing a long series of many pulses. Some of the pulses, now, seemed to be missing, or were much reduced in size.

Dan picked out the gaps with a fat finger. 'See? On average, these events seem to have around half the neutrino count of the others. So half the energy.' He looked at Emma, trying to see if she understood. 'This is *exactly* what we'd expect if somebody downstream has some way of suppressing the advanced-wave neutrinos. The apparent retarded neutrinos then would have only half the strength –'

'But it's such a small effect,' Emma said. 'You said yourself neutrinos are hard to detect. There must be other ways to explain this, without invoking beings from the future.'

'That's true,' Dan said. 'Though if this sustains itself long enough we're going to be able to eliminate other causes. Anyhow, that's not all. We have enough data now to show that the gaps *repeat*. In a pattern.'

Malenfant growled, 'This is new to me. A repeating pattern. *A signal?*'

Dan rubbed his greasy hair. 'I don't see what else it could be.'

'A signal,' said Malenfant. 'Damn. Then Cornelius was right.'

Emma felt cold, despite the metallic stuffiness of the chamber.

Dan produced a simplified summary of several periods of the pattern, a string of black circles and white circles. 'Look at this. The blacks are full-strength pulses, the whites half-strength. You get a string of six white. Then a break of two black. Then an irregular pattern for twelve pulses. Then two black, six white, and a break. Then another set of twelve black-whites, "framed" by the two black and six white combination. I think we're seeing delimiters around these two strings of twelve pulses. And this is what repeats: over and over. Sometimes there are minor differences, but we think that's caused by the experimental uncertainty.'

Malenfant said, 'If it's a signal, what does it mean?'

Emma said, 'Binary numbers. The signals are binary numbers.'

They both turned to her.

Malenfant said, 'Huh? Binary numbers? Why?'

She smiled, exhausted, jetlag-disoriented. 'Because signals like this always are.'

Dan was nodding. 'Yes. Right. I should have thought of that. We have to learn to think like Cornelius. The downstreamers know us. Maybe they *are* us, our future selves. And they know we'll expect binary.' He grabbed a pad and scribbled out two strings of 1 and 0:

$$1\ 1\ 1\ 0\ 1\ 0\ 1\ 0\ 1\ 0\ 0\ 1$$
$$0\ 1\ 1\ 1\ 1\ 1\ 0\ 0\ 0\ 0\ 1\ 0$$

He sat back. 'There.'

Malenfant squinted. 'What's it supposed to be?'

Emma found herself laughing. 'Maybe it's a Carl Sagan picture. A waving downstreamer.' Shut up, Emma.

'No,' Dan said. 'It's too simple for that. They have to be numbers.' He cleared his softscreen and began tapping in a simple conversion program. After a couple of minutes, he had it running.

$$3\ 7\ 5\ 3$$
$$1\ 9\ 8\ 6$$

They stared. Malenfant said, 'What do they mean?'

Dan began to feed the raw neutrino counts through his conversion program, and the converted signals – live, as they were received in the film-emulsion detector – scrolled steadily up the screen.

$$3\ 7\ 5\ 3$$
$$1\ 9\ 8\ 6$$
$$3\ 7\ 5\ 3$$
$$1\ 9\ 8\ 6$$
$$3\ 7\ 5\ 3$$
$$1\ 9\ 8\ 6$$

'Someone should call Cornelius,' Dan said. 'And –'

Malenfant said, 'What?'

'We only ran for a week before we picked this up. How did the downstreamers know when we were ready, when to switch on?'

Malenfant grinned. 'Because they already knew when we'd be here.'

Emma didn't share his evident glee at this result.

She felt dwarfed. She imagined the world wheeling around her, spinning as it carried her through darkness around the sun, around the rim of the Galaxy – and the Galaxy itself sailing off to its own remote destination, stars glimmering like the windows of a great ocean liner . . .

Messages from the future. Could it be true? – that there were beings, far beyond this place and time, trying to signal to the past, to her, through this lashed-up physics equipment?

Was Cornelius right? Right about everything? Right, too, about the Carter catastrophe, the coming extinction of them all?

It couldn't be true. It was insanity. An infection of schizophrenia from Cornelius, that was damaging them all.

Malenfant, of course, was hooked. She knew him well enough to understand he would be unable to resist this new adventure, wherever it took him.

And how, she wondered, was she going to be able to persuade him to do any work at all, after *this*?

3 7 5 3

1 9 8 6

3 7 5 3

1 9 8 6

. . .

Reid Malenfant:

The puzzle of the Feynman radio message nagged at Malenfant, even as he threw himself into his myriad other projects. He would write out the numbers on a pad, or have them scroll up on a softscreen. He tried taking the numbers apart: factorizing them, multiplying them, dividing one by the other.

He got nowhere.

Cornelius Taine was equally frustrated. He would call Malenfant at odd time-zoned hours. *Mathematics, even numerology, must be the wrong approach.*

'Why?'

What do you know about math, Malenfant? Remember the nature of the signal we're dealing with here. Remember that the downstreamers are trying to communicate with us – specifically, with you.

'Me?'

Yes. You're the decision-maker here. There has to be some simple meaning in these numbers for you. Just look at the numbers, Cornelius urged. *Don't think too hard. What do they look like?*

$$1\ 9\ 8\ 6$$

$$3\ 7\ 5\ 3$$

'Umm, 1986 could be a date.'

A date?

1986: the year of *Challenger* and Chernobyl, a first overseas posting for a young pilot called Reid Malenfant. 'It wasn't the happiest year in history, but nothing so special for me . . . Hey. Cornelius. Could 3753 *also* represent a date?' His skin prickled. 'The 38th century – Christ, Cornelius, maybe that's the true date of the Carter catastrophe.'

Cornelius's softscreen image, slightly blurred, showed him frowning. *It's possible, but any date after a couple of centuries is very unlikely. Anything else?*

'No. Keep thinking, Cornelius.'

Yes . . .

And Malenfant would roll up the softscreen and return to his work, or try to sleep.

Until the day came when Cornelius, in person, burst into a BDB project progress meeting.

It was an airless Portakabin at the Mojave test site. Malenfant was with George Hench, poring over test results and subcontractor signoffs. And suddenly there was Cornelius: hot, dishevelled, pink with sunburn, tie knot loosened, white gypsum staining his lower legs, clinging to the fabric of his suit pants.

Malenfant couldn't keep from laughing. 'Cornelius, at last I've seen you out of control.'

Cornelius was panting. '*I have it.* The numbers. The Feynman numbers. I figured it out, Malenfant. And it changes everything.'

Despite the heat of the day, Malenfant felt goosebumps rise on his bare arms.

He made Cornelius sit down, take his jacket off, drink some water.

Cornelius brusquely cleared clutter from the tabletop – battered softscreens, quality forms, a progress chart labelled with bars and arrows, old-fashioned paper blueprints, sandwich wrappers and beer cans – and he spread his own softscreen over the desk.

'It was staring us in the face the whole time,' Cornelius said. 'I knew it had to be connected to *you*, Malenfant, to your interests. Your obsessions, even. And it had to be something you could act on now. And what –' he waved a hand '– could be a grander obsession than *this*, your asteroid mission?'

George Hench paced around the room, visibly unhappy.

Cornelius glanced up at George. 'Look, I'm sorry to disrupt your work.'

George glared. 'Malenfant, do we have to put up with this bull?'

'Whatever it is, it ain't bull, George. I've seen the set-up –'

'Malenfant, I spent my career fending off handwaving artistes like this guy. Colour co-ordinators. Feng Shui artists. Even astrologers, for Christ's sake. Sometimes I think the US is going back to the Middle Ages.'

Malenfant said gently, 'George, there was no US in the Middle Ages.'

'Malenfant, we have a job to do here. A big job. We're going to a fucking asteroid. All I'm saying is, you need to focus on what's important here.'

'I accept that, George. But I have to tell you I've come to believe there's *nothing* so important as the downstreamers' message. If it's real.'

'Oh, it's real,' Cornelius said fervently. 'And what it means is that you're going to have to redirect your mission.' Cornelius eyed George. 'Away from Reinmuth.'

George visibly bristled. 'Now, you listen to me –'

Malenfant held up a hand. 'Let's hear him out, George.'

Cornelius tapped at his softscreen. 'When I began to wonder if the numbers referred to an asteroid, I thought 1986 might be a discovery date. So I logged onto the Minor Planet Center in Massachusetts.' A table of numbers and letters scrolled down the screen; the first column, of four digits and two letters, all began with '1986'. 'This is a list of all the asteroids first reported in 1986. This first code is a provisional designation –'

'What do the letters mean?'

'The first shows the half-month when the asteroid was discovered. The second is the order of discovery in that half-month. So 1986AA is the first asteroid to be discovered in the first half of January, 1986.'

Malenfant eyed the numbers with dismay. 'Shit. There must be dozens, just for 1986.'

'More in later years; asteroid watches have got better . . .'

'So which one is ours?'

Cornelius smiled and pointed to the second column. 'As soon as enough observations have been accumulated to determine the asteroid's orbit, it is given an official designation, a permanent number, and sometimes a name.'

The official numbers, Malenfant saw with growing excitement, were in the range 3700–3800. Cornelius scrolled down, until he came to a highlighted line.

1986TO 3753 0.484 1.512 0.089 . . . .

The key numbers jumped out at Malenfant. 1986 3753.

'Holy shit,' he said. 'It's there. It's *real*.'

'Not only that,' said Cornelius. 'This little baby, 1986TO, is like no other asteroid in the Solar System.'

'How so?'

Cornelius smiled. 'It's Earth's second Moon. And nobody knows how it got there.'

George Hench stomped out to 'go bend some tin', glaring at Cornelius as he did so.

Cornelius, unperturbed, called up more softscreen data and told Malenfant what little was known about asteroid number 3753.

'3753 is not in the main belt. In fact, it's a near-Earth object, like Reinmuth. What the astronomers call an Aten.'

Malenfant nodded. 'So its orbit mostly lies inside Earth's.'

'It was discovered in Australia. Part of a routine sky watch run out of the Siding Springs observatory. Nobody's done any careful spectral studies or radar studies. But we think it's a C-type: a carbonaceous chondrite, not nickel-iron, like Reinmuth. Water ice, carbon compounds. It probably wandered in from the outer belt – far enough from the sun that it was able to keep its volatile ices and organics – or else it's a comet core. Either way, we're looking at debris left over since the formation of the Solar System. Unimaginably ancient.'

'How big is it?'

'Nobody knows for sure. Three miles wide is the best guess.'

'Does this thing have a name?'

Cornelius smiled. 'Cruithne.' He pronounced it *Crooth-knee*. 'An ancient Irish name. The ancestor of the Picts.'

Malenfant was baffled. 'What does that have to do with Australia?'

'It could have been worse. There are asteroids named after spouses, pets, rock stars. The orbit of Cruithne is what made it worth naming.' Cornelius pointed to numbers. 'These figures show the asteroid's perihelion, aphelion, eccentricity . . .'

Asteroid 3753 orbited the sun in a little less than an Earth year. But it did not follow a simple circular path, like Earth; instead it swooped in beyond the orbit of Venus, out further than Mars. 'And,' said Cornelius, 'it has an inclined orbit . . .' Cornelius's diagrams showed 3753's orbit as a jaunty ellipse, tipped up from the ecliptic, the main Solar System plane, like Frank Sinatra's hat.

Malenfant considered this looping, out-of-plane trajectory. 'So what makes it a moon of the Earth?'

'Not a moon exactly. Call it a companion. The point is, its orbit is locked to Earth's. A team of Canadian astronomers figured this out in 1997. Watch.'

Cornelius produced a display showing the orbits of Earth and Cruithne from a point of view above the Solar System. Earth, a blue dot, sailed evenly around the sun on its almost-circular orbit. By comparison, Cruithne swooped back and forth like a bird.

'Suppose we follow the Earth. Then you can see how Cruithne moves in relation.'

The blue dot slowed and stayed in place. Malenfant imagined the whole image circling, one revolution for every Earth year.

Relative to the Earth, Cruithne swooped towards Venus – inside Earth's orbit – and rushed ahead of Earth. But then it would sail out past Earth's orbit, reaching almost to Mars, and slow, allowing Earth to catch up. Compared to Earth it traced out a kind of kidney-bean path, a fat, distorted ellipse sandwiched between the orbits of Mars and Venus.

In the next 'year' Cruithne retraced the kidney-bean – but not quite; the second bean was placed slightly ahead of the first.

Cornelius said, 'Overall 3753 is going faster than the Earth around the sun. So it spirals ahead of us, year on year . . .' He let the images run for a while. Cruithne's orbit was a compound of the two motions. Every year the asteroid traced out its kidney bean. And over the years the bean worked its way along Earth's orbit tracing out a spiral around the sun, anti-clockwise.

'Now, what's interesting is what happens when the kidney bean approaches Earth again.'

The traced-out bean worked its way slowly towards the blue dot. The bean seemed to touch the Earth. Malenfant expected it to continue its spiralling around the sun.

It didn't. The kidney bean started to spiral in the opposite direction: clockwise, back the way it had come.

Cornelius was grinning. 'Isn't it beautiful? You see, there are resonances between Cruithne's orbit and Earth's. When it comes closest, Earth's gravity tweaks Cruithne's path. That makes Cruithne's year slightly *longer* than Earth's, instead of shorter, as it is now. So Earth starts to outstrip the kidney bean.' He ran the animation forward. 'And when it has spiralled all the way back to where it started –' Another reversal. 'Earth tweaks again, and makes Cruithne's year shorter again – and the bean starts to spiral back.'

He accelerated the timescale further, until the kidney bean ellipses arced back and forth around the sun.

'It's quite stable,' said Cornelius. 'For a few thousand years at least. Remember a single kidney bean takes around a year to be traced out. So it's a long time between reversals. The last were in 1515 and 1900; the next will be in 2285 and 2680 –'

'It's like a dance,' said Malenfant. 'A choreography.'

'That's exactly what it is.'

Although Cruithne crossed Earth's orbit, its inclination and the tweaking effect kept it from coming closer than forty times the distance from Earth to Moon. Right now, Malenfant learned, the asteroid was a hundred times the Earth-Moon distance away.

After a time Malenfant's attention began to wander. He felt obscurely disappointed. 'So we have an orbital curiosity. I don't see why it's so important you'd send a message back in time.'

Cornelius rolled up his softscreen. 'Malenfant, NEOs – near-Earth objects – don't last forever. The planets pull them this way and that, perturbing their orbits. Maybe they hit a planet, Earth or Venus or even Mars. Even if not, a given asteroid will be slingshot out of the Solar System in a few million years.'

'And so –'

'And so we have plausible mechanisms for how Cruithne could have been formed, how it could have got into an orbit close to Earth's. But *this* orbit, so finely tuned to Earth's, is unlikely. *We don't know how Cruithne could have got there,* Malenfant. It's a real needle-threader.'

Malenfant grinned. 'And so maybe somebody put it there.'

Cornelius smiled. 'We should have known. We shouldn't have needed a signal from the downstreamers, Malenfant. That Earth-locked orbit is a red flag. Something is waiting for us, out there on Cruithne.'

'What?'

'I have absolutely no idea.'

'So now what?'

'Now, we send a probe there.'

Malenfant called back George Hench. The engineer prowled around the office like a caged animal.

'We can't fly to this piece of shit, Cruithne. Even if we could reach it, which we can't, Cruithne is a ball of frozen mud.'

'Umm,' Cornelius said. 'More to it than that. We're looking at a billion tons of water, silicates, metals, and complex organics – aminos, nitrogen bases . . . Even Mars isn't as rich as this, pound for pound. It's the primordial matter, the stuff they made the Solar System out of. Maybe you should have planned to fire the probe at a C-type in the first place.'

Malenfant said evenly, 'George, it's true. We can easily make an economic case for Cruithne –'

'Malenfant, Reinmuth is made of steel. My God, it *gleams*. And you want to risk all that for a wild goose chase with your la-la buddy?'

Malenfant let George run on, patiently. Then he said, 'Tell me why we can't get to Cruithne. It's just another NEO. I thought the NEOs were easier to reach than the Moon, and we got *there* forty years ago.'

George sighed, but Malenfant could see his brain switching to a different mode. 'Yeah. That's why the space junkies have been campaigning for the NEOs for years. But most of them don't figure the correct energy economics. Yes, if you look at it solely in terms of delta-vee, if you just add up the energy you need to spend to get out of Earth's gravity well there are a lot of places easier to get to than the Moon. But you need to go a chart deeper than that. Your NEO's orbit has to be *very* close to Earth's: in the same plane, nearly circular, and with almost the same radius. Now, Reinmuth's orbit *is* close to Earth's. Of course it means that Reinmuth doesn't line up for low-energy missions very often; the orbits are like two clocks running slightly adrift of each other –'

'So tell me,' Malenfant said heavily, 'why Cruithne is so much more difficult.'

George ticked the problems off on his fingers. 'Cruithne is twenty degrees out of the plane of the ecliptic. Plane changes are *very* energy-expensive. That's why the Apollo guys landed close to the Moon's equator. Two. Cruithne's orbit is highly eccentric. So we can't use the low-energy Hohmann trajectories we employ to transfer from one circular orbit to another, for instance in travelling from Earth to Mars. Changes to elliptic orbits are also energy-expensive. Three –'

Malenfant listened a while longer.

'So you've stated the problem,' said Malenfant patiently. 'Now tell me how we do it.'

There was more bluster and bullshit and claims of impossibility, which Malenfant weathered.

And then it began.

George produced mass statements for the BDB and its payload, began to figure the velocity changes he would need to reach Cruithne, how much less manoeuvring capability he would have, how much less payload he could carry there compared to Reinmuth. Then he began calling in an array of technicians, all of whom started just as sceptical as himself, most of whom, in the end, were able to figure a reply. They called up Dan Ystebo at Key Largo to ask him how little living room his pet squid really, truly could survive in. Dan was furious, but he came back with answers.

It took most of the day. Slowly, painfully, a new mission design converged. Malenfant only had to sit there and let it happen, as he knew it would.

But there was a problem.

The present spacecraft design packed enough life support to take Sheena 5 to Reinmuth, support her work there, and bring her home again: she was supposed to come sailing into Earth's atmosphere, behind a giant aeroshell of asteroid slag.

But there was no way a comparable mission to Cruithne could be achieved.

There was a way to meet the mission's main objectives, however. In fact it would be possible to get Sheena to Cruithne much more rapidly.

By cutting her life support, and burning everything up on the way out.

For Sheena, a Cruithne voyage would be one way.

Emma Stoney:

From Emma's perspective, sitting in her office in Vegas, everything was starting to fall apart.

The legalistic vultures were hovering over Malenfant and his toy spaceships, and meanwhile the investors, made distrustful by rumours of Malenfant's growing involvement with bizarre futurian types, were starting to desert.

If Malenfant had made himself more available, more visible to shore up confidence, it might have made a difference. But he didn't. Right through Christmas and into the New Year Malenfant remained locked away with Cornelius Taine, or holed up at his rocket test site.

It seemed to Emma events were approaching a climax. But still Malenfant wouldn't listen to her.

So Emma went to the Mojave.

Emma stayed the night in a motel in the town of Mojave itself. She was profoundly uncomfortable, and slept little.

Her transport arrived before dawn. It was an Army bus. When she climbed aboard, George Hench was waiting for her. He had a flask of coffee and a bagel. 'Breakfast,' he said. She accepted gratefully; the coffee was industrial strength, but welcome.

The other passengers were young engineers, trying to sleep with their heads jammed in corners by the windows.

The drive out to the BDB test site was dull but easy. The sun had risen, the heat climbing, by the time they hit the thirty-mile road to Malenfant's BDB launch complex – or *launch simplex*, as he liked to call it.

Hench jammed open the bus window. 'Natural air conditioning,' he said, cackling.

She glanced back. One or two of the youngsters behind them stirred.

Hench shrugged. 'They'll sleep.'

At the site the bus passed through the security fence and pulled over, and Emma climbed down cautiously. The light glared from the sand that covered everything, and the heat was a palpable presence that struck at her, sucking the moisture from her flesh.

The test site had grown. There were a lot more structures, a lot more activity even at this hour of the morning. But it was nothing like Cape Canaveral.

There were hardly any fixed structures at all. The place had the air of a construction site. There were trailers scattered over the desert, some sprouting antennae and telecommunications feeds. There weren't even any fuel tanks that she could see, just fleets of trailers, frost gleaming on their tanks. People – engineers, most of them young – moved to and fro, their voices small in the desert's expanse, their hard hats gleaming like insect carapaces.

And there was the pad itself, the centre of attention, maybe a mile from where she stood, bearing the *Nautilus*: Bootstrap's first interplanetary ship, Reid Malenfant's pride and joy. She saw the lines of a rust-brown Shuttle external tank and the slim pillars of solid rocket boosters. The stack was topped by a tubular cover that gleamed white in the sun. Somewhere inside that fairing, she knew, a Caribbean reef squid, disoriented as all hell, would some day ride into space.

Hench said gruffly, 'I'll tell you, Ms Stoney –'

'Emma.'

'Working with those kids has been the best part of this whole damn project, for me. You know, these kids today come out of graduate school, and they are real whizzes with Computer Aided This and That, and they do courses in science theory and math and software design . . . but they don't get to bend tin. Not only that, they've never seen anything *fail* before. In engineering, experience gained is directly proportional to the amount of equipment ruined. No wonder this country has fallen behind in every sphere that counts. Well, here they've had to build stuff, to budget and schedule. Some of the kids were scared off. But those that remained flourished . . .'

And here came Malenfant. He was wearing beat-up overalls – he even had a spanner in a loop at his waist – and his face and hands and scalp were covered in white dust patches. He bent to kiss her, and she could feel gritty sand on her cheek.

'So what do you think of *Nautilus*? Isn't she beautiful?'

'Kind of rough and ready.'

Malenfant laughed. 'So she's supposed to be.'

An amplified voice drifted across the desert from the launch pad.

'What was that?'

Hench shrugged. 'Just a checklist item.'

'You're going through a checklist? A launch checklist?'

Malenfant said, 'Demonstration test only. We're planning two tests today. We've done it a dozen times, already. Later today we'll even have that damn squid of Dan Ystebo's up in the payload pod, on top of a fully fuelled ship. *We're ready*. And Cruithne is up there waiting for us. And who knows what lies beyond that. As soon as you can clear away the legal bullshit –'

'We're working on it, Malenfant.'

Malenfant took her for a walk around the booster pad, eager to show off his toy. Malenfant and Hench, obviously high on stress and adrenaline, launched into war stories about how they'd built their rocket ship. '. . . The whole thing is a backyard rocket. It has Space Shuttle engines, and an F-15 laser gyro set and accelerometer, and the autopilot and avionics from a MD-11 airliner. In fact the BDB thinks it's an MD-11 on a peculiar flight path. We sent the grad school kids scouring through the West Coast aerospace junkyards, and they came back with titanium pressure spheres and hydraulic actuators and other good stuff. And so on. Assembled and flight-ready in six months . . .'

He seemed to know every one of the dozens of engineers here by name. He was, by turns, manipulative, bullying, brutal, overbearing. But he was, she thought, always smart enough to ensure he wasn't surrounded by sycophants and yea-sayers.

Maybe that's why he keeps me on.

'How safe is all this, Malenfant? What if the ship blows up, or a fuel store –'

He sighed. 'Emma, my BDBs will blow up about as often as a 747 blows up on take-off. The industries have been handling LOX and liquid hydrogen safely for half a century. In fact I can prove we're safe. We've kept the qual and reliability processes as simple as possible – no hundred-mile NASA paper chains – and we put the people on the ground in charge of their own quality. Qual upfront, the only way to do it.' He looked into the sun, and the light caught the dust plastered over his face, white lines etched into the weather-beaten wrinkles of his face. 'You know, this is just the beginning,' he said. 'Right now this is Kitty Hawk. You got to start somewhere. But some day this will be a true spaceport.'

'Like Cape Canaveral?'

'Oh, hell, no. Think of an airport. You'll have concrete launch pads with minimal gantries, so simple we don't care if we have to rebuild them every flight. We'll have our own propellant and oxidizer manufacture facilities right here. The terminal buildings will be just like JFK or O'Hare. They'll build new roads out here, better rail links. The spaceport will be an airport too. We'll attract industries, communities. People will *live* here . . .'

But she heard tension in his voice, under the bubbling faith. She'd gotten used to his mood swings, which seemed to her to have begun around the time he was washed out of NASA. But today his mood was obviously fragile, and, with a little push, liable to come crashing apart.

The legal battle wasn't won yet. Far from it. In fact, Emma thought, it was more like a race, as Bootstrap lawyers sought to find a way through the legal maze that would allow Malenfant to launch, or at least keep testing, before the FAA inspectors and *their* lawyers found a way to get access to this site and shut everything down.

Tomorrow, she told herself. Tomorrow I have to confront him with the truth. The fact that we're losing the race.

As the sun began to climb down the blue dome of sky, Emma requested an Army bus ride back to her motel in Mojave. There she pulled the blinds and spread out her softscreen. She fired off mails, ate room service junk, tried to sleep.

. . . The phone rang, jarring her awake. It was Malenfant.

Go to your window.

'What?'

I'm simplifying a few bureaucratic processes, Emma.

He sounded a little drunk. And dangerous. She felt a cold chill settle at the pit of her stomach. 'What are you talking about?'

Go to the window and you'll see. I've been talking to Cornelius about Doctor Johnson. Once Johnson was asked how he would refute solipsism. You know, the idea that only you exist, all else is an illusion constructed by your mind . . .

She opened her shutters. In the direction of the test range, a light was spreading over the bottom half of the sky: a smeared yellow-white rising fast, not like a dawn.

Johnson kicked a rock. And he said, 'I refute it thus' . . .

'Oh, Malenfant. What have you done?'

They came to shut me down, Emma. We lost the race with those FAA assholes. One of those smart kids of George's turned out to be an FBI plant. The inspectors arrived . . . They would have drained

95

the Nautilus *and broken her up. And then we'd never have reached* *Cruithne. I decided it was time to kick that rock. Emma, you should* *see the dust we're raising!*

And now a spark of light rose easily from the darkened horizon, climbing smoothly into the sky. It was yellow-white, like a fleck of sunlight, and it trailed a pillar of smoke and steam that glowed in the light spark.

She knew what that was, of course. The yellow-white was the burning of the solid propellants of the twin boosters, half-combusted products belching into the air; the central hydrogen-oxygen main engine flame was almost invisible. Already, she could see, the arc of the climbing booster was turning east, towards the trajectory that would take it off the planet.

And now the noise arrived, rocket thunder, billowing over her like the echo of a distant storm.

This is just the beginning, Malenfant whispered.

DOWNSTREAM

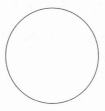

And so some day
The mighty ramparts of the mighty universe
Ringed around with hostile force
Will yield and face decay and come crumbling to ruin . . .

— Lucretius

Sheena 5:

Drifting between worlds, the spacecraft was a miniature planet, a bubble of ocean just yards across.

The water was sufficient to protect its occupants from cosmic and solar radiation. And the water sustained concentric shells of life: a mist of diatoms feeding off the raw sunlight, and within them, in the deeper blue water, a shell of krill and crustaceans and small fish schools, hunting and browsing.

And, at the centre of it all, a single enhanced cephalopod.

. . . Here was Sheena, swimming through space.

Space: yes, she understood what that meant, that she was no longer in the wide oceans of Earth, but in a small, self-contained ocean of her own that drifted through emptiness, a folded-over ocean she shared only with the darting fish and the smaller, mindless animals and plants on which they browsed.

She glided at the heart of the *Nautilus*, where the water that passed through her mantle, over her gills, was warmest, richest. The core machinery, the assemblage of devices that maintained life here, was a black mass before her, suspended in dark water, lights winking over its surface, weeds and grasses clinging to it. Sheena saw no colours; she swam through a world of black, white and grey. But she could discern polarized light; and so now she saw that the light which gleamed from the polished surfaces of the machinery was subtly twisted, this way and that, giving her a sense of the solidity and extent of the machinery.

When the ship's roll took her into shadow, she hunted and browsed.

She would rest on the sand patches that had been stuck to the metal, changing her mantle colour so as to be almost invisible. When the fish or the krill came by, all unawares, she would dart out and snatch them, crushing them instantly in her hard beak, ignoring their tiny cries.

Such simple ambushes were sufficient to feed her, so confused did the fish and krill appear in this new world which lacked up and down and gravity. But sometimes she would hunt more ambitiously, luring and stalking and pursuing, as if she was still among the rich Caribbean reefs.

But all too soon the ship's languid roll brought her into the light, and brief night gave way to false day.

Rippling her fins, she swam away from the machinery cluster, away from the heart of the ship, where she lived with her shoals of fish. As she rose the water flowing through her mantle cooled, the rich oxygen thinning. She was swimming out through layers of life, and she sensed the subtle sounds of living things washing through the sphere: the smooth rush of the fish as they swam in their tight schools, the bubbling murmur of the krill on which they browsed, and the hiss of the diatoms and algae which fed *them*, and the deep infrasonic rumble of the water itself, compression waves pulsing through its bulk.

And just as each successive sphere of water was larger than the one it contained, so Sheena knew there was a hierarchy of life. To sustain *her*, there had to be ten times her weight in krill, and a hundred times in diatoms.

And if there had been other squid, of course, those numbers would increase. But there was no other squid here but herself.

For now.

She could see, through misty, life-laden water, the ship's hull, a membrane above her like an ocean surface. Except that it *wasn't* above her, as it would be in a true ocean. And there was no sandy ocean floor below. Instead the membrane was all around her, closed on itself, shimmering in great slow waves that curled around the sphere's belly.

This was self-evidently a complex world, a curved world, a world without the simple top and bottom of the ocean; and the light was correspondingly complex, its polarization planes random, or else spiralling down around her.

But Sheena hunted in three dimensions. She could come to terms with all this strangeness. She knew she must, in fact.

She reached the wall of the ship.

The membrane was a firm, if flexible, wall. If she pushed at it, it pushed back. Human eyes could see that the wall was tinted gold.

Dan had told her how beautiful this great golden egg had been in the skies of Earth, as it receded to the stars. *Sheena ship good pretty,* he said. *Like Earth. Ship people see, gold bubble, ship of water . . .*

Grass algae grew on the wall, their long filaments dangling and wafting in the currents. Crabs and shellfish grazed on the grass algae. The benthic grazers helped feed her, and in the process kept the walls clean.

Every creature in this small ocean had a part to play. Here, for instance, she drifted past a floating bank of seaweed. The seaweed cleaned the water, and used up drifting food that the algae and diatoms could not consume. And the seaweed was useful in itself. One of Sheena's jobs was to gather the weed, when it grew too thick, and deliver it to a hopper in the machinery cluster. There it could be spun into fibres that Dan called sea silk. The sea silk would be used when she got to her destination, to make and repair the equipment she would use there.

Now the ship's slow rotation carried Sheena into the light of a milky, blurred disc. It was the sun – dimmed by the membrane so it did not hurt her eyes – with, near it, a smaller crescent. That, she knew, was the Earth, all its great oceans reduced to a droplet. The craft scooted around the sun after Earth like a fish swimming after its school, seeking the rock that was the target for this mission.

Once, swimming under the arching membrane like this, she had been startled by a starburst of light, only a few moments' swim from her. It had disappeared as soon as it had occurred – but it seemed to her that there was a flaw in the membrane, a small patch that had lost its lustrous glow; and she could see from the muddled polarization how the composition of the water had been disturbed beneath the flaw.

Then she had seen something moving, outside the membrane. She cowered, flashed signals of false threat and concealment, thinking it was some deep space predator.

It was no predator. It was just a box that squirted back and forth, emitting gentle little farts of glittering crystals. It was pulling a patch over the hole.

Dan told her it was a firefly robot, a smart little box with its own power supply and fuel and miniaturized machinery and cameras and machine intelligence. The ship carried a shoal of these small craft for external inspection and repairs like this.

But the little craft's life was limited, intended for a single use only, and it could achieve only one thing, which was to fix the membrane –

unlike Sheena, who could do many different things. When its job was done, its fuel expended, the craft neatly folded away its tool-bearing arms, and used the last breath of its fuel to push itself away from the ship. Sheena had watched as the little craft, discarded, dwindled to a sunlit point.

She had learned that her ship leaked all the time anyway, from tiny flaws and miniature punctures. And every few days the throwaway robots would scuttle over the membrane, tracking the vapour clouds, fixing the worst of the leaks, before sacrificing themselves.

She let the lazy, whale-like roll of the ship carry her away from the glare of the sun, and she peered into the darkness, where she could see the stars.

The stars were important. She had been trained to recognize many of them. When she had memorized their positions around the ship she would return to the machinery cluster and work the simple controls Dan had given her. By this means she could determine her position in space far more accurately than even Dan could have, from far-off Earth.

Then the rockets would flare, sending hails of exhaust particles shooting into space. They would push at the hide of the ship like a squid shoving at the belly of a whale. Waves, flaring with light, pulsed back and forth across the meniscus, illuminating the drifting clouds of algae, and Sheena could detect the subtle wash of gravity around her as the great mass of water was nudged back to its proper trajectory.

But to Sheena the stars were more than navigation beacons. Sheena's eyes had a hundred times the number of receptors of human eyes, and she could see a hundred times as many stars.

To Sheena the universe was *crowded* with stars, vibrant and alive. The Galaxy was a reef of stars beckoning her to come jet along its length.

But there was only Sheena here to see it.

She found it hard to rest.

Sheena was utterly alone. Though she knew there were no predators here, that she was as safe as any squid had ever been, she could not rest: not without the complex protection of the shoal around her, its warnings and sentinels. And, of course, without the shoal she was cut off from the society of the squid, the mating and learning and endless dances of daylight.

Dan had provided a kind of dream shoal for her: squid-like shapes that swam and jetted around her, glimmering. But the polarization of the light from their false hides was subtly wrong, and the fake shoal was no comfort. She was surprised Dan had not understood.

As the mission progressed, as she grew progressively more weary, her loyalty to Dan crumbled, grain by grain.

e-CNN:

. . . And we return to our main story, the developing crisis around the illegal space launch by the Bootstrap corporation from their Mojave facility. It has become clear that the authorities, far from granting the approvals Bootstrap is seeking, were in fact moving to close down the operation completely. Joe . . .

. . . Thanks, Madeleine. We do know that Cruithne was not the original target of Reid Malenfant's interplanetary ambitions. Originally he was planning to head for Reinmuth, another asteroid that is much richer in metals than Cruithne. So, why Cruithne?

It's now emerged, from sources inside Bootstrap itself, that in recent months Malenfant has become convinced that the world itself may be coming to an end. And this global doom is somehow linked to asteroid Cruithne. What are we to make of this remarkable twist in this spectacular story?

We've been trying to determine if there is more to Malenfant's fears about the future than mere paranoia. It is said there are respectable scientists who claim that it is a statistical fact that the world will end, taking all of us with it, in just a few centuries. Apparently this has been known in government circles since the 1980s. Again the Administration declined to comment. Madeleine . . .

Joe, Reid Malenfant, fifty-one, is highly charismatic and popular. Since the announcement of his interplanetary venture he has become something of a cult figure. In fact last year's best-selling Christmas toys were models of Bootstrap's so-called Big Dumb Booster, along with action figures and animated holograms of the intelligent squid crew, and even of Reid Malenfant himself.

But, while undoubtedly an attractive figure, Malenfant has long been regarded by commentators as an unstable personality.

However Bootstrap spokespersons are saying this is all scurrilous rumour put out by enemies of Reid Malenfant, perhaps within his own corporation . . .

John Tinker:

Yes, they threw me out of the Flying Mountain Society. Screw them.

And screw Reid Malenfant. Malenfant is a wimp.

Yes, he got his bird off the ground. But to continue to launch with 1940s-style chemical rockets is at best a diversion, at worst a catastrophic error.

People, you can't lift diddley into space by burning chemicals.

There has been a solution on the drawing boards since the 1960s. Project Orion.

You take a big plate, attach it by shock-absorbers to a large capsule, and throw an atomic bomb underneath.

Your ship will move, believe me.

Then you throw another bomb, and another.

For an expenditure of a small part of the world's nuclear stockpile you could place several million pounds in orbit.

I believe in the dream. I believe we should aim to lift a *billion* people into space by the end of the century. This is the only way to establish a population significant enough to build a genuine spacegoing industry infrastructure – and, incidentally, the only way to lift off enough people to make a dent in the planet's population problem.

Yes, this will cause some fallout. But not much, compared to what we already added to the background radiation. What's the big deal?

Malenfant is right; we are facing a crisis over the survival of the species. Hard times make for hard choices. Omelettes and eggs, people.

Anyhow, those bombs aren't going to go away. If America doesn't use them, somebody else will . . .

Art Morris:

My name is Art Morris and I am forty years old. I am a Marine, or used to be until I got disabled out.

My most prized possession is a snapshot of my daughter, Leanne.

In the snap she's at her last birthday party, just five years old, in a splash of Florida sunshine. The snap's one of those fancy modern ones that can show you movement, and it cycles through a few seconds of Leanne blowing at her cake. And it has a soundtrack. If you listen under the clapping and whoops of the family and the other kids, you can just hear her wheeze as she took her big breath. What you can't see off the edge of the picture is me, just behind Leanne's shoulder, taking a blow myself to make sure those damn candles did what she wanted them to do, making sure that something in her world worked, just once.

It wasn't long after that that we had to put her into the ground. I didn't understand half of what the doctors told me was wrong with her, but I got the headline.

She was a yellow baby, a space baby, a rocket baby.

Maybe by now she would have been one of these smart kids the news is full of. But she never got the chance.

I rejoiced when they shut down the space program. But now those assholes in the desert have started firing off their damn rockets again, regardless.

I keep Leanne's picture taped to the dash of my car, or in my pocket.

Look what you did, Reid Malenfant.

Reid Malenfant:

Madame Chairman, this is not some wacko stunt. It is a sound business venture.

Here's the plan from here on in.

Cruithne is a ball of loosely aggregated dirt: probably eighty per cent silicates, sixteen per cent water, two per cent carbon, two per cent metals. This is an extraordinarily rich resource.

Our strategy is to aim for the simplest technologies, fast return, fast payback.

The first thing we're going to make up on Cruithne is rocket fuel. The fuel will be a methane-oxygen bipropellant.

Then we'll start bagging up permafrost water from the asteroid, along with a little unprocessed asteroid material. We'll use the propellant to start firing water back to Earth orbit – specifically, a type of orbit called HEEO, a highly eccentric Earth orbit, which in terms of accessibility is a good compromise place to store extraterrestrial materials.

Thus we will build a pipeline from Cruithne to Earth orbit.

This will not be a complex operation. The methane rockets are based on tried and trusted Pratt and Whitney designs. The cargo carriers will be little more than plastic bags wrapped around big dirty ice cubes.

But in HEEO this water will become unimaginably precious. We can use it for life support and to make rocket fuel. We think *Nautilus* should be able to return enough water to fuel a further twenty to fifty NEO exploration missions, at minimal incremental cost. This is one measure of the payback we're intending to achieve. Also we can sell surplus fuel to NASA.

But we are also intending to trial more complex extraction technologies on this first flight. With suitable engineering, we can extract not just water but also carbon dioxide, nitrogen, sulphur, ammonia, phosphates – all the requirements of a life support system. We will also be able to use the asteroid dirt to make glass, fibreglass, ceramics, concrete, dirt to grow things in.

We are already preparing a crewed follow-up mission to Cruithne which will leverage this technology to establish a colony, the first colony off the planet. This will be *self-sufficient*, almost from day one.

And the colonists will pay their way by further processing the Cruithne dirt to extract its metals. The result will be around ninety per cent iron, seven per cent nickel, one per cent cobalt, and traces. The trace, however, includes platinum, which may be the first resource returned to the surface of the Earth; nickel and cobalt will probably follow.

(Incidentally I'm often asked why I'm going to the asteroids first, rather than the Moon. The Moon seems easier to get to, and is much bigger than any asteroid besides. Well, the slag that is left over after we extract the water and volatiles and metals from asteroid ore – the stuff we'd throw away – that *slag* is about equivalent to the richest Moon rocks. That's why I ain't going to the Moon.)

Later we'll start the construction of a solar power plant in Earth orbit. The high-technology components of the plant, such as guidance, control, communications, power conversion and microwave transmission systems, will be assembled on Earth. The massive low-tech components – wires, cables, girders, bolts, fixtures, station-keeping propellants and solar cells – will all be manufactured in space from asteroid materials. This plan reduces the mass that will have to be lifted into Earth orbit several-fold. This plant will produce energy – safe, clean, pollution-free – we can sell back to Earth.

And that's the plan. In the next few years Cruithne volatiles will support the Space Station, more Earth-orbital habitats, and missions to the Moon and Mars, as well as the first self-sufficient off-Earth colony.

That little lot ought to see *me* through to retirement.

But what about beyond that?

Beyond that, the Galaxy awaits, and all the universe. Virgin territory. All we need is a toehold. And that's what Bootstrap will give us. America has discovered a new frontier, and we will become great again.

Frankly, Madame Chairman, I think I've spent enough time in front of Congressional committees like this and other boards of inquiry. All I need is for you to let me carry on and do my job. And I don't see I have a damn thing to apologize for.

Thank you.

Sheena 5:

Swimming through space, despite her consuming weariness, Sheena 5 had work to do.

She explored the complex knot of equipment that was the centre of her world. It was like swimming around a sunken boat.

The machinery was covered with switches and levers, labelled with black and white stripes and circles so she could recognize them. And there were dials designed for her eyes – dials coated with stripes like the hide of a squid, dials which could send out pulses of twisting polarized light. The dials told her what was happening inside the equipment, and if anything was wrong she was trained to turn the levers and switches to make it right.

Sometimes she had to chase away curious fish as she did so.

If anything more serious was wrong she could ask Dan for help, and he always knew the answer, or could find it out. She would fit the plastic cup to her eye, and speckled laser light would paint images on her retina, distorted diagrams and simple signs which showed her what to do.

The machinery contained whirring motors which drove pumps and filters: devices that, coupled with the flow of heat from the sun, drove steady currents. The currents ensured that the waters mixed, that no part became too hot or cold, too rich with life or too stagnant. Otherwise the diatoms and algae would cluster under the bubble's skin, where the sunlight was strongest, and would grow explosively until they had exhausted all the nutrients available and formed a dank cloud so thick the water would die.

And the filters removed waste from the water, irreducible scraps that no creature in this small world could digest. But something had to be done with those wastes, or gradually they would lock up all the nutrients in the water. So the machine contained a device which could burn the wastes, breaking them down into their component parts. The products, gas and steam and salts, could then be fed back to the plants and algae.

Thus, in Sheena's spacecraft, matter and energy flowed in great loops, sustained by sunlight, regulated by its central machinery as if by a beating heart.

Dan told her that she was already a success: in her management of the equipment, she had shown herself to be much smarter and more adaptable than any human-made machine they could have sent in her place.

She knew that in their hearts the humans would prefer to send machines, mindless rattling things, rather than herself. That was because they knew they could control machines, down to the last clank and whirr. But they could never control *her* . . . as was proven by the remnants of the spermatophore she still guiltily hoarded in her mantle cavity, cemented to the inner wall.

Perhaps they were jealous.

How strange, she thought, that her kind should be so well adapted to this greater, infinite ocean, so much better than humans. As if this was somehow meant to be. It seemed to Sheena that it must be terribly *confining* to be a human, to be confined to the skinny layer of air that clung to the Earth.

. . . At first she had found it strangely easy to accept that she would die without seeing Earth's oceans again, without rejoining the shoals. She suspected this was no accident, that Dan had somehow *designed* her mind to accept such instructions without fear.

Which was, of course, not true.

But as her restlessness and tiredness gathered, as her isolation increased, the importance of Dan and his mission receded, and her sense of loss grew inexorably.

And, of course, there was a final complicating factor nestling in her mantle cavity.

She would have to release her eggs eventually. But not yet. Not here. There were many problems that day would bring, and she wasn't ready for them.

So, swimming in starlight, Sheena cradled her unhatched young, impatiently jetting clouds of ink in the rough shape of the male she had known, the male with the bright, mindless eyes.

Michael:

It was some weeks after the woman had come to the village that Stef called him.

'I have to go away,' said Stef. 'So do you.'

Michael didn't understand. Stef, with his machines and his food and his girls, was the most powerful person in the village, far more powerful than the head man or the herbalist. Who could make *him* do things?

And besides, Michael had never been more than a few hundred yards outside the village, never slept anywhere but in a village hut. He wasn't sure what 'going away' might actually mean, what he would be made to do.

It seemed unreal. Perhaps it was all some game of Stef's.

'I don't want to go,' Michael said. But Stef ignored him.

He slept, trying not to think about it.

But the very next day they came for him.

A car pulled up outside the village. Big smiling women got out. Cars came to the village every day, stayed a few hours, left again. But this day, for the first time in his life, Michael would have to get into the car, and leave with it.

He took his clothes, and the flashlight Stef had given him. Stef had given him new batteries too, long-life batteries that would not run down so quickly. Michael didn't want to go, but the big women, their smiles hard, made it clear there was no choice.

'I'm sorry,' Stef said to Michael. 'We never finished our lessons. But you'll be okay. You'll keep learning.'

Michael knew that was true. He knew he couldn't stop learning. Even when he was alone, even in the dark, he would just keep working, learning, figuring out.

Even so he was frightened.

'Take me with you,' he said.

But Stef said no. 'They won't even let me take Mindi,' he said. Mindi had been his favourite girl. Now, pregnant, she had gone back to her mother, because no man would have her. 'They'll look after you,' Stef said to Michael. 'You're a *Blue*.'

That was the first time Michael heard that word, the English word, used like that. He didn't know what it meant.

He wondered if he would ever see Stef again.

He was taken through a series of bright buildings, a barrage of voices and signs, nothing of which he could understand. Even the smells were strange.

At one point he was in an airplane, looking down over parched land and blue sea.

Afterwards he thought he must have slept a great deal, for his memories of the journey were jumbled and fragmented, and he could put them in no logical order.

So he came to the School.

Emma Stoney:

Thanks to the unauthorized launch, the spectacular sight of the golden spacecraft leaving Earth orbit, Malenfant had become a popular hero. This was his Elvis year for sure, the media advisers were telling them; and they were working hard on making him even more mediagenic.

But he had made an awful lot of very powerful enemies. Opposition to Malenfant had erupted, as if orchestrated, right across the financial and political spectrum. Right now, it seemed to Emma, they were further away than ever from being certificated to fly again, and further still from being licensed to keep any money they made out of Cruithne, assuming *Nautilus* actually got there.

Emma called a council of war in the Bootstrap offices in Las Vegas: herself, Malenfant, Maura Della. She didn't invite him, but Cornelius Taine came anyhow.

Malenfant stalked around the office. 'I can't believe this shit.' He glared at Emma. 'I thought we figured out our prebuttals.'

'If you're blaming me I'm out of here,' she said. 'Remember, you never even warned me you were going to fire off your damn rocket.'

Maura said evenly, 'I know what you tried to do, Malenfant. You thought that by simply launching, by proving that your system worked safely, you could cut through the bureaucratic mess, as well as prove your technical point.'

'Damn right. Just as I will prove my economic point when we start bringing the goodies home.'

Maura shook her head. 'You're so naïve. You showed your hand. All you did was give your opponents something to shoot at.'

'But we *launched*. We're going to Cruithne. That is a physical fact. All the staffers on the Hill, all the placeholders in the NASA centers, can't do a damn thing about that.'

Cornelius Taine steepled his elegant fingers. 'But they can stop you from launching again, Malenfant.'

'And they can throw you in jail,' Emma said softly. 'We mustn't argue among ourselves. Let's go over it point by point.' She tapped the tabletop; it turned transparent, and an embedded softscreen brought up a bullet chart. 'First, the NASA angle.'

Malenfant laughed bitterly. 'Fucking NASA. I couldn't believe the immediate one-eighty they pulled about the feasibility of my BDB design, *after* it flew.'

Cornelius Taine said, 'Why are you surprised? They hoped you would fail technically. Now that is not possible, they intend to ensure you fail politically.'

'Yeah, that or take me over . . .'

It seemed to be true. With indecent haste – leading Emma to suspect they had been working on precisely this move in advance, and waiting for the moment to strike – NASA had come up with counter-proposals for BDB designs, issuing formal Requests for Proposals to prospective industry partners. NASA claimed they could start flying BDBs of their own, in five or ten years' time – after ensuring that all the relevant technologies were 'understood and in hand'.

Not only that, they were absorbing Malenfant's long-term goals as well, with proposals for an international program to reach and exploit the asteroids.

Maura said, 'I'm not sure how we can win this one – after all, NASA is supposed to be *the* agency that develops spacecraft.'

'But,' Cornelius said heavily, 'this process of assimilation is precisely how NASA has killed off every new space technology initiative since the Shuttle.'

'Yeah,' Malenfant growled. 'By turning it into another aerospace industry cartel feeding frenzy –'

Maura held her hands up. 'My point is NASA may well win. If they do, we need a way to live with that.'

We, Emma thought. Even in the depths of this tense meeting, she found time to wonder at the way Malenfant had, once again, turned a potential enemy into a friend.

'Next,' Emma said warily. 'Congressional funding.'

'We're not reliant on federal funds,' Malenfant snapped.

'That's true,' Maura said dryly. 'But you've been happy to accept whatever general-purpose funding you could lay your hands on. And that's turning into a weakness. We're being caught between authorization and appropriation. You need to understand this, Malenfant. These are two phases. Authorization is a wish-list. Appropriation is the allocation of funds to the wish-list. Not every authorized item gets funded.' She paused. 'Let me put it simply. It isn't wise to spend authorized money as if it was appropriated already. That's what you did. It was a trap.'

'It was peanuts,' Malenfant growled. 'And anyhow I don't know why the hell you Congress critters can't just make a simple decision.'

Maura sighed. 'Federal government is a complex thing. If you don't use the processes right . . .'

'And,' Emma said, 'next year looks even worse. The bad guys have identified all sources of federal funding we budgeted for and have put in place recision and reprogramming processes to –'

'Then we rebudget,' said Malenfant. 'We cut, trim, rescope, find new funds.'

'But the investors are being frightened off,' Emma said. 'That's the next point. It started even before the launch, Malenfant. You knew that. Now they're haemorrhaging. The problems we've had with the regulatory agencies have scared away even more of them.'

'. . . But,' said Cornelius Taine evenly, 'we must continue.'

Oh, Christ, Emma thought.

Cornelius looked from one to the other, his face blank. 'Don't any of you understand this? Who do you *want* to appropriate the Solar System? The Russians? The Chinese? Because if we fail now, that's what will happen.'

Emma said sharply, 'I'll tell you the truth, Cornelius. From where I'm sitting you're part of the problem, not the solution. No wonder the investors took flight. If any of your kook stuff has leaked out –'

Cornelius said, 'The Carter catastrophe is coming no matter what you think of me.'

Maura frowned. 'The *what*?'

Emma took a breath. 'Malenfant, listen to me. Everything we've built up so far will be destroyed. Unless we start to take action.'

'Action? Like what? A sell-out to NASA?'

'Maybe. And you have to cut your links with this character.'

Cornelius Taine smiled coldly.

Malenfant's hands, clasped behind his back, showed white knuckles.

The meeting broke up without agreement on a way forward. And on the way out, Maura whispered to Emma, 'Carter? Who the hell is Carter?'

Emma didn't get to her apartment until midnight that night. When she walked in the door she told the TV to turn itself on. And there, on every news channel, was Cornelius Taine.

Cornelius Taine:

So, Dr Taine, you're saying that these people from the future – the ones you call downstreamers – have reached into the past, to us. To send a message.

Yes. We believe so.

But you're assuming these are downstreamers who have survived this catastrophe of yours. Will survive. Whatever. Right? So why did they need to send a message?

You're asking me about causal paradoxes. The downstreamers are saving their grandmothers, us, from drowning. But if she *had* drowned they wouldn't even exist, so how can they save her? Right?

Umm . . . yeah. I guess –

There's a lot we don't understand about time. What happens if you try to change the past is top of the list. Let me try to explain. It is a question of transactions, back and forth in time.

The Feynman radio works on the notion of photons – electromagnetic wave packets – travelling back in time. Fine.

But photons aren't the only waves.

Waves lie at the basis of our best description of reality. I mean, of course, the waves of quantum mechanics. These waves represent flows of – what? Energy, information? Certainly they criss-cross space, spreading out from every quantum event like ripples.

We have good equations to tell us how they propagate. And if we know the structure of the waves we can tell a great deal about the macroscopic reality they represent. A clumping of the waves *here* means this is the most likely place to find that travelling electron emitted from over *there* . . .

But, like electromagnetic waves, quantum wave packets emitted from some event travel both forward and back in time. And these backward waves are vital to the structure of the universe.

Suppose you have an object of some kind that changes the state of another: a source and a detector, maybe of photons. The source changes state and sends quantum waves off into future and past. The future-travelling wave reaches the detector. In turn this emits waves travelling into both future and past, like echoes.

Here's the catch. The quantum echoes cancel out the source waves, both future and past, *everywhere* – except along the path taken by the ordinary retarded waves. It's like a standing wave set up between source and receiver. Because no time passes for a wave travelling at lightspeed, all of this is timeless too, set up in an instant.

It's called a transaction, as if source and detector are handshaking. 'Hi, I'm here.' 'Yes, I can confirm you are . . .'

So there really are waves travelling back in time?

So it seems. But you don't have to worry about them.

I don't?

No. There are no back-in-time paradoxes, you see, because the backwards waves only work to set up the transaction; you can't detect them otherwise.

And that's how our reality works. As the effects of some change propagate through space and time, the universe knits itself into a new form, transaction by transaction, handshake by handshake.

Umm. And this is quantum mechanics, you say? So what happened to all that quantum funny stuff? The collapsing wave function, and Schrödinger's cat, and the Many Worlds Interpretation, and –

Oh, you can forget all *that*. We study that today the way we study Roman numerals. Now that we know what quantum mechanics is *really* all about, it's hard to imagine how people in those days thought like that. Do you follow?

Umm . . . Madeleine?

Let me get this straight. If I go back and change the past, I create a new universe that branches off at that point . . . right? If I kill my grandmother, I get two universes, one where she lived and I was born, one where she dies and I was never born –

No. Perhaps you haven't heard me. It just doesn't work like that.

There is only one universe at a time. New universes may bud off from others, but they are not 'parallel' in the way you say. They are separate and entire, with their own self-consistent causalities.

So what happens if I go back in time and do something impossible, like kill my granny? Because if she dies, I could never be born, and could never have killed her . . .

Each quantum event emerges into reality as the result of a feedback loop between past and future. Handshakes across time. The story of the universe is like a tapestry, stitched together by uncountable trillions of such tiny handshakes. If you create an artificial timelike loop to some point in spacetime within the negative light cone of the present –

Woah. In English.

If you were to go back in time and try to change the past, you would nullify all those transactions, the handshakes between future and past. You would damage the universe, erasing a whole series of events within the time loop.

So the universe starts over, from the first point where the forbidden loop would have begun to exist. The universe, wounded, heals itself with a new set of handshakes, working forward in time, until it is complete and self-consistent once more.

Then changing the past is possible.

Oh, yes.

Tell me this, Dr Taine. According to this view, even if you do

go back and change the past – how do you know you succeeded?
Won't you change along with the past you altered?

We don't know. How could we? We never tried this before. But we think it's possible a conscious mind *would* know.

How?

Because consciousness, like life itself, is structure. And structure persists as the cosmic tapestry changes.

Think about a DNA molecule. Some of the genes are important for the body's structure; some are just junk. If you could perturb reality, consider possible alternate destinies for that molecule, you could see a lot of variation in the junk without affecting the operation of the molecule in any significant way. But if there's a change in the *key* structural components, those that contain information, the molecule may be rendered useless. Therefore, the key structure must be stable in the face of small reality changes.

So if in some way our minds span reality changes –

Then maybe we'll be able to perceive a change, an adjustment of the past. Of course this is speculative.

And what about free will, Doctor Taine? Where does that fit into your grand plan?

Free will is a second order effect. Even life is a second order effect. Light dancing from the rippled surface of time's river. It is not the cause even of the ripples, let alone the great majestic flow itself.

That's one gosh-darned gloomy view.

Realistic, however.

You know, our time is just a bubble far upstream that must seem utterly insignificant compared to the great enterprises of the future. But it isn't insignificant, because it's the *first* bubble. And if we don't survive the Carter catastrophe, we lose everything – eternity itself . . .

Emma Stoney:

The media types had it all: the Carter prediction, the message from the future, the real reason for the redirection of the *Nautilus*. All of it.

Emma was convinced it was Cornelius himself who had leaked the Carter stuff. It increased the pressure on Bootstrap hugely, but that only seemed to reinforce Malenfant's determination to fight his way through this, to maintain his links with Cornelius, and continue on to Cruithne, and launch again.

Which, of course, was exactly what Cornelius wanted. She had been outflanked.

She spent a sleepless night trying to figure out what to do next.

Michael:

At first the School seemed a good place to Michael. Better than the village, in fact.

The clothes were clean and fresh. The food was new and sometimes tasted strange, but there was always a lot of it. In fact there were refrigerators that lit up with food and drink inside, food the children could help themselves to whenever they wanted. Michael found he missed baobab fruit, though.

There were lots of children here, from very small to young teenagers. They lived in dormitories, which were bright and clean.

At first the children had been wary of each other. They had no common language, and children who could speak to each other tended to gather in groups. There was nobody who spoke Michael's language, however. But he was used to being alone.

This was a place called Australia. It was a big empty land. He saw maps and globes, but he had no real understanding of how far he had come from the village.

Except that it was a long way.

There were lessons. The teachers were men and women called Brothers and Sisters.

Sometimes the children would be gathered in a room, ten or fifteen of them, while a teacher would stand before them and talk to them or have them do work, with paper and pen or softscreen.

Michael, like some of the other children, had a special softscreen which could speak to him in his own tongue. It was comforting to hear the little mechanical voice whisper to him, like a remote echo from home.

The best times of all were when he was allowed to go explore, as if the softscreen was a window to another world, a world of pictures and ideas.

He had no interest in languages or music or history. But mathematics held his attention from the start.

He drank in the symbols, tapping them onto his softscreen or scratching them on paper, even drawing in the dust as he used to at home. Most of the symbols and their formalism were better than the ones he had made up for himself, and he discarded his own without sentiment; but sometimes he found his own inventions were superior, and so he kept them.

He loved the strict rigour of a mathematical proof – a string of equations, statements of truth, which nevertheless, if manipulated correctly, led to a deeper, richer truth. He felt as if his own view of the world was crystallizing, freezing out like the frost patterns he watched inside the refrigerators, and his thinking accelerated.

Soon, in math class, he was growing impatient to be forced to work at the same pace as the other children.

Once, he grew restive.

That was the first time he was punished, by a Sister who yelled at him and shook him.

He knew that was a warning: that this place was not as friendly as it seemed, that there were rules to learn, and the sooner he learned them the less harm would come to him.

So he learned.

He learned to sit quietly if he was ahead of the rest. He could do his work almost as effectively that way anyhow.

Michael seemed to be the one who enjoyed mathematics the most. But most of the children had one or two subjects in which they excelled. And then it was Michael's turn to sit and struggle, and the others' turn to race ahead, risking the wrath of the teachers.

Any children who showed no such talent were soon taken out of the School. Michael didn't know what happened to them.

It was a paradox. If you weren't smart enough you were taken out of the School. If you were too smart you were punished for impatience. Michael tried to learn this rule too, to show just enough ability but not too much.

It didn't matter anyhow. Most of his real work he did in his head, in the dark, and he never told anybody about it.

There were many visitors: adults, tall and dressed smartly, who walked around the classes and the dormitories. Sometimes they brought people with cameras who smiled as if the children were doing something of great importance. Once a woman even took away Michael's softscreen, looking at the work he had recorded there with exclamations of surprise. He was given another soft-screen, but of course it was empty, containing none of the work he had completed. But that didn't matter. Most of it was in his head anyhow.

There was a girl here called Anna, a little older and taller than the rest, who seemed to learn the rules more quickly than the others. She had big grey eyes, Michael noticed, grey and watchful. She would speak to the others – including Michael, through his softscreen – trying to help them understand what was wanted of them.

It meant she was in line for punishment more often than most of the others, but she did it anyway.

Many of the children drew blue circles on their books or their soft-screens or their skin or the walls of the dormitories. As did Michael, as he had for a long time. He didn't know what that meant.

Those days – in retrospect, strange, bright days – didn't last long.

Michael couldn't know it, but it was the publicizing of the Carter prophecies – the end of the world news – that forced the change in the Schools, including his own.

Because suddenly people grew afraid: of the future, of their own children.

Leslie Gandolfo:

Frankly our biggest problem, since this damn end-of-the-world Carter bullshit broke, has been absenteeism. We're up over a hundred per cent nationally. Not only that but productivity is right down, and our quality metric program shows a massive decline in all functions. (Except Accounting, for some reason.) We've also had a number of incidents of violence, immoral behaviour and so forth in the workplace, some but not all related to alcohol and/or drugs.

It's as if they all *believe* this pseudo-science bullshit about there being no tomorrow. But of course the clockpunchers expect *us* to keep on providing salaries and bonuses and medical benefits, presumably right up until doomsday itself, with maybe an advance or two.

I know our competitors are suffering too. But we can't go on like this, ladies and gentlemen; our costs are skyrocketing, our profits haemorrhaging.

I'm pleased to see the federal government is finally taking some positive action. Grey-suited spokesmen denouncing Carter and Eschatology as moonshine were all very well. What they are doing now, pumping out free twenty-four-hour sports, comedy, softsoaps and synth-rock on TV, is a somewhat more practical response.

We've already installed giant video walls in our workplaces in Tulsa and Palm Beach. Productivity took a hit, of course, but happily nowhere near as bad as in other sites without the wall-to-wall pap. We've also provided free e-therapy up to four hours a week per permanent employee. For now I agree with the government analysis that an anaesthetized workforce is preferable to a workforce plunged into existential gloom.

But this is just a palliative. We have to find a long-term way to handle this. The end of the world may or may not be inevitable. Our stockholder meeting *is* inevitable, however. I'm open to further suggestions . . .

'The Voice of Reason':

> . . . Mail this on to ten people you know, and tell them to send it to ten people they know, and so on. We have to inoculate the species against the contagion of madness which is plaguing mankind, or this damn Carter hypothesis is going to become a self-fulfilling prophecy.
> HOW TO DEBUNK CARTER
> 1) First of all, don't dismiss it as nonsense. The hypothesis may be wrong-headed but it's not irrational and it's not illogical. We aren't dealing with the usual airhead crap here. It's more potent than that.
> 2) Don't insult your opponent. Start with the premise that people aren't stupid, whether they know science and math or not. If you insult them you'll be seen as arrogant, and you'll lose the argument.
> 3) The best attack on Carter is the notion that the cosmos is radically indeterministic. You can argue from quantum physics to justify this, if you can keep your audience with you, or from free will if not. There is no way, even in principle, to say how many humans might exist in the future. So the Carter analogy between humankind and balls in an urn breaks down.

> 4) If your audience is sophisticated enough, remind them that the whole argument is based on Bayesian statistics, which is a technique to refine probabilities of an event *given a knowledge of prior probabilities.* But in this case we have no prior probabilities to work with (we can only guess about the long-term future of mankind). So the Bayesian technique can't be valid.

> 5) Reduce the argument to the trivial. It's trivially obvious that people discussing Carter's argument find themselves alive today, not hundreds of years in the future. But nothing non-trivial follows from a triviality. Since no humans of the future are yet alive, it isn't in the least surprising that we aren't among them.

> 6) You could try a reductio ad absurdum. On any scale an exponential curve looks the same. You always seem to be at the beginning, minuscule compared to what is to come. So the catastrophe will always be just over the horizon. (Of course this argument falls down unless the exponential curve of the human population really does extend to infinity. Any finitude and something like Carter comes into play. But you don't have to mention that unless challenged.)

> 7) Appeal to common sense. Look back in time. A human of, say, AD 1000 would likewise have been sitting on top of an exponential curve reaching back to the Palaeolithic. Would she have been correct to deduce she was in the last generations? Of course not, as we can see with retrospect. (You may find Carter proponents countering this one by saying this is a false analogy; humanity today faces far graver extinction threats than in AD 1000 because of our technological advancement, the way we have filled up the Earth, etc. And it took our modern-day sophistication to come up with the Carter argument in the first place. So we have formulated the Carter prophecy at precisely the moment it is most applicable to us. But then you can argue that they are appealing beyond the statistics.)

   <continuing list snipped>

> Remember, though! *None of the counter-arguments is definitive.* You may find yourself up against somebody with as much or more understanding of statistics than

you. In that case, escalate the argument until you blind the general audience with science.

> The objective here isn't to disprove Carter – that may be impossible; you can hole the argument but you can't sink it, and anyhow the one true invalidation will be our continued survival in 201 years – but we must stop this ludicrous panic over Carter before it eats us all up like a brush fire . . .

Maura Della:

Doom soon was all rather difficult to believe, a month after Cornelius had gone public, as Maura endured the usual Potomac hell: breakfasts with reporters, morning staff meetings, simultaneous committee meetings to juggle, back-to-back sessions with lobbyists and constituents, calls, briefings, speeches, receptions, constant implant-pager tingles to make quorum calls and votes on the run. And then there were the constituency issues she couldn't neglect: 'casework' – distributing small favours, funded by the federal pork-barrel and otherwise – and targeted mail and fundraising shots and chat-room surgeries and online referenda and appearances, in person, e-person or simulated. It was all part of the constant campaign, a treadmill she knew she couldn't fall off if she expected to get elected again.

But this was just the general grind of federal government. It was as if illegal rocket launches in the desert, the dire warnings of doom, had never happened.

The federal government think tanks who had tried to flesh out the Carter catastrophe hypothesis had provided her with some gloomy reading.

On the one hand, nobody could definitively undermine the argument itself on philosophical or mathematical grounds. No tame expert would stand up and say he or she could demonstrate the damn thing was bullshit in simple enough terms for the President to deliver to the nation, the panicking world.

On the other hand the think tanks could come up with a lot of ways the world *might* end.

War, of course: nuclear, biological, chemical.

A disaster from genetic engineering, malevolent or otherwise. The report recalled one near-miss in the early '00s in Switzerland, concerning a birth control vaccine. A genetically altered salmonella bacterium had been supposed to cause a temporary infection in the female gut that triggered antibodies against sperm. It had, of course, mutated and got out of control. A hundred thousand women had been rendered permanently infertile before the bug was stopped.

Environmental catastrophes: the continuing collapse of the atmosphere's structure, the greenhouse effect.

Eco terrorism. People waging war both for and against the environment. Witness the ground-to-air missile that had recently brought down the *Znamya*, the giant inflatable mirror that should have been launched into orbit to light up the night sky over Kiev. Witness similar attacks on the reef balls on the Atlantic ocean shelf, the giant concrete hemispheres intended to attract fast-growing algae and so soak up excess atmospheric carbon dioxide. (Maura was grimly amused to see that Bootstrap had been a major investor in both these projects.)

But much worse was possible. The environment was essentially unstable, or at least only quasi-stable. If somebody found a way to tip that stability, it might only need a small nudge . . .

That was the man-made stuff. Then there were natural disasters. That hoary old favourite, the asteroid strike, was still a candidate.

And the Earth, she read, was overdue for a giant volcanic event, of a scale unseen in all of recorded history. The result would be a 'volcano winter' comparable to nuclear-war aftermath.

Or the radiation from a nearby supernova could wipe the Earth clean of life; she learned that the Earth, in fact, was swimming through a bubble in space, blown clear in the interstellar medium by just such an explosion.

And here was something new to her: perhaps a new ice age would be triggered by the Earth's passage through an interstellar cloud.

The report concluded with more outlandish speculations. What about annihilation by extraterrestrials? What if some alien species was busily transforming the Solar System right now, not even aware that we existed?

Or how about 'vacuum decay'? It seemed that space itself was unstable, like a statue standing on a narrow base. It could withstand small disturbances ('small', in this case, including such things as galactic core explosions) but a powerful enough nudge, properly applied, could cause the whole thing to tip over into – well, a new form. The take-home message seemed to be that such a calamity would be, not just the end of the world, but the end of the universe.

Et cetera. The list of apocalypses continued, spectacular and otherwise, at great length, even to a number of appendices.

The report authors had tried to put numbers to all these risks. The overall chance of species survival beyond the next few centuries it put as sixty-one per cent – the precision amused Maura – a result they described as 'optimistic'.

That wasn't to say the world would be spared all the disasters; that wasn't to say the human race would not endure death and suffering on giant scales. It wasn't even a promise that human civilization in its present form would persist much longer. It was just that it was unlikely that the world would encounter a disaster severe enough to cause outright human extinction.

Relatively unlikely, anyhow.

Whether or not the world was ending, the prediction itself was having a real effect. The economy had been hit. Crime, suicides, a loss of business confidence. There had been a flight into gold, as if *that* would help. This was, the think-tankers believed, ironically a by-product of a recent growth in responsibility. After generations of gloomy warnings about Earth's predicament, people had by and large begun to take responsibility for a future that extended beyond the next generation or two. Perhaps in the 1950s, the world two centuries hence would have seemed impossibly remote. Now it seemed around the corner, awfully close, within the bounds of current plans and thinking.

It was ironic that people had begun to imagine the deeper future just as it was snatched from them.

. . . Above all we must beware Schopenhauerian pessimism, she read. *Schopenhauer, obsessed with the existence of evil, wrote that it would have been better if our planet had remained lifeless, like the Moon. From there it is only a short step to thinking that we ought to make it lifeless. It may be that this motivates some of the destructiveness seen recently in our urban communities, although the disruption caused by the so-called 'Blue children' phenomenon at a fundamental level – that is, nuclear family level – is no doubt contributing . . .*

It was a complex of responses, an unstable species sent in to a spin by the bad news from the future. Perhaps what would bring down mankind in the end was not nature, or science, but a creeping philosophical disaster.

In the midst of all this, Malenfant was summoned to appear before the House Committee on Space, Science and Technology in Washington, DC, an appearance which might be – as Maura realized immediately – his last chance to save his sorry ass.

Emma Stoney:

On the morning Malenfant was due to give his testimony, Emma – nervous, unsleeping – was up early.

She took a walk around Washington, DC. It was a hot, flat morning. The traffic noise was a steady rumble, carried through the sultry air.

She followed the Mall, the grassy strip of parkland that ran a mile from the Capitol building to the Lincoln Memorial. The grass was yellow, the ground baked hard and flat, though it was only April. The heat rose in waves, as if she was walking across a hot plate. From here she could see several of the nation's great buildings: seats of government, museums. A lot of neo-classical marble, grandly spaced: this was an imperial capital if ever there was one, a statement of power, if not of good taste.

She considered going to see the asteroid-exploration VR gallery Malenfant had donated to the Air & Space Museum. Typical Malenfant: influencing public opinion with what was ostensibly a gesture of generosity. Maybe another day, she thought.

She reached the Washington Monument: simple and clean, seamlessly restored since its '08 near-demolition by Christian libertarians. But the flags which ringed it were all at half-mast in recognition of the American lives lost in the latest anti-USA terrorist outrage in – she'd forgotten already – France, was it?

And then she turned, and there was the White House, right in front of her: still – arguably – the most important decision-making centre on the planet. There was what looked like a permanent shanty town on the other side of the road, opposite the White House, panhandlers and protesters and religious crazies doing their stuff in full view of the Chief Executive's bedroom window. Police drones buzzed overhead, languidly.

DC was dense, real, crusted with history and power. Compared to this, Malenfant's endeavours in the desert and off in space seemed foolish, baroque dreams.

Nevertheless, here Malenfant was, ready to fight his corner.

*　　*　　*

Maura eyed Emma. 'So, Malenfant. What is it with you two?'

'Umm?'

'I can't understand how come you're still together.'

'We're divorced.'

'Exactly.'

Emma sighed. 'It's a long story.'

Maura grunted. 'Believe me, at my age, everybody has a long story.'

To loosen them both up, Maura Della said, she had brought Emma as a special guest to the House gym, in the basement of the Rayburn House Office Building. It was smaller than Emma had expected, with a pool, steam and massage rooms, a squash court and exercise equipment. Maura and Emma had opted for a swim, steam and massage, and now Emma felt herself relax as her mechanical masseur pounded her back with plastic fingers.

They had married young – he in his thirties, she her twenties. Emma had her own career. But she had been excited at the prospect of following his charming, childlike, outlandish dreams of a human expansion into space. She knew her public role would be as an Air Force wife, perhaps a NASA wife, and those institutions were so old and hide-bound that she knew she would be forced to let her career shadow his. Raising Air Force brats, in fact. But the truth was they were partners, and would be for life.

But Malenfant had washed out of NASA at the first hurdle. She had been stunned.

He had come back silent, sullen. He had never told her what went wrong; she had learned not to press him on it.

And after that, nothing had been the same.

He was floored by his setback for a whole year, before he resigned from the Air Force, and started finding other directions to channel his energy. That had been the start of Bootstrap Inc., of Malenfant's journey to riches and power. Emma had worked with him, even in those early days.

But he had started to push her away.

'I still don't understand why,' she told Maura. 'We'd planned children, family years, a home somewhere. Somehow, all that had disappeared over the horizon. And then –'

'You don't have to tell me.'

Emma smiled, feeling tired. 'It's in the gossip columns. He had an affair. I found them together. Well, the marriage was finished.

I'll tell you the strangest thing. I've never seen him so unhappy as at that moment.'

In fact it had seemed to her that Malenfant was working to finish it, digging at its foundations: that he had taken his lover not for herself but to drive away Emma.

Her e-therapists said he was reacting to the thwarting of his true ambition. Now that he knew he would never achieve his dreams, Malenfant was playing with the toys of youth one more time, before the coffin lid started to creak down over him.

Or maybe, some of the therapists argued, it was just some hideous andropause thing.

'The only advantage of e-therapists,' Maura murmured, 'is that their horseshit is cheaper than from humans.'

'Well, whatever, it hurt.'

'And it still does. Right?'

Emma shrugged. 'Someday I'll understand.'

'And then you'll walk out the door?'

'That's my plan. So. You think we're going to get through today?'

'I think so,' Maura said briskly, turning to business. 'The danger man is Harris Rutter, from Illinois. One of the Gingrich generation. You know, once they arrive here people never leave, in office or not. You have strata of power, going back decades . . . Rutter has a *lot* of power. He's on a number of appropriations subcommittees, sluiceways for federal money. But Rutter's power is all negative. He likes to filibuster, raise delaying amendments, stall appointments – all means to frustrate the will of the majority, until he gets his own way, whatever *that* is. But I think I managed to blindside him this time.'

'How?'

'Federal pork. Or at least, the promise of a slice, if Malenfant gets his way.'

'That's looking a long way ahead, isn't it?'

'You have to stay ahead of the power curve in this town, Emma,' Maura murmured, and she closed her eyes with a sigh, as her massager went back to work. 'Did you know they didn't let women in this gym until 1985? . . .'

The hearing, here in the Rayburn building, took place in a cramped, old-fashioned conference room cooled by a single inadequate air-conditioner. There were two rows of conference tables down the middle of the room, with name plates for the Representatives on one side, and for the testifiers on the other. It was a place of judgment, of confrontation.

Malenfant was here. He looked crisp, calm, confident, composed, his bald pate gleaming like a piece of a weapons system.

Emma looked into his eyes. He looked as innocent and sincere as if he'd just been minted.

Malenfant took the stand, and Emma and Maura took seats side by side at the back of the room. Two Representatives took the lead: Harris Rutter, the former lawyer, and Mary Howell of Pennsylvania, once a chemical engineer. Both of them were Republicans.

The purpose of the hearing was for Malenfant to justify, once more, why he shouldn't be shut down. Rutter questioned Malenfant hard about the dubious legality of his operations, particularly his first launch.

Malenfant's answers were smooth. He allowed himself to sound irritated at the maze of conflicting legislation Bootstrap had had to tiptoe through, and he launched into a rehearsed speech about his manned space program to come: how he had four astronaut candidates, already in training, chosen to be representative of the US's demographic mix. 'It wasn't hard to find volunteers, sir, even though we emphasized the dangers to them – not of the space mission, but of being grounded without making the flight.'

A little sympathetic laughter.

'In this country we have a huge reservoir of expertise in launching space missions, reserves of people laid off by the space and defence industries, people champing at the bit to be let to work again. In my view it's a crime to waste such a skilled resource . . .' Then he went on to how the mission was being assembled mainly from components supplied, not by the usual aerospace cartels, but by smaller – sometimes struggling – companies right across the US. Malenfant was able to outline a glowing future in which the benefits of the new, expansive space program would flow back from the Mojave in terms of profits and jobs to districts right across the country, not least to Illinois and Pennsylvania, home states of his inquisitors.

Emma whispered to Maura, 'Laying it on thick, isn't he?'

Maura leaned closer. 'You have to see the big picture, Emma. Most big pork-barrel projects gain broad support in their early stages, when there are a lot of Representatives who can still hope for a slice of the ultimate pie. If Malenfant can promise to bring wealth to as many districts as possible, all for a modest or even zero government outlay, then he's convincing people at least to give him the benefit of the doubt . . .'

Anyhow Malenfant seemed to have survived Rutter's grilling. But now – to Emma's surprise – into the attack came Howell, the engineer from Pennsylvania. She was a tough, stockily built woman of about fifty, her defiantly grey hair tied back in a bun. She looked sharp, vigorous and spoiling for a fight.

'Colonel Malenfant. Bootstrap is about more than engineering, isn't it?'

'I don't know what you mean.'

Howell held up a copy of the *Washington Post*, with a splash headline about the Feynman radio at Fermilab, an animated picture beneath of Cornelius Taine repeating some Carter-catastrophe sound-bite. She quoted, 'Exclusive statements from an Eschatology spokesperson . . . Fermilab managers furious at the misuse of their facilities . . .'

'That news release was nothing to do with me.'

'Come, Colonel Malenfant. I've absolutely no doubt that news management like this goes on only with your tacit approval. So the question is why you feel this kind of message-from-the-future mumbo jumbo helps your cause. Now you have a background in engineering, don't you, Colonel? As I do.' She eyed him. 'I dare say we're about the same age. So we've both witnessed the same changes in our society.'

'Changes?'

'The distrust of technology. The loss of faith in scientists, engineers – in fact, a kind of rejection of the scientific method itself, and of the scientific explanation of the world. Do you agree that we've seen a flight to the irrational?'

'Yes. Yes, I agree with that. But I don't necessarily agree with your implication, that the irrational is all bad.'

'Oh, you don't.'

'There are many mysteries science has not dealt with, perhaps never will. What is consciousness? Why does anything exist, rather than nothing? Why am I alive here and now, and not a century ago, or a thousand years from now? We all have to confront such questions in the quiet of our souls, every minute of our lives. And if the irrational is the only place to look for answers, well, that's where we look.'

Representative Howell rubbed her temples. 'But, Colonel Malenfant, you must agree that it is our brains, our science, which have made the world around us. It is science which has given the planet the capacity to carry many billions of people. "It is only the intelligent management of the future which can get us through the next decades, assure us of a long-term future." I know you agree with that, because it's a direct quote from your own company report last year. Now. Let's not hear any more bullshit philosophizing . . .'

Maura leaned over to Emma. 'Representatives get to edit the Congressional Record. Witnesses don't, unfortunately.'

'Do you really believe it is responsible to try to gain public support for your highly dubious activities by whipping up hysteria over nonsense about the end of the world and messages from the future? –'

But now Rutter from Illinois was leaning forward. 'Will the lady yield on that? If you'll yield for a moment I have something to ask.'

Howell glared at him, realizing her attack was being dissipated.

Rutter was a corpulent, sweating man with an anachronistic bow tie. To Emma he looked as if he hadn't been out of Washington in twenty years. He said, 'I was interested in what you had to say, Colonel Malenfant. Most of us don't see any ethical problems in your links with organizations like Eschatology. Somebody has to think about the future constructively, after all. I think it's refreshing to have a proposal like yours in which there is a subtext, as you might call it, beyond the practical. If you can go to the stars, bring home a profit *and* something – well, something spiritual, I think that's to be applauded.'

'Thank you, Representative.'

'Tell me this, Colonel. Do you think your mission to Cruithne, if successful, will help us find God?'

Malenfant took a deep breath. 'Mr Rutter, if we find everything we hope to find on Cruithne, then yes, I believe we will come closer to God.'

Emma turned to Maura Della, and rolled her eyes. Good grief, Malenfant.

There were follow-on questions from Howell among others. But that, as far as Emma could tell, was that.

Maura was grinning. 'He had them eating out of his hand.'

'All but Representative Howell.'

'The question he planted with Rutter put a stop to her.'

Emma goggled. 'He *planted* it?'

'Oh, of course he did. Come on, Emma; it was too obvious, if anything.'

Emma shook her head. 'You know, I shouldn't be shocked any more by anything Malenfant does. But I have to tell you he is not a Christian, and he does not believe in God.'

Maura pursed her lips. 'Lies told to Congress, shock. Look, Emma, this is America. Every so often you have to push the God button.'

'So he won.'

'I think so. For now, anyhow.'

Representative Howell, the engineer from Pennsylvania who had argued for rationalism, pushed between them with a muttered apology. Howell looked distressed, frustrated, confused.

Malenfant, when he emerged, was disgustingly smug. 'To Cruithne,' he said.

Maura Della:

'Ladies and gentlemen,' Dan began, 'welcome to JPL. Today, June 18 2011, a US spacecraft piloted by a genetically enhanced cephalopod is due to rendezvous and dock with near-Earth object designated 3753, or 1986TO, called Cruithne, a three-mile-diameter C-type asteroid. We should be getting images from a remote firefly camera shortly, and a feed from the *Nautilus* herself . . .' He stood in a forest of microphones, a glare of TV lights. Behind him a huge softscreen was draped across the wall like a tapestry. It showed a mass of incomprehensible graphic and digital updates.

As Dan lectured his slightly restive audience, Maura allowed her attention to drift.

JPL, the Jet Propulsion Laboratory, had turned out to look like a small hospital, squashed into a cramped and smoggy Pasadena-suburb site dominated by the green shoulders of the San Gabriel Mountains. A central mall adorned with a fountain stretched from the gate into the main working area of the laboratory. And on the south side she had found the von Karman auditorium, the scene of triumphant news conferences and other public events going back to NASA's glory days, when JPL had sent probes to almost every planet in the Solar System.

Absently she listened to the talk around her, a lot of chatter about long-gone times when spirits were high, everybody seemed to be young, and there was a well-defined enemy to beat.

Heady days. All gone now.

Well, today the big old auditorium was crowded again, almost like the old days, mission managers and scientists and politicians and a few ageing sci fi writers, all crammed in among the softscreen terminals.

Just as NASA had declared that Malenfant's BDB design was a criminal joke that could never fly until it *had* flown, so its experts had declared that Bootstrap's cephalopod-based asteroid expedition was irresponsible and absurd – until it had survived out in deep space, and, more important, had started to gather some approving public attention.

And so, as Sheena 5 neared Cruithne, here everybody was, basking in reflected cephalopod glory.

As they waited for the rendezvous, Dan launched stiffly into a formal presentation on the technical aspects of the spacecraft.

'. . . The membrane that is the core of the ship's design is based on technology Bootstrap developed for undersea methane extraction operations. As far as the biosphere itself is concerned, efficiency is the key. Phytoplankton, one of the most efficient life forms known, can convert seventy-eight per cent of available nitrogen into protein. The simplicity of the algae – no stems, leaves, roots or flowers – makes them almost ideal crop plants, one hundred per cent foodstuff. Of course the system is not perfect – it's not completely closed, and imperfectly buffered. But it's still more robust, in terms of oper-ational reliability, than any long-duration mechanical equivalent we can send up. And a hell of a lot cheaper. I have the figures which –'

What about the problems, Dan?

He looked uncomfortable. 'Sheena has had to spend more time acting as the keystone predator than we expected.'

Say what?

'Culling pathological species that get out of hand. And you have to understand that the system is inherently unstable. We have to manage it, consciously. Or rather Sheena does. We have to replace leaked gases, regulate the temperature, control the hydrological cycle and trace contaminants . . .'

And so on. What Ystebo didn't say, what Maura knew from private briefings, was that this could be a very near thing. It's so fragile, Maura thought. She imagined the tiny droplet of water containing Sheena drifting in the immensity of interplanetary space, like a bit of sea foam tossed into the air by a wave, never to rejoin the ocean.

. . . What about Sheena herself?

At that question, Dan seemed to falter.

Maura knew that Sheena had been refusing to participate in her 'medical briefings', or to interface with the remote diagnostics that Dan used to monitor her health. Not that Dan, or anybody else, knew *why* she was refusing to cooperate. Maura tried to read the emotions in Dan's bearded, fat-creased face.

'You understand I can only speak to her once a day. When the spacecraft is above the horizon at Goldstone. She is in LOS – loss of signal – for fifteen hours a day . . .'

How do you feel about the fact that she's not coming home?

Again Dan blustered. 'Actually the simplification of the mission goals has worked benefits throughout the profile. The cost of the return – the mass penalty of return leg propellant and comestibles and the aerobrake heat shield – multiplied through the whole mission mass statement.'

Yeah, but it's become a one-way trip for your squid. The Calamari Express.

Uncomfortable laughter.

Dan was squirming. 'Bootstrap have plans to deal with the ethical contingencies.'

Technocrat bullshit, thought Maura; whoever coached this poor sap did a bad job. But she pitied Dan, nonetheless. He was probably the only person on the planet who truly cared about Sheena 5 – as opposed to the sentimental onlookers on TV and on the net – and here he was, having to defend her being sentenced to death, alone in space.

. . . And now, at last, an image came through on the big wall-mounted softscreen. Pictures from space. A hush spread over the hall.

It took Maura some seconds to figure out what she was seeing.

It was an asteroid.

It was misshapen and almost black, the craters and cracks of its dusty surface picked out by unvarying sunlight, a potato left too long on the barbecue. And a spacecraft of rippling gold was approaching, dwarfed by the giant rock.

There was applause, whooping. *Way to go, Dan! Right down US One.*

133

Dan fumbled at a touchpad, and a new image came up on the softscreen: Sheena 5, a Caribbean reef squid, drifting in blue-gold shadows, live from *Nautilus*. Eerily, her head was hidden by a metal mask which trailed wires back to a mass of machinery.

Then the cephalopod pulled back, leaving the metal mask dangling in the water, and she began an elaborate dance. It was enchanting: her chromatophore organs pulsed with colours and shapes, black and orange and aquamarine and ochre, and her tentacles and arms flashed as she arced, twirled and pirouetted through the tank. She was very obviously producing signals: one, even two a second, signals that flowed into each other, varying remarkably in their intensity.

Can you interpret what she's saying, Dan?

Hesitantly he began to translate.

'*Stop and watch me. Stop and watch me* . . . You have to understand her language elements are based on those she inherited from the cephalopod shoals. This is a signal she might use to distract prey, or even a predator . . . Now this is what we call the pied pattern. *Court me. Court me.* She's asking for admiration. She's proud. *Asteroid. Come near, come near.* Another mating signal. It's as if she's luring the asteroid. *Star shoal all around. No danger, no danger.* Literally, no predators. But she means that her navigation has been a success, that the systems are working nominally. *Stop and watch me. Court me* . . .'

His posture was stiff as he stared at the screen, the separation from his dancing friend a tangible, painful thing.

The audience was silent, Maura noted absently: stunned by this shard of cheap emotion.

The digital displays told her the moment of rendezvous was near. The remote firefly-camera images returned to the softscreen, a stop-start sequence updated every few seconds. The gold spark tracked across the blackened surface.

Sheena 5:

The asteroid was big, now, covering almost half of the sky.

She could see the asteroid's surface, as if she was drifting over Caribbean sandflats. It was dull and dark. But its polarization was rich. She was searching for the shading and twinkling that meant frozen water. *Here* was a patch where the twisting of the light was muddy and random, and Dan had taught her that meant bare metal. *Here* the light was strongly polarized, and the surface was probably coated with thick, sticky dust. It seemed wonderful to Sheena that she could clearly see, just by looking at the sparkling, twisting light, what this strange deep space fish was made of.

. . . *There*. It looked like a hole in surface, and it had a shallow, sloping floor that sparkled and gleamed with the look of water.

Sheena touched her waldoes, and the ship hovered above the depression.

She knew it would take a long time for Dan to learn of her success. She trembled with anticipation.

Gripping the circular support with her arms, Sheena inserted her two long tentacles into the smooth, flexible sheaths, and touched the central pad with her beak.

Two three-hundred-foot cables began to unwind from the hull of *Nautilus*. Sheena extended her tentacles, and small puffs of gas from the pads at the cable ends sent them stretching towards the asteroid. She allowed the cables to droop to their limits, then flashed *down* to the ship's software.

She sensed the tentacles touch the bottom, touch the asteroid. Contact.

She flexed her suction cups to grip the surface. Slowly she contracted her tentacles, drawing herself down until she could see the smallest details of the asteroid, even her ship's small shadow.

She had practised this manoeuvre in deep space, over and over. It was probably the most important task she would ever have to complete, after all; if she failed at this one thing, the mission itself would fail . . .

Finally she felt a gentle pressure wave pulse through the water and through her own body, letting her know that she had come to rest.

The asteroid, this great black whale of space, was her prey, and she, the hunter, had captured it.

Pride surged, chromatophores pulsing over her body.

Maura Della:

The gentle impact came unspectacularly, with a silent turning of digits from negative to positive.

There was a small splash of grey dust. And then Maura could see the ship, a green-gold fragment of Earth embedded in the hide of the asteroid.

On the interior camera image, Sheena, free of her waldoes, was jetting from one side of her habitat to another, stopping to stare at the asteroid landscape with her dark, saucer-like eyes before racing for a different view, her carapace flashing colours, posturing elaborately with her head and mantle and eight arms.

Maura sneaked a peek at the faces in the audience. Everyone was grinning.

Dan, tell us what she's saying.

Hesitantly, Dan translated. '*I am strong and fit. I am large and fierce. See my weapons. See my strength.* A mixture of mating signals and deimatic patterns designed to drive off predators. See those fake eye rings? . . .' Dan turned to his audience, grinning. 'She's bragging. That's what this means. It seems we have reached Cruithne.'

The applause swelled. The chairwoman on the stage hugged Dan Ystebo, and Maura found herself with tears in her eyes. Damn this space stuff, she thought. Why does it have to be so magnificent?

Sheena 5:

. . . And on Cruithne:

Drifting in cool Earth water, Sheena 5 could feel the feather-touch of new gravity. Above her the sky wheeled, the sun's glare cycling to the dazzle of a billion stars; she could feel how she was spinning, wheeling in three-dimensional space, as this small world turned.

Beneath the translucent skin of the habitat she could see a grainy, grey-black ground. Dan told her it was a substance older than all the rocks of the Earth, older than the oceans themselves, older perhaps than the Solar System. And, through the curving walls of the ship, she was able to see this world's jagged horizon, barely tens of yards away.

She flashed her triumph, her mantle skin tingling as the tiny muscles pulsed her chromatophores.

Gabriel Marcus:

. . . Some minor planets, of course, already have roles in astrology. Since these worlds weren't known to the ancients, their roles are the subject of modern interpretation and some debate.

So it is proving with Cruithne.

Perhaps we can take some guidance from the derivation of the name. 'The Cruithne' was the old Irish name for the Pictish people. In the 12th-century Irish document 'List of Pictish Kings', Cruithne is given as the eponymous ancestor of the Pictish people, and it was his seven sons who have lent their names to the divisions of the Pict kingdom in Scotland.

But 'the Cruithne' was also used by the Irish to describe a group of aboriginal people living in Ireland before the coming of the Gaels. They seem to have been at one time the predominant power in Ulster.

A further blurring of the name's meaning comes from the fact that some early writers claim that Pictish lineage was traditionally taken from the mother's line, not the father's. So perhaps Cruithne – if such an individual existed at all – was not a man, but a woman.

As far as its astronomical properties go, Cruithne is again an unusual world.

Perhaps uniquely among astrological subjects it wanders far from the plane of the ecliptic and so far from the traditional Houses; in fact at times it can be seen, by telescope, above (or beneath) Earth's poles. And yet it is intimately linked to Earth; we know that its peculiar 'horseshoe' orbit is dominated by Earth's gravity.

And, of course, the most direct link of all has now been established, as the squid, Sheena, has become the first Earth creature since the Apollo astronauts to reach another world.

Cruithne: mother-father, person and people, linked to Earth by spidery webs of influence and life. Little wonder that this tiny, remote, ambiguous world is causing such a stir in astrological circles.

It is of course true, but irrelevant, that the name 'Cruithne' was a late choice among the Australian astronomers who named the minor planet. An earlier suggestion was an irreverent nickname for one of their number, 'The Chunder Wonder'. We can be grateful – if not surprised – that destiny guided the correct choice . . .

Sheena 5:

She could not leave her water habitat; yet she was able to explore.

Small firefly robots set off from the habitat, picking their way carefully over the surface of the asteroid. Each robot was laden with miniature instruments, as exquisite as coral, all beyond her understanding.

But the fireflies were under her control.

She used the waldo, the glove-like device into which she could slip her long prehensile arms and so control the delicate motions of each firefly. Cameras mounted in the carapace of the firefly brought her a view through her laser eye-cup of what the firefly was seeing, as if she was swimming alongside it. The gravity was so low that a careless movement would have sent the little metal devices spinning away from the surface, to be lost for ever. So the limbs of the fireflies carried hooks and suction devices to ensure that at every moment they were anchored to the thin regolith. And, with delicacy and care, she was able to ensure the fireflies avoided ravines and deep craters, and so were never in danger.

Her fireflies scuttled hundreds of yards from the slumped membrane of *Nautilus*.

Sheena thought all this was remarkable.

She had come to awareness in a universe that was three-dimensional and infinite. Slowly she had come to understand that the ocean she inhabited was part of the skin of a giant sphere. She had seen that ocean-world from outside, seen it diminish to a pale dot of light.

And now she had come to a world which was so small she felt she could enclose its curve in her outstretched arms, and her eyes picked out the starry universe through which this little world swam. Entranced, munching absently on the krill the currents brought to her beak, she watched the new world – *her* world – unfold.

Her world. She had not expected to feel like this, so triumphant.

Her weariness, her edgy isolation, were forgotten now. She pulsed with pride, her chromatophores prickling.

And she knew, at last, she was ready.

Emma Stoney:

Mission control for the *Nautilus* was not what Emma had come to expect from cliché images of Houston – the rows of gleaming terminals, the ranks of young, bespectacled engineers sweating through their neat shirts as the astronauts ran into yet another crisis on orbit. *That* was the manned space program. *This* was rather different. The JPL flight operations room was cluttered, cramped, the decor very dated. There were big mass storage units and immense filing cabinets, some of them open to reveal yellowing files, mounds of paper. Everything looked stale, ageing.

Dan had a cubicle to himself. He had a softscreen draped over his lap, and he wore a virtual reality helmet that fitted tight over his head, like a swimming cap, hiding his eyes behind rubber pads. There was kipple everywhere: pictures – of the *Nautilus* leaving orbit, shots of the ship splashing against the rock, pin-ups of Sheena 5 herself – as well as a lot of the usual techie junk, toy spaceships and plastic aliens and soda cans and candy wrappers and movie posters.

Dan turned to them and smiled. It was disconcerting, his eyes concealed. 'Yo, Malenfant, Emma. Welcome to the geekosphere . . .' Maybe, for him, they were floating against coal-black Cruithne. But she noticed he seemed to be able to work his softscreen, despite its awkward draping over his lap, without glancing down. 'You want coffee, or soda? There's a Shit machine –'

'Just give me some news, Dan,' Malenfant said. 'As good as possible.' His voice sounded tight with stress.

Dan pushed his VR hood off his face. His eyes were reddened and sore, and the mask had left white marks across his forehead and cheeks. He said, 'Pay dirt. The carbonaceous ore contains hydrogen, nitrogen, methane, carbon monoxide and dioxide, sulphur dioxide, ammonia –'

'Water?' Emma asked.

He nodded. 'Oh, yes. As permafrost and hydrated minerals. Twenty per cent by mass, by God. Every prediction fulfilled, exceeded in fact.'

Malenfant smacked his hands together. 'It's a warehouse up there.'

Dan plastered a big softscreen over the posters and photos and memos and other crap on the wall, and tapped its surface. Up came an image of the asteroid's surface – gritty and crumpled, Emma thought, like roadside slush – and there was one of the microrobots they were calling 'fireflies'.

As she watched, a tiny puff of vapour vented from the base of the firefly. It jetted sharply up away from the asteroid ground, swivelled neatly, then shot out a little dart that trailed a fine cable, like fishing line. The dart buried itself in the loose rock. The line went taut and began to haul itself in, neatly dragging the firefly back to the surface.

Dan said, 'The fireflies are working great. We should be able to find a hundred applications for these babies, in LEO, other asteroids, even on the Moon. The propulsion system is neat. It's a digital propulsion chip: a little bank of solid rocket motors, and you can address the motors individually, *pop pop pop*, to get a high degree of manoeuvrability and control –'

Emma asked, 'And Sheena is running these things?'

'Oh, yes.' Dan grinned proudly. 'She has a big waldo glove in the habitat she can fit her whole body right inside. Of course that took some designing. Because she lacks bones, Sheena doesn't have a good sense of where her arms are in space. So the waldoes feed back information about pressure and texture . . . She does a fine job. She can run *eight* of these babies at once. In many ways she's smarter than we are.'

'And yet we sent her out there, to die,' Emma said.

There was an uncomfortable silence, as if she'd been impolite to mention such a thing.

Dan pulled his VR mask over his face and started to scroll through more results from the asteroid, and Emma went in search of a coffee machine.

Sheena 5:

. . . And on Cruithne, Sheena laid her eggs.

They were cased in jelly sacs, hundreds of them in each tube. There was no spawning ground here, of course. So she draped the egg sacs over the knot of machinery at the heart of her miniature ocean, which had now anchored itself to the surface of Cruithne. The gardens of egg cases dangled there, soft and organic against the hard machinery.

Small schools of fish came to nose at the eggs. She watched until she was sure that the fish were repelled by the jelly that coated the eggs, which was its purpose.

She had no instinct to return to the eggs, to cradle them. But she knew this was an unusual circumstance; this small ball of water, collapsed to a fat lens against the asteroid, was no enriching ocean. So she developed a habit of visiting the eggs every few hours, of squirting gentle water jets over them to keep them aerated.

All this was out of sight of Dan's cameras. She did not tell him what she had done.

Michael:

More children arrived, but now they seemed bewildered and frightened. They always had blue circles crudely stitched onto their shirts or jackets. The children would complain and cry, until they learned the first of the rules Michael had learned, which was never to complain or cry.

Some children were taken away, too.

Many were taken by concerned-looking people, who would put their arms around a frightened child. Michael didn't know what this meant. Perhaps it was a trick.

The children taken away all had white skin. The children who were brought in mostly had black or brown skin. Soon, most of the children who were left behind, including Michael, had brown or black skin. He didn't know what this meant either.

One day he saw a Brother wearing a gold ring.

Michael was fascinated to see gold again, the deep lustre of the time-stretched electrons in its structure. He came forward and stared at it. The Brother smiled at him and held out his hand so he could see.

Then, without warning, the Brother swung back his arm and slammed his fist into the side of Michael's head. Michael could feel the ring dig into his flesh, warm blood spurting. The Brother smiled and walked away.

To his shame, Michael was crying.

He ran back to his dormitory. He ran across the floor towards his pallet. But there was a Sister here and she grabbed his arm and shouted at him. He didn't understand, but then she pointed at the floor. He had left a trail of blood. He had to get a mop and bucket and scrape his drying blood off the floor. But still the blood flowed, and he had to work harder to keep it off the floor, and it seemed as if it would never stop.

That snapshot, the incident with the ring, divided Michael's life in two, as light from dark.

The visitors grew fewer, until they stopped coming altogether.

And the lessons were more infrequent. Sometimes they were replaced by work sessions, in which the children had to paint the huts or clean floors or mop out the toilet blocks. Sometimes they were just cancelled altogether.

The refrigerators and bowls of food were taken away. Now there was only food at meal times, twice a day.

The children were no longer issued fresh clothes. They were given shirts and shorts and shoes which were marked with small blue circles, just one set per child. The clothes soon became dirty and threadbare.

The last lessons were stopped, and the softscreens were taken away.

Many of the children wept and fought at that, but not Michael.

He had expected this to happen some day. The School had been like a strange dream anyhow.

He would be able to work in his head. As long as he was left alone, as he had been in the village.

Emma Stoney:

Each morning now, Emma had to run the gauntlet of the noisy mobs outside Bootstrap's Vegas office. This morning, as her car approached, a few of them burst through the police line. The car sensed warm human bodies ahead and slowed to a halt. Emma made sure her windows were sealed up, overrode the SmartDrive and inched the car forward.

Slowly the people parted, but not before they got close enough to scream in through the windscreen at her. There were eco types in body paint, a lot of religious groups she couldn't identify, and also counter-protesters, people actually in favour of Bootstrap and its projects, mostly young white males with US flags and other national emblems, chanting about pioneers and the new frontier. Some of them wore animated T-shirts with an image of Malenfant making a speech somewhere, a few words and a smile, cycled over and over on the crumpled cloth. She grimaced; she wondered how much money some remote corner of Bootstrap was making out of *that*. A line of cops, supplemented by company security people (racking up one hell of an expense, as Emma knew too well) kept the factions apart.

Here was a beefy guy with shaven hair, dressed in a green T-shirt and pants, as if he was some kind of veteran. He was limping, one of his legs betraying him. He was carrying a blown-up picture of a sickly-looking kid blowing candles on a birthday cake. He was shouting. 'Yellow babies! Look what you did, Malenfant! Look what you did!'

Emma recoiled from his anger.

But once she was inside, and the gate had sealed itself shut behind her, she couldn't even hear the protesters' chants any more: only a soft white noise, barely audible, like rushing water.

Almost soothing.

She arrived at the conference room late. She took a seat quietly at the back of the darkened, half-empty room, and tried to follow what was going on.

George Hench was chairing an engineering seminar on the design of a hab module for the proposed human-manned follow-up missions to Cruithne.

At the front of the room a technical type was standing at a lectern; a softscreen the size of a curtain was hanging on the wall behind him. Other techs sat around the first few rows, their arms draped over the backs of their chairs, their feet up before them.

These technicians were mostly men, mostly badly dressed, generally bearded. They were laden with doctorates and other qualifications. Many of them came from NASA itself, from corners of that sprawling bureaucratic empire called things like the Mission Definition Office or the Mars Exploration Studies Office. Behind each of these guys lay a whole fleet of beautiful spacecraft which had existed only in blueprints and mass estimates and a few items of demonstration technology, and which had landed on the Moon or Mars only in clean, software-generated NASA imagery, and in the dreams of their creators.

After Malenfant's electrifying first launch, and his announcement that he was proposing manned missions to Cruithne and beyond – and despite the outstanding legal difficulties the company faced – Bootstrap had had no difficulty recruiting guys like these.

The speaker was describing the high-level design of the Cruithne mission's hab module. He spoke in a mumble, directly to his softscreen, and the screen behind him showed a blizzard of bewildering images.

The hab was little more than a can, fifteen yards long. It had a small Earth-return capsule – a cone shape like an Apollo capsule – glued to its lower end. The capsule would also serve as a solar storm shelter. Big wing-like solar cell panels were fixed to struts extending from the can's sides. Various antennae, thruster assemblies and ports were visible through layers of powder-white insulation blankets. It reminded Emma a little of prehistoric images of Skylab. But in the animated image the hab was spinning, end over end, to provide the crew with artificial gravity, at least at the can's extremities. The speaker made great play of the mass limitations the craft was going to work under; it seemed that the whole design was right at the limit of what Malenfant's BDB could throw into space.

Life support systems engineering was far from Emma's area of expertise. But attending meetings like this was all part of her general ongoing strategy to contain Reid Malenfant. She'd been around Malenfant long enough to know that it was worth her while to cast her net as wide as possible, to follow as much as possible, to anticipate as much as she could. Because, even here at the heart of Reid Malenfant's secretive empire, she could never be sure under which rock the next rattlesnake lay coiled.

It was characteristic of Malenfant to be pressing ahead with the design, assembly and even fabrication of his asteroid-pioneer spacecraft while the slow wheels of official approval still ground on. Not only that, he had become even more unobtainable than usual, because he had launched himself into every aspect of the training of Bootstrap's cadre of prospective astronauts, even to the extent of racking up flying hours and time in the centrifuge.

Meanwhile, Bootstrap's destiny remained unresolved.

The fact that this next flight would (if it flew at all) be carrying human passengers just made the bureaucratic tangle that much worse. It had shocked Emma to learn that even comparatively unambitious human spaceflights incurred a *lot* of danger, much of it unacceptable to bodies like OSHA, the Occupational Safety and Health Administration.

Beyond the shelter of Earth's magnetic field, for example, the astronauts would be bombarded by radiation, sporadically violent flares from the sun and a steady drizzle of cosmic rays: fast-moving particles, relics from remote parts of the universe, a single particle of which, George Hench once told her, could pack as much punch as a baseball. Then there were the familiar hazards of zero gravity: bone decalcification, immune and cardiovascular system degradation, muscular atrophy.

Emma formed a bleak image of the crew limping across space in a cramped, stinking, spinning module, earnestly pounding away at their treadmills just to keep alive, cowering every time the sun belched. There was something un-American about it, she thought, something dogged and Soviet.

What might save Bootstrap was once again the weakness and ambiguity of the current regulatory regime. For example, OSHA actually had no radiation exposure standards for human space missions. NASA had adopted supplementary standards drawn up by bodies like the National Academy of Sciences and the National Council on Radiation Protection and Measurements as the agency's standard for crew dose limits. But even then NASA had left loopholes, saying the standards should be applied to all but 'exceptional exploration missions'.

Where NASA led, Reid Malenfant was happy to follow.

The presenter was nearing the end of his talk, and he had started to wax philosophical. *Before Copernicus, humans believed humanity was walled off from the heavens by a set of crystal spheres. Well, those spheres are still there, but they aren't made of glass, but of fear. Let's do this. Let's smash those spheres.*

Whoops, raised fists, a scattering of applause.

These technicians had tunnel vision, she thought. To them the mission was everything, the various obstacles a frustration that stopped them from doing things. And when they were forced to confront those obstacles they resorted to hopeful button-pushing: Ptolemaic spheres, the frontier, the American dream, can-do, the spirit of Wright and Lindbergh and Armstrong, the organizational will that enabled us to cover a continent, win the Second World War, blah blah.

But, she thought, maybe they *had* to be that way to get anything done at all. Dreams had to be uncomplicated to be achievable.

Now another technician got up to show a new type of chart. It represented a flow of raw materials to a schematic of the hab's manufacture: electrical components from factories around the US, structural parts from the big aerospace companies, raw materials from a variety of producers, a web of sources, flows and sinks.

There was one box at the lower left corner which Emma had trouble reading. She sat forward and squinted.

The source box was marked 'Dounreay'. And the product flowing out of it was 'enriched U-235'.

And Emma had spotted her rattlesnake.

She got out of her seat and slipped out of the room.

When she got back to her office she booted up her softscreen and started to find out about Dounreay.

And, immediately after that, she booked a flight to Scotland.

She arrived at a place called Sandside: a tiny village, just holiday homes and a pub. She got out of the car – no SmartDrive – and climbed a low hill at the edge of the village.

She was on the north coast of Scotland, just a few miles from John O'Groats, the miniature tourist trap that was the northernmost point of mainland Britain. There was a sweeping beach before her, and then the sea itself, wild and grey under a flat lid of sky. On the horizon she glimpsed more landmasses, the Old Man of Hoy and the Orkneys. It was a rugged place, suffused by wind noise, poised between sea and sky, and the wind seemed to suck the warmth from the core of her body.

And there, sprawled across the eastern horizon, was Dounreay: a mile-long sprawl of buildings, a giant golfball shape, huge grey and brown sheds and chimneys. Somehow, oddly, even though she knew what this place represented, it did not offend the eye.

Here came Malenfant, his gaunt frame swathed in a giant quilted coat. He climbed up the little hillock beside her.

'You look ill,' she said.

He shrugged. 'I don't think the climate suits me. Even though I've got some Scottish blood. Maybe all that Vegas sunshine has diluted it.'

'What have you been up to this time, Malenfant?'

He sighed. 'Doing what needs to be done.'

She faced him. 'Listen to me for once, you asshole. If you're planning to launch nuclear materials into space, if you're even intending to move nuke stuff around the planet, you're committing a whole series of offences. And if you're going to involve Bootstrap in that – if you're going to involve me – then tell me about it.'

'I will, I will,' he soothed. 'But we don't have a choice.'

'Oh, Malenfant. You never do . . .'

He took her arm, and they walked along the hillock.

He picked out some of the sights of Dounreay for her. This was the second largest nuclear installation in Britain, after Sellafield. Once it had generated power, made medical isotopes, run three reprocessing lines and a nuclear waste packaging plant. The golfball shape was a fast reactor, built in 1959. It had caught fire and overheated several times. Now it was shut down and preserved, bizarrely, by a heritage ministry. The big grey sheds were for reprocessing nuclear waste, extracting usable fuel from spent material. Behind the golfball there was a waste shaft, two hundred feet deep, fifteen thousand tons of waste mixed with uranium and plutonium. Very unstable; it had already suffered two hydrogen explosions, spraying radioactive waste everywhere.

'Jesus,' she said. 'What a folly. Another generation's dreams of cheap power. And we have to live with the shit for evermore.'

'Well, it didn't go entirely to plan,' he conceded. 'Originally this was going to be a nuclear park. Six reactors. But the technology was ahead of its time.'

'*Ahead of its time?*'

'Everything was within the guidelines of the time. Even the secrecy, if you want to know. You have to remember it was the Cold War. They didn't have the same obsession with safety we have now. An obsession that has stunted us since, conservatively, 1970. And guess what – the local people now love the plant. If it never produces another watt, Dounreay is going to be around for a hundred years. Four generations of high-quality, highly-skilled local employment. Because it will take that long to decommission it.'

'So tell me something else. If the UK government shut this place down in the 1990s, how come you managed to acquire enriched uranium here?'

He said gently, 'There's nothing illegal.'

'My God, Malenfant.'

'Look.' He dug a small, crumpled softscreen out of his pocket, unfolded it with stiff fingers. It showed an image of something like a rocket engine, a sky-blue nozzle mounted by complex machinery, tall and skinny. The diagram was labelled with spidery text much too small to read. Malenfant said, 'This is what we're building. It's a nuclear reactor, designed for space missions. Here's the reactor at the top.' He pointed with a thumbnail and worked his way down. 'Then you have pumps, shielding and a radiator. The whole thing stands about twelve feet tall, weighs about a ton. The reactor has a thermal output of 135 kilowatts, an electrical supply of 40 kilowatts . . .

'Emma, you have to understand. If we have humans aboard a new *Nautilus*, we have a mission an order of magnitude more power-hungry than Sheena's. And then there are the power requirements for surface operations. To generate the juice we need from a solar array you'd need an area half the size of a football field, and weighing maybe ten times as much. Even the BDB couldn't lift it.'

'And this is what you're planning to build? . . . Oh. You're *already* building these things. Right?'

He looked pleased with himself. *Look what I did.* 'We hired Russian engineers. Dug some of them out of retirement, in fact. The US never developed nuclear power sources beyond the radio-isotope heat generators we flew on unmanned missions. In fact the Clinton administration shut down our space nuclear power research program. What can you do but condemn that? – when we gave up nuclear power, we gave up the future.

'But the Russians flew nuclear power sources on reconnaissance missions back in the 1960s, and they even test-flew a design called Topaz, which is what we based this baby on. Of course we were able to tune the design a hell of a lot.'

'Malenfant –'

He tapped the little screen. 'All we need is fifty pounds of enriched U-235, in the form of uranium dioxide pellets. The moderator is zirconium hydride, and you control the reaction by rotating these cylinders on the outside of the core, which –'

'How are you smuggling this shit into the Mojave?'

'Smuggling is a harsh word.'

'Come on, Malenfant. Those desert skies are pretty clear. Surveillance satellites –'

'You really want to know? All the satellites' orbital elements are on the net. You can work out where they will be at any minute. You just shut down until they've passed overhead. Even better, make sure you hit the night shift at the National Imagery and Mapping Agency down at Fairfax. There's always something more interesting to look at than pictures of an old buzzard like me jerking off in the desert.'

'Act now, justify later. Like the BDB launch. Like most of the actions in your life.'

'Emma, you have to trust me on this one. If I can run a Topaz or two, prove it's safe, I can get the authorizations I need. But I have to get the nuke stuff to run the tests in the first place.'

'And the citizens of Las Vegas have to trust you too, until enriched uranium comes raining down out of the sky? You know, you're a dreamer, Malenfant. You actually believe that one day we will all come to our senses and agree with you, and hail you as a hero.'

'I'm already a hero.' He winked. 'There are T-shirts that say it. Look, Emma – I won't pretend I'm happy with everything I'm having to do. No more than you are. But we have to go on. It's not just Bootstrap, the profits, not even the big picture, our future in space –'

'Cornelius. The Carter catastrophe. Messages from the future.'

He eyed her. 'I know how you're dealing with this. You've put it all in a box in your mind, that you only open when you have to. *But it's real*, Emma. We both saw those neutron pulses.'

'Neutrinos, Malenfant,' she said gently.

'We're in this too deep, Emma. We have to go on.'

She closed her eyes. 'Malenfant – patience has always been your strength. You don't need lousy Russian reactors and dubious uranium shipments. Take your time and find another way to build your spaceship.'

His voice was strained. 'I can't.'

And, of course, she knew that.

He bent down and kissed the top of her head.

She sighed. 'You know I won't betray you. I've been sucked in too deep with you for a long time, for half my life. But do you ever consider the ethics of implicating me, and others, in this kind of shit? . . . You have to be open with me, Malenfant.'

'I will,' he said. 'I promise.'

She knew, of course, that he was lying.

In fact she was more useful to him if she *didn't* know. It made her denials that much more effective. It probably even protected her a little too.

But that wouldn't be uppermost in his mind; it was just an incidental. What drove Malenfant was maximizing her utility in the drive towards his ultimate goals. Just like any of the tools he deployed.

She understood all that. What she really didn't know, in her heart of hearts, was why she continued to put up with it.

She linked her arm through his, and they huddled together against the wind, looking over Dounreay. Mist swept in off the sea, covering the plant in greyness.

Reid Malenfant:

How can we turn asteroid rock into rocket fuel? Sounds like magic, doesn't it?

... First we'll crack asteroid water into hydrogen and oxygen with electrolysis. Remember high school science classes, the pyrex beakers and the wires and the batteries? All you have to do is pass an electric current through water to break it down. That's what we do. But the units we use are a little more advanced.

Slide, please.

This is a solid polymer electrolyte, or SPE, electrolyzer. What you have is sandwiched layers of electrolyte-impregnated plastic separated by metal meshes. The whole assembly is compressed by metal rods running the length of the stack.

SPEs have been used extensively on nuclear submarines and on the Space Station. They run for thousands of hours without maintenance.

As for the methane, we will extract some directly from the asteroid material, and more by processing carbon dioxide. We use something called a Sabatier reactor. Slide. We liquefy the hydrogen from the electrolyzer banks, and feed it into the reactor with carbon dioxide. Out the other side comes water and methane – which is just a compound of carbon and hydrogen. The reaction is very efficient, ninety-nine per cent in fact, and is exothermic, which means it requires no input of heat to make it work, just the presence of a ruthenium catalyst.

Sabatier units have been used in space before, for life support applications. They have been tested by NASA and the Air & Space Force and have also been used on the Space Station.

There is further information in your packs on how we intend to optimize the ratios of the methane-oxygen bi-propellant, and various subsidiary processes we need. We can show you a demonstration breadboard prototype. Oxygen-hydrogen is of course the most powerful chemical-rocket propellant of all. But hydrogen is difficult to liquefy and store: low temperature, large bulk. Methane is like oxygen, a soft cryogenic, and that guided our choice.

All this sounds exotic. But what we have here is very robust engineering, gaslight era stuff, technologies centuries old, in fact. It's just a novel application.

Ladies and gentlemen, mining an asteroid is easy.

Slide, please.

Sheena 5:

The babies were already being hatched: popping out of their dissolving eggs one by one, wriggling away, alert, active, questioning. With gentle jets of water, she coaxed them towards the seagrass where they would browse until they were mature.

She tried not to think about what would happen then.

Meanwhile, she had work to do.

When Sheena powered up the rock eater, she was more nervous than at any time since the landing itself. She lay as still as she could inside her waldo glove, and tried to sense the eater's systems: the gripping tracks that dug into the asteroid's loose surface, the big gaping scoop of a mouth at the front, the furnace in its belly like a warm heart, as if she herself had become the fat clanking machine that would soon scuttle crab-like across the asteroid floor.

She understood why she felt so tense.

The rock eater was a complex machine. It would need monitoring as it chewed its way around the asteroid, to make sure it didn't burrow too deeply into the surface, or spin its tracks on some loose patch of rock and throw itself into the emptiness of space, beyond retrieval.

But it was no more difficult to control, in principle, than the little firefly robots, and she was used to *them* by now; in fact she had come to enjoy deploying six, seven, eight of them at once, a shoal of robots, relishing the chance to show off her skill to Dan.

It wasn't even the importance of this operation for her mission. She knew the fireflies had done no more than measure, weigh, analyse, monitor. Now, for the first time, she was going to do something that would *change* the asteroid, to make something out of its loose, ancient substance. To fail would mean that she could not succeed with her great task of bringing this asteroid's incomprehensible riches back to Earth.

But that wasn't why she was so anxious.

To fail would mean that her young would die here, as she would, cut off from the shoal, for no reason. *That* was what mattered to her. To die was one thing; to die for no purpose was quite another. It was a fear that never left her, a knowledge that seemed to circle around her, like a predator, waiting for her to weaken.

Therefore – exhausted, ageing as she was – she would not weaken, would not fail.

It was time. She pushed at the glove.

. . . And she felt the eater dig its scoop-like jaw into the loose soil at the surface of Cruithne.

Her first motions were clumsy. From the microcameras embedded in the eater's upper surface she saw chunks of regolith sail up before her, dust and larger fragments. The fragments disappeared from her view, following loose, looping paths, some of them escaping the asteroid's tiny gravity field altogether and sailing off on new orbits of their own, new baby asteroids circling the sun.

Patiently she slowed, tried again, adjusted the angle of the scoop and the speed at which its ploughed into the surface. Soon she had it right, and a steady stream of asteroid rock worked its way in through the scoop to the eater's hopper.

Now little belts and shovels forced the captured regolith into the processing chambers. First the ore was ground up and sieved by rocking mechanical jaws and rollers and vibrating filter screens. Next, magnetic fields sucked out nickel-iron metal granules. Then the crushed ore was passed to a furnace, powered by the sun's focused heat.

Liquid, baked from the rock, began to gather in the condenser tanks, big low-gravity globules drifting around the thin walls.

This one roving rock eater, patiently working its way over the asteroid's surface, would deliver pounds of precious water every day from the unpromising rock of the asteroid. The water would be processed further and used in many of the other, more complex machines. And so this asteroid would be transformed from a lump of ancient slag into something wonderful, something alive.

When she was happy with the eater's operation, she pulled herself out of the glove. She swam down to where the pipe trailing back from the eater met the habitat membrane. And she found a trickle of fresh asteroid water.

She swam through the asteroid stream, let it wash under her carapace and through her gills. It was warm, perhaps from the heater at the heart of the rock-eating robot, and there was only a trickle of it, seeping into the great mass of the habitat. But Sheena swam back and forth through it, her hide pulsing excitedly.

She was the first creature from Earth to swim in water not of her native planet, water that had formed before the sun itself – water that had lain dormant, bound into this dark lump of rock, until *she* had liberated it.

She knew this was Dan's mission, not hers; she knew she was Dan's creature, not her own. But she was proud, because she was the first; no other creature who had ever lived or ever would live could claim this honour from her.

She swooped and pulsed her joy.

Sheena sent the fireflies to converge at one pole of Cruithne. There, patiently, piece by piece, she had them assemble a small chemical factory, pipes and tanks and pumps, and a single flaring nozzle which pointed to the sky. Borers began to dig into the surface of Cruithne, drawing up surface regolith and the rock and ice which lay deeper within. Precious solar panels, spread over the dusty surface of the asteroid, provided power, via cables strung out over the regolith.

The factory began its work.

The whole process seemed remarkable to Sheena. To take ancient rock and ice, and to transform it into something new . . .

At last, under Sheena's control, simple valves clicked open. Through firefly cameras, in the images relayed to the laser projectors cupped over her eyes, Sheena could see a flame erupt from the nozzle, flaring up into the sky. And now combustion products emerged, ice crystals that caught the sunlight, receding in perfectly straight lines. It was a fire fountain, quite beautiful.

Humans could control operations from Earth from now on. Asteroid water and raw, unprocessed rock would be swallowed into giant bags and, pushed by rockets like this test rig, steered through the empty ocean of space towards Earth, as if by a squid's mantle jet.

Dan would tell her there was much celebration, within Bootstrap. He did not say so, but Sheena understood that this was mainly because she had finished her task, before dying.

She turned away from the waldo glove and the imagers, the human machines, and sought out her young.

They were growing explosively quickly, converting half of all the food they ate to body mass.

At first they had been asocial, foraging alone in the beds of seagrass. But already – though still tiny – they had developed shoals. She watched the males fighting: aggressive signalling, fin-beating, chasing and fleeing – miniature battles prefiguring the greater conflicts to come at breeding time.

Some of the young were already hunting the smaller fish, adopting behaviour patterns her kind were hatched with, even talking to each other in the simple, rich sign language which Dan said was hard-wired into their brains by millions of generations of ancestors: *I am large and fierce. Look at my weapons. I am seagrass, I am no squid. I am strong. Look at me!*

She knew that Dan must be aware of the existence of the young by now. The growing imbalance in the small ecosphere could surely not be ignored. But he said nothing; and she volunteered nothing.

Most of the young were dumb. Four were smart.

She took the smart ones to one side. She swam at the heart of their small shoal. She was growing old now, and tired easily. Nevertheless she taught the smart ones how to hunt, sophisticated techniques beyond their dumber siblings.

She taught them how to lure foolish fish. They would hold up their arms with blanched tips, waving them, distracting the attention of the fish from the far more dangerous tentacles, waiting to strike.

She taught them how to stalk, gradually approaching a fish from behind, where its vision was poorest.

She taught them how to chase, pursuing a fleeing prey with careful watchfulness until close enough to make the final, decisive lunge.

She taught them to hunt, disguised. They would mimic sargassum weed, hanging in the water with arms dangling, ready to dart out at incautious fish. Or they would swim backward with false eye spots and arms held together and waved like the tail of a fish.

They practised on the smaller fish, and some of them eyed the other squid, their siblings.

She taught them about the reef, the many creatures that lived and died there, how they worked together, even as they competed and fought and hunted. She tried to teach them about predators. She role-played, swooping down on them like a moray eel, trying to catch them with her arms and beak. But they were young and agile and easily evaded her, and she sensed they did not believe her stories of monsters that could nip off a squid's arms, or even swallow a squid whole, enhanced brain or not.

And she taught them language, the abstract signs Dan had given her. As soon as they had the language their mantles rippled with questions. *Who? Why? Where? What? How?*

She did not always have answers. But she showed them the machinery that kept them alive, and taught them about the stars and sun, and the nature of the world and universe, and about humans.

The young ones seemed to understand, very quickly, that Sheena and all her young would soon exhaust the resources of this one habitat. The habitat had been designed to support one squid, herself, for a fixed period of time, a time which was almost expired. Already there had been a number of problems with the tightly closed environment loops: unpredictable crashes and blooms in the phytoplankton population, depletions or excessive concentrations of trace elements, with corresponding impacts on the krill and the fish.

The young were *very* smart. Soon they were able to think in ways that were beyond Sheena herself.

For instance, they said, perhaps they should not simply repair this fabric shell, but *extend* it. Perhaps, said the young, they should even make *new* domes and fill them with water.

Sheena, trained only to complete her primary mission, found this a very strange thought.

There weren't enough fish, never enough krill. The waters were stale and crowded.

This was clearly unacceptable.

So the smart young hunted down their dumb siblings, one by one, and consumed their passive bodies, until only these four, and Sheena, were left.

Michael:

His memories were jumbled.

When tourists had come to the village they would take snapshots with their cameras, and sometimes they would send them to the village. Michael would see himself in the pictures, a person who no longer existed, smiling up at somebody who was no longer there, like two ghosts. Sometimes the pictures would arrive out of order, so he would see himself in a T-shirt with a hole in it, and in the next picture there he would be, a little shorter maybe, with the T-shirt magically fixed.

When he had been taken out of the village he had understood almost none of what happened to him, and his memories had become jumbled, like the snapshots.

But there was still a sky above him, with stars and a Moon, even though they were in different places from when he was in the village.

And when he closed his eyes – on his pallet at night, in the stillness of his blanket, with no sound or sensation – he could feel deep inside himself that time wore on, passing inexorably, measured invisibly by the evolution of his own thoughts. It didn't matter that his memories didn't make sense, that what had happened to him had no logic or explanation. It was enough that he knew, deep inside, that the universe still worked.

The rules, here in the School, became simple.

Food was everything.

You could not be sure when another meal might come, so you had to eat or hoard every scrap of food you could find.

In fact it was better to hoard as much as possible, to hide it in your clothes or in a cache, like Michael's store in the wall of the dormitory hut, to make it last longer.

If you had food you had power. If another had food, they had power over you.

There were other rules.

For example: at night the children were not allowed to go outside their dormitory room to relieve themselves. There was always a Sister or a Brother in the dormitory to ensure this was so. There was a single slop-bucket at night, set in the middle of the floor. It was not big enough and soon filled up. If it spilled on the floor, you would be punished. If you made a mess, if you wet your bed or relieved yourself where you shouldn't, you would be punished. Many of the younger children were quite clumsy, and so would often knock over the bucket, or otherwise mess the place up. They were punished often.

At night Michael would hear children crying in pain as they tried to resist the temptation to use the bucket. And he would hear Anna's quiet, grave voice, helping them stay quiet, overcome the discomfort.

New children, arriving here in their shirts marked with crude blue circles, would often cry and complain, and suffer when they broke the rules. They soon learned, however.

Michael had one possession he cared about. It was the flashlight Stef had given him. Michael used the flashlight sparingly, and the new batteries had hardly dimmed.

At night, he would crawl under his bed, in utter silence. He had some pieces of scrap metal, into which he had knocked small holes with a headless nail.

He shone the flashlight on one metal scrap and looked at the spot of yellow light he cast on the wall. He saw a bright central spot, surrounded by a band of half-shadow, and darkness beyond. Then he put another scrap in that spot, punctured by a second hole, so that the light he cast was stretched thinner.

The spot of light cast by the second hole was different. He saw the central spot and the outer darkness, but between them there were intricate patterns of light and dark, concentric rings. There was colour here, blue and orange and red rings overlapping. The rings, in the silent dark, were quite beautiful. He was seeing waves, like ripples on a pond, places where the bits of light – *photons* – were washing against each other, falling together in the bright places or nudging each other out of the way in the dark.

He found a scrap of cellophane, bright blue, and put that over one of the holes. Now he saw a simpler system of concentric rings, painted in blue only. He found the blue circles comforting. He imagined they were doors painted on the wall, and that he might pass through them, to go home to the village, or somewhere even better.

He kept pulling his apparatus apart. Perhaps he could stretch it

157

so much that only one light bit at a time, one photon, would pass through the holes. He never managed that, but it didn't matter; he could see in his mind what the result would be.

He would see a stream of photons speckling against the wall, nudging and jostling, working together to make the glowing bands.

But one photon, alone, separate from the others, was like a thrown stone. What was affecting *it*? How could it *know* which parts of the wall to land on, and which not?

The answer was obvious. The photon was being nudged and jostled into the right place, just as it had been when part of a flood. So there must be something coming from the holes to jostle the photon, even when only one photon at a time passed through the holes. Something that behaved exactly like photons, except he could not see them.

They were ghost photons, he thought. Partners of the 'real' one, the one he could see. The real photon reached forward in time, inquiring. And a flood of ghosts from the future came crowding back in time, along every possible path it could take. And yet they *were* real, for they jostled the genuine photon just as if it was part of a dense bright beam.

For every photon, there was an uncounted flood of ghosts, of possible futures, just as real as the photon he saw.

And so, surrounding every person, there must be a flood of future ghosts, representing all the unrealized possibilities, all equally real.

Michael, with his flashlight and metal scraps, surrounded by ghosts, smiled in the dark. Perhaps the future Michaels were happy.

One day a Brother found his food cache, and the flashlight, and the scraps of metal, all buried in the wall.

The children in the dormitory were made to stand in a line, before their beds, while the Brother barked at them. Michael did not understand the words, but he knew what would happen. The Brother wanted the owner of the cache to step forward. If nobody volunteered as responsible, all the children would be beaten. And then, when the Brothers were gone, the other children would beat Michael.

Still, he waited. Sometimes a child, one who was not responsible, would step forward, and take the punishment for another. Anna often did this, but today she was not here. Michael had done it once, to spare a sickly boy.

Today, nobody came forward.

Michael took a step.

His punishment was severe.

And later the Brother stamped on the flashlight, smashing it. Michael was made to sweep up the pieces, the bits of broken glass, with his bare hands. The fragments of glass that stuck in his fingers made them bleed for days.

Shit Cola Marketing:

Adopt a baby space squid!

Thanks to Shit's commercial tie-up with the Bootstrap corporation we can offer a once-in-a-lifetime opportunity to purchasers of Shit Cola or other Shit products to become official adopters of one of the infant squid on the asteroid Cruithne.

Every squid is different. We have recognition software, designed in conjunction with leading scientists, which can distinguish *your* baby squid by its shape, markings and characteristic movements. You can name him/her, monitor his/her progress, even (pending legal approval) send him/her messages and tell him/her something of yourself.

Numbers are limited!

To apply, laser-swipe 100 pull-tabs from cans of Shit Cola or related soft drink products and mail the codes, together with your completion in no more than ten words of the phrase: *Shit will be the downstream drink of choice because* ... to the following e-address ...

Maura Della:

When the storm broke about the baby squid, Maura flew straight out to Vegas to confront Malenfant and Emma.

She found them in Emma's office. Emma was sitting at her desk, her head in her hands. Malenfant was hyped up, pacing, hands fluttering like independent living things. Maura said quietly, 'You fool, Malenfant. How long have you known?'

He sighed. 'Not long. A couple of weeks. Dan had suspicions

before we got confirmation, the actual pictures from Cruithne. Imbalances in the life support systems –'

'Did you know she was pregnant before the launch?'

'No. I swear it. If I'd known I'd have taken her off the mission.'

She looked sceptical. 'Really? Even given the launch window constraints and all of that technical crap? It would have meant scrubbing the mission.'

'Yes, it would. But I'd have accepted that. Look, Congresswoman. I know you think I'm some kind of obsessive. But I do notice how the world works. A mission like Bootstrap needs public support. We've known the ethical parameters from the beginning.'

'But we're not sticking to those parameters any more, are we? We'd got to the point where the bleeding-heart public would have accepted Sheena's death. The asteroid colony, a permanent tribute to a brave and wonderful creature. But this has changed everything . . .'

It was true. Since the latest leak, support for Bootstrap's Cruithne project and its grandiose goals had evaporated.

All the tabloid-fed hysteria, the religious ravings, the pompous and hostile commentaries, made no sense, of course. If to abandon ten or a thousand sentient squid was a crime, so was abandoning one.

But when, she thought sourly, had sense and rationality been a predominant element in public debates on science and technology?

Malenfant spread his hands. 'Look, Representative, we spent the money already. We have the installation on Cruithne. *It's working*. Baby squid or not, we have achieved the goal, begun the bootstrap.'

'Malenfant, we are soon going to have an asteroid full of sentient-squid corpses up there. People will think it is – monstrous.' She blinked. 'In fact, so will I.'

He thought that over. 'You're talking about shutting us down?'

'Malenfant, the practical truth is you're already dead. The body hasn't gone cold yet, is all.'

'It isn't your decision. The FAA, the White House people, the oversight committees –'

'Without me, and a few others like me, Bootstrap would have been dead long ago.' She hesitated, then reached for his shoulder. 'I'm sorry, Malenfant. Really. I had the same dream. We can't sell *this*.'

Emma said slowly, 'We'll do it with decency. We won't kill Sheena. We'll let her die in comfort.'

'And the babies?'

She shrugged. 'We'll turn away the communications dishes, and let nature take its course. I just hope they forgive us.'

'I doubt that,' Malenfant said, and he began pacing again, back and forth, compulsively. 'I can't believe we're going to be blocked by this, this one small thing.'

Maura said to Emma, 'Are you going to be okay?'

'Yes.' Emma looked up and contrived a smile. 'We've been lower than this. We'll manage.'

Meaning, Maura realized, she will manage Malenfant. Bring him through this. You don't deserve your friends, Malenfant, she thought.

They began to go through details.

Sheena 5:

She could feel the soft tug of Cruithne's gravity field pulling her to the dark base of the habitat. She drifted, aching arms limp, dreaming of a male with bright, mindless eyes.

There were no fish left, scarcely any krill or prawns. The water which trickled through her mantle was cloudy and stank of decay. She felt life pulse through her, ever faster, as if eager to be done. And she seemed so weak, as if her muscles themselves were being consumed; it was a long time since the great ring muscles of her mantle had been strong enough to send her jetting freely, as once she had done, through this ocean she had brought across space.

But the young wouldn't let her alone. They came to her, shook her limbs, seeking guidance. She summoned the will to open her chromatophores.

I am grass. I am no squid.

No. Smart eyes swam into her vision. *No. Danger near. You die we die.* They were flashing the fast, subtle signals employed by a shoal sentinel, warning of the approach of a predator. There was no predator here, of course, save the ultimate: death itself, which was already consuming her . . .

And it would soon consume these hapless young too, she knew. Dan and Bootstrap had promised to keep her alive. But they would shut down the systems when she was gone. She wondered how the young knew this. They were smarter than she was.

When they swam out of her field of view, oddly, she forgot they were there, as if they ceased to exist when she could not see them. Her mind itself was weakening. She knew she could never hunt again, even if she had the strength.

But then the children would return, clamouring, demanding.

Why, they said. *Why here now this. Why die.*

And she tried to explain it to them. Yes, they would all die, but in a great cause, so that Earth, the ocean, humans, could live. Humans and cephalopods, a great world-spanning shoal. It was a magnificent vision, worthy of the sacrifice of their lives.

Wasn't it?

But they knew nothing of Dan, of Earth. They wanted to hunt in shoals and swim through the ocean, unhindered by barriers of soft plastic.

They were like her. But in some ways they were more like their father. Bright. Primal.

She could see them chattering, rapidly, one to the other, too fast for her to follow.

She probably hadn't explained it as well as Dan could. She tried again.

No. You die we die . . .

Dan Ystebo:

At JPL, at the appointed time, Dan logged on for his daily uplink to the *Nautilus.*

There had been nothing but inanimate telemetry for days. He wasn't even sure – couldn't tell from the muddled telemetry – if Sheena was in fact still alive.

Maybe this would be his last contact. He'd be glad if he could spare himself any more of this shit.

He was clearing his desk. He looked around the cubicle he was dismantling, the good old geekosphere, a comfortable mush of old coffee cups and fast-food wrappers and technical manuals and rolled-up softscreens, the multi-poster on the partition which cycled through classic *Twenty Thousand Leagues Under the Sea* scenes.

Dan was going back to Key Largo. He planned to resign from Bootstrap, get back to the biorecovery and gen-eng work he'd started from. To tell the truth he was looking forward to moving back to Florida. The work he would do there would be all for the good, as far as he was concerned. None of the Nazi-doctor ethical ambiguities of Bootstrap.

But he was hoping to hang around JPL long enough to be with Sheena when she died. And the bio-signs in the telemetry indicated that wouldn't be so long now. Then the Deep Space Network radio telescopes would be turned away from the asteroid for the last time, and whatever followed would unfold in the dark and cold, unheard.

. . . Here was a new image in his softscreen. A squid, flashing signs at him, a mixture of the passing cloud, and a sign he'd taught Sheena himself, the very first sign: *Look at me. Dan. Look at me. Dan. Dan. Dan.*

He couldn't believe it. 'Sheena?'

He had to wait the long seconds while his single word, translated to flashing signs, was transmitted across space.

Sheena 6.

'. . . Oh.' One of the young.

The squid turned, strong and confident, and through a forest of arms predator eyes seemed to study him.

Dying.

'Sheena 5? I know.'

Water. Water dying. Fish. Squid. Danger near. Why.

She's talking about the habitat biosphere, he realized. She wants me to tell her how to repair the biosphere. 'That's not possible.'

Not. Those immense black eyes. *Not. Not. Not.* The squid flashed through a blizzard of body patterns, bars and stripes pulsing over her hide, her head dipping, her arms raised. *I am large and fierce. I am parrotfish, seagrass, rock, coral, sand. I am no squid, no squid, no squid.*

He had given Sheena no sign for 'liar', but this squid, across millions of miles, bombarding him with lies, was doing its best.

But he was telling the truth.

Wasn't he? How the hell could you extend the fixed-duration closed-loop life support system in that ball of water to support *more* squid, to last much longer, even indefinitely?

. . . But it needn't stay closed-loop, he realized. The *Nautilus* hab was sitting on an asteroid full of raw materials. That had been the point of the mission in the first place. In fact Sheena 5 had already opened up the loops a little, replacing hab membrane leakage with asteroid water.

You'd need machinery to get at all that stuff. But there *was* machinery. The rocket propellant factory. Pilot plant for the pro-duction of other materials. The fireflies, robots to do the work.

If he could figure a way to do this. *If* he could figure how to re-engineer all that equipment to process carbonaceous ore into some kind of nutrient soup, maybe, for the hab biosphere. And *if* he could find a way to train these new squid. He'd had years to work with Sheena; he'd have weeks, at best, with these new guys. Still . . .

His brain started to tick at the challenge.

But there were other problems. When the comms uplink shut down in a few weeks, he wouldn't be able to run the operation.

In that case, he realized, he'd just have to train up the squid in the principles of what they were building. How to run it, repair it for themselves. Even extend it.

It might work. Sheena had been smart.

It would be a hell of an effort, though. And for what?

What's this, Ystebo? Are you growing a conscience, at last? Because if you are, that damn piece of calamari up there knows how to play on it.

And besides, he thought, maybe I can convince Reid Malenfant that this is the best thing to do, a way to keep the greater goals of the project in progress, with official sanction or not. If the squid, by their own efforts, refuse to die, maybe we can turn around public opinion one more time . . .

Do it now, justify later. Isn't that what Malenfant says?

'I'll help you,' he said. 'I'll try. What can they do, fire me?'

Dan placed a call to Malenfant. And then a second, to Florida, to tell the people there he wouldn't be joining them just yet.

The squid turned away from the camera.

Emma Stoney:

Cornelius Taine came to Emma's office.

'We think it worked,' he said, breathless. 'We found him.'

Emma was not glad to see Taine once more. 'Found who? What are you talking about?'

Cornelius handed over a document. It was a report prepared by a professor of physics from Cal Tech. Emma leafed through it. It was heavy on text and laden with equations, difficult to skim.

Cornelius said, 'It's an analysis of material found on a softscreen.

The math was difficult to decipher. Unconventional formalism. But it's all there.'

'*What* is?'

Cornelius sat down, visibly tried to be patient. 'It's a sketch of the foundations of a theory of quantum gravity. Which is a unification, awaited for a century, of general relativity and quantum theory, the two great pillars of physics.'

'I thought we had that. String theory.'

'String theory is part of it. But string theory is mathematically dense – after thirty years the theorists have only extracted a handful of predictions from it – and it's limited besides; it doesn't incorporate curved space in a natural way. And –'

Emma pushed the report away. 'What does this have to do with us?'

He smiled. 'Everything. The material turned up in a Foundation School in Australia, their Northern Territory. Produced by one of the inmates there.'

Inmates. 'You mean one of the Blue children?'

'Yes. A ten-year-old from Zambia.'

He handed over a photograph. A frightened-looking boy, strong white teeth, round eyes. 'My God,' she said. 'I know this boy.'

'I know.' Taine looked at the image hungrily. 'He's the one we've been looking for. Don't you see?'

'No, I don't.' She thought over what he had said. 'You're saying that finding this one boy was the objective of the whole program?' She pushed away the report. 'Cornelius, I'm amazed you've come to me with this. In case you're not aware of it, we're being shut down, up on Cruithne. In three months of surface operations we've discovered nothing to justify the diversion of the mission, away from Reinmuth, with all the complication that brought us.'

'We've gone over this many times,' he said tightly. 'You're well aware that the firefly robots have been restricted to a small area around the *Nautilus*. We have been marking time. There's a *lot* of surface area to explore. And besides, we *know* there's something to be found. We have the Feynman radio message –'

'Sure,' she said harshly. 'Or maybe all we were picking up was the Fermilab air conditioning turning itself on and off. What do you think?'

He eyed her, eyes bright, mouth small and tense. He seemed to be rocking back and forth in his chair, almost imperceptibly. 'Emma, there is much, *much*, you've yet to understand about what's going on here. Remember we believe we are fighting for the destiny of the species.'

She sighed. 'So now what?'

'Now we have to go get him.'

'We?'

'Perhaps he will remember you.'

Sheena 6:

Sheena 6 was the smartest of the young.

It was no privilege. She had to work hard to absorb the new signs and concepts Dan sent to her.

And there was much work to do.

She learned to use the glove-like systems that made the firefly robots clamber over the asteroid ground, that strange place beyond the ship wall where there was no water. The mining equipment, designed to extract methane and water for the rocket fuel, was adapted to seek out essentials for the phytoplankton, nitrates and phosphates. No more sacks of water and dirt were fired to Earth. Under her command, fireflies took apart the methane rocket plants at the poles, and began to haul the parts over the surface for new uses.

Even in the hab itself there was much to do. Dan showed her how to keep the water pure. Oxygen could be produced by the great metal cells, to keep the water fresh and vitalizing. There were beds of charcoal filters through which the water was pumped. But the charcoal had to be replaced by carbon extracted from asteroid material, burned in sun fire.

Dan also tried to show her how to interpret the elaborate automatic monitoring systems, which checked that the closed loops remained healthy. But this was no use to her. Squid senses were delicate. If the water was unbalanced, she could see, taste, smell it as it passed through her mantle, over her gills. She could see the twisting polarization of the light caused by murky pollutants. She could even hear the tiny cries of the plankton. She *knew* when the water was unhealthy. It was enough that she had the means to fix it.

The processes were complex. But at heart, she learned, there was a simple principle. Her world, this droplet of water clinging to a rock, was so small it could not sustain itself. She took food out of it by feeding on krill; so she must find ways, direct or indirect, of returning raw materials for that food to the world.

Very well.

In the midst of this activity, Sheena 5 grew weaker. Sheena 6 tried to pummel her awake, a few hours longer.

At last, though, Sheena's black eyes clouded. Her young gathered around her. *Look at me. Court me. Love me.*

Last confused words, picked out in blurred signs on a mottled carapace, stiff attempts at posture by muscles leached of strength.

Sheena 6 hovered close to her mother. What had those darkening eyes seen? Was it really true that Sheena 5 had been hatched in an ocean without limits, an ocean where hundreds – thousands, millions – of squid hunted and fought, bred and died?

Sheena 5's arms drifted purposelessly, and the soft gravity of Cruithne started to drag her down for the last time.

Sheena's young fell on her, their beaks tearing into her cooling, sour flesh.

With time, the *Nautilus* hab was stabilized. As long as the machines survived, so would the hab's cargo of life.

But it was too small.

It had been built to sustain one squid. There were four of them now, four of Sheena's young.

The shortage of food wasn't the only problem. At times Sheena 6 ached with the need to rip open the mantle of her most foolish brother.

So Sheena, under instruction from Dan, went to work. Under her guidance the firefly robots began to assemble new engines, new flows of material. Dan tried to teach her sign-labels for the chemical processes involved.

Here was a small plant, for instance, that burned hydrogen and carbon dioxide to produce water and carbon monoxide. Then the carbon monoxide burned with further hydrogen to produce water and ethylene, and then the ethylene was used to produce polyethylene and polypropylene . . .

The truth was she understood little of this. But she understood the end product.

Plastics.

With plastics she could make anything. She had the firefly robots toil over the plastic sheets and artefacts, cutting and joining. The shining sheets spread around the rocket at the pole and the glimmering habitat of *Nautilus*.

These toy factories had been intended as trials of technologies and manufacturing processes that would have supported a human colony on Cruithne. But no humans had come to Cruithne.

Soon there were four habs, linked by tunnels, one for each of Sheena's young, the smart survivors.

The habs filled up with water from melted asteroid substance. The krill and diatoms bred happily to fill the volume available. The habs were splashes of water and life on the asteroid's crumbling, coal-dark surface; they looked like living things themselves, spawning and breeding.

But already another cephalopod generation was coming: sacs of eggs clung to asteroid rock, in all the habs.

So they extended the habs further.

And the greater volume required more power. Sheena extended the solar cell arrays that coated the surface of the asteroid, around the pole.

But this wasn't enough. So Sheena 6 found a way to make glass from Cruithne silicon compounds, and ceramics to make frames that held great wings of solar receptors in space, away from the surface.

Unremarked by humans, the young of Sheena swarmed over their asteroid.

The third generation emerged from their shells and started to look at their expanding world with new, curious, resentful eyes.

Perhaps a fifth of them were smart. A fifth seemed a small number.

As the young hunted their mindless brothers, Sheena wondered if there were ways to increase that proportion. And to make the squid smarter.

And live longer.

Sheena 6 thought about the future.

It wouldn't stop, Sheena 6 saw, more generations of young and more habs, until the asteroid was full, used up. What then? Would they turn on each other at last?

But there was nobody to discuss her ideas with.

The truth was, Sheena was isolated. Her siblings, even her own young, were remote from her.

This new shoal had been hatched in the strangeness of space, and they swam in asteroid water, not the oceans of Earth. That was true of Sheena 6 also, of course, but she had worked with humans, with Dan, as had her mother before her. Perhaps she was closer to Earth than they were.

Sheena 5 had talked about the great shoals of Earth, their dreaming songs of the million-year-deep past. These new squid cared nothing for Earth, nothing for the past. And their dreams, their dances and songs, were of the future.

The siblings found new ways to control the firefly robots. They had begun to send firefly robots to explore the asteroid, places neither Sheena 5 nor even Sheena 6 had seen. They signed pictures to each other Sheena 6 couldn't recognize: great starburst explosions, squid writhing and dying.

It seemed they had found something on the far side of the asteroid. Something strange.

They would not discuss it with her. When she sent a firefly robot crawling over there to investigate, they turned it around and sent it back.

The siblings took to wearing sigils on their chromatophore-rich hides. Bright circles. Dan told her they were blue.

Sheena 6 swam restlessly through the *Nautilus* hab, alone.

She longed for the shoal. But she had never known the companionship of the true shoal; she had been born too late to have shoaled with the great clouds of squid on Earth, too early to join with these new, bright-eyed creatures of space. She was neither one nor the other.

She had no purpose. She may as well die.

Still, the restlessness burned in her, and curiosity itched. What was it that the others had found, on the far side of the asteroid?

She sent another firefly, but it too was turned back.

Once, Sheena 5, her mother, had crossed space, travelled between worlds. Perhaps it would be appropriate if Sheena 6 – the closest of Sheena 5's young, the last to have communicated with a human – were to do something similar.

She gathered her remaining machines and began to plan something new.

Michael:

There were legs before Michael when he opened his eyes. Pillars of cloth. A man's legs.

He tried not to move. He closed his eyes again. Perhaps if the man thought Michael was asleep he would go away, choose someone else. There was a strange, unearthly silence in the room. He imagined the others lying rigid, feigning sleep as he did.

The Brothers hardly ever came here. The Sister, in her glass-fronted office at the end of the dormitory, would only come out if someone had done something wrong, like spill the slop bucket.

It was never good when something unusual happened, because it meant that somebody was going to get hurt. All you could do was find ways to stop it being you.

But tonight, it seemed, it was Michael's turn.

The man's voice barked. It was the language they spoke here, not Michael's language, and so he didn't understand. Best not to say anything.

But the man was still speaking to him, angrier now, too loud for him to ignore, to feign sleep.

And now a fist the size of a child's head came down and grabbed Michael's grubby T-shirt. He felt the cloth dig under his arms and he heard a seam rip. Michael was lifted up, bodily, his legs dangling.

He hung there limp. A face like a cloud, puzzled and angry, loomed before him.

He was set down on his bare feet, hard. He stood there and looked up at the man. It wasn't one of the Brothers. The man turned away and spoke some more, this time to the Sister, who was standing at the end of Michael's bed.

The Sister took hold of Michael's hand. He made a fist so she couldn't take his fingers, but she shook his hand, hard, until his fingers uncurled, and then she grabbed them and squeezed them tightly.

The Sister dragged him out of the dormitory. It was early morning. The grey of dawn had washed out, leaving the sky an empty blue, as always, and the bleached buildings of the School stretched away around him.

The Sister took him to a smaller building, a place he'd never been into before. She opened the door and pushed him inside.

He thought it was the cleanest place he had ever seen. The walls were white and so smooth they looked like skin. There were gleaming metal fixtures set in the roof, and bright strip lights that turned the air grey.

The Sister started pulling at his clothes, lifting or ripping them off him. He endured this passively. He would get them back later.

He reached out and touched the smooth wall. The grime on his palm left a mark. He snatched back his hand and looked at the Sister, wondering if she would punish him for that, but she didn't seem to have noticed.

When she had removed all his clothes she pushed him into the middle of the room, away from the walls. Then she walked out of the door and pulled it closed behind her.

He just stood there in the middle of the room, because nobody had told him to do anything else.

And then water began to gush from the ceiling, hard needle jets of it. It hissed against the walls, and battered at his flesh. At first he thought it might be rain. There used to be rain at home, in the summer. But there was never rain here.

The roof rain grew harder, so hard it stung. There was an odd smell in it, like the smell of the liquid the Sisters sometimes used to hose out the dormitory. And it was getting hotter. He stumbled back, fetching up against the hard, slippery wall, but the rain seemed to follow him and there was nowhere to run, not even other children to hide behind.

Perhaps this was his punishment, then. Perhaps it was because of the flashlight.

He huddled down in the corner, wedged into the angle of the walls. He could see water trickling off his body into a hole in the middle of the floor. The water was stained brown and black, but after a time it began to run clear.

Emma Stoney:

Emma had become increasingly dismayed by the bad news that surrounded the Blue-children Schools. Nothing, however, could have prepared her for the reality of Red Creek.

Red Creek turned out to be an Aboriginal reserve in Australia's Northern Territory, reinstated by the Terra Nullius national government. A section of it had been hastily cordoned off to site this Foundation School. They were shown around by a 'Brother' – a young Portuguese, darkly handsome and composed, dressed in a flapping black gown and dog-collar.

It was a bleak place.

There were huts, like barracks, which had once been painted white, but the paint had faded to an indiscriminate pink. Otherwise there seemed to be no colour at all, save the greyish red of the dust, here at the baked, eroded heart of Australia. The dust lay everywhere; as she walked she was trailed by a great cloud of it. Away from the reception area there seemed to be absolutely no vegetation, not a blade of grass. There was a hot, dry smell, of dust, dirty clothing, faeces and urine.

They weren't allowed into the huts. She saw no children.

Here in Red Creek, three hundred children lived in administered squalor. Cornelius and the Brother remarked on none of this. The Brother talked instead of economies-of-scale joint administration of the School and the rest of the *gin* reservation.

Gin. This word referred to Aborigines. It seemed to be a word of casual abuse. Likewise the Brother referred to the children here, of course, as *Blues*. Even though, he said in what was apparently meant to be a joke, most of the children here were black.

Terra Nullius – the name of Australia's governing party – meant 'empty land'. It referred to the old fiction that Australia was unoccupied when Captain Cook planted the flag here, that the Aborigines had no rights to the lands they had inhabited for millennia. A good name for the policies the government followed ruthlessly.

The native Australians had suffered a couple of centuries of persistent discrimination, with the dispossession of land, the separation of children from parents for indenture as servants and labourers, and so on. There had been a brief summer of hope, in the 1970s and after, when liberal, if flawed, protective legislation had been passed. It had all evaporated when the economy down-turned at the start of the new century, and the soil erosion began to hit.

Today, black children made up three per cent of the youth in Australia, but sixty per cent of those in prison. International human rights groups and Aboriginal organizations talked of torture and beatings. And so on.

Modern Australia was a good place for a school like this. And the people who staffed it.

The Portuguese Brother belonged to a Christian group called the Order of Christ. This was part of the shadowy coalition which supported the Milton Foundation. The Order turned out to have roots going back to the fourteenth century. It was a religious-military society originally set up to attack Islam in its own territories. The Order had included Vasco da Gama, for example, one of whose specialities was hanging Muslims from his masts and using them for crossbow practice . . .

In the year 2011, here was the Order in the black heart of Australia, running a school. And it was partly funded by Bootstrap, with money which had passed through Emma's control.

Appalled, ashamed, she drew Cornelius aside. 'Dear God, Cornelius.'

He frowned. 'You're distressed.'

'Hell, yes. I never imagined –'

'There is no crime here,' Cornelius said smoothly. 'The Brothers are actually here to protect the children. The Blues.'

'Does Malenfant know about this?'

Cornelius smiled. 'What do you think?'

Emma took deep breaths. Compartmentalize, Emma. One issue at a time.

'Cornelius, how can a child, alone and uneducated, in this God-forsaken School in Australian outback, come up with a theory of everything?'

'I could point to Einstein. He was a patent clerk, remember. His education was flawed. He didn't even have access to experimental evidence. He just dreamed up relativity from first principles, by *thinking hard*. And –'

'What?'

'Well, it's possible Michael has had a little help.'

'What kind of help?'

He looked into the air, his pale blue eyes milky with light. 'You have to think like a downstreamer. Anticipate them.'

'You really are insane, Cornelius.'

He smiled. He turned and walked away after the Portuguese Brother.

She had no choice but to follow him.

They returned to the reception area, and waited for the child, Michael, to be brought to them.

Michael:

In the rain house, the water stopped. He sat, shivering.

Then warm air gushed from the ceiling over him. The light grew strange, and he felt his skin tingle.

The door banged open, and the Sister returned.

He cowered, burying his hands between his thighs, but she hauled his hands out and dragged him to his feet.

She pulled him from the room into the open air. The sun felt harsh on his skin, which no longer had its warm screen of dirt. There were clothes here, but they weren't his. She prodded him. Her meaning was clear.

Reluctantly he bent down and picked up the clothes, and pulled them on. They were crisp and white, a T-shirt and long trousers and even socks and a pair of shoes. But they scratched his denuded skin. Besides, they had no blue circle, and he was confused.

When he was dressed, the Sister grabbed his hand again and dragged him once more.

Now they walked the length of the School compound. The Sister took great long strides with a harsh, regular gait, and he had to half-run to keep up. Once he almost fell. She screamed at him, evidently concerned he might have dirtied his new clothes.

They soon left behind the dormitory blocks, their paint peeling in the endless sunlight.

He started to feel frightened again. Although it was just a short walk from his own block, he didn't recognize the buildings here. He must have been brought past them when he arrived here, but he didn't remember, and he had never been so far since. Would he know his way back to his dormitory again? He tried to memorize the buildings he passed, but there was too much newness here.

He tried dragging his toe in the dirt, so as to leave a trail he might follow to get back. But when the Sister saw him she shouted at him, because he had soiled his new white shoes, and she cuffed his head.

They were coming towards one of the buildings now. It had an open door, darkness inside. There was a fence beyond this building, and beyond that the desert stretched away, flat and empty.

The Brothers had told them all about the desert. It stretched away a long way from the School, so far you would soon collapse of thirst, and even if you did manage to cross it you would find people who would punish you and send you back. So even if you somehow got out of the School there was nowhere to go, nobody to help you.

The Sister dragged him towards the dark doorway. He couldn't help but pull back. This was the end of the journey, and whatever awaited him, whatever he had been prepared for in the building with the rain and the light, was here, inside this building.

Sometimes children were taken away from the dormitory and never came back. Would he find their bleached bones piled up here?

The Sister dragged him inside, and he tried not to scream.

Cornelius Taine:

I can tell you now why I believe Michael is so important.

I have had long arguments with Malenfant over this: Malenfant, who feels it is callous to manipulate the lives of children so.

But Michael is not merely a child.

The Milton project was, of course, a cover. We have our own theory on the origin of the Blues, the bright children.

We believe the downstreamers must be trying to signal us. Because *we* would, if we knew what they know. But we're not convinced that some technological gadget is the correct solution, even though we've got to try.

Perhaps instead the downstreamers are also targeting something else. Perhaps they are targeting the most widespread programmable information storage system on the planet.

I mean, of course, the human brain. Especially the brains of the young: empty, impressionable, easily shaped.

We don't know how. We don't know what it would *feel* like. We don't seem to hear downstreamer voices in our heads.

Or perhaps we do – perhaps we always have – but we just don't recognize them.

Quite a thought, isn't it? Is it possible that Michael – born into ancient dust and squalor, unable to read or write, and yet dreaming of a four-dimensional universe – is more than some precocious genius, that he is actually being influenced, somehow, by time-traveller beams from the future?

175

It may sound fantastic, a dip into insanity.

But what if it's true?

And – what if Michael's generation aren't the first? There have always been isolated geniuses, with insights and wisdom that seem to transcend the time and place they were born into.

Perhaps this has been going on a long time.

Michael is a treasure beyond price. Malenfant seems to understand this now.

None of us yet knows where this extraordinary multifaceted journey is taking us. But it is clear to me that the boy, Michael, and this man, Malenfant, together are the key element.

I feel I have been groping in the dark. And yet I feel proud to have reached so far, to have been the catalyst to this essential relationship.

The first time Malenfant met Michael he seemed electrified, as if by recognition.

The fate of the other Blue children, incidentally, is irrelevant.

Michael:

Inside the building it was *cold*. Air blew on his skin, chill and dry. There was a table and chairs and doors, no people here, no children.

The Sister pushed him to a chair opposite the table. He sat down.

The Sister went to one of the doors. She opened it, and he glimpsed people beyond, adults talking and holding glasses, drinks. The door closed behind the Sister and he was left alone.

He glanced around. There was nobody here. He could see no cameras or softscreens.

He slid off the chair and crossed to the table, feet padding on the hard floor. There was a paper plate on the table with something on it, curling and dry and brown. Perhaps it was the rind of some fruit. He crammed a piece of it into his mouth, and pushed the rest inside his shirt. The rind was sharp on his tongue, tough and hard to chew.

The door opened abruptly. He turned. People came in, the Sister and another woman.

When the Sister saw him with the plate her face twisted. He saw her fist bunch, but something made her keep from hitting him.

Instead she bent down and grabbed his face, pinching his cheeks until he had to spit out the rind onto the floor.

The other woman came forward. She looked familiar.

Memory floated into his head, unwelcome. She had come to the village, in the days before. *Stoney.* Stef had called her Stoney.

Suddenly he knew what they were going to do to him. After Stoney had come to the village, he had been taken to this School. Now here she was again, and he would be taken away again, somewhere worse than this, where he would have to learn the rules, over again.

Stoney took a step towards him.

He fell to the ground, covering his belly and head, waiting for the blows.

But Stoney was reaching for him with open hands. She stroked his back. He looked up in surprise.

She was doing something he had never seen an adult do before. Something he'd thought only children did.

She was crying.

Emma Stoney:

A week after Emma got back from Australia, Cornelius called a meeting at the Mount Palomar observatory, from where he had been trying to observe Cruithne.

Emma – working furiously, unable to sleep, unable to put out of her mind what she'd seen in Australia – tried to veto this. But of course she was overruled.

And so, at the behest of Cornelius Taine and his bright insanities, she was dragged across the country once more.

To reach Mount Palomar, Emma had to fly into San Diego, and then she faced an hour's drive east up into the San Jacinto Mountains. The highway was modern. Her driver, a chatty, overweight woman, told her the highway had been laid by prisoners from a local jail. They reached the group of telescopes that made up the observatory. The site was dominated by the dome of the giant 200-inch reflector: a national monument, its heart a mirror made of twenty tons of honeycombed glass. But tonight, even though the skies were clear – if stained a little by sodium-lit smog – the big dome was closed up.

Cornelius Taine met Emma from her car. She turned away from him, refusing to speak.

Apparently undisturbed, he led her to a small support building. Brightly lit, the hut was crammed with humming information technology, much of it looking a little antiquated. There were a few junior researchers working here, quietly bullshitting as they gave up another night of their lives to this slow, obsessive work, waiting for Earth to pass through the starlight shadow of some rock in space. The dedication, the ingenuity with which data was squeezed out of such invisibly small opportunities, was awesome.

They aren't here, she thought, unlike Cornelius, because of the Carter catastrophe, whatever Cruithne means for him. They aren't even paid well. They just do it because –

Actually, she didn't really understand why they did it.

In this nervous, overcompensating crew, Cornelius in his black suit looked ice-cool and in control.

They reached a small, cluttered office. Emma had arrived late; the others, it seemed, had already started.

Malenfant was pacing the room, his movements large and aggressive and exaggerated. She hadn't seen him since she got back from Australia. Dan Ystebo was sitting there, cradling a doughnut, looking obscurely pleased with himself.

And Emma was deeply disturbed to see that Michael was here: the boy from Africa, who she had retrieved from the nightmare camp in the Australian desert. He was wearing loose, clean clothes. He was sitting in a corner of the office with his back to a wall. He was playing with a prism, letting its scattered light wash over his eyes.

She hissed to Malenfant, 'What is he doing here?'

Malenfant said, 'I don't know yet, Emma. I know it seems wrong. But I don't think we have any choice.'

She frowned. He sounded frightened.

Cornelius stood by them. 'Michael is safe and well, his situation legally controlled.' His eyes were very pale, like pieces of glass. 'You know, Emma, if you were so concerned about this boy, you could have taken the initiative. Tried to find him a guardian of your choice, for instance. But you didn't. You're like all the bleeding hearts who have been shouting loud and long recently about the Schools and the treatment of the Blue children. As long as the kids were out of sight you didn't care what happened to them.'

She found she couldn't meet his eyes.

She noticed that even as Michael watched his prism, his eyes flickered, his gaze travelling over the adults. He doesn't trust us, she thought. He's expecting us to turn on him again, as we – the adult world – have done before.

She sat down, troubled. 'Let's get this over.'

Tense, excited, Malenfant said, 'You got something, haven't you? Something on Cruithne.'

Cornelius nodded curtly. 'To business. One thing at a time, yes? Thanks to our friend Dan here, the squid have survived on Cruithne.' He tapped at touchpads embedded in the table surface. 'Unfortunately they aren't talking to us. They are even turning away fireflies controlled by the squid faction who have remained in the primary *Nautilus* hab bubble – a faction who seem to be reasonably loyal. We're trying to establish direct control of the fireflies ourselves, bypassing the cephalopods. In the meantime, ironically, we have had to rely on remote sensors, from Earth and Earth-orbital satellites, to figure out what is happening up there.'

Malenfant said to Emma, 'Ironic because we sent the squid up there in the first place to give us a better look at Cruithne.'

Cornelius started to bring up data – graphs, bar charts – on the softscreens embedded in the tabletop. 'You'd be surprised how much we can figure out about an asteroid just by looking at it. We can see how bright our asteroid is by comparing it with nearby stars, see how fast it's moving by watching it against the background sky, see how its brightness changes so we can guess its shape, see what colour the rocks are and so guess what they're made of. Also we use radio telescopes to bounce radar beams off Cruithne's surface. By comparing the echo with the outgoing beam, we can tell even more about the asteroid: its shape, rotation, surface properties, position and velocity, composition . . .

'We've found that the surface morphology of some parts of the asteroid is unusual. And not just because of the presence of the squid habs. We did manage to pick up a signal from one of the firefly drones that got close enough to return an image, a partial image, before it was turned away.'

Malenfant snapped, 'Close enough to what?'

For answer, Cornelius flashed up an image in the tabletop softscreens.

Emma shared a firefly's view of Cruithne:

A star field, a lumpy horizon, a broken, pitted, dark grey surface highlighted by a light source somewhere behind her, presumably fixed to the robot whose electronic eyes she was looking through.

She saw bits of the firefly in the foreground: a metal manipulator arm, a couple of tethers pinning the drone to the surface. Her view was restricted; the drone was low, hugging the surface, bringing the asteroid's horizon in close.

And on that horizon she saw –

What?

It was an arc, bright blue. It seemed utterly smooth, geometrically pure. It stretched from one side of the frame to the other, obviously artificial.

She felt cold. This was strange, utterly unexpected.

'Holy shit,' said Malenfant. 'It's an artefact, isn't it?'

'*That*,' said Cornelius, 'is what our AWOL squid have dug out on Cruithne. What you see is only part of the structure. After sending this the firefly was turned back. I can show you an image of the whole thing.' He tapped at his softscreen. 'Taken from the ground, however. Distressingly remote, blurred.'

Emma leaned forward. She saw a potato-shaped object – grey, lumpy and scarred – against a dark background. 'Cruithne,' she said.

The image was animated; Cruithne rotated, gracefully, about its long axis, bringing something into view. Standing in a pit, deep and neatly round, there was a structure.

It was a blue circle.

Over-enlarged, it was just a ring of blocky pixels. It was obviously the extension of the arc the firefly had approached. She had no way of gauging its size. There were squid habs clustered around the circle, golden splashes, not touching it directly.

Within the circle itself there was only darkness.

'It's about thirty feet tall. We tried bouncing radar and laser signals off the artefact. It doesn't have the same reflective properties as the rest of the asteroid. In fact we don't seem to be getting any radar echo at all. It's hard to be definitive. The clutter from the surrounding surface –'

Malenfant said, 'So what does that mean?'

'Maybe it's perfectly absorbent. Or maybe it's a hole.'

Malenfant frowned. 'A hole? What kind of hole?'

'An infinitely deep one.' Cornelius smiled. 'We're looking for a better explanation. We've also detected other anomalies. Radiation, high-energy stuff. Some oddities, pions and positrons. We think there must be high-energy processes going on there.' He shrugged. 'It doesn't seem to reflect light. That blue glow comes from the substance itself. It has no spectral lines. Just a broad-spectrum glow.'

Emma shook her head. 'I don't understand.'

He said patiently, 'If it was made of atoms, any kind of atoms, it would emit precise frequencies. Because the electrons in atoms jump between quantized energy levels.'

'So this isn't made of atoms,' said Dan, wondering.

Cornelius said, 'We should soon get back direct control of a couple of robots. Then, if this is a hole in space, let's find out where it leads. We'll send in a firefly.'

Malenfant paced, obsessive, exultant. 'So it's true. It's an artefact, out there on Cruithne. You were right, Cornelius. *This* will stick it to those assholes at the FAA and NASA and Congress . . .'

Emma looked inside herself, searching for awe, even terror perhaps. She found only numbness.

Malenfant's mind was immediately on the implications for his projects, Emma realized, his business. Not on the thing itself, its blunt reality. And yet, if this was real, everything was different.

Wasn't it?

Cornelius was smiling. Dan was sitting with his mouth open. Michael's prism-lit eyes were on her, empty and open.

It took Cornelius another week to set it up.

Sitting in her office in Vegas autumn sunlight, trying to deal with her work – the complex, drawn-out destruction of Bootstrap, the various related scandals concerning the end of the world and the Blue children and the squid, with her softscreens scrolling financial reports and projections, press statements, shareholder reports – what she had seen on Mount Palomar seemed – well, unreal. A light show.

Artefacts on an asteroid? A hole in space?

It couldn't *possibly* be real.

And yet she found it unaccountably hard to concentrate.

Malenfant, during this period, was a pain in the ass. He threw himself into Bootstrap affairs, but it was obvious he was trying to distract himself: angry, vigorous, frustrated, burning up nervous energy. Emma did her best to keep him away from the press.

At last Cornelius called Emma and Malenfant to a meeting at Eschatology's offices in New York. Emma considered ignoring the request: excluding Cornelius, and the strain of madness and inhumanity he had introduced into her life.

But, she found, she couldn't. She had to *know*.

With a sense of dread, she put her affairs on hold, and flew out with Malenfant.

Cornelius met them at reception and led them to a conference room.

At the closed door – a mundane oak panel in this plain carpeted corridor – he paused. 'Be warned,' he said.

Emma's hand crept into Malenfant's.

Cornelius opened the door.

And Emma found herself on Cruithne: black sky, dull black surface curving under her feet, the light from a powerful sun, hanging above her, drowning the stars. And, in a neatly excavated pit, there was a blue artefact in front of her: thirty feet tall, shining, perfectly circular, like some piece of blunt municipal sculpture. Waiting.

She walked forward, hesitantly, her eyes slowly adjusting. When she looked down she saw that her feet were a little below the coal-black asteroid surface, as if she was paddling in a shallow pool. Of course, she felt nothing.

Cornelius said, 'We papered the walls with softscreens. Not quite immersive VR . . . Much of the imagery comes directly from the various camera feeds we're managing to operate up there. The rest is software extrapolation. I've been preparing our firefly robot probe. But –'

Malenfant said, 'But what?'

Cornelius sighed. 'An hour ago this happened.' He tapped at a desk surface.

A firefly robot materialized from a pixel hail in front of them. Using its cables and pitons to drag at the coarse surface, it made its painstaking way towards the artefact. Lines trailed back from it, out of their view.

Malenfant said, 'That's our robot?'

'No. Not ours. Just watch . . .'

And now an object like a huge beach ball, attached to the long lines, came washing into the virtual reconstruction, towed by the firefly. It was water, Emma saw, a droplet wrapped up in a shimmering golden blanket, complex waves moulding its surface as it bounced gently on the regolith.

Within the blanket something was moving.

'It's a squid,' said Emma.

'Yes.' Cornelius rubbed his nose. 'We think it's a Sheena. That is, from the faction that still inhabits the *Nautilus*. They, it, seem to retain some of the mission's original imperative. Watch what happens now . . .'

The firefly, with a neat pulse of microrockets, leaped through the portal. It was briefly dwarfed by the great blue circle. Then it disappeared; Emma glimpsed a red flash.

The cables that trailed back to the beach ball oscillated, but they did not grow slack. The golden beach ball sat on the surface, quivering.

Malenfant stepped forward, hands on hips, studying the image. 'Where did the firefly go? Did it come out the other side of the hoop?'

'We think so,' said Cornelius. 'But the other side doesn't seem to be on Cruithne.'

There was a long silence.

The squid in the golden beach ball jetted back and forth, patient. Then the cables grew taut again, and began dragging the beach ball forward.

Watching the cables disappear into the artefact, apparently not connected to anything, was eerie.

It took just seconds for the beach ball to complete its series of awkward, slow bounces to the blue circle. Then, after a single liquid impact with the blue circle itself, the beach ball shimmered through the hoop. As the curved golden wall hit the dark disc, it seemed to flatten out, Emma thought, quickly reddening to darkness. At last the beach ball was squashed to an ellipse, dimmed to a sunset glimmer.

Then it was gone, not a trace remaining.

'Holy shit,' Malenfant said.

Cornelius held his hand up. 'Wait –'

There was a screech, loud enough to sting Emma's eardrums. 'What was that?'

'A radio signal,' Cornelius said. 'Very high intensity. Coming from the artefact. I cleaned it up, and got this.'

It was a TV image of a squid: coarse, the colours distorted, in golden gloom. She was repeating a simple sign, over and over.

'She's saying *reef*,' Cornelius said.

Cornelius had chairs and coffee brought in. They sat under Cruithne's wheeling black sky, legs crossed, sipping latte. Emma watched Earth and Moon climb through Cruithne's fifteen-minute night, blue spark with pale grey-brown companion.

'I have only partial answers.' Cornelius's face was heavily shadowed, its expression impossible to read. 'The Sheena obviously survived. She used a camera in her hab bubble to send back that message. But she's . . . somewhere else. I suspect we're dealing with an Einstein-Rosen bridge here.'

'A what?'

'A multiply connected space.' He waved his hands. 'A bridge between two points in space and time, otherwise separated. Or maybe even between two different spacetimes altogether, different levels of the manifold.'

'The manifold?' Emma asked.

'The ensemble of possible universes,' Cornelius said. He took his softscreen and folded it over, pinching two places together with thumb and forefinger. 'You must be familiar with the principle. If I take this flat space, two-dimensional, and fold it over in the third dimension, I can connect two points otherwise far separated. And the point where they meet, the place between my thumb and finger, is a circle, a flat place.'

'So if you fold over our three-D space in four dimensions –'

'The interface you get is three-dimensional. A box of some kind, where the two spaces touch.'

'You're talking about a wormhole,' Malenfant said.

Cornelius said seriously, 'A wormhole is only one possibility. An Einstein-Rosen bridge is a generic term for any such interface, which is Lorentzian. That is, it transforms like special relativity –'

Malenfant snapped, 'I thought you needed a lot of energy to make a wormhole. Funny physics.'

Cornelius sighed. 'You do indeed. To keep their throats open, wormholes have to be threaded with exotic matter.' He looked at them. 'That means negative energy density. Antigravity.'

Emma said, 'I didn't see any antigravity machines out there on the asteroid.'

Cornelius shook his head. 'You don't understand. General relativity is barely a century old. We haven't even observed a black hole directly yet. And we believe that relativity is only a partial description of reality anyhow. We have no idea how a sufficiently advanced society might set up an Einstein-Rosen bridge: what it might look like, how it might behave. For example, it's possible the ring itself contains something like cosmic string. Channels of unified-force energy. Very massive, very powerful gravity fields.'

Emma said, 'How could you manipulate such stuff?'

'I don't know.' He smiled.

Malenfant said, 'How that thing works is less important right now than what it does. If the ring is some kind of wormhole, a gateway to somewhere else –'

'Or some*when*.'

'Then the Sheena isn't dead. And if she stepped through that gateway, she can step back again. Right?'

Cornelius shook his head. 'We think this particular bridge is one way. That's theoretically possible. The Kerr-Newman singularity, for instance –'

Emma faced him. '*Why* do you think our portal is one way?'

'Because we can't see through it. Because light falling on it, even sunlight, is absorbed completely.' He gazed at her. 'Emma, if it was two way, we'd be able to see Sheena. Wherever she is.'

Malenfant growled, 'So what do we do?'

Cornelius smiled. 'Why, we send through our firefly, as we planned.'

They invested another hour, while Cornelius finalized the set-up of his firefly robot. It had been loaded up with every sensor Cornelius could think of, mostly stuff Emma had never heard of.

Emma stretched, paced around this strange VR representation of Cruithne.

None of this is real, she thought. It is a light show from the sky. None of it matters, compared to the mountain of mails that must be mounting up in her in-tray even now, compared to the complexities of the human world in which she had to survive. And when it all proves to be some dumb illusion, then we'll get back to work.

Or not.

Without warning Cornelius collapsed the VR walls. Emma found herself in a bare, black-walled room, illuminated by a single wall-mounted softscreen. The screen showed a slab of dark sky, a stretch of regolith; it was the single point of view returned by their firefly's camera.

Cornelius, working at a desktop softscreen, sent a command.

Long time-delayed minutes later, the firefly started trundling towards the portal. The screen image shuddered, ground and sky lurching, as the firefly snaked its way across Cruithne's battered surface. Data returned in a chattering stream to Cornelius's software.

Then the firefly stopped, maybe six feet short of the portal itself.

The portal loomed against a star-scattered sky, bright blue, a hole of emptiness.

'This is it,' whispered Cornelius. 'Well. I wonder what we're going to see.' He grinned coldly.

The robot, autonomous, moved forward once more.

The portal surface loomed larger, the blue ring at its boundary passing out of the image, only a thin dusting of Cruithne regolith at the base of the image giving any sense of motion.

There was a blue flash. Then darkness.

Leon Coghlan:

Did you *see* it? It was on all the channels. Jesus Christ. If this is real – Spike, think about the implications.

If Reid Malenfant's light show from Bootstrap has any validity at all – and our experts here at the think tank, e and otherwise, have reached a consensus that it does – then the old arguments about mutually assured destruction, the nuclear winter and so forth, no longer apply. *We know that no matter what we do today, the species will emerge strong and destined for a long and glorious future.*

The only question is who will control that future.

We *know*, Spike, that our enemies are wargaming this, just as we are. We're *already* in a game of chicken, we're in those two onrushing cars locked eyeball to eyeball with the other guy, and it's a game we have to win.

Many of us think our best strategy right now is to throw out the steering wheel.

And that's why we must consider a first strike.

I know this is a controversial view, Spike. But you have a seat on Marine One. If anybody has a chance to enact this, to press it on the President, it's you.

Emma Stoney:

The image broke up into static, restabilized.

Emma felt bewildered. 'Has the firefly gone through?'

Cornelius said, 'We lost a couple of systems. Overloads. I think . . .'

Emma leaned forward. The screen was empty, dark ... No, not quite. Something at the base. Broken ground, regolith, asteroid soil.

The firefly seemed to be rolling forward. A spot of ground directly in front of it was lit up by the small floodlights it carried. Further out the ground was illuminated by a softer glow: not sunlight, or even starlight, she realized; the light seemed diffuse, as if from some extended source, a glowing ceiling somewhere out of her view.

There were no stars in the sky.

Suddenly a bright yellow light washed over the regolith, drowning the firefly's feeble glow.

Emma was dazzled. 'What's that? Is something wrong?'

'No. I just turned on the floods. We can't see into the portal, but we can fire light beams through from the other side.'

Malenfant said, 'I think the firefly is panning the camera.'

The image crept sideways. Empty sky, broken regolith in a wash of light.

'Shit,' said Malenfant. 'It looks like Cruithne.'

'I think we *are* still on Cruithne. Or a version of Cruithne. The firefly has a gravimeter, and instruments to study the surface material. The data's patchy. But the composition looks same as Cruithne's, at first glance. The gravity strength is actually a little down, however.'

'What does that mean?'

'Cruithne has lost a little mass.'

'How?'

Cornelius just glared.

A blue ring scanned slowly into the picture. Its interior was shining, bright and yellow.

'The portal,' said Cornelius. 'That light is our flood, shining through. In fact when the sun comes up on our side, the sunlight should reach the far side −'

'If this is Cruithne,' said Malenfant, 'where the hell are we? The far side, the pole?'

'You don't understand,' whispered Cornelius.

The firefly was moving its own small spotlights. The glowing ellipses swept across the regolith, and fell on the portal.

Malenfant grabbed a softscreen and began flicking through camera angles. 'If it *is* possible to get back through that portal −'

'We should be able to see the firefly's glow, coming back through this side,' Cornelius said. 'Good thinking.'

They found a stable external image of the portal – from *this* side; the asteroid ground here was littered with instruments and fireflies. The portal stayed dark. Emma stared hard, hoping to see a twinkling glow, like a flashlight shone out of a dark pit. There was nothing.

Cornelius nodded, looking pleased.

Emma snapped, 'Damn it, Cornelius. This means the Sheena won't be able to get back. Doesn't it?'

He seemed surprised by her anger. 'But we knew that already. This just reinforces the hypothesis.'

'And that pleases you.'

'Of course it does.' He was puzzled.

Emma took a breath to calm herself.

'If the firefly's light isn't making it back,' said Malenfant, 'how come its radio signal is?'

'I don't think it is. I think the portal – the far end – is picking up the firefly's transmissions and rebroadcasting them, maybe through some kind of Feynman radio. And I think the portal at *our* end is picking the Feynman stuff up, and transmitting them again as radio signals, which we *can* pick up.'

'Like Sheena's initial screech.'

'Yes.'

'What kind of Feynman radio? Neutrinos?'

'There is a higher neutrino flux coming from the portal since we started this,' said Cornelius. 'But I'm guessing. We're dealing with capabilities far beyond our own . . .'

The firefly's camera angle continued to scan across the asteroid's horizon; the eerily glowing portal, standing alone, started to move out of the picture.

A crater came into the field of view: so vast and deep only its near rim, high and sharp, was visible.

Malenfant said, '*Look* at that. It must be a mile across. *That* isn't on our Cruithne.'

'Not yet,' murmured Cornelius.

Malenfant said, '*Not yet?* You think the Sheena has gone into the future? Is that what you're saying?'

'Think about it. If there had been a crater like that on Cruithne in the past – what could have erased it?'

'How far in the future?'

'I've no way of telling,' said Cornelius. 'There's no sign of residual radioactivity from that crater. If it was caused by a nuclear weapon – the detonation must have been ten, a hundred thousand years ago.'

'*A hundred thousand years?*'

'That's a minimum. The maximum . . .' He checked another datum. 'The firefly is carrying thermocouples. I programmed it to check the background radiation temperature of the universe. The cooling glow of the Big Bang . . . I can't see a change within the tolerance of the equipment from the present value, three degrees above absolute.'

'What does that mean?'

'Hard to say. We've gone forward less than a billion years, perhaps.'

Emma said, 'My God, Cornelius. You *expected* this, you were prepared to track giant jumps in time, by measuring changes in the temperature of the universe?'

'I didn't know what we would find. I didn't want to rule out anything.'

'How can you think that way?'

He smiled slyly. 'I'm an obsessive. You know me, Emma.' He tapped his forehead.

'. . . There,' Malenfant said, pointing at the big softscreen. 'The Sheena.'

The golden beach ball was sitting on the asteroid ground, under the black sky. And something was reflected in the golden meniscus: something above the frame of the image, up in the sky. Swirling light, washing across the gold.

A shadow swam within the beach ball.

Emma said, 'Can we speak to her?'

'We can pass radio signals into the portal, like our floodlights. The Sheena should be able to pick them up.'

'And presumably she can speak to us, through the Feynman mechanism.'

'If she wants to.' Cornelius tapped his softscreen. 'Just speak. The software will translate.'

Malenfant said, 'Sheena? Sheena, can you hear me?'

They waited patiently through the time delay.

On the screen, the squid turned to look at the firefly. Cornelius's software picked up a sign: simple, iconic.

Dan.

'Not Dan. Friends. Are you healthy?'

They waited out another long pause.

Reef.

Malenfant said tightly, 'What in hell is she looking at? How can I ask her –'

Cornelius said, 'We can do better than that.' He tapped his softscreen.

At Cornelius's command, the firefly's camera swivelled away from the beach ball, tipped up towards the sky, the way the Sheena was looking.

A ceiling of curdled light filled the camera's frame.

'Shit,' said Malenfant. 'No wonder there were no stars . . .'

Emma found herself staring at a galaxy.

It was more complex than Emma had imagined. The familiar disc – shining core, spiral arms – was actually embedded in a broader, spherical mass of dim stars. The core, bulging out of the plane of the disc, was bigger than she had expected, a compact mass of yellowish light. Delicately blue spiral arms – she counted them, one, two, three, four, wrapped tightly around the core – were much brighter than the core itself. She could see individual stars blazing there, a granularity, and dark lanes traced between each arm.

There was a surprising amount of structure, she thought, a lot of complexity; this galaxy was quite evidently an organized system, not just some random mass of stars.

'So, a galaxy,' said Malenfant. '*Our* Galaxy?'

'I think so,' Cornelius said. 'Four spiral arms . . . It matches radio maps I've seen. I'd say our viewpoint is a quarter of a galactic diameter away from the plane of the disc. Which is to say, maybe twenty-five thousand light years away. The sun is in one of the spiral arms, about a quarter of the way from the centre.'

'How did we *get* here?'

'I'd guess that Cruithne evaporated out of the Solar System.'

'Evaporated?'

'It suffered a slingshot encounter, probably with Jupiter, that hurled it out of the System. Happens all the time. If it left at solar escape velocity, which is around a three-thousandth of lightspeed –'

Emma worked it out first. '*Seventy-five million years,*' she said, wondering. 'We're looking at images from seventy-five million years into the future. That's how long it took that damn asteroid to wander out there.'

Cornelius said, 'Of course if that *isn't* our Galaxy, then all bets are off . . .'

Seventy-five million years was a long time.

Seventy-five million years ago on Earth, the dinosaurs were dominant. Emma's ancestors were timid mammals, the size of rats and shrews, cowed by the great reptiles. Look at us now, she thought. And in another seventy-five million years, what will we have achieved?

Cornelius's voice was tense, his manner electric. He's waited all his life for this, Emma realized, this glimpse of the far future through an alien window. 'This opportunity is unprecedented. I'm no expert on cosmology, the future of the Galaxy. Later we have to consult people who can interpret this for us. There is probably an entire conference to be had on that Galaxy image alone. For now I have some expert systems. I can isolate them, keep them secure –'

Emma said, 'What did she mean, *reef*?'

Cornelius said, 'I think she meant the Galaxy. The Galaxy has, umm, an ecology. Like a coral reef, or a forest.' He looked up. 'You can make out the halo, the spherical cloud around the main disc. Very ancient, stable stars. And the Population II stars in the core are old too. They formed early in the Galaxy's history: the survivors are very ancient, late in their evolution.

'Most of the star formation going on now is happening in the spiral arms. The stars condense out of the interstellar medium. Which is a rich, complex mix of gas and dust clouds.' Checking with his softscreen, he pointed to the spiral arms. 'See those blisters? The e-systems are telling me they are bubbles of hot plasma, hundreds of light years across, scraped out by supernova explosions. The supernova shock waves enrich the medium with heavy molecules – carbon, oxygen, iron – manufactured inside the stars, and each one kicks off another wave of star formation.'

'Which in turn creates a few new giant stars, a few more supernovae –'

'Which stirs up the medium and creates more stars, at a controlled rate. So it goes, a feedback loop, with supernova explosions as the catalyst. The Galaxy is a self-regulating system of a hundred billion stars, the largest organized system we know of, generations of stars ending in cooling dwarfs or black holes. The spirals are actually waves of stellar formation, lit up by their shortest-lived, brightest stars, waves propagating around the Galaxy in a way we don't understand . . .'

'Like a reef, then,' Emma said. 'The Sheena was right.'

Cornelius was frowning at his softscreen. 'But –'

'What's wrong?'

'There's something not right. I – the e-systems – don't think there are *enough* supernovae. In our time the hot plasma bubbles should make up around seventy per cent of the interstellar medium . . . That looks a *lot* less than seventy per cent to me. I can run an algorithm to check –'

'What,' said Malenfant evenly, 'could be reducing the number of supernovae?'

Cornelius was grinning at him.

Emma looked from one to the other. 'What is it? I don't understand.'

'Life,' Malenfant said. '*Life*, Emma.' He punched the air. 'I knew it. We made it, Emma. That's what the supernova numbers are telling us. We made it through the Carter catastrophe, got off the Earth, covered the Galaxy.'

'And,' Cornelius said, 'we've started farming the stars. Remarkable. Mind has spread across the stars. And just as we are already managing the evolution of life on Earth, so in this future time we will manage the greater evolution of the Galaxy. Like a giant life support system. Closed loops, on a galactic scale . . .'

Malenfant growled, 'I got to have this visual next time I give a speech in Delaware.'

Emma said, 'If this *is* intelligence, how do you know it's human?'

Malenfant said, 'What else could it be?'

Cornelius said, 'He is right. We seem to be surrounded by a Great Emptiness. The nearest handful of sun-like stars show no signs of civilization-produced radio emissions. The Solar System appears to be primordial, in the sense that it shows no signs of the great engineering projects we can already envisage: for example, Venus and Mars have not been terraformed. The face of the Moon appears to have been essentially untouched since the end of the great bombardment four billion years ago.

'Even if They are long gone, surely we should see Their mighty ruins, all around us. But we don't. Like an ant crawling around a Los Angeles swimming pool, we might have no idea what Their great structures are for, but we would surely recognize them as artificial . . .'

Malenfant said, 'Today, there's just us; in the future, *somebody* spreads across the Galaxy. Who else but us? Anyhow seventy-five megayears is more than you need to cover the Galaxy. You know, we should look further out. Another few megayears for the biosphere to reach Andromeda, three million light years away –'

Cornelius said, 'The nearest large galaxy cluster is the Virgo

Cluster. Sixty million light years out. It's plausible the biosphere might have reached that far by now.'

'We have to look,' said Malenfant. 'Send through more fireflies. Maybe we could establish a science station there, on the future Cruithne.'

Emma said, 'Christ, Malenfant, it's a one-way trip.'

'Yeah, but there are resources on future Cruithne, just as there are now. Enough to sustain a colony for centuries. We'd have no shortage of volunteers. For half a buck I'd go myself. Maybe we could contact the downstreamers directly.'

Malenfant and Cornelius talked on, excited, speculating.

But they are missing the point, Emma thought. Why are we being shown this? What do the downstreamers *want*?

. . . There was a blur of movement in the corner of the softscreen image. Out of focus, a flash of golden fabric.

'There's the Sheena,' she snapped. 'Cornelius, the camera. Fast.'

Cornelius, startled, complied. Again the agonizing wait as Cornelius's command crept across space, through the portal, to this startling future.

The picture tipped up drunkenly, and Galaxy light smeared across the image. But they could see that the beach ball was rolling across the surface towards the portal.

Emma said, 'She's going to come back through.'

'You don't understand,' Cornelius said tightly. 'She won't come *back* anywhere. The portal isn't two-way.'

'So if she steps through it, she will go –'

'Somewhere else.'

On the screen, the golden beach ball sailed into the interface, reddening, slowing, disappearing.

The firefly rolled forward, through soft Galaxy light, toward the downstreamer gateway.

Maura Della:

Open journal. October 22 2011.

Can it be true? Can it possibly? Do we *want* it to be true?

People seem to think I have a more privileged access to Malenfant and his projects than is the reality. I can't tell whether those now-famous downstream images are a hoax, or a misinterpretation, or if they are real. I can't tell if they represent the only future available to us, or one of a range of possibilities.

I don't even know whether it has been to Malenfant's help or hindrance to release the images. When you're trying to build credibility in Congress it generally does not help to have most of the media and every respectable scientist on the planet calling you a wacko.

But I do know the effect of the images on the world, real or false, has been astounding.

It has all been cumulative, of course: the hysteria over the Carter predictions, the strange, eerie, shameful fear we share over the Blue children, and now this downstream light show. And all of it wrapped up with Reid Malenfant's outrageous personality and gigantic projects.

We shouldn't dismiss the more extreme reactions we're seeing. Violence, suicide and the rest is regrettable of course, and there are a number of 'leaders', even some here on the Hill, who need, I would say, to keep a clearer head.

But how are we *supposed* to react? As a species we've never before had a proper debate about the structure of the future. And now we're all online, all our voices joined, and everybody is having a say.

None of us knows what the hell we're talking about, of course. But I think it's healthy. The debate has to start somewhere.

Maybe it's all part of our growing up as a race. Maybe every technical civilization has crises to survive: the invention of weaponry that can destroy its planet, acquiring the capability to trash its environment. And now here is a philosophical crisis: we must come to terms with the prospect of our own long-term destiny, or demise.

Just as each of us as individuals must at last confront death.

Emma Stoney:

Another flash of blue light. And –

And nothingness.

The darkness before Emma was even more profound than the intergalactic night. And there was no sign of the Sheena.

'Shit,' said Malenfant.

'Everything's working,' said Cornelius evenly. 'We're actually retrieving an image. And I'm picking up other telemetry. That *is* what the firefly is seeing.'

Emma said tightly, 'Then where's the Sheena?'

'Have it pan,' Malenfant said.

Cornelius said, 'I'll try. But I don't think we can communicate with the firefly any more. It's passed through the portal again, remember, so it must have crossed a second Einstein-Rosen bridge. There's no longer a line of sight connecting us. The communication is one way now, through the Feynman radio –'

'Then what do we do?'

Cornelius shrugged. 'We wait. The firefly has onboard autonomy. It's programmed to investigate its own situation, to return what data it can.'

A blur, a wash of light, passed over the corner of the screen, before the image stabilized.

Now Emma saw a battered plain, slightly tipped up, receding to a tight, sharp horizon. The craters and ridges were low, eroded, shadows streaming away from the viewpoint.

'The light's too poor to return any colour,' Cornelius said.

'What's the light source?'

'Floods on the firefly. Look at the way the shadows are pointing away from us. But the use of those floods is going to exhaust the batteries fast. I don't know why it's so dark . . .'

'Cruithne looks *older*,' Emma said. The firefly was panning its camera across an empty landscape; the shadows streamed away. 'Those craters are eroded flat, like saucers.'

Malenfant said, 'Micrometeorite impacts?'

Cornelius said, 'It's possible. But the micrometeorite sandblasting must be slow. I assume we're still out in intergalactic space. Matter's pretty thin out here.'

'How slow?'

Cornelius sighed. 'I'd say we're further into the future by several orders of magnitude compared to the last stop.'

Emma asked Malenfant, 'What's an order of magnitude to a physicist?'

Malenfant grimaced. 'A power of ten.'

Emma tried to take that in. Ten times seventy-five million. Or a hundred, a thousand times . . .

The viewpoint was shifting. The landscape started to rock, drop away, return. Slowly more features – ancient, eroded craters – loomed up over the horizon.

Cornelius said, 'The firefly is moving. Good.'

'The Sheena,' Emma said.

The beach ball was sitting on Cruithne's surface once more, complex highlights picked out by the firefly's light. Within, a shadow was visible, swimming back and forth.

'How extraordinary,' Cornelius said. 'To see a living thing across such immense spans of time.'

'She looks healthy,' Emma said. 'She's moving freely; she looks alert.'

'Maybe not much longer,' Malenfant growled. 'That damn water ball will freeze.'

'Do you think she understands any of what she is seeing?'

Cornelius murmured, 'I doubt it.'

Now she looked carefully Emma saw that the shadows the floods cast on the golden ball weren't completely dark. The shaded areas were lit by some deep red glow.

'There's something in the sky,' she said. 'A light source.'

The image started to pan away from the cephalopod, jerkily. More Cruithne craterscape slid across their field of view.

Then the landscape dropped out of sight, leaving a frame filled with darkness once more.

'The firefly's panning upwards,' said Malenfant. 'Come on . . .'

And a new image resolved. 'Oh, my,' he said.

At first Emma could make out only a diffuse red wash. Perhaps there was a slightly brighter central patch. It was surrounded by a blood-coloured river of light, studded here and there by dim yellow sparkles. But the image kept breaking up into blocky pixels, and she wondered if the shapes she was perceiving were real, or artefacts of her imagination.

'We're right at the limit of the optical system's resolution here,' Cornelius said. 'If the firefly is smart – *there*. We switched to the infra-red detectors.'

The picture abruptly became much brighter – a wash of white and pale pink – but much more blurred, in some ways more difficult to see. Cornelius laboured at his softscreens, trying to clean up the image.

Emma made out that great central glow, now brightened to a pink-white ball. It was embedded in a diffuse cloud; she thought she could see ribbons, streamers in the cloud, as if material was being dragged into that pink maw at the centre.

The core and its orbiting cloud seemed to be embedded in a

ragged disc, a thing of tatters and streamers of gas. Emma could make out no structure in the disc, no trace of spiral arms, no lanes of light and darkness. But there were blisters, knots of greater or lesser density, like supernova blisters, and there was that chain of brighter light points – yellow before, now picked out as bright blue by the enhancement routines – studded at regular intervals around the disc. Filaments seemed to reach in from the brighter points towards the bloated central mass.

'It looks like a galaxy,' said Malenfant.

Emma saw he was right. It was like a caricature of the Galaxy she had watched just minutes before. But that central mound was much more pronounced than the Galaxy's core had been, as if it was a tumour that had grown, eating out this cosmic wreck from the inside.

Cornelius was consulting his softscreen, asking questions of the hierarchy of smart software that was poring over the images. 'It probably *is* a galaxy. But extremely old. Much older than our Galaxy is at present – even than when we saw it at the Sheena's last stop –'

Malenfant said, 'Is it *the* Galaxy? Our Galaxy?'

'I don't know,' Cornelius said. 'Probably. Perhaps Cruithne entered some wide orbit around the centre. Or Cruithne might have had time to reach another galaxy. There's no way of knowing.'

'If that's our Galaxy,' Emma said, 'what happened to all the stars?'

'They're dying,' Cornelius said bluntly. 'Look – all stars die. Our sun is maybe half-way through its life. In five billion years or so, it will become a red giant, five hundred times its present size. The inner planets will be destroyed. The sun will span the sky, and Earth will be baked, the land hot enough to melt lead . . .'

'But there will be other stars,' Emma said. 'The Galaxy reef.'

'Yes. And the smallest, longest-lived dwarfs can last for maybe a hundred billion years, a lot longer than the sun. But the interstellar medium is a finite resource. Sooner or later there will be no more new stars. And eventually, one by one, *all* the stars will die. All that will remain will be stellar remnants, neutron stars and black holes and white dwarfs, slowly cooling.' He smiled, analytic. 'Think of it. All that rich, complex dust and gas we saw before, locked up in the cooling corpses of dead stars . . .'

Malenfant said grimly, 'And then what?'

'And then, *this*.' Cornelius pointed. 'The wreck of the Galaxy.

Some of the dying stars have evaporated out of the Galaxy. The rest are collapsing into the great black holes – those blisters you see in the disc. That central mass is the giant black hole at the core. Even in our time it has around a million times the mass of the sun. And it's still growing, as star remnants fall into it . . . You see the way the matter streams are straight, not twisted? That means the central hole isn't rotating. Wait.'

'What now?'

'The firefly is returning the relic temperature. The Big Bang glow. Well, well. It's down to one per cent of one degree above absolute zero. A little chilly.'

Malenfant growled, 'What does that mean?'

'It means I know where we are. Or rather, *when*. The universal temperature is declining as the two-thirds power of time.' He hesitated, and when he spoke again, even he sounded awed. 'The data is chancy. But the consensus of my software colleagues here is that we're around ten to power fourteen years into the future. That's, umm, a hundred thousand billion years – compared to the universe's present age, which is around twenty billion years – *five thousand times* as far downstream as at present.' He nodded, as if pleased.

The numbers seemed monstrous to Emma. 'I can't take that in,' she said.

Cornelius glared at her. 'Then try this. These powers of ten are zoom factors. With every extra power of ten you zoom out another notch, shrinking everything. You see? This downstream universe is so old that the whole history of our world – from its formation to the present – compares to this desert of future time as, let me see, as your own very first day of existence compares to your whole life.'

Malenfant, looking stunned, his mouth tight, just shook his head.

'So this is the end,' Emma said. 'The end of life.'

'Oh, no.' Cornelius sounded surprised. 'Not at all.' He pointed to the clusters of brighter light around the rim of the galactic corpse. '*These* seem to be normal stars: small, uniform, but still glowing in the visible spectrum.'

'How is that possible?' said Malenfant. 'I thought you said all the star stuff was used up.'

'So it is, by natural processes,' said Cornelius.

'. . . Oh. So these stars can't be natural.'

'That's right.' Cornelius turned to Emma, his pale eyes shining. 'You see? Somebody must be gathering the remnant medium, forming artificial birthing clouds. Somebody is still gardening the Galaxy, even so far downstream. Isn't it wonderful?'

'*Wonderful?* The wreck of the Galaxy?'

'Not that. The existence of downstreamers. And they still need stars and planets, and warmth and light. *They are still like us*, these descendants of ours. Maybe they even remember us.' He rubbed his face. 'But those stars are small and cold. Designed for longevity. Their worlds must be huddled close – probably gravitationally locked, keeping one face in the light, one in the dark . . .'

'Good God, Cornelius,' said Malenfant. 'That's a lot to deduce from one smudgy image.'

'I've been thinking about this all my life,' said Cornelius. 'Plotting the survival of mankind, of intelligent life, into the far future. Mind games, played against an unyielding opponent – time – with the laws of physics as the rules. And the further downstream we look, the more we are constrained by the laws of physics. The future *has* to be like this.'

Now the image lurched. The wrecked Galaxy slid out of the frame, to be replaced by a glaring wash of light. The firefly adjusted its receptor to visible light and the floodlit plain of Cruithne was revealed once more.

There was no sign of the golden bubble, or the firefly patiently towing it.

'The Sheena has gone,' said Malenfant immediately. 'She must have gone back to the portal again.'

'Christ,' said Emma. 'She's trying to get home.'

'But she's only succeeded in travelling further downstream,' said Cornelius. The image lurched again, as the firefly began to toil towards the portal once more. 'And so, it seems, must we. The firefly doesn't know what else to do.'

Emma found she was making a fist, so hard her nails were digging into her palm. 'I don't want to see any more.'

'I don't think there's a choice,' Malenfant said grimly.

The image of the portal expanded out of the camera's field of view, and once more that deep black, blacker than galactic night, confronted Emma.

There was a flash of electric blue.

Another black sky, another Cruithne. The patient firefly crept forward, shining its own fading light over the crumpled surface of the asteroid, seeking the Sheena.

Emma would not have believed that the ground of Cruithne could look more aged than it had before. And yet it did, its craters and ridges and scarps all but invisible under a thick blanket of dust. As the firefly laboured Emma could see how its pitons and cables kicked up great sprays of regolith.

The three of them watched in sombre silence, oppressed by time's weight.

'How long, Cornelius?' Malenfant asked, his voice hoarse.

Cornelius was studying his data. 'I don't know. The relic temperature is too low to read. And . . .'

And there was a dawn, on far-downstream Cruithne.

Emma gasped. The sight was as unexpected as it was beautiful: a point of yellow-white light, sun-like. The light rose in clumsy stages as the firefly laboured toward it. Shadows of smooth eroded crater rims and ridges fled across the smooth landscape toward her, like bony fingers reaching. It was so bright it seemed to Emma she could feel its warmth, and she wondered if somehow this long journey through time had looped back on itself, returning her to the dawn of time, the birth of the Solar System itself.

But, she quickly realized, this was no sunrise.

A glaring point was surrounded by a tilted disc, glowing red, within which she could trace a tight spiral pattern. And there seemed to be lines of light tracing out from the poles of that central gleam, needle-thin. Further out she saw discs and knots of dull red matter, much smaller than the big bright core object. The central light actually cast shadows through the crowded space around it, she saw, shadows that – if this was a galactic scale object – must have been thousands of light years long.

It was oddly beautiful, a sculpture of light and blood-red smoke. But it was chilling, inhuman, even compared to the last grisly galactic vision; there was nothing she could recognize here, nothing that looked like a star.

'Our Galaxy?' Malenfant asked.

Cornelius studied his data. 'Perhaps. If it is, it's extremely shrunken. And I'm seeing objects away from the disc itself now, a scattering of low-energy infra-red sources, all around the sky. Stellar remnants, I think.'

Malenfant said grimly, 'What you said. Evaporated stars. Right?'

'Yes.' Cornelius studied the screen. 'At a guess, I'd say ninety per cent of the objects in the Galaxy have evaporated away, and maybe ten per cent are gathering in the core object.'

200

'The black hole. That's what we're seeing.'

'Yes. We've come a long way, Malenfant, and our strides are increasing. These processes are *slow* . . .'

Emma barely listened.

The camera swung from the bright black hole structure, to the folded asteroid dirt, to sweeping empty sky.

'No sign of Sheena,' she murmured. 'Maybe the portals don't always work consistently. Maybe she's been sent on somewhere else, out of our reach –'

Malenfant briefly hugged her. 'Emma, she's been out of our reach since the first time she bounced through that portal. Whether we see her or not hardly matters.'

'But it feels like it does. Because we're responsible for her being there.'

'Yes,' he said at length.

They fell silent, but they stayed close to each other. Emma welcomed Malenfant's simple human warmth, the presence of his flesh, the soft wash of his breath on her face. It seemed to exclude the endless dark of the future.

Meanwhile Cornelius was staring up at the image, interrogating the smart systems, speculating, theorizing, obsessing.

'. . . The light we see is coming from that central accretion disc, where matter is falling into the black hole and being absorbed. Intensely bright, of course, probably more energetic than the combined fusion energy of all the Galaxy's stars in their heyday. The hole itself is probably a few light-months across. Those beams coming from the poles – perhaps they are plasma directed by the magnetic field of the disc, or maybe the hole itself. Like a miniature quasar.' He frowned. 'But that's *wasteful*. It's hard to believe they don't have a way to harness that radiant energy. Perhaps they're signalling –'

'Wasteful?' Malenfant snapped. 'What are you talking about, Cornelius? Wasteful to who?'

'The downstreamers, of course,' Cornelius said. 'The downstreamers of this era. Can't you see them?' Cornelius froze the camera's shuddering image. 'Can't you see? Look at these smaller satellite holes. Look how uniform their size is, how regular the spacing . . .'

'You're saying this arrangement of black holes is artificial,' Emma said.

'Why, of course it is. I suspect the downstreamers are using the smaller holes to control the flow of matter into the central hole.

They must be regulating every aspect of this assemblage: the size of the satellite holes, the rate at which they approach the central core. I think the downstreamers are mining the Galaxy-core black hole of its energy.'

'Mining? How?'

He shrugged. 'There are a whole slew of ways even we can dream up. If you coalesce two black holes, you get a single, larger hole – with an event horizon ringing like a bell – but you also get a monumental release of gravitational energy. Much of a spinning hole's energy is stored in a great tornado-like swirl of space and time, dragged around by the hole's immense inertia. You could tap this energy by enclosing the hole in a great mesh of superconducting cables. Then you could thread the tornado swirl with a magnetic field, to form a giant electrical power generator. Or you can just throw matter into the central hole, feeding off the radiation as it is crushed . . . No doubt there are better ways. They've had a long time to work it out.'

'*How* long?'

Cornelius tapped his softscreen. 'A guess, based on the nature of that black hole? Ten to power twenty-four years: a trillion trillion years. Ten *billion* times as old as the last images we saw, the age of the star farmers.'

'Jesus,' said Malenfant. 'A long time.'

Cornelius said testily, 'Remember the zoom factors. We just zoomed out again. The universe must have expanded to, umm, some ten thousand *trillion* times its size in our day. Compared to the age of the Galaxy remnant we see here, the evolution of our universe was as brief, as insignificant, as the first three *hours* after the Big Bang is to us . . .'

'And yet there is still life,' Emma said.

'. . . The Sheena,' Malenfant said.

There was the golden beach ball, lurching over the surface, cables glimmering in the fireflies' floods. A cephalopod was clearly visible within, swimming back and forth, curious. The camera swept the Cruithne landscape, as the firefly turned to follow the Sheena.

'She's going back to the portal,' Malenfant said. 'She's going on.'

Something shrank, deep inside Emma. Not again, she thought.

'Perhaps it's a kind of morbid curiosity,' Cornelius said dryly. 'To keep on going forward, on and on, to the end of things.'

'No,' said Emma. 'You saw her. She's not morbid.'

'Then what?'

'It's as if she's looking for something. But what? The more I see of this future universe, the more it seems –'

'Pointless?' asked Malenfant.

She was surprised at that, from him. 'Yes, exactly.'

His face wore a complex expression. He's taking it hard, she thought, this cold, logical, working-out of his dreams. Malenfant campaigns for an expansive future for mankind: survival, essentially, into the far downstream. Well, here it is, Malenfant, everything you dreamed of.

And it is appalling, terrifying: proof that if we are to survive we must sacrifice our humanity.

Cornelius shrugged. '*Pointless?* What a trivial response. We are the first, the only intelligence in the universe. We have no objective, save endurance: nothing to do but survive, as long as we can.

'And in fact *this* era may be the peak, when we learn to tap these giant energy sources, the greatest in the universe, sources so great they outshine our fusion-driven stars as if they were candles.'

'The manhood of the race,' Emma said dryly.

'Perhaps. And –'

'And are they like us?' Emma asked.

'What does it matter? Your thinking is so small. Modern humans could never handle such projects as this. We can't imagine how it is to be such a creature, to think in such a way.

'Perhaps there is no real comparison between them and us, no contact possible. But it does not matter. They are magnificent.'

She was repelled. She thought: *you're wrong.* There had to be something more to strive for than that, more than simple survival in a running-down universe.

But then, she had no children. So these black hole miners, however remote, however powerful, were not *her* descendants; she was cut off, a bubble of life lost in the far upstream.

The firefly worked its painful way across the time-smoothed landscape towards the portal.

Damien Krimsky:

. . . Anyhow that's why I went AWOL for so long, Mr Hench. I hope you can understand that.

I support Bootstrap. I'm a big fan of Reid Malenfant and every-thing he's trying to do. The time I spent working with you on those BDBs in the Mojave desert was probably the most meaningful of my life.

It's just that, when all that Carter stuff came out of the media, well, maybe I went a little crazy. If the world's going to end anyhow, what's the point of paying taxes?

That was why I, umm, disappeared.

Anyhow I saw what Malenfant broadcast, the galaxies and the black holes and all. And now I feel different. Who wouldn't? Now I know my children have a chance to grow old and happy, and *their* children too, on and on until we've conquered the stars.

Life is worth living again.

I know there are those who say it doesn't matter. That if the future is going to be so wonderful anyhow we don't need to do anything *now*. But I feel a sense of duty. It's the same way I felt when I saw my own kid in my wife's arms for the first time. At that moment I knew how I would spend the rest of my life.

So I'm coming back to the Mojave. I have clearances from the rehab and detox clinics, as well as from the parole board. I hope you'll welcome me back.

Your friend,
Damien Krimsky

'Moondancer':

People have been arguing for months about whether this Carter stuff can be correct. And now they're arguing about whether the far-future visions are hoaxes.

Of course they can't both be true.

And it's amazing that you have stock market crashes and suicide cults and wackos who think they need to rip up the cities because the end of the world is coming, and another bunch of nuts doing exactly the same thing because the end of the world *isn't* coming.

Of *course* the far future visions are all genuine.

This is our fate. And it's fantastic! Wonderful! Don't you think so?

Have you even thought where you'd like to travel if you had a time machine, and could go anywhere, past or future? Maybe you would go hunt T Rex, or listen to Jesus preach, or sail with Columbus. What do you think? I know what I'd do. I'd ride off to join the black hole miners in the Incredible Year Four Hundred Billion AD. Man, will those guys party.

. . . What? How come I know the future stuff is real? Because I've seen it myself. Also, as you probably know, there were secret codes in the *LA Times* write-up comprehensible only by other Travellers, confirming the veracity of the pictures.

I have a Cap – careful with it! – and when I wear it, it *projects my sense of self astrally* . . .

Emma Stoney:

This time the golden beach ball was visible as soon as the firefly emerged from the blue flash of transition. The beach ball was standing on a smooth, featureless plain, square in the middle of the softscreen. An arc of the portal was visible beside the beach ball, a bright blue stripe.

The sky was dark. The black hole rose had disappeared. The only light falling on the beach ball seemed to be the glow of the firefly's dimming floods. The belt of horizon Emma could see looked like a perfect circular span, unmarked by ridges or craters.

The squid swam through her bubble of water, lethargic.

Emma watched the Cruithne landscape slide past the firefly's panning camera lens. Its smoothness was unnerving, unnatural. She felt no awe, no wonder, only a vague irritation.

'That damn asteroid has taken a beating,' said Malenfant. 'Look at that mother. Smooth as a baby's butt –'

'You *don't* understand,' said Cornelius testily. 'I – or rather my electronic friends – think there's more than simple erosion here. The gravimeters on the firefly are telling me the morphology of Cruithne has changed. I mean, the asteroid's shape has changed. Out here in the dark, it has flowed into a sphere.'

Malenfant said, 'A sphere? How the hell?'

'I think this is liquefaction. If that's so, it means that proton decay lifetimes must exceed ten to power sixty-four years – and *that* means –'

'Woah, woah.' Malenfant held up his hands. '*Liquefaction?* You're saying the asteroid flowed like a liquid? How? Did it heat up, melt?'

'No. What is there to heat it up?'

'What, then?'

'Malenfant, over enough time, the most solid matter will behave like a very viscous liquid. All solid objects flow. It is a manifestation of quantum mechanical tunnelling which –'

Malenfant said, 'I don't believe it.'

'You're seeing it,' said Cornelius tightly. 'Malenfant, the far future is *not* the world you grew up in. Marginal processes can come to dominate, if they're persistent, over long enough timescales . . .'

'*How long?*' Malenfant snapped.

Cornelius checked his softscreen. 'A minimum of ten to power sixty-five years. Umm, that's a hundred thousand trillion trillion trillion trillion trillion . . . Look. Start with a second. Zoom out; factor it up to get the life of the Earth. Zoom out *again*, to get a new period, so long Earth's lifetime is like one second. Then nest it. Do it again. And *again* . . .'

The camera image swept away from the beach ball, away from the blank liquefied ground, and swept the sky.

Malenfant pointed. 'What the hell is *that*?'

It was a blur of grey-red light in an otherwise empty sky. The firefly switched to infra-red, and Cornelius cleaned up the image. Emma saw a rough sphere, a halo of motes of dim light which hovered, motionless, around –

Around what? It was a ball of darkness, somehow darker even than the background sky. It looked about the size of the sun, seen from Earth; the motes were like dim-glowing satellites, closely orbiting a black planet.

Cornelius sounded excited. 'My God. Look at this.' He magnified the image, picking out a point on the rim of the central ball, enhancing as he went.

Emma saw rings of red light, running around the rim, parallel to the surface.

'What is it?'

'Gravitational lensing. Bent light. That means – it must be –'

He scrolled through expert system interpretations, speed-reading. 'We're looking at a black hole. A giant.

'This is probably the remnant of a supercluster. Just as what's left of a galaxy after star evaporation collapses into the central hole, so galactic clusters will collapse in turn, and then the superclusters . . . That hole might have a mass of anything from a hundred trillion to a hundred *thousand* trillion solar masses, an event horizon radius measured in hundreds of light years.'

'I don't understand,' said Emma. 'Where did the Galaxy go?'

'Our Galaxy hole was surely carried to the heart of the local galactic cluster black hole, and then the supercluster.'

'And we were dragged along with it.'

'If it's a hole it has no accretion disc,' Malenfant said.

'Malenfant, this thing is ancient. It ate up everything a hell of a long time ago.'

'So how come those motes haven't been dragged down?' Malenfant said.

'Life,' said Emma. 'Even now. Feeding off the great black holes. Right?'

'Maybe,' said Cornelius grimly. 'Maybe. But if so they aren't doing enough. Even gravity mines can be exhausted.'

'Hawking radiation,' said Malenfant.

'Yes. Black holes evaporate. The smaller the hole, the faster it decays. Solar mass holes must have vanished already . . . In their last seconds they become energetic, you know. Go off with a bang, like a nuke.' He smiled, looking tired. 'The universe can still produce occasional fireworks, even this far downstream. But ultimately even this, the largest natural black hole, is going to evaporate away. What are the downstreamers going to do then? They should be planning now, working. There will be a race between the gathering and management of energy sources and the dissipative effects of the universe's general decay.'

Malenfant said, 'You'd make one hell of an after-dinner speaker, Cornelius.'

The camera had panned again, and found the Sheena in her beach ball.

'I think her movements are getting laboured,' Emma said.

Cornelius murmured, 'There's nothing we can do. It's *cold* out there, remember, in the far downstream. Her heater will surely expire before long. Maybe she won't even suffocate.'

They watched in silence.

Sheena's firefly, tethered to the beach ball, jerked into motion. It floated towards Emma's viewpoint, across the eerily smooth surface of the liquefied asteroid.

It drifted to a halt, and reached out with a grabber arm to touch its human-controlled cousin. In the softscreen image, the arm was foreshortened, grotesquely huge.

Then the firefly turned and drifted out of shot, towards the portal, towing the beach ball.

'Onwards,' Emma whispered.

Another transition, another blue flash.

The camera performed a panorama, panning through a full three hundred and sixty degrees. The portal, a glaring blue ring still embedded in the asteroid ground, slid silently across the softscreen. There was the Sheena's bubble, resting on the surface, lit only by the robot's lights and by the soft blue glow of the portal itself. The Sheena tried to swim, a dim dark ghost behind the gold. But she fell, languidly, limbs drifting.

And then, beneath a black sky, there was only the asteroid surface, smooth, utterly featureless, rubbed flat by time.

'It's just like the last stop,' Emma said. 'As if nothing will ever change again.'

'Not true,' said Cornelius. 'But this far downstream, the river of time is flowing broad and smooth –'

'Down to a sunless sea,' Emma said.

'Yes. But there is still change, if only we could perceive it.'

The camera tipped up, away from the asteroid, and the softscreen filled up with black sky. At first Emma saw only darkness, unrelieved. But then she made out the faintest of patterns: charcoal grey on black, almost beyond her ability to resolve, a pattern of neat regular triangles, covering the screen.

When she blinked, she lost it. But then she made out the pattern again. Abruptly it blurred, tilted, and panned across the screen.

Now the triangles showed up pinkish-white, very blurred, but regular, a net of washed-out colour that filled space.

'The firefly is using false colour,' Cornelius said.

The pattern slid across the screen, jerkily, as the remote firefly panned its camera. And beyond the net Emma saw a greenish surface, smoothly curved, as if the netting contained something.

Emma said, 'It must cut the universe in half.'

More of the framework slid through the screen, blurring as

the camera's speed outstripped the software's ability to process the image.

'It looks like a giant geodesic dome,' Malenfant said.

Cornelius said, 'I think it is a dome. Or rather, a sphere. Hundreds of thousands of light years wide. A net. And there's only one thing worth collecting, this far downstream.' He pointed to the complex, textured curtain of greenish light visible through the interstices of the dome. 'Look at that. I think we're seeing black hole event horizons in there. Giant holes, galactic supercluster mass and above. They are orbiting each other, their event horizons distorting. I think the holes have been gathered in there, deliberately. They are being merged, in a hierarchy of more and more massive holes. I imagine by now the downstreamers can manage hole coalescence without significant energy loss.'

'How the hell do you move a black hole? Attach a tow rope?'

Cornelius shrugged. 'I don't know. Maybe you use Hawking radiation as a rocket. The details hardly matter . . . The dome seems to be an energy collector. Like a Dyson sphere. Anything still alive must be living on those struts, feeding off the last free energy: the slow Hawking radiation of the black holes. But it's a damn thin trickle.' He glanced at his softscreen. 'We can postulate strategies for survival. Maybe they eke out their dilute resources by submitting to long downtimes. Hibernation, slow computation rates, stretching an hour of awareness across a million years . . .'

Perhaps, Emma thought. Or perhaps they are conscious, continually, even now, in this ruin of a universe. Frozen into their black hole cage, unable to move, trapped like Judas in the lowest circle of Hell.

Cornelius said, 'It may seem strange to you how much we can anticipate of this remote time. But the downstreamers are walled in by physical law. And we know they will have to manage their black hole resources. The supercluster holes are the largest to have formed in nature, with masses of maybe a hundred trillion suns. But even they are evaporating away.

'So they *have to* harvest the holes. If you combine two holes you get a more massive hole –'

'Which will be cooler.' Malenfant nodded. 'It will evaporate more slowly. So you can stretch out its lifetime.'

'They're probably coalescing holes in hierarchies all over the reachable universe. This site, immense as it is, might be just a rung on the ladder.

'The engineering details are tricky. You have to bring the holes together fast enough that they don't evaporate away before you've harvested them. On the other hand it mustn't be so rapid that you form a hole so huge it evaporates too slowly and you are starved of usable energy ... Remarkable,' Cornelius breathed, staring at the dim, ghostly images. 'To think that mind has now encompassed the universe – that the future evolution of the universe actually depends on conscious choices – made by *our* descendants.'

Cooperation, Emma thought, spanning a universe, projects lasting millions, even billions of years. Whatever these people have become, she thought, they are *not* human.

'Oh, Jesus. *Look* at that.'

Emma turned back to the screen, where Malenfant was staring.

Across a broad circular region the geodesic network was disrupted. It looked as if some immense fist had punched through it from the inside, ripping and twisting the struts. The tips of the damaged struts were glowing a little brighter than the rest of the network; perhaps there was some form of repair effort underway.

And beyond the damaged network she could see the event horizons of giant coalescing black holes – each, perhaps, the mass of a supercluster of galaxies or more – the horizons distorted, great frozen waves light years long visible in their cold surfaces.

'What do you think?' Emma said. 'Some kind of breakdown?'

'Or war,' said Malenfant.

'War? Here, so far downstream? That's insane.'

'Maybe not,' said Cornelius. 'These people have responsibility for the whole of the future. They are managing the last of the universe's energy resources. With responsibility comes tension, disagreement. Conflict.'

Malenfant said, 'To have come so far, to see this. How depressing.'

'No,' said Cornelius irritably. 'We have no idea what kind of minds inhabit these giant structures. They may inhabit hierarchies of consciousness far above us. Their motivations are probably so far removed from ours that we can't even guess at them –'

'Maybe,' Malenfant growled. 'But I'm just a poor *H Sap*. And if I lived in that dome, I'd want to survive, no matter how huge my brain was. And it seems to me they are doing a damn poor job.'

Reluctantly, Emma asked, 'How far have we come?'

Cornelius studied his softscreens again. 'Even the e-systems are giving up on me now ... Suppose we've taken another scale-factor jump downstream of the same kind of size as last time. That puts us at around ten to power one hundred years remote. What does that mean?' He rubbed his forehead. 'To these downstreamers, the early days of their empire – zoom factors of ten or a hundred or ten thousand back, maybe, when even medium-sized black holes could still exist – *those* days were the spring time of the universe. As for us, we're a detail, back in the detail of the Big Bang somewhere, lost in the afterglow.

'Malenfant, I once asked you if you understood, *really* understood, what it would mean to carry your off-Earth colonization project through to its final conclusion. To challenge eternity. This is what it means, Malenfant. *This*.

'And the responsibility is immense. We have to spread across the universe, make it possible for human descendants of the far downstream to have the power to do *this*, to survive the winter as long as possible. Because this is the last refuge.'

'But this is a process without limit.' Malenfant frowned. 'This is a strategy which offers the prospect of eternal life . . . doesn't it?'

'No,' said Cornelius sadly. 'At least we don't think so. There's a paradox. You have to have some kind of framework, a structure to gather your energy, house your souls.'

'The Disneyland sphere.'

'Yes. The structure grows with time. And even if matter is stable, which it may not be, the structure has to be upgraded, repaired. The maintenance requirements go up with time, because the structure is getting bigger, but the energy available is going down with time . . . It's a squeeze, Malenfant. And it isn't possible to win. This black hole management policy is a good idea – the last, best idea – but in the end, *it's doomed to fail*.'

Abruptly the camera angle swung again. The smoothed-out asteroid, the portal, tilted crazily.

The beach ball was moving, half-bouncing, half-rolling towards the portal. It left a trail of pits and scrapes in the smooth metallic-dust surface of the asteroid.

Emma said sadly, 'So Sheena hasn't yet found peace.'

The camera swung around once more, and Emma got a last glimpse of the mighty, broken empire of the black hole engineers.

It was magnificent, she thought, and it would last an unimaginable time, zoom-factors beyond puny human scales. But it was an epic of futility.

'What now?' Malenfant muttered. 'What is left?'

Emma didn't know. But, she found, she welcomed the obliterating blue flash.

Once more, emptiness.

A piton, trailing a tether, was drifting across the field of view. The little gadgets were lit up brightly by the firefly's floods, a brightness that only contrasted with the illimitable darkness beyond.

Malenfant growled, 'So why can't we see the asteroid?'

'Because we aren't on a solid surface. The firefly's accelerometers show it is rolling, tumbling in space.'

Now there was something new in the frame, beyond the writhing tether. It was a blue circle, suspended in the darkness, glowing bright, turning slowly. And alongside it was a slack golden ball, oscillating in space, returning languid highlights.

Emma said, 'That's the artefact. And Sheena. Is she –'

The camera zoomed in on the ball, until it filled the screen. The squid within was turning slowly, gently drifting. The only light falling on her, save for the soft blue glow of the portal, was from the firefly's dimming flood.

'She's receding,' Emma said. 'Moving away from the firefly, and the portal.'

'Yes,' Cornelius said. 'Her momentum, as she came through the hole, is taking her away.'

Malenfant asked, 'So what happened to the asteroid?'

'Proton decay,' said Cornelius immediately. 'I've been expecting this.' He checked his expert systems for details. 'There are three quarks inside a proton, you know; if you wait long enough you'll see them come together to form a miniature black hole which immediately explodes . . . Well. The details of the mechanism don't matter –'

'Are you saying that *matter itself* is unstable?'

'On the longest timescales, yes. But it's slow. The fact that you're standing there – that you can survive your own mass – tells us proton decay must take at least a billion billion years. Your body contains so many protons and neutrons that any faster decay rate would give rise to enough energetic particles to kill you by cancer. Now we've *seen* that the rate is a lot slower than that.'

Malenfant said, 'So the asteroid just evaporated.'

'Yes. It got smaller and smaller, warmed gently by the annihilation of electrons and positrons in its interior, a thin smoke of neutrinos drifting out at lightspeed . . .'

Emma asked, 'How long this time?'

'The theories are sketchy. If you want me to put a number on it, I'd say ten to power a hundred and seventeen years.' Even Cornelius looked bewildered now. 'More zoom factors.'

The cephalopod hab dwindled in the softscreen image, turning, receding.

'So where is everybody?' Malenfant snapped.

Cornelius turned to him, looking lost. 'You're not listening. There *is* no more. When proton decay cuts in, *nothing* is left: no dead stars, no rogue asteroids like Cruithne, no cold planets, no geodesic empires. This far downstream, all the ordinary matter has disappeared, the last black holes evaporated. The universe has swollen, its material stretched unimaginably thin.

'Even if the black hole farmers tried to gather more material to replace what decayed away, they would have been beaten by the timescales. Matter was decaying faster than it could be collected and used to record information, thoughts, life. And when their structure failed, the last black hole must have evaporated.' He looked misty. 'Of course they must have tried. Fought to the last. It must have been magnificent.'

Emma studied Malenfant. 'You're *disappointed*. But we've seen so much time. So much room for life –'

'But,' Malenfant said, 'I hoped for eternity.'

Cornelius sighed. 'The universe will presumably expand forever, on to infinity. But we know of no physical processes which will occur beyond this point.'

Emma said, 'And all life, of any form, is extinct. Right?'

'Yes.'

'In that case,' Emma said softly, 'who is Sheena talking to?'

Sheena was blurred with distance now, her habitat a golden planet only dimly visible in the light of the robot's failing lamps. Maybe Emma's imagination was projecting something on her, like the face of the man in the Moon.

But still –

'I'm sure I can see her signing,' she said.

'My God,' said Malenfant. 'You're right.'

Emma frowned. 'There *must* be someone here. Because the portal's here. And it called to us – right? – through a relay of portals, upstream through the zoom factors, to the present. Maybe it called to Sheena, and brought her here.'

'She's right,' said Cornelius, wondering. 'Of course she's right. There has to be an entity here, a community, manipulating the neutrino bath and sending signals to the past.'

'So where are they getting the energy from, to compute, to think?'

Cornelius looked uncomfortable; obsessively he worked his softscreen, scrolling through lists of references. 'It's very speculative. But it's possible you could sustain computation without expending energy. We have theoretical models . . . What actually uses up energy during computation is discarding information. If you add two numbers, for instance, clearing out the original numbers from your memory store eats up energy. But if your computation is logically reversible – if you never discard information – you can drive down your processing costs to arbitrarily small values.'

'There has to be a catch,' said Malenfant. 'Or somebody would have patented it.'

Cornelius nodded. 'We don't know any way of interacting with the outside universe without incurring a loss. No way of inputting or outputting data. If you want to remain lossless, you have to seal yourself off, in a kind of substrate . . . But then, nothing significant is going to change, ever again. So what is the use of perception?'

'Then what's left?'

'Memory. Reflection. There is no fresh data. But there may be no end to the richness of understanding . . .'

Malenfant said, 'If these ultimate downstreamers are locked into the substrate, how can Sheena talk to them?'

'Sheena is a refugee from the deepest past,' said Cornelius. 'Perhaps they feel she is worth the expenditure of some of their carefully hoarded energy. They must be vast,' he said dreamily. 'The last remnant particles orbit light years apart. A single mind might span the size of a galaxy, vast and slow as an empire. But nothing can hurt them now. They are beyond gravity's reach, at last immune to the Heat Death.'

Emma said, 'And these are our ultimate children? These wispy ghosts? The manipulation of structures spanning the universe, the endless contest of ingenuity versus entropy – was it all for *this*?'

'That's the deal,' said Cornelius harshly. 'What else is there?'

Emma said simply, '*Purpose* . . . We're losing her.'

Sheena was drifting out of the picture.

Cornelius tapped his console. 'The firefly is nearly out of attitude control gas.'

Every few minutes the beach ball drifted through the frame of the softscreen, as the firefly's helpless roll carried it around. The image was dim, blurred, at the extreme range of the failing camera. Emma took to standing close to the softscreen frame, staring at the squid's image, trying to read any last signs.

It's like a wake, she thought.

Cornelius murmured, 'We have to consider our next step.'

Malenfant frowned. '*What* next step?'

'Look at the image. *Look* at it. We've found an artefact, a non-terrestrial artefact, on that asteroid. Exactly where the down-streamers pointed us. And they used it to teach us about the future: the trillions upon trillions of years that await us, if we can only find a way around the Carter catastrophe – *which must be possible*. My God, think of it. We caught the barest glimpse today, a flyby of the future. What if we established monitoring stations in each of those downstream islands? Think of what we'd achieve, what we'd see . . . We have to retrieve that artefact. If we can't get it off the asteroid, we have to study it in situ. Malenfant, we have to send people to Cruithne. And we must show this to Michael.'

A look of unaccountable fear crossed Malenfant's face.

In the softscreen Sheena was a blurred patch of light, shadows moving across her sides. Sheena signed once more – Emma struggled to see, and a translation scrolled over the image – and then the screen turned a neutral grey.

'It's over,' Cornelius said. 'The firefly's dead. And so is Sheena.'

'No,' said Emma. 'No, I don't think so.'

Somehow, she knew, Sheena understood what was happening to her. For the last thing Sheena had said, the last thing Emma could recognize before the image failed, was a question.

Will I dream?

Maura Della:

Open journal. October 22 2011.

I've never forgotten the first time I flew the length of Africa. The huge empty deserts, the mindless blankets of green life, the scattered humans clinging to coasts and river valleys.

I'm a city girl. I used to think the human world was the whole world. That African experience knocked a hole in my confidence of the power of humans, of us, to change things, to build, to survive. The truth is that humans have barely made an impression on Earth – and Earth itself is a mote in a hostile universe. This shaped my thinking. If humanity's hold on Earth is precarious, then, damn it, we have to work to make it less so.

It's only a generation since we've been able to see the whole Earth. And now, it seems, we can see the whole future, and what we must do to survive. And I hope we can cope.

I admit, though, I found the whole thing depressing.

It is of course the logical conclusion of my own ambition, which is that, on the whole, the human race should seek not to destroy itself – in fact, that it is our destiny to take over from the blind forces of inanimate matter and guide the future of the cosmos.

It's just it never occurred to me before that, in the end, all there will be out there to conquer is rubble, the cooling ruins of the universe.

I'm sixty-one years old. I'm not in the habit of thinking about death. I suppose I always had a vague plan to fight it. To use all my resources, every technique and trick I can find and pay for, to live as long as possible.

But is it worth it? To cling to life until I'm drained of strength and mind and hope? But isn't that exactly what we saw in the far future, a senile species eking out the last of its energies, struggling against the dark?

It seems to me that age, growing old, is a war between wisdom and bitterness. I'm not sure how I'll come out of that war myself, assuming I get so far.

Maybe some things are more important than life itself.

But what?

Emma Stoney:

Even as his representatives wrestled with the bureaucratic demons that threatened to overwhelm him – even as the world alternately wondered at or mocked his light-and-shadow images of the far future – Reid Malenfant sprung another surprise.

He went on TV and the nets and announced a launch date for BDB-2, tentatively called *O'Neill*.

And as Malenfant's nominal, fictional, technically-plausible-only launch date approached, events seemed to be coming to a head. On the one hand a groundswell of popular support built up for Malenfant, with his enterprise and defiance and sense of mystery. But on the other hand the forces opposing him strengthened and focused their attacks.

Look at it this way. If all this legal bullshit evaporates, and I'm ready to launch, I launch. If I ain't ready to launch, I don't launch. Simple as that. What am I wasting?

Come watch me fly.

He was wasting a few million bucks, actually, Emma thought, with every aborted launch attempt. But Malenfant knew that, and it wouldn't stop him anyhow, so she kept it to herself.

And she had to admit it worked: raising the stakes again, whipping up public interest to a fever pitch. *Nothing like a countdown to focus the mind.*

Then, a couple of days before the 'launch date' itself, Malenfant asked Emma to come out from Vegas. *Things are hotting up, babe. I need you here . . .*

She refused Malenfant's offer of a flight out to the compound. She decided to drive; she needed time to rest and think. She turned on the SmartDrive, opaqued the windows, and tried to sleep.

It was only when the car woke her, some time before dawn on Malenfant's 'launch day', that she began to be aware of the people.

At first there was just a handful of cars and vans parked off the road, little oases of light in the huge desert night. But soon there were more: truck-camper vans, and cars with tent-trailers, and converted buses, and jeeps with houses built on the back, and Land Rovers, and Broncos with bunks. There were tents lit from inside, people moving slowly in the pre-dawn greyness. There were people sleeping in the cars, or even in the open, on inflatable mattresses and blankets.

As she neared the Bootstrap site itself the density of people continued to increase, the little groups crowded more closely together. She saw a place where a blanket spread out under the tailgate of an ancient convertible was almost overlapping the groundsheet of a much more elaborate tent. In another, right next to an upmarket mobile home, she saw an ancient Ford, its hood held in place by duct tape, with a child sleeping in the open trunk and dirty bare feet protruding from all the windows. And as dawn approached people were rising, stirring and scratching themselves, making breakfast, some climbing on top of their cars to see what was going on at the Bootstrap compound.

She spotted what looked like a military vehicle, a squat, fierce-looking jeep of some kind, with black rectangular tinted windows. A man was standing up, poking his head out of a sun-roof. He was beefy, fortyish, shaven-haired. He shifted, as if he was having trouble standing. He was watching the compound with big, professional-looking binoculars. She thought he looked familiar, but she couldn't think where from.

When she looked again the jeep had gone. It could only have driven off, away from the crowded road, into the desert.

Further in she spied uniforms and banners. There were religious groups here, both pro and anti Malenfant. Some of them were holding services or prayer sessions. There were animal rights campaigners holding animated posters of Caribbean reef squid, other protesters holding up images of sickly yellow babies. And then there was the spooky fringe, such as a group of women dressed in black shifts painted with bright blue circles, holding up sky-blue hoops to the sky. *Take me! Take me!*

But these agenda-driven types were the minority, Emma realized, flecks of foam on the great ocean of ordinary people who had gathered here, on the day of Malenfant's 'launch'. There were whites, blacks, Asians, Latinos, native Americans. There were young people, some infants in arms, and a lot of oldsters who probably remembered Apollo 11. There was no reason to suppose they weren't just as thickly crowded as this on every approach to the Bootstrap compound.

So how many? A million?

But why where they here? What had drawn so many of them from so far?

. . . It was faith, she realized. Faith in Malenfant, faith that he could once more defy the various forces ranged against him: Reid Malenfant, an old-fashioned American can-do hero, who had already brought back postcards from the future, now about to launch a rocketship and save the species single-handed.

I have to admit, Malenfant, you hit a nerve.

And as she thought it through, as that realization crystallized in her, she understood, at last, what was happening today.

My God, she thought. *He's actually going to do it.* He's going to launch, come what may. That's what this is all about.

And she felt shock, even shame, that these strangers, so many of them, had understood Malenfant's subliminal message better than she had. *Come watch me fly*, he'd told them; and here they were.

She pressed forward with increasing urgency.

At last she was through the crowds and the security barriers and inside the compound. And there – still a couple of miles away – was Malenfant's ship, BDB-2, called *O'Neill*.

She could see the slim profile of the booster stack: the angular Space Shuttle boat-tail at the base, the central tank with its slim solid boosters like white pencils to either side, the fat tube of the payload module on top. There were splashes of red and blue that must be the Stars and Stripes Malenfant had insisted must adorn all his ships, and the hull's smooth curve glistened sharply where liquid air had frozen out frost from the desert night. The tower alongside the BDB looked minimal, slim and calm. There were clouds of vapour alongside the booster, little white knots which drifted from the tanks.

Bathed in a white xenon glow, the booster looked small, remote, even fragile, like an object in a shrine. This was the flame to which all these people had been drawn.

She got out of her car and ran to George Hench's control bunker.

The blockhouse was small, cramped, with an air of improvisation. One wall was a giant window, tinted, giving a view of the pad itself, the splash of light around the waiting booster. Facing the window were consoles – just desks piled with manuals and softscreens and coffee cups – each manned by a young T-shirted technician. At the back of the room were more people, arguing, running back and forth with manuals and piles of printout. Cables lay everywhere, in bundles across the floor and along the ceiling.

In one doorway, being shepherded by one of Malenfant's flunkies, there was a gaggle of what looked like federal government types, grey suits and ties and little briefcases. One of them, protesting loudly, was Representative Mary Howell, Emma realized with a start, the former chemical engineer who had given Malenfant such a tough ride in the Congressional hearings.

In the middle of all this, surrounded by people, yelling instructions and demanding information, there was Malenfant himself, with Cornelius – and Michael, the boy from Zambia. Cornelius was holding Michael's hand, which was balled into a fist. Malenfant hurried forward. 'Emma. Thank Christ you're here.'

She couldn't think of a damn thing to say. Because all three of them, Malenfant, Cornelius and Michael, were wearing one-piece orange garments, covered in pockets and Velcro patches.

They were flight pressure suits. Spacesuits.

Art Morris:

Art could see the rocket ship from the driving seat of the Rusty. But he was parked well away from the roads, on a patch of scrub it had been no trouble at all for the Rusty to reach.

This Rusty – strictly a Reconnaissance, Surveillance and Targeting Vehicle, or RST-V – was the Marine Corps's replacement for the jeep. Like the jeep it was all but indestructible. And it ran with a hybrid electric power system, which used a diesel-power generator to produce power for electric motors mounted on each wheel. The design was slighter and much more compact than mechanical drive trains, and there was built-in reliability: if one wheel failed, he could just keep motoring on three, or even two if they weren't on the same side. And the wheels worked independently; the Rusty could turn around and around, like a ballerina.

Best of all, when he turned off the generator and ran on batteries, there was no engine noise, no exhaust gases that might give away his position to any thermal sensors deployed by those guys on the fence.

Art loved this Rusty. But it wasn't his, of course. The only personal touch Art allowed himself was the snapshot of his daughter, Leanne, taped to the dash.

The Rusty had been borrowed for him for the occasion by his good friend Willy Butts, who was still in the Marine corps. Art's first idea had just been to walk up to the compound and start blasting, but Willy had talked him out of it. *You won't get past the gate, man. Think about it. And you'll still be a couple miles from the rocket. What you need is a little transport. Leave it to me . . .*

And Willy, as he always did, had come through, and here was Art, and there was the rocket, waiting for him.

He touched the ignition button. The Rusty's engine started up with the quietest of coughs. He rolled forward, the big adjustable suspension smoothing out the ride for him over the hummocky ground.

No more yellow babies, Malenfant. He tapped his photo. His little girl blew her candles one more time.

Art switched over to silent running.

Emma Stoney:

Mary Howell stepped forward. 'This is a joke. Malenfant, I could ground you under child protection legislation if I didn't already have *this*.' She waved a piece of paper in his face. 'You are in breach of federal aviation regulations parts 23, 25, 27, 29 and 31, which govern airworthiness certification. I also have clear evidence that your maintenance program does not follow the procedures spelled out in FAA advisory circular AC 120-17A. Furthermore –'

Malenfant glared at Howell. 'Representative, this has nothing to do with FAA regulations or any of that bullshit. This is personally vindictive.'

George Hench, a headset clamped to his ears, growled to Malenfant, 'If we're going to stand down I have to know now.'

Somehow the sight of Malenfant and Cornelius and a child, for God's sake, trussed up in these astronaut suits, surrounded by the clamour of this out-of-control situation, summed up for Emma how far into lunacy Malenfant had slipped. 'Malenfant, are you crazy?'

'We're going to fly, Emma. We have to. It's become a duty.'

'What about the four astronauts we trained up, at vast expense?'

'They were training *me*,' Malenfant said. He smiled, looking almost wistful.

Cornelius Taine shrugged. 'That was always the plan. Who is better qualified?'

'Another blind, Malenfant?'

'Yeah . . . All but one. Jay. The girl. She had the right training.'

'What for?'

'To care for Michael.'

George Hench was picking up something on his headset. He grimaced at Malenfant. 'More inspectors incoming.'

'Who is it this time?'

'Atomic Energy Commission.'

Howell's gaze flicked from George to Malenfant. 'AEC? What's this about the AEC?'

'Scottish uranium,' Emma said grimly. 'If they're here it's all unravelling. We'll be lucky to avoid jail.'

'But I've no choice.' Malenfant stared at her, as if trying to force her to agree with him through sheer power of personality. 'Don't you see that? I've had no choice since the moment Cornelius talked his way into your office.'

'This isn't about mining the asteroids any more. Is it, Malenfant?'

'No. It's about whatever is waiting for us on Cruithne.'

Cornelius grinned coldly. 'And who knows what that might be? The answers to everything, perhaps. The purpose of life. Who can say?'

Malenfant said desperately, 'The logic of my whole life has led me to this point, Emma. I'm trapped. And so is Michael. He's been trapped ever since he was born, with that damn blue circle turning in his head. *And I need you.*'

She felt oddly dizzy, and the colours leached from the world, as if she was about to faint. 'What are you saying?'

'Come with me.'

'*To Cruithne?*'

'It's the only way. Michael is terrified of me. And Cornelius, come to that. But you –'

'For God's sake, I'm no astronaut. The launch would kill me.'

'No, it won't. It's no worse than a roller coaster. And once we're gone we're gone. These assholes from the FAA can't reach us in outer space . . . Anyhow, at least you'll be out of the country when they prosecute.'

She sensed the great divergent possibilities, of past and future – for herself, Malenfant, perhaps the species itself – that flowed through this moment, as if her awareness was smeared across multiple realities, dimly lit.

She said, 'You're frightened, aren't you?'

'Damn right. I'm terrified. I just wanted to go mine the asteroids. And now, *this.*' He looked down at Michael's round eyes. 'I don't know what the hell I'm doing here, Emma. But I can't get off the ride. I need you with me. Please.'

But now the others were crowding around Malenfant again. Here was Mary Howell, yammering about her FAA regulations. Cornelius had picked up a headset and was shouting about how the gate guards were going to have trouble stalling the AEC inspectors. And George Hench, his face twisted, was watching the clock and following his endless pre-launch checks.

Michael was crying.

Howell stepped forward. 'Face it, Colonel Malenfant. You're beaten.'

Malenfant seemed to come to a decision. 'Sure I am. George, get her out of here. We have a spaceship to fly.'

George Hench grinned. 'About time.' He wrapped his big arms around Howell and lifted her bodily off the floor. She screamed in frustration and kicked at his legs and swung her head back. She succeeded in knocking his headset off, but he just thrust her out of the room and slammed the door.

Emma was glaring at Malenfant. 'Malenfant, have you any idea –'

George said, 'Enough. You can debate it in space. Get out of here. I'll take care of the rest.'

Malenfant clasped George's beefy shoulder. 'Thank you, my friend.'

George pushed him away. 'Send me a postcard from Alcatraz.' He snatched another headset and started to yell at the technicians at their improvised consoles.

Malenfant faced Emma. He reached out and took her hand, and gave it the gentlest of tugs.

As if in a dream, she followed him, as she always had, as she knew she always would.

As they walked out of the blockhouse into the grey of the Mojave dawn, she heard screaming, a remote crackle.

Gunfire.

Art Morris:

The Rusty performed beautifully. It was built to reach seventy on regular roads and maybe forty on *anything*, from sand dunes to peat bogs. Meanwhile he was sitting inside a shell of carbon-fibre composite and ceramic plating that was tough enough to stop a rifle bullet. Art didn't have to do much more than point and hope.

He drove hell for leather at the fence. In his IR viewer he saw company guards running along inside the fence, pointing to where he was coming from, then getting the hell out of the way.

He laughed.

He hit the fence. He barely noticed it as it smashed open around him.

223

Guards scattered before him. He heard the hollow slam of bullets hitting the armour. He hit the ignition and powered up the diesel; there was no point in running silent now. The engine roared and he surged forward, exhilarated.

'Look what you did, Malenfant!'

He saw the pad ahead of him, the booster lit up like a Disneyland tower. He gunned the engine and headed straight for it.

Emma Stoney:

It was as if time fell apart for Emma, disintegrated into a blizzard of disconnected incidents, acausal. She just endured it, let Malenfant and his people lead her this way and that, shouting and running and pulling, through a blizzard of unfamiliar places, smells and equipment.

Here she was in a suiting room. It was like a hospital lab, gleaming fluorescents and equipment racks and medical equipment and a stink of antiseptic. She was taken behind a screen by unsmiling female techs, who had her strip to her underwear. Then she was loaded into her pressure suit, tight rubber neck and sleeves, into which she had to squeeze, as if into a shrunken sweater. The techs tugged and checked the suit's seals and flaps, their mouths hard.

Gloves, boots.

Here was a helmet of white plastic and glass they slipped over her head and locked to a ring around her neck. Inside the helmet she felt hot, enclosed, the sounds muffled; her sense of unreality deepened.

She heard Michael, elsewhere in the suiting room, babbling in his own language. *Give me back my clothes! Oh, give me back my clothes!* Her heart tore. But there was no time, nothing she could do for him.

In some other world, she thought, I am walking away from here. Talking calmly to Representative Howell, fending off the AEC people, figuring out ways to manage this latest disaster. Doing my job.

Instead, here I am being prepped for space, for God's sake, for all the world like John Glenn.

She was hurried out of her booth. The others were waiting for her, similarly suited up. Malenfant peered out of his helmet at her, the familiar face framed by metal and plastic, expressionless, as if he couldn't believe he was seeing her here, with him.

... And now, after a ride in an open cart, she was hurrying across the compound, towards the glare of light that surrounded the booster. Pad technicians ran alongside her, *applauding*.

Then they had to climb, with a single burly pad rat, into the basket of a cherry-picker crane, enduring a surging swoop as it lifted them into the air. They rose through banks of vapour, thin, translucent, smelling of wood smoke. She saw smooth-curving metal, sleek as muscle and coated in condensation and frost, just feet away from her, close enough to touch.

Michael seemed to be whimpering inside his helmet; Cornelius was still gripping the kid's fist, hard. The pad rat watched this, his expression stony.

The cherry-picker nudged forward until it banged against the rocket's hull. The tech stepped forward and began to fix a ramp over the three hundred feet drop that separated them from the booster.

Malenfant went first.

Then it was Emma's turn. Hanging on to the pad tech's arm, she stepped forward onto the ramp. She was looking through a gaping hole cut into the fairing which covered the spacecraft itself. The hull was covered by some kind of insulating blanket, a quilt of powder-white cloth. There was a hatchway cut into the cloth, rimmed with metal. Inside the hatch was a grey conical cave, dimly lit, the walls crusted with hundreds of switches and dials. There were reclining bucket seats, just metal frames covered with canvas, side by side. They looked vaguely like dentist's chairs, she thought.

There was the smell of a new machine: the rich flavour of oil, a sharp tang of welded steel and worked brass, the sweet scent of canvas and wall coverings not yet pumped full of stale body odour. The cabin looked safe and warm and snug.

Again, the crackle of gunfire, drifting up from the ground.

George Hench:

For George Hench, in these final minutes, time seemed to slow, flow like taffy.

He tried to step back from the flood of detail. Now that the politicos and bureaucrats had been slung out of here, there was a welcome sense of engineering calm, of control. He heard his technicians work through the pre-launch events, calling 'Go' and 'Affirm' to each other. Both the hydrogen and oxygen main tanks were filled and were being kept topped up. Inertial measurement units had been calibrated, which meant the BDB now had a sense of its position in three-dimensional space as it was swept around the Earth by the planet's rotation. The propulsion system helium tanks were being filled, antenna alignment was completed . . .

His ship was becoming more and more independent of the ground.

Now the external supply was disconnected. The valves to the big oxygen and hydrogen tanks were closed, and the tanks brought up to pressure. With a minute to go, he handed over control to the BDB's internal processors.

It was then he got the word in his ear.

He pulled himself away from the consoles and studied the images in the security camera feeds. The picture was blurred, at the limit of resolution.

He saw a smashed section of fence. Guards down, lying on the ground. Some kind of vehicle, a boxy military kind of thing, slewed around in the dirt. Somebody was standing up in the vehicle, lifting something to his shoulder. Like a length of pipe. Pointed at the booster stack.

'Oh, Jesus.'

George. Do I have your authorization?

The bad of the bad. 'Do it, Hal.'

He could see the guards in the picture struggling to pull on their funny-faces, their M-17 gas masks. Meanwhile the guy in the truck was readying his weapon, clumsily.

It might have been comical, a race between clowns.

The guards won. A single shell was lobbed towards the truck.

George could barely see the gas that emerged. It was like a very light fog, colourless. When it reached the truck, the guy there started

226

coughing. He dropped his bazooka, whatever it was. Then he started vomiting and convulsing.

A masked guard ran forward and jammed something into the hatchway in the top of the truck. George knew what that was. It was a willy pete, a white phosphorus grenade.

The truck filled with light, and shuddered. The guards moved closer.

There had been no sound. It was eerie to watch.

Three minutes.

George turned back to the booster stack, which stood waiting for his attention.

Emma Stoney:

The curving flank of the booster, just a couple of feet away from her, swept to the ground, diminishing with perspective, like a piece of some metal cathedral. On the concrete pad at the booster's base she could see technicians running, vehicles scattering away like insects. Further out she could see the buildings of the compound scattered over the churned-up dirt, the fence, and the people swarming beyond: a great sea of them, cars and tents and faces, under the lightening dawn sky.

In one place the fence was dark, as if broken. She saw guards running. The distant crackle of gunfire drifted through the air. She saw a truck, a man dangling out of it, some kind of mist drifting, guards closing in.

She turned to the hatch. There was Malenfant, his thin face framed by his helmet, staring out at her.

'GB,' he said. 'It was GB. That's what the military call it.'

'Sarin. Nerve gas. My God. You used *nerve gas.*'

'It was brought here to be incinerated in the waste plant . . . Emma, I have always been prepared to do whatever I have to do to make this mission work.'

I know, she thought. I know more than I want to know.

I shouldn't be here. This is unreal, *wrong.*

He held out his hand to her. Through the thick gloves, she could barely feel the pressure of his flesh.

Without looking back, she entered the humming, glowing, womb-like interior of the spacecraft.

George Hench:

Pale fire burst from the base of the stack. Smoke gushed down the flame trenches and burst into the air like great white wings, hundreds of feet wide. And now the solid boosters lit, and the light was extraordinarily bright, yellow and dazzling as the sun.

The stack started to rise. But the noise hadn't reached him yet, and so the booster would climb in light and utter silence, as if swimming into the sky.

George had worked on rockets all his life. And yet he never got over this moment, this instant when the great blocky machine, for the first and only time, burst into life and lifted off the ground.

And now the sound came: crackling and popping, like wet wood on a fire, like oil overheated in a pan, like a million thunderclaps bursting over his head. The rocket rose out of the great cauldron of burning air, trailing fire, rising smooth and graceful. At the moment it lifted off the booster was burning as much oxygen as half a billion people taking a breath.

George, exhilarated, terrified, roared into the noise.

3

CRUITHNE

Darest thou now O soul,
Walk out with me toward the unknown region
Where neither ground is nor any path to follow?
— WALT WHITMAN

Emma Stoney:

Rockets, it turned out, were unsubtle.

The launch was a roaring vibration. She'd been expecting acceleration. But when each booster stage cut out, the engine thrust just died – suddenly, with no tail-off – so that the reluctant astronauts were thrown forward against their restraints, given a couple of seconds of tense breathing and anticipation, and then the next stage cut in and they were jammed back once more. After a couple of minutes of this Emma felt bruises on her back, neck and thighs.

But the thrust of the last booster stage was gentle, just a push at her chest and legs. Then, finally, the thrust died for good.

. . . And she was drifting up, slowly, out of her seat, as far as her restraints would let her. She felt sweat that had pooled in the small of her back, spreading out over her skin.

The rocket noise was gone. There was silence in the cabin, save for the whirr of fans and pumps, the soft ticking of instruments, Malenfant's quiet voice as he worked through his shutdown checklist.

And she heard a gentle whimpering, oddly high-pitched, like a cat. It must be Michael. But he was too far away for her to reach.

Now there was a series of clattering bangs, hard and metallic, right under her back, as if someone was slamming on the hull with great steel fists.

'There goes the last stage,' called Malenfant. 'Now we coast all the way to Cruithne.' He grinned through his open faceplate. 'Welcome to the *Gerard K. O'Neill*. Don't move yet; we aren't quite done . . .'

This cabin was called the Earth-return capsule. The four of them sat side by side, their orange pressure suits crumpled in their metal-frame couches. Emma was at the left-hand end of the row, jammed between Malenfant and the wall, which was just a bulkhead, metallic and unfinished. She was looking up into a tight cone, like a metal tepee. She was facing an instrument panel, a dashboard that spanned the capsule, crusted with switches, dials and softscreen readouts. On the other side of the panel she could see clusters of wires and optical fibres and cables, crudely taped together and looped through brackets. This was *not* the Space Shuttle, rebuilt and quality-certified after every flight; there was a home-workshop, improvised feel to the whole shebang.

Obscurely, however, she found that comforting.

The light, greenish grey, came from a series of small fluorescent floods set around the walls of the capsule; the shadows were long and sharp, making this little box of a spaceship seem much bigger than it was. But there were no windows. She felt deprived, disoriented; she no longer knew which way up she was, how fast she was travelling.

Malenfant reached up and took off his helmet. He shook his head, and little spherical balls of sweat drifted away from his forehead, swimming in straight lines through the air. 'All my life I dreamed of this.' The helmet, released, floated above his belly, drifting in some random air current. He knocked it with a finger and it started to spin.

Emma found her gaze following the languid rotation of the helmet. Suddenly it felt as if the helmet was stationary, and it was the rest of the ship which was rotating, and her head was a balloon full of water through which waves were passing. She closed her eyes and pressed her head back against the headrest of her couch, until the spinning sensation stopped.

There was a sound like a cough, a sharp stink of bile.

Emma opened her eyes and tried to lift her head, but her vision swam again. 'Michael?'

'No,' said Cornelius, his voice tight. And now she saw a big ball of vomit, green laced with orange, shimmering up into the air above them. Complex waves crossed its surface and it seemed to have ten or a dozen smaller companions travelling with it.

'Oh, Christ, Cornelius,' said Malenfant. He reached under his couch and pulled out a plastic bag that he swept around the vomit ball. When the vomit touched the surface of the bag, it started to behave 'normally'; it spread out all over the interior of the bag in a sticky, lumpy mess.

It was like nothing Emma had seen before; she lay there and watched the little drama unfold, mindless of the stink.

There was a new series of low bangs, like guns firing, from beyond the wall beside Emma. With each bang she felt a wrench as her couch dragged her sideways.

'Take it easy,' Malenfant said to them all. 'That's just the hydrazine attitude thrusters firing, spinning us up. We're feeling transients. They'll dampen out.'

There were metallic groans from the hull, pops and snaps from the latches which docked the Earth-entry module to the rest of the spacecraft cluster. It was like being in a huge, clumsy fairground ride.

But at length, as the spin built up, she felt a return of weight, a gentle push that made her sink back into her seat once more.

The attitude thrusters cut out.

'Right on the button,' said Malenfant. 'We is pinwheeling to the stars, people. Let's go open up the shop.'

He released his restraints. He stood up in his couch, his feet bouncing above the fabric, and he pulled at levers and straps until a central section of the instrument panel above him folded back. It was like rearranging the interior of a station wagon. Beyond the panel was a short tunnel, leading to a hatch like a submarine's, Emma thought, a heavy iron disc with a wheel at the centre.

Malenfant said, 'One, two, three.' He took a jump into the air. He drifted upwards easily, floated sideways and impacted the wall of the tunnel, gently. He grabbed on to a rung, his boots dangling. 'Coriolis force,' he said. 'Piece of cake.' He pulled himself further into the tunnel, reached up and hauled at the wheel.

But the wheel was jammed, presumably by the vibration of launch. What an anticlimax, Emma thought. Malenfant had to have Emma pass up a big spanner, and he used this to hit the wheel until it came loose. At last Malenfant had the wheel turning, and he pushed the hatch upward and out the way. He floated easily through the hatch, his booted feet trailing after him. Emma, looking up beyond him, saw a disc of grey fluorescent light.

She glanced at Cornelius. 'Me next?'

Cornelius's face, still inside his helmet, was actually green. 'I'll pass Michael up.'

She took off her own helmet and stowed it carefully on Malenfant's vacated couch. Then, breathing hard, she unclipped her restraints and laid them aside. She pushed down at her chair, cautiously. She drifted into the air a little way, fell back slowly. It was like wading through a waist-deep swimming pool.

She was aware of Michael watching her, his eyes round and bright inside his helmet.

She tried to think of something to say to him. But of all of them he seemed the most centred, she sensed, the most at home in this starkly new environment. How strange that was.

Without giving herself time to think about it, she bent her knees and pushed up.

She had leapt like an Olympic athlete, but she drifted away from her course, and slammed, harder than Malenfant, against the wall of the tunnel. But she managed to grab onto a rung. Then she hauled at the rungs to pull herself through the tunnel. She seemed as light as a feather.

She emerged into a small chamber, a cylinder maybe ten feet across. The light was a flat fluorescent grey-white. There was an odd smell, metal and plastic, a mix of staleness and antiseptic, air that had never been breathed. The walls were thick with equipment boxes, cables, pipes, softscreens and displays. Above her there was a partition ceiling, an open-mesh diamond grill, beyond which she glimpsed more cylindrical chambers. Ducts and pipes coated with silver insulation snaked up through gaps cut in the ceiling. There were no windows here either, and her sense of enclosure increased.

Malenfant was standing here. He bent and grabbed under her shoulders, and hauled her up as if she were a child. 'How do you feel?'

'For now, fine,' she said.

He pushed himself up into the air by flexing his toes. He seemed exhilarated, boyish. As he descended, slow as a feather, he was drifting sideways; and when he landed he staggered a little. 'Coriolis. Just a little reminder that we aren't under true gravity here, but rotating.'

'Like a bucket on a rope.'

'Yeah. This compartment is what you might call ops. Controls for the cluster, computer hardware, most of the life support boxes. We'll use the Earth-return module as a solar storm shelter. Come on.'

He led her to a ladder at the centre of the chamber. It ran straight up through a hole in the ceiling, like a fireman's pole.

Emma walked forward cautiously. With every step she bounced into the air and came down swimmingly slowly, and the Coriolis forces gave her a small but noticeable sideways kick as she moved.

It was disorienting, every sensation subtly unfamiliar, like walking through a dream.

Malenfant grabbed the ladder and began to pull himself upwards. He moved effortlessly, like a seal.

Emma took the ladder but moved much more cautiously, taking the rungs one at a time, making sure her feet were firmly anchored. With every rung she climbed the weight dropped off her shoulders. But as if in compensation the sideways Coriolis push seemed that much more fierce, a tangible sideways shove prising her loose of the ladder.

Malenfant had grabbed onto a strut. He reached down, took her hand, and helped her float up the last few feet. She seemed to drift over the open-mesh floor like a soap bubble. Malenfant babbled about cleated shoes he had brought along, but she found it hard to concentrate.

He said, 'This is the zero G deck, the centre of gravity of the cluster, the place we're pinwheeling around. There are two more compartments above us. In here we have everything that needs a stable platform: astronomy, navigation, radar, antennae. We even have coelostats, little devices that will spin the opposite way to the ship, if we need them . . .'

'Malenfant, with this act – by launching again, by absconding from Earth – you've wrecked Bootstrap. You know that, don't you? They'll take apart everything you built up.'

'But it doesn't matter, Emma. Because we're here, now. On our way to Cruithne, and the downstreamer artefact, and *everything*. Nothing else matters.' He grinned and pulled at her hand. 'Come see.'

She let herself be led towards small curving windows set in the wall. Each window was a disc of darkness. She pressed her face to cool glass and cupped her hands around her eyes.

The module's hull was a fat, curving wall. Fastened to the outside she could see thick blankets, insulation and meteorite shielding. Solar cell wings, seen edge-on, were filmy sheets of bluish glass, and slow ripples passed along them in response to some complex vibration mode. She was almost facing the sun here; the hull and the solar wings were brilliantly lit, and she could see no stars.

But now, swimming into her view, came the Earth.

It was a crescent, blue and white and brown. She could see a fringe of atmosphere, brilliantly bright, and the arc shape cupped a pool of darkness that was broken by strings of orange stars – cities, she realized, spread along the edge and river valleys of some continent on the night side of Earth. The ship's rotation made the Earth turn, smooth as an oiled machine, over and over.

And as she watched, the Earth was growing smaller, visibly receding, as if she was riding into the sky in some glass-bottomed elevator.

She clutched Malenfant's arm.

'I know,' he said, his voice tight. 'Not even the Apollo astronauts saw it like this. They did a couple of orbits of Earth, time enough to get used to the situation before they lit out for the Moon. Not us; we've been thrown straight into the out.'

She checked her watch implant. She had a meeting with some East Coast investors, booked *right now*.

On some level, deep in her mind, she sensed that *this was wrong*: not just the illegality and unexpectedness of it, but the very nature of the situation. She felt that she shouldn't be here, that this was unreal; she felt as if she was outside the scene, somehow, looking in through a glass barrier.

She shouldn't be here. And yet she was.

Perhaps she was in some form of shock.

The crescent Earth shrank, becoming more round, more three-dimensional, more vividly blue against the empty blackness of space, a planet rather than a world. And, she wondered, could it be really true that all the mind and love and hope in the universe was confined to that thin blue film of dirt and water and air?

Infomercial:

You know me.

Nowadays you probably know me better from my Shit Cola ads than for the one big successful glorious thing I did in my life. Which was to walk on the Moon.

Once. In 1971.

After that the whole damn thing was shut down.

Back in 1971 I thought that by now we would be well on the way to colonizing space. Why not? Airlines operate at just three times fuel costs. Why shouldn't space operations be just as economical? Spacecraft are no more complex than airplanes – in fact, less so.

But since 1970 or thereabouts going to space has not been part of our national agenda.

NASA has kept complete control over space. But since 1970 NASA has produced paper, not spaceships. This was the agency, remember, which destroyed the Saturn V rather than allow it to launch cheap-and-cheerful Skylabs which would have threatened its bloated Space Station program.

In 1980 I joined the study group which convinced President Ronald Reagan that the statesman who led mankind to space would be remembered for millennia after Isabella the Great was forgotten. For a while, it looked as if something revolutionary might be done.

But then came the assassination attempt, and Cold War problems, and various other issues. The President left space to other people, who couldn't get it done.

NASA won its turf wars. We lost access to space.

But the dream – the reasons we *need* spaceflight, now more than ever – none of that has gone away.

Which is why I for one am fully behind Malenfant's launch from the Mojave.

What else was he supposed to do? You just *know* those federal paper-pushers were going to find every way they could to block him.

I want to emphasize that my personal problems are not the issue here, nor is my own career trajectory and related difficulties. To put it bluntly, I haven't drunk a drop in four years, and my new marriage is working out just fine. What I am concerned about is that future generations should not be denied the opportunities denied to my own children and grandchildren.

That's why I agreed to appear in this infomercial. Support Reid Malenfant. If you can't bring yourself to do that, get off his back. The man is out there risking his hide for you, and your children.

Give him a break.

Emma Stoney:

Malenfant started up the life support systems. Pumps and fans clattered into life, and Emma felt a breeze, flat and warm, in her hair. Then Malenfant clambered back up to the zero G deck to check the ship's comms systems and navigation alignment.

The others gathered on the ops deck and stripped off their fat orange pressure suits. They changed into lightweight NASA-type jumpsuits that lacked a lot in style, but were warm and practical and covered in pockets and Velcro strips. They shoved the pressure suits down the hole into the Earth-return capsule and dogged closed the hatch.

The boy, Michael, had to be manhandled through all this. He was passive, unresponsive, like a week-old infant; it was possible to move him around, even strip and clean and dress him like a doll, but he seemed to have no will of his own. Emma let Michael stay on the ops deck, and made sure at least one of them was there with him the whole time.

She realized that she had a sneaking, selfish gratitude that Michael was aboard. Having someone else to think about would take her mind off her own utter disorientation.

She climbed the fireman's-pole ladder to go up – or down – to the module's other two compartments. The disorientation of the changing vertical wasn't so bad if she spent a few seconds in the zero G bay giving herself time to adapt. Then she could put out of her mind the fact that the ops deck had just been *down*; now it was *up*, and the ladder *down* now led her to the other decks that used to be above her head.

It worked fine provided she didn't look up through the mesh and see people dangling from the ceiling like chandeliers.

The bio sciences deck was a mix of lab and field hospital. There was some medical equipment, a collection of pills and lotions and bandages and inflatable splints, and more heavy-duty equipment, scary-looking stuff like a defibrillator. The small lab area was pretty much automated, with little requirement from the crew but to pump in regular samples of blood and urine. Everything was colour-coded and labelled and built into smart little plastic units you could just pop out of the wall to repair and replace.

The lowest deck – called, with nerdish humour, the meatware deck – was up against the outer bulkhead of the craft, and so was the furthest from the cluster's centre of gravity. They would eat and sleep here, under the strongest gravity available – about equivalent to the Moon, a sixth of Earth normal. It wasn't exactly possible to walk normally here, but at least she could move around without getting a kick sideways the whole time.

There was exercise gear, foldaway treadmills and an exercise cycle. Bunks were neatly stacked against one wall. They had private curtains, zip-up sleeping bags, nightlights and little personal stowage pockets. She looked inside one of the pockets and found a small softbook and music player with headset, a sleeping mask and ear plugs, all marked with Bootstrap logos. It was cute, like an airline give-away pack.

The john – strictly speaking the Waste Management System – looked like it would be less fun. It was the old Space Shuttle design, a lavatorial veteran of decades of spaceflight. There was a commode with an operating handle and, God help her, a control panel. Liquid waste would be captured and pumped away for recycling. Solid waste wasn't recycled; a valve would open to the vacuum of space to dry out the faeces, and it would then be dumped overboard. When she turned the handle a vent opened and air started sucking its way down into the commode, big vanes turning in a very intimidating way.

The toilet could only be used four times an hour, she noted with apprehension. She suspected that in the early days at least they would need more capacity than that.

Each crew member had a personal hygiene kit, more airline-complimentary stuff: a little fold-up toothbrush, toothpaste, dental floss, nail clippers, soap, a comb, a brush, anti-chap lipstick, skin lotion, stick deodorant, a tube of shaving cream and a shaver that, bizarrely, worked by clockwork. There was a little hand-washing station, a hole in the wall through which you thrust your hands, and jets of hot and cold water played over your skin. It was also, thankfully, possible to take a shower, with a hosepipe and a nozzle that you passed over your body inside a concertina-type wraparound curtain. But the curtain was imprinted with stern instructions about the importance of washing down the shower properly after use, to avoid algal growths.

The galley was a neat little unit the size of a domestic freezer. It had hot and cold water dispensers, serving trays, a range of plastic plates and cutlery, and a teeny-tiny microwave oven. On the door of the galley was a complete food list, everything from apple sauce to turkey tetrazzini. The food, stowed under the galley, came in dehydrated packages, sliced meats with sauce or gravy in foil packages, plastic cans with tear-off lids. There were also a few treat items like candy bars in, the labels said, 'their natural form'. There was even a tap that would dispense Shit Cola, the relic of some long-forgotten sponsorship deal. Experimentally she found a cup, a globe with an inlet valve and nipple, and tried a little of the Shit. The carbonation didn't seem to be working right – no doubt some low gravity problem – and it tasted lousy.

There was enough food for the four of them for two hundred days in space: ninety days out, ninety back, twenty at the asteroid. No doubt that could be stretched by rationing if it came to it, but it did give a finality to the mission duration.

She was unstowing all of this from its launch configuration when Malenfant called her from the zero G deck. She glanced at her watch, and was startled to find that already twelve hours had elapsed since the launch.

She pulled herself up the ladder to join Malenfant by a window. He grinned and took her arm. 'You'll want to see this. We're here for a gravity assist. In fact, we'll be doing this twice . . .'

Quietly, he talked about the difficulty of reaching Cruithne, with its highly elliptical and tilted-up orbit. To that end the impulse from the rocket stack would be boosted with gravity slingshots around the Moon. The ship would whip right around the Moon, to be hurled inward past the Earth, and then out past the Moon a second time. The theft of momentum by the *O'Neill* would mean that the Moon would forever circle the Earth a fraction slower.

She let his words wash over her. For, beyond the small, curving window, she saw black, grey, brown-white, a mesh of curves and inky darkness, sliding across her view like oil. It was a crescent bathed in sunlight, pocked with craters, wrinkled by hills. On the plains she could see boulders, pinpoints of brightness sending long, needle-fine shadows across the dusty ground. And the crescent was *growing*. The ship was flying into the shadow of the Moon: towards the terminator, the line between night and day.

The sunlit crescent narrowed, even as it spread across space. It was soon too large to be captured by a single window, and she leaned forward to see the sweep of the Moon, from horn to skinny horn. At last the crescent narrowed to invisibility, and she was flying over the shadowed Moon, a hole in the stars.

She found she was holding her breath. The noises of the ship's systems, little gadgets humming and ticking, seemed sacrilegious in this huge dark quiet.

There was an explosion of light. She craned to see.

Far ahead of the craft, the sun was rising over the Moon. A line of fire had straddled the horizon, poking through the mountains and crater rims there. The light fled across the bare surface, casting shadows hundreds of miles long from mountains and broken crater walls. The smaller, younger craters were wells of darkness in the flat light.

She checked her watch. It was early evening in Vegas. Right now, she thought, I am supposed to be wrapping up the day's work, making my way out through the protesters to my apartment . . .

Instead, *this*. Already Earth, her life, seemed a lot further away than twelve hours, a mere quarter-million miles.

The craft sailed over brightening ground.

'You know,' Malenfant said, 'when we pass the orbit of the Moon we'll already have travelled further than anybody has ever gone before.' He cupped her chin, and turned her head to him. He ran his thumb over her cheek. It came away wet. She was surprised.

'I'm sorry,' she said. 'I didn't know it would be like *this*.'

He smiled. 'I know it's wrong. I know I'm selfish. But I'm glad you're here.'

She let him hold her, and they stared out at the fleeing Moon.

But suddenly Michael was here, pushing between them, warm limbs flashing. *Watch the Moon, Malenfant. Watch the Moon!*

'Jesus,' Malenfant snapped. He was terrified, Emma realized.

Maura Della:

Maura had to decide whether to endorse a military response to Bootstrap's activities.

It was a big decision. Maybe the biggest of her life.

It may be, proponents of the military option concluded, that there was something on the asteroid that was indeed essential to the future of mankind. If *that* was so, then surely it couldn't be left in the hands of Reid Malenfant: a rogue, a maverick, out of control. And who best to take control but the US government?

Well, perhaps.

She tried to call Bootstrap's various offices. All she got was voice jail, endless automated phone systems. Occasionally a cop or FBI officer picked up, as a break from impounding Bootstrap files and property. Eschatology, similarly, was being raided and shut down.

Meanwhile she read through the reports her staff assembled for her, and watched TV, and scoured the net, and tried to get a sense of where the world was heading, now that the Carter prediction doom-soon gloom had been so confounded and confused by the far-future light show from the sky.

The e-psychologists likened it to the trauma, at an individual level, of learning the date of one's death – and then unlearning it, like a mock execution.

There were some positive aspects, of course. Thanks to the far-future visions the science of cosmology seemed to be heading for an overnight revolution – at least, in the minds of those who were prepared to entertain the notion that the Cruithne images might be genuine. Similarly – in ways she failed to understand, relating to constraints on particle-decay lifetimes and so forth – various other branches of physics were being turned over. On the other hand, some philosophers argued it was bad for the mental health of the species to be given answers to so many questions without the effort of discovery.

The churches had pretty uniformly condemned the downstream visions for their godless logic. Science fiction sales in all media had taken a hammering – not that that was necessarily a bad thing, in Maura's opinion – though she had heard that there were already several digital dramas being cooked up in Hollywood's banks of story-spinning supercomputers, set against the death of the Galaxy, or orbiting a black hole mine.

And on a personal level, there were many people who seemed simply unable to cope with it all.

There were some estimates that the downstream hysteria had claimed more than a thousand lives nationally already. People were killing themselves, and each other, because they believed the shadowy future visions weren't real, that Carter must be right after all; others were killing themselves because they thought the Cruithne future *was* real.

A lot of the fear and violence seemed to have focused on the Blue children – and, just as distressing, those who were suspected of being Blue. Perhaps it was inevitable, she thought; after all the children live among us, here and now. How convenient it is to have somebody to hate.

Meanwhile the FBI had reported on a new ritual murder sect. The adherents believed they were 'fast-forwarding' their victims to a point where they would be revived by the black hole miners or some other group of downstreamers, and live in peace and harmony, forever in the future.

And so on. More and more she got the sense that she was stuck in the middle of an immature species' crisis of adolescence.

Which shaped her view on the decision that faced her.

Personally Maura had severe doubts there would be anything to find on Cruithne, except for ancient dusty rock and Dan Ystebo's peculiar squid. What was more important was the symbolism of the military action.

The government would act to show it was still in control of events: that it was not paralysed by the Carter prediction, that even Reid Malenfant was not beyond its jurisdiction. It seemed to Maura that this was what Americans always strove to do: to take a lead, to take control, to *do* something.

And that was the subtext, the real purpose behind the military response. The think tank report argued that the resonance of *action* was essential now to restore the social cohesion of a wired-up planet.

And Maura, reluctantly, found she agreed.

Sorry, Malenfant, she thought.

She registered her recommendation, and turned, with relief, to other matters.

Reid Malenfant:

Removed from the swirling currents of humanity, the crew of the *Gerard K. O'Neill* sailed into darkness.

After just a couple of days, though Earth's clouds and blue-green oceans were still visible, its disc had shrunk to the apparent size of the Moon from the ground. And the next day, it was smaller still. It would take ninety days of such phenomenal travelling to reach

Cruithne, tracing out its own peculiar orbit all of forty million miles from home.

The celestial mechanics of the ship's trajectory were complex.

Both Earth and Cruithne rounded the sun in about a year. Cruithne, tracing its ellipse, moved a tad faster. It meant that the *O'Neill* had to leap between two moving rocks, like a kid hopping from one roundabout to another. After the impulse given it by its booster throw, the ship was coasting through its own orbit independently of the Earth, a rounded ellipse that cut inside Earth's path.

By the time they reached Cruithne the ship would be around twelve degrees in advance of Earth: twelve out of three-sixty, a thirtieth of the circumference of the planet's orbit.

Malenfant liked to think he would be a couple of weeks ahead in time of the folks back home.

He treated the first bouts of motion sickness with Scop-Dex; he was glad when he could wean his crew off that because of the drowsiness it caused. They all suffered from low-G problems like the facial puffiness and nasal irritation caused by body fluid redistribution. They were peeing too much as a result of their bodies' confusion over this, and their hearts, with less work to do, were relaxing. And so on. Despite the artificial G and the exercise regime he imposed, their muscles were wasting, their hearts were shrinking and their bones were leaching away.

It was all anticipated and well understood, of course. But that didn't help make it easier to accept. Most of their deconditioning, in fact, had happened in the first *nine hours* in space, when they were still inside the orbit of the Moon. And after the nominal mission, after two hundred days in space, they would all be walking with a stick for months.

So it goes.

He kept Cornelius and Emma busy by cross-training them on the medical equipment. There was simple stuff like cardio-pulmonary resuscitation procedures, how to administer electroshock paddles, the use of chemicals like sodium bicarb. He gave them familiarization training on the drugs the ship carried, along with blood products. There were more grisly exercises, such as emergency tracheotomy, and how to secure an intravenous catheter (the fat saphenous veins of the inner thigh were the best bet).

Of course he was no medic himself. He relied heavily on recordings and softscreen simulations to keep him on the right track.

But both Cornelius and Emma were intelligent; they both soon figured out the subtext of their training, which was that in the event of any real emergency there was little that could be done. A single serious injury would likely exhaust their medical supplies. And even if the patient, whichever unlucky sap it was, could be stabilized long enough to be kept alive and brought home, the others would have to nurse a non-functioning invalid all the way back to Earth.

Malenfant didn't share with the others the training he'd gotten for himself on euthanasia, or on how to conduct a scientifically and legally valid autopsy.

During those first weeks they stayed healthy enough, luckily.

But once the adrenaline-rush excitement of the launch and the novelty of the mission wore off, all three of the adults – himself included – came crashing down into a feeling of intense isolation. He had expected this. He'd gotten some psychological training, based mainly on Russian experience, on long-duration spaceflight. Cornelius, for example, seemed locked in a bubble-world of his own, his odd, smoothed-over personality cutting him off from the others, like a second spacesuit. Malenfant left him alone as much as possible.

The general depression seemed to be hitting Emma hardest, however.

Oddly, when he looked into her eyes, it sometimes seemed as if she wasn't there at all, as if there was only a fragment of the Emma he knew, looking out at him, puzzled. *How did I get here?* It was understandable. He had, after all, shanghaied her, utterly without warning.

It would help if there was something to fill up her time, here on the *O'Neill*. But there was no real work for her to do beyond the chores and the training. He had softbooks, of course, but he'd only brought along technical manuals, a few books for the kid . . . Not a novel in the whole damn memory, and not even a yellowing hardcopy paperback. It would be easy enough to have stuff uploaded from Earth, of course, but although the reports and telemetry he downloaded daily were surely being picked up by the NASA deep space people, nobody down there seemed inclined to talk back to him.

He tried to handle his own deep sense of guilt.

He'd felt he needed to bring her along, on a whole series of levels. He still felt like that. But it would, after all, have been easy to push her away, there in the critical moments in the Mojave. To have kept from stealing her life from her.

If not for his Secret, maybe they'd be a little more open with each other. Of course, if not for the Secret, they wouldn't be here at all.

But what was done, was done.

Anyhow he'd refused to waste processor capacity on e-therapy programs, or any of that other modern crap which he regarded as mind-softening junk, despite recommendations from a slew of 'experts' during the mission planning. The truth is, he knew, there *were* no experts, because nobody had gone out as far as this before. They would just have to cope, learn as they went along, support each other, as explorers always had.

He did worry about the kid, though. Even though Michael spooked him half to death. Wherever *that* came from, it surely wasn't the kid's fault . . .

Flight in deep space was, after all, utterly strange – even for Malenfant, who felt as if he'd spent his whole life preparing for this.

It was possible to forget, sometimes, that they were locked up here in this tiny metal bubble, with *nothing* out there save for a few lumps of floating rock which came to seem less and less significant the further they receded from Earth.

But most times, *everything* felt strange.

If he walked too rapidly across the meatware deck, he could feel the Coriolis cutting in, a ghostly sideways push that made him stagger. Even when he washed or took a drink, the water would move around the bowl in huge languid waves, pulsing like some sticky, viscous oil. If he immersed his hands it felt like water always had, but it clung to his flesh in great globules and ribbons, so that he had to scrape it off and chase it back into the bowl.

And so on. *Everything* was strange. Sometimes he felt he couldn't cope with it, as if he couldn't figure out the mechanics or logic of the environment. Perhaps, he thought, this is how Michael feels all the time, living in this incomprehensible, fragmented world.

It was a relief to retreat to his bunk, eyes closed, strapped in, shut out from all stimuli, trying to feel normal.

But even here, in deepest space, with no sensory input at all, he could still feel *something*: the evolution of his own thoughts, the sense of time passing as he forged downstream into the future, the deepest, most inner sense of all.

There was no science to describe this. The laws of physics were time-reversible: they ran as happily backwards as forwards. But he knew in his deepest soul that time was *not* reversible for him, that he was bound on a one-way journey to the future, to the deepest downstream.

How strange, how oddly comforting that was.

He drifted into sleep.

Milton Foundation e-spokesperson:

It distresses all of us that the general psychological reaction to the news of the future has focused on the Blue children. You have to understand that Foundation Schools have always worked for the children's protection as much as their development.

When the children's nature was first publicized, the Schools first established, the effect was, at first, beneficial for everybody concerned. Families started to understand they weren't alone, that their super-intelligent children were part of a wider phenomenon. But after all, there is much about the children we do not understand. Their common obsession with blue-circle motifs, for instance.

There have been many theories to explain the children's origin, their sudden emergence into the world. Perhaps this is all some dramatic example of morphic resonance. Perhaps they are aliens. Perhaps they represent an evolutionary leap – maybe we have *Homo superior*, living among us, soldiers from the future who will enslave us. And so on.

Hysteria, perhaps. But people are *afraid*.

At first the general fear manifested itself in subtle ways: a general shunning of the Schools by surrounding communities, starving them of resources and access to local infrastructure, blocking approvals for extensions, that sort of thing.

Lately, matters have taken a turn for the worse. Much worse.

Foundation Schools in cities and towns around the planet – buildings, staff and students – have been attacked. Some children have been injured; one child is dead.

And even beyond the Schools, in the homes, we know that parents have turned on their own children.

We deeply regret several unfortunate incidents within Foundation Schools. We have tried to ensure that our supervision of the children has been of the highest quality. However I have to emphasize that the Milton Foundation has no direct control over the Schools. The Schools are independent establishments run under national and regional educational policies; we aren't responsible for this. We have actually acted to mitigate the conditions many children are kept in.

We do not oppose the closure of our Schools, the taking of the children into federal custody. It's easy to be judgmental. But what are we to do?

Besides, some of the worst Schools have been American.

Oh. You didn't know that?

(Name and Address Withheld):

Sir,

There has been a great deal of speculation in these columns and elsewhere over the origin of the so-called 'Blue child' phenomenon.

Perhaps this is just a statistical fluke – maybe these superkids have always been among us and we never even noticed. Some, of course, believe the Blue children may have some supernatural or even divine origin. It seems rather more likely to me they are mutant products of the ecocollapse.

For example, many children have difficulty digesting proteins, such as casein and gluten, contained in cows' milk and wheat. These proteins may be broken down, not into amino acids, but into peptides that can interfere with the hormones and neurotransmitters used by the brain, where they interfere with the brain's development. Perhaps some such physical cause is the solution. Certainly we seem to be suffering a parallel 'plague' of developmental illnesses that includes attention deficit syndrome, hyperactivity and dyslexia.

Whatever the truth I believe the focus of the debate must now shift: away from the origin of the children, to their destiny.

I believe the children represent a discontinuity in the history of our species. If they are truly superior to us, and if they breed true, they are the greatest threat to our continued survival since the Ice Age.

The resolution to this situation is clear.

First. The existing children must be sterilized to prevent their breeding and further propagation.

Second. Tests must be developed (perhaps they already exist) for assessing the developmental potential of a child while still in the womb. Such tests must be applied – nationally and internationally – to all new pregnancies.

Third. Foetuses which fail the tests, that is which prove to have Blue attributes, must be terminated immediately.

This must be done without sentiment and with maximum efficiency, before the children accrue the power to stop us.

At present they are young, small and weak and unformed and vulnerable. They will not always be so.

It will be hard. If governments will not listen, it is up to us, the people, to take action. Any and all sanctions are morally defensible. This is a time of racial survival, a crux.

I would point out that we emerged from the Ice Age crisis transformed as a species, in strength and capability. So we must purge our souls again. These need not be dark days, but a time of glorious bright cleansing.

Turning to the comparable issue of the enhanced cephalopods . . .

Burt Lippard:

We've all seen the future now. That Reid Malenfant stuff. Holy smoke. The one thing we know for sure is human beings, us, won't be able to cope with *that*.

We shouldn't fear the Blues. They're smarter than us, is all. So what? Most people are smarter than me anyhow.

I say we should give up our power to them. Sooner one Blue child running the world than a thousand so-called democrats. I'll work with them, when the day comes.

I say this. The Blues are the future. Anyone who lays a finger on them now will have me to answer to.

Maura Della:

Maura flew to Sioux Falls and spent the night.

The next morning was bright, clear, the sky huge. On a whim she gave her driver the day off. She set off, heading towards Minnesota. Past Worthington she turned into Iowa. The sun was high and bright in a blue cloudless sky. She drove past huge Day-Glo fields of rape and corn. This was a place of farms, and worked earth, and people living in the same houses their great-grandparents did. Even the agri-chemical corporate logos, painted by gen-eng on the corn fields, seemed unobtrusive today.

In these days of gloom and eco-disaster, after too long buried in the orange smog of Washington, she'd forgotten that places like this still existed. And in her district too.

Was all the Malenfant stuff – talk of the future, messages from time, the Carter catastrophe, the destiny of mankind – just an airy dream? If there was no way to connect the grandiose dreams of the future to *this*, the day-to-day reality, the small, noble aspirations, of the people of Iowa, could they be said to have any meaning?

I should spend more time out here, she thought.

In fact, maybe it was time to retire – not in a couple of years – but now.

She was too old for children of her own, of course, but not for the whitewashed farmhouse, the couple of horses. Anyhow, she knew when she looked into her heart, she'd never really wanted kids anyhow. She'd seen how kids dropped from the sky and exploded people's lives like squalling neutron bombs. She was honest enough to admit she was too selfish for that; her life, her only life, was her own . . .

Of course that didn't qualify her too well for the visit she must make today.

She had received a plea for help.

It had come into Maura's office, remarkably, by snail-mail. She opened the envelope and found a picture of a wide-eyed five-year-old, a letter hand-written in a simple, childish hand, far beyond the reach of any spellchecker software and replete with grammatical and other errors.

Reading a letter was a charge of nostalgia for Maura, in these days of electronic democracy.

The letter was from a family in a town called Blue Lake, in northern Iowa, right at the heart of her district, the heart of the Midwest. It was a college town, she recalled, but she was ashamed to find she couldn't remember the last time she'd been out there. The letter was from two parents baffled and dismayed because the government was demanding they give up their son. It was all part of the greater scandal that had broken out nationally – indeed, world-wide – about the treatment of Blue children.

The thing of it was, Maura couldn't see a damn thing she could do about it.

She reached for her softscreen, preparing to post an e-reply. Somehow, though, as she sat here holding the simple scrap of paper, the old-fashioned still photo with its smiling kid, that didn't seem enough.

She had glared out the window at the dull Washington sky, heard the wash of traffic noise. She needed a break from all this hothouse shit, the endless Malenfant blamestorming.

She started going through her diary.

Blue Lake – *pop. 9000* – seemed to be a classic small town, built around the wide, glimmering lake that had given it its name. The downtown, brick buildings and family-owned stores, was solid and immortal-looking. There was a park at the edge of the lake, and from it ran a whole series of broad, leafy streets lined with big nineteenth-century homes. One of these turned out to be the street she was looking for.

She stopped the car and got out.

The air was fresh, silent save for a distant growl of traffic, a rustle of leaves over her head. The sidewalk felt oddly soft under her feet. It was smart concrete, of course: self-repairing, unobtrusive. She walked up a path past a glowing green lawn. There was a bicycle, child-sized, bright red, dumped on the grass. The house itself might still be in the middle of the nineteenth century, save for the solar collection blanket draped over the roof, the button-sized security camera fixed to the door, the intelligent garbage can half-hidden by foliage. Thus technology could be used to improve the world: not to change it, or spin it out of touch with humanity. Sometimes we get it right, she thought; the future doesn't have to destroy us.

This is a good place, she thought, a human place. And the federal government – no, Maura, admit your responsibility, *I* – I want to take away a child, spirit him off from this beautiful place to some Godforsaken centre in Idaho or Nevada or maybe even overseas.

She rang the doorbell.

Bill Tybee turned out to be thirty-ish, slim, a little overawed by this Congresswoman who had parachuted into his life. He welcomed her in, talking too fast. 'My wife's away on military assignment. She was thrilled you were coming out to see us. Tommy's our older child. We have a little girl, Billie, not yet two; she is at a crèche today . . .'

She put together a picture of the Tybees' life from the little clues around the house: the empty box of fatbuster pills, the big softscreen TV plastered over one wall, the ticking grandfather clock, obviously ancient, a run-down cleaner microbot the size of a mouse in the middle of the living room carpet that she nearly stepped on; Bill kicked it out of the way, embarrassed.

Bill wore a silver lapel ribbon, the med-alert that marked him out as a cancer victim. Every time she looked, Maura counted more cancer victims among her electors than seemed reasonable. No doubt something to do with the breakdown of the environment.

Bill led her upstairs to a bedroom door. There was a sign, cycling around like a Times Square billboard: TOM TYBEE'S ROOM! DO NOT ENTER! SANTA CLAUS ONLY!

Bill knocked. 'Tom? There's a lady to see you. Can we come in?'

Uh huh.

Bill pushed open the door – there was some kind of junk behind it, and he had a little trouble – and he led Maura into the room.

It was painted bright yellow, with a window that overlooked the garden. Along one wall there was a wardrobe and a bunk bed with a giant storage locker underneath, against the other wall a big chest of drawers. The wardrobe and chest were both open, and clothes and other stuff just spilled out, all over the floor and the bed, to such an extent it was hard to believe it was possible, even in principle, to stow it all away. The spare acreage of walls was covered with posters: a map of the world, sports pennants, some aggressive-looking superhero glaring out of a mask.

It was a typical five-year-old boy's room, Maura thought to herself. Not that she was an expert on such matters.

The most striking thing about the room was a series of photographs and posters, some of them blown up, that had been stuck to the walls at about waist height – no, she thought, at little boy

252

eye-level – some of them even lapping over the precious sports pennants. They were pictures of star fields. Maura was no astronomer but she recognized one or two constellations – Scorpio, Cygnus maybe. A river of light that ran through the images, a river of stars. The photographs made up, she realized, in a kind of patchwork way, a complete three-hundred-and-sixty degree map of the Milky Way as it wrapped around the sky.

Tom himself – the kid, the Blue – was a very ordinary five-year-old, small, thin, dark, big-eyed. He was sitting in the middle of the kipple-covered floor. He was playing some kind of game, Maura realized; he had toys – cars, planes, little figures – set out in a ring around him. He had a Heart, one of those electronic recording gadgets, sitting on the floor beside him.

'Hello,' said the boy.

'Hello, Tom.'

Bill kneeled down, with a parent's accustomed grace. 'Tom, this lady is from Congress.'

'From Washington?'

Maura said, 'That's right.' She picked up one of his toys, some kind of armed lizard in a blue cape. 'What are you making? A fort?'

'No,' Tom said seriously. He took back the lizard and put it back in its place in the circle. He didn't expand, and Maura felt very dumb.

She stood up and pointed at the Milky Way photos. 'Did you find all these yourself?'

'I started with that one.' He pointed. It was Cygnus, an elegant swan shape, bright Vega nestling alongside. 'I found it in my dad's book.'

'An old astronomy encyclopaedia,' Bill said. 'Fixed-image. I had it when *I* was a kid. He found the other pictures himself. From books, the net. I helped him process them and get them to the same scale, match them. But he knew what he was looking for. That's when we first suspected he might be –'

Solitary. Brilliant. Obsessive. Uncommunicative. Pursuing projects beyond his years. *Blue.*

Tom said, 'I have a telescope.'

'You do? That's great.'

'Yeah. You can see it's made up of stars.'

'The Milky Way?'

'The Galaxy. And it goes beyond Cygnus.' He pointed at his walls. 'It starts in Sagittarius, over there. Then it goes through Aquila and

Cygnus, and it brushes Cassiopeia, and past Perseus and Orion and Puppis, and then you can't see it any more. I wanted to see it from the other side.'

Bill said, 'He means the southern hemisphere. His mother brought him home a couple of images from postings in the Pacific.'

Tom pointed to his photos. 'It goes to Carina, and you can see a lot more of it. And it goes to the Southern Cross and Centaurus and the tail of Scorpio, and it gets brighter, and then it goes to Sagittarius where it's really wide and has a dark line in the middle. And then it goes on to Aquila and to Cygnus . . .'

'Do you know what it is, Tom? The Milky Way, I mean, the Galaxy.'

'It's stars. And it's a big whirly.'

'A spiral?'

'Yeah. Look, you can see. There's the middle of the Galaxy, in Sagittarius, where it gets fat and bulgy. And all the arms wrap around that.

'We're inside an arm. You can see one of the other arms between us and the centre, there going through Centaurus and the Southern Cross and Carina. And there –' he pointed to the bright cloud in Carina '– that's where it turns away from us, and you see it end on, and that's why it looks so bright, like a road full of cars coming at you. And then there's a lane of dust and stuff that looks dark, the stuff between the arms, and that's the black stripe down the middle. And then on the other side of Carina you can see the arm that wraps around the outside of the sun, and it goes –' he turned around and pointed to his northern sky '– there, all the way across . . .'

Bill shrugged. 'He figured all this out for himself.'

'He *figured out* he's in the middle of a spiral galaxy?'

'All by himself. Yes.'

The kid, Tom, talked on. He might have been any five-year-old – cute, friendly enough, a little subdued – except for his subject. Most kids his age, the kids in the neighbourhood here, were surely barely aware they were in Iowa. Little Tom was already a galactic traveller.

She felt a brush of fear.

It was, she thought, this mix of the mundane with the strange – the childish toys and mess with the visions of galactic geography – that was so unsettling about these Blue children. A kid wasn't supposed to *be* like this.

And she noticed, now, that every one of Tom's toys, the cars and boats and figures he had put in a protective ring around himself, was blue.

Maura accepted some coffee, tried to put Bill at his ease.

Bill Tybee was a stay-at-home parent, the homemaker. He showed her, shyly, an animated postcard of his wife, June. It had been taken on an air base somewhere. She was a short, slightly dumpy blonde, a wide Iowa smile, dressed in a crisp USASF uniform; when Bill lifted it into the sunlight the postcard cycled ten seconds of her saluting and grinning, over and over. She was enlisted, a technical specialist in a special forces unit.

After a few minutes, Bill started to open up about his fears for the boy. 'I know he's Blue. The school assessment proved it –'

'Then you should be proud. You know that means he's exceptional.'

'I don't want him to be exceptional. Not if it means he has to go away.'

'Well, that's the law, Bill. I know how you feel. I know you're concerned for his safety, and you've every right to be after what happened to him before.'

'They failed to protect him, and they expelled him, Ms Della. I wasn't going to give him back just because they said they changed their minds.'

'But you can't keep him at home. The new centres aren't run by some private organization like the Miltons, but by the federal government. There's nothing to fear. It's the best for him.'

'With respect, Ms Della, I don't think you know what's best for my kid.'

'No,' she said. 'No, I probably don't. That's why I'm here.'

'So he's smart. But he still needs to grow, to have a life, to play with other kids. Is he going to get all of that at one of these fancy centres?'

'Well, that's why the centres were set up, Bill.'

'I know the theory,' said Bill. 'But that's not how it *is*. That's not what it's like to live with this thing.' Bill talked on about the effect of TV and the nets: the talk shows featuring kids with giant plastic dome heads, the TV evangelists who claimed that the kids were a gift from Jesus or a curse from Satan, and so on. 'It's a drip, drip, drip. There's a whole host of "experts" telling the world it's okay to pick on my kid, because he's *different*. And I've seen the reports

255

of those schools overseas, in Australia and places, where they beat up the kids and starve them and –'

'That's not happening here, Bill.' She leaned forward, projecting a practised authority. 'And besides, I'll ensure Tom is protected.'

Or at least, she thought, I will strive to minimize the harm that is done to him. Maybe that is my true vocation.

Bill Tybee burst out, '*Why us*, Ms Della? Why our kid?'

To that, of course, she had no answer.

Emma Stoney:

Emma tried to care for Michael. Or at least to maintain some kind of human contact with him.

But the boy would barely stir from his sleeping compartment down on the meatware deck. He seemed to spend the whole time sitting on his bunk bent over some softscreen program or other.

When they did force Michael out of his bunk, for food and exercise and hygiene breaks, the kid seemed to veer between catatonia and a complete freak-out, an utter inability to deal with the world. He would rock back and forth, crooning, making strange flapping motions with his hands. Or he would find some control panel light, flickering on and off, and stare at it for hours.

Meanwhile, no amount of encouragement or attention seemed able to root out Michael's fundamental suspicion of them.

It disturbed Emma. She knew that when Michael looked at her, he just saw another adult in the long line who had mistreated him, subjected him to arbitrary rules, punished him endlessly. From Michael's point of view, this new environment was just another set-up, the kind hands and smiling voices just part of a new set of rules he had to learn.

Eventually, the punishment would return.

Once she tried to push him, with the help of a softscreen translator. 'Michael. What are you thinking about?'

I am nothing.

'Tell me what that means.'

It means I am not special. I am nowhere special. I am in no special time. I would not know if the whole world were suddenly made one day older, or one day younger. I would not know if the whole world were moved to the left, this much. He hopped sideways, like a frog;

256

briefly he grinned as a child. *It means that the world was born, and will die, just as I will.* He said this calmly, as if it was as obvious as the weather.

Cornelius stirred. 'This is new. It sounds like the Copernican principle. No privileged observers. Every day he surprises me.'

Emma felt baffled, distracted by Michael's software-translated voice, which sounded like a middle-aged American woman, perhaps from Seattle. 'Tell me how you know that, Michael.'

Because the sky is dark at night.

It took her some minutes of cross-examination, and cross-reference with sources she accessed through her softscreen, to figure out his meaning.

It was, she realized slowly, a version of Olbers' paradox, an old cosmological riddle. Why should the sky be dark at night? If the universe was infinite, and static, and lasted forever, then Earth would be surrounded by an array of stars, going off to infinity. And every direction Michael looked, his eye would receive a ray of light from the surface of a star. The whole sky ought to glow as bright as the surface of the sun.

Therefore, since the sky was dark – and since Michael had figured out that he wasn't in a special place in the universe, and so there *were* no special places – the universe couldn't be eternal and infinite and static; at least one of those assumptions must be wrong.

So the stars must have been born, as I was born, said Michael. *Otherwise their light would fill up the sky. People born, people fade, people die. I was born, I fade, I die. So the stars were born, the stars will fade, the stars will die. It is okay.*

Big Bang to Heat Death, just from looking at the stars.

Cornelius said, 'Maybe it comes from his belief system. His people had Christianity imposed on them, but the Lozi have kept many of their old beliefs. They believe in an afterlife, but it isn't a place of punishment or reward. *This* world, of illness and crop failure and famine and short, brutal lives, is where you suffer. In the next life you are happy. They wear tribal markings so that when they die they are placed with their relatives.'

She asked Michael if he believed there would be a happy life for the world and the stars, after they died.

Oh yes, the translating machine said. *Oh yes. But not for people. We have to make it right for others. Do you see?*

'Moses,' Malenfant growled. 'Moses and the Promised Land. Are we, humans, Moses, Michael?'

Yes, oh yes.
But she was not sure if they had understood each other.

One day, cleaning up, Emma found, behind a ventilation grille, a cache of food – just scraps, crumbs in cleaned-out bags, fragments of fruit bars, a few dehydrated packets which had been chewed on, dry, as if by a rat. She left it all exactly as she had found it.

Cornelius Taine:

In a way Michael's soul is the essence of the mathematician's.

I know what he is feeling. I remember how strange it was when I realized that if I became a mathematician I could spend my life in pursuit of a kind of mystical experience few of my fellow humans could ever share.

Mystical? Certainly. Data can serve only as a guide in the deepest intellectual endeavours. We are led more by a sense of aesthetics, as we manufacture our beautiful mathematical structures. We believe that the most elegant and simple structures are probably the ones which hold the greatest truth. That is why we seek unified theories – ideas which underpin and unite other notions – in mathematics as well as physics.

We're artists, we mathematicians, we physicists.

But more than that. There is always the hope that a mathematical construction, a product of the human imagination, nevertheless corresponds to some truth in the external world.

Perhaps you can understand this. When you learned Pythagoras's theorem, you learned something about every right-angled triangle in the world, for all time. If you understood Newton's laws, you grasped something about every particle that has ever existed. It is a sense of reach, of joy – of power.

For most of us such transcendent moments are rare. But not for Michael. The whole universe is the laboratory for his thought experiments. And given the most basic of tools to work with – even scratchings in the dirt – he attains that state of grace easily. He is in a kind of –

Ecstasy? Well, perhaps.

– Of course it may be his genius is associated with a deeper disorder.

There is a mild form of autism called Asperger's Syndrome. This is characterized by introversion and a lack of emotion; it results in an unwillingness and difficulty in communicating, a lack of awareness of and sympathy for the emotions of others. But it is also associated with a narrow focus, adherence to an obsession that takes precedence over mere social satisfaction.

Surely such a nature is essential for any intellectual success.

Emma Stoney claims that Michael's withdrawn and suspicious nature has nothing to do with any autism, but is a direct result of how he has been handled by us, the adult world. Well, perhaps.

There are six classic symptoms of Asperger's. I would claim Michael exhibits five of these.

I should know. I recognize four in myself.

June Tybee:

For June Tybee, the pace of the training was ferocious. As a tech specialist who seemed likely to go into battle, her own workload was mostly physical stuff and combat.

She was put through parachute drops. She endured the rigours of a centrifuge in a big Navy lab in Pennsylvania. She floated for hours underwater in weighted-down pressure suits fighting mock battles against experienced NASA astronauts who would come swarming at her from any which way (*think three-D! think three-D!*). The training was clearly intended to desensitize her against the experiences of the upcoming spaceflight. There would be time enough during the mission, the long flight to Cruithne, to brief them all on operations at the asteroid itself.

And, suddenly, it was shipping-over time.

In the week before she was to be flown to California, she paid a last visit to Tom's centre in Nevada. Bill was here to meet her, of course. He'd been working as an unpaid assistant at the centre since Tom had been brought here, leaving Billie with his sister back home.

They spent an unhappy, sleepless night in a motel, and then Bill drove her in to the centre.

The security operation was ferocious. But it was obviously necessary. Bill pointed out a place where the desert sand was blackened and scarred, the wire fencing obviously repaired.

June, crisp in her Air & Space Force uniform, wished she was wearing a weapon.

'I hate to think of you and Tommy in here, with this shit going on.'

Bill said tiredly, 'Junie, don't you follow the news? The whole damn world is going crazy. In here is about the safest place in the country we could be right now.'

Maybe so, June thought, as she returned the glare of the scowling grunt on the gate. As long as those goons don't turn around and start firing inward.

They found Tom in a lab room filled with science equipment. Bill said the children worked on physics here.

'Physics? How can Tom be working on physics? He's five years old.'

'June, things here are – different. Until you work with them, you wouldn't believe it.'

And now here came little Tom himself, straight and serious in his gold uniform with that ugly blue band on his breast. He was still carrying the electronic Heart she had given him. At first he walked solemnly, almost cautiously, holding onto the hand of a girl, an older kid, tall and blonde and staring.

But then Tom broke away and ran to his mother, and he was just Tommy, for a few moments more. She knelt down and grabbed his squirming warm body and buried her face in his hair, determined not to show him any tears.

She played with him for a while, and he showed her his work. Some of it was frankly beyond her, strings of symbols crossing bright plastic softscreens. But some of it was just kids' stuff, paintings of stick people and fluffy yellow clouds, clumsy models of rockets and animals made of paper and clay.

The mix of the weird wonder-kid stuff and normal, everyday childishness was unnerving. She stole glances at Bill, and saw that he understood how she was feeling.

And the whole time the older girl, Anna, stayed near Tom, always watching, always silent.

When her time was up, June knelt down again and faced her son. 'Tommy . . . You know I have to go away.'

'Into space. Dad told me.'

'I don't know how long I'll be gone.'

'Will you come back?'

A quick answer came to her lips, a mother's white lie, but she bit back on it. She glanced up at Bill's weary bafflement – into the grey, clear eyes of the girl, Anna – into the deep, unfathomable eyes of her own son.

'I don't know,' she told him. It was the truth, of course.

He nodded gravely.

When she let him go, he went to the girl, Anna. She took him by the hand and led him to a group of the others, and soon he was immersed in physics, or quantum mechanics, or whatever the hell they were doing over there. And he was animated, engaged.

More than with her, his mother.

Bill wiped tears from her cheek. 'Some space ranger you're going to make.'

'We're losing him,' she said. 'That isn't Tom any more.'

'It is Tom. It's just that he's found something more – *interesting* – than anything we can offer him.'

'I'm going to be away for months,' she said.

'I'll be here when you come back,' said Bill. 'We'll have each other. Even if that's all.'

And he held her a long time.

And then, before she knew it, she found herself assembled with fifty others parade-ground style on a slab of concrete at Vandenberg Air & Space Force Base, California.

They were on a rise here, a foothill of the Casmalia Hills in fact, and she got a fine view of the AFB facilities – blocky vehicle assembly buildings, gantries, gleaming fuel storage tanks – and the Pacific itself beyond, huge and blue and sleek like some giant animal, glimmering in the sun.

C-in-C Space Command, a four-star Air & Space Force general, took the stand before them. He glared at them with hands on hips and addressed them through a booming PA: *The USASF's proudest moment since we took command of the high frontier on the occasion of our sixtieth anniversary in 2007 . . . The finest candidates from all the services . . . a rigorous selection process . . . the first US spaceborne troops . . .*

The fifty of them were dressed in their spacesuits: bright silver with service epaulettes and name patches, white helmets under their arms, gloves neatly folded. Why the hell the suits should be silver she didn't know – she looked like a cross between John Glenn and Buck Rogers – but she had to concede they looked magnificent, shining in the California sun, and maybe that was the point. TV cameras hovered around them, beaming their smiling faces across the planet. Symbols, she thought. But that made her feel good, to be a symbol of strength and reassurance in these difficult times. She stood a little taller.

And now there was action at the launch facility itself. One of the assembly structures started to roll back.

. . . From the major conflicts of history we learn conclusive lessons. The Trojan Horse. Hannibal's crossing of the Alps. The retreat of Napoleon's infantry from Moscow. All of these underscore the strategic necessity for effective transportation of troops and their support equipment. Each new era of human progress has brought with it an urgency for an expanded military transport capability, most recently to global ranges, and now to the truly interplanetary scale . . .

A spacecraft was revealed.

It was a blunt cylinder. It was capped by a truncated, rounded nose cone, and fat auxiliary cylinders – expendable fuel tanks? – were strapped to the hull. She looked at the base, searching for rocket nozzles, but she saw only a broad dish shape, like a pie dish. The hull was coated with what looked like Space Shuttle thermal blankets and tiles, black and white, and there were big USASF decals and lettering. TV camera drones buzzed around the walls like flies.

This new vessel is over two hundred feet tall, taller than the Space Shuttle, with a base diameter of eighty feet and a gross weight of fourteen million pounds. We have thirty-six combustion chambers and eighteen turbo-pumps; the fuel system is liquid hydrogen and oxygen. The rocket engines are the most advanced available, developed by Lockheed Martin for the VentureStar. They are based on the 'aerospike' principle which, I am assured, will ensure optimal operation at all altitudes, from ground to interplanetary space . . .

The bird looked like a toy, gleaming in the sun. She couldn't see how it could be big enough to lift all of them to orbit, let alone all the way to an asteroid.

It was only when she saw a technician walking past – an orange-hatted insect – that she got a sense of the ship's true scale.

It was immense.

. . . We call her Bucephalus. *She is the outcome of a whole series of covert projects mounted since we were effectively grounded by the* Challenger *debacle. She is built on studies developed over decades, but she has been designed, tested, constructed in a couple of months.*

This is US can-do at its best, rising to this new challenge. Bucephalus *will develop a takeoff thrust of eighteen million pounds, which is two and a half times as much as the Saturn rocket that took us to the Moon, and it will be so damn loud our major problem will be preventing it shaking Vandenberg to pieces* . . .

Laughter at that. Nervous, but laughter.

Ladies and gentlemen, she is named after Alexander the Great's charger. Now she is your steed. Ride her out now into the great out there, ride her to victory beyond the sky itself! . . .

They cheered, of course. They even threw their white space helmets into the air. You had to make the four-star feel good about his project.

But June knew she wasn't the only one who gazed down on the giant fat ship – scrambled together in just months and now destined to hurl them all off the planet – with deep, stomach-churning dismay.

Reid Malenfant:

The night before they reached the asteroid, Malenfant had trouble sleeping.

Every time he turned over he would float up out of his bunk, or find his face in the breeze of the air conditioning vent. When he took off his eye shield and ear plugs the noise of the air system's mechanical rattling broke over him, and the dimmed lights of the meatware deck leaked around the curtain into his compartment.

He dozed a little, woke up alone, one more time. He decided to pop a pill. He climbed out of his bunk and made for the galley.

There was movement far overhead. It was Emma, visible through the mesh ceiling.

For a heartbeat he was shocked to find her there, as if he'd forgotten she was here on the ship. He had to think back, to remember how he'd coerced her onto the ship at the Mojave . . .

She was up on the zero G deck. She seemed to be spinning in the air, as if she was performing somersaults.

He pulled himself up the ladder and joined her. When he arrived she stopped, looking sheepish. She was wearing a loose cotton coverall.

He whispered, 'What's up?'

'Just trying to see Earth.'

He looked out the window. There were Earth and Moon, neatly framed, a blue pebble and its wizened rocky companion, still the brightest objects in the sky save for the sun itself. They were spinning, of course, wheeling like the stars behind them, four times a minute.

'You know,' she said, 'it's funny. Every time I wake up I'm surprised to find myself here. In this ship, in space. In my dreams I'm at home, I think . . .'

'Let me try.' He braced himself on the struts behind her. He took her waist. He took his guide from the Earth, the Moon turning around it like a clock hand, and soon he had her turning in synch. She stretched out her arms and legs, trying to keep herself stable. Her hair, which she was growing out, billowed behind her head like a flag, brushing his face when it passed him. When she slowed, he was able to restore her motion with a brushing stroke of her bare arm or leg. She laughed as he spun her, like a kid.

Her skin was soft, warm, smooth, full of water and life in this dusty emptiness.

Afterwards he wasn't sure how it happened, who initiated what. It did take a certain amount of ingenuity, however. The key, Malenfant discovered, was to brace himself against a strut for leverage.

Afterwards she clung to him, breathing hard, her face moist with sweat against his chest, their night clothes drifting in a tangled cloud around them.

'Welcome to the Three Dolphins Club,' he whispered.

'Huh?'

'How to have sex in free fall. If you can't brace against anything, you do it like the dolphins do. You need a third person to push.'

She snorted laughter. 'How do you *know*? . . . Never mind. This was stupid.'

'We're a long way from home, Emma. All we have out here –'

'Is each other. I know.' She stroked his chest. 'Your skin is hard, Malenfant. That time in the desert toned you up. I think I can still smell it on you. Dry heat, like a sauna. You smell like the desert, Malenfant . . . I still don't understand why you wanted me on this flight. I have a feeling you planned this whole damn thing from the beginning.'

Warm in his arms, she was waiting for an answer. He said, 'You have things I don't, Emma. Things I need.'

264

'Like what?'

'A moral centre.'

'Oh, bullshit.'

'Really.' He waved a hand. 'Remember the note left by that crazy, Art Morris, the guy who tried to shoot down the BDB. *Look what you did, Malenfant.*'

'He *was* crazy. You didn't hurt his kid.'

'I know. But I have hurt a lot of people, to get us here. For example they probably threw poor George Hench in jail. *Look what I did.* I think it's worth it, all of this. I think it's justified. But I don't *know*.' He studied her. 'I need you to tell me, Emma. To guide me.'

'You screwed somebody else. You wanted a divorce. I disagree with everything you do. I don't even understand how you feel about me.'

'Yeah. But you're *here*. And as long as that's true I know I haven't yet lost my soul.'

She pulled away from him, holding her arms; her face was a pool of shadow, her eyes invisible.

Emma Stoney:

In the last hours Cruithne swam out of the darkness like some deep-ocean fish. Malenfant despun the *O'Neill*, and all of them – even Michael – crowded around the windows and the big light-enhanced softscreen displays to see.

Emma saw a shape like a potato, a rough ellipsoid, three miles long and a mile wide, tumbling lethargically, end over end. Cruithne was not a world, neat and spherical, like the Earth; it was too small for its gravity to have pulled it into a ball. And it was *dark*: so dark she sometimes lost it against the velvet blackness of space, no more than a hole cut out of the stars.

The *O'Neill* crept closer.

Emma began to make out surface features, limned by sunlight: craters, scarps, ridges, valleys, striations where it looked as if the asteroid's surface had been crumpled or stretched. Some of the craters were evidently new, relatively anyhow, with neat bowl shapes and sharp rims. Others were much older, little more than circular scars overlaid by younger basins and worn down, perhaps by a billion years of micrometeorite rain.

And there were colours in Cruithne's folded-over landscape, spectral shades that emerged from the dominant grey-blackness. The sharper-edged craters and ridges seemed to be slightly bluish, while the older, low-lying areas were more subtly red. Perhaps this was some deep space weathering effect, she thought; aeons of sunlight had wrought these gentle hues.

Cruithne's form was a dark record of its long and violent gestation. Cruithne had been born with the Solar System itself, shaped by the mindless violence of impacts in the dark and cold, and hurled around the System by the intense gravity field of the planets. And now here it was, drifting through the crowded inner System, locked into its complex dance with Earth.

Emma's own brief life of a few decades, over in a flash, seemed trivial compared to the silent, chthonic existence of this piece of debris. But right now, in this moment of light and life, she was *here*. And she was exhilarated.

Malenfant pointed at the asteroid's pole. 'The methane plant is *there*. So that's where we're heading. We're closing at forty feet per second, three feet per second cross-range, and we're still go for the landing. Time to check out the hydrazine thrusters . . .' Though immersed in the detail of the landing procedure, he took time to glance around at his motley crew. 'Everything's under control. Remember your training.'

After endless rehearsals in the weeks out of Earth, they all knew the routine for the next few days. They would land close to the methane plant, make the *O'Neill* secure, then seek supplies to replenish their life support – principally water, nitrogen and oxygen. Then they would refill *O'Neill's* fat fuel tanks with asteroid methane, to ensure they had an escape route, a fast way off this dirty rock and home. Once that was done, they would be free to pursue the main objectives of the mission, and –

And a golden droplet erupted from the surface of Cruithne.

They stood and watched, as if stunned, in the ticking calm and fluorescent light of this zero G deck. Emma could see how the droplet's shape deformed as it rose from Cruithne's shallow gravity well, oscillating like a jellyfish, and complex waves criss-crossed its surface, gleaming in sunlight. Emma glimpsed movement inside the translucent golden surface: small, strong shapes, darting in shoals, blurred and grey.

It was quite beautiful, a soundless ballet of water and light, utterly unexpected.

And it was growing, blossoming like a flower, heading towards *O'Neill*.

There was a jolt, a groan of torn metal. Red emergency lamps started to flash, and a harsh buzzing klaxon roared rhythmically.

'Master alarm,' Malenfant shouted. He was clutching Michael against his chest. 'Everybody grab something.'

Emma looked around. The deck was spinning around her. She reached for a strut, but it was too far away.

'*Emma!*'

The open-mesh floor swept up to meet her.

'. . . Earth. Tell those fucking squid we're from Earth. God damn it, Cornelius.'

'I *told* them. I just don't think they believe us . . .'

Emma found herself lying on a mesh partition, loosely restrained by a couple of strips of bandage around her waist and legs. Michael's face was hovering over her like a moon, small and round, split by white teeth, bright eyes. He seemed to be mopping the side of her face –

'. . . *Ow.*'

– where something stung. She could smell the sharp stink of antiseptic ointment.

Am I in my office? What happened?

Here came Malenfant. Michael backed away.

. . . She remembered it all. I'm in the spacecraft, in deepest space, not where I *should* be. Reality seemed to swim around her.

Malenfant braced on a strut and peered down at her. 'You okay?'

She touched the side of her face. She felt open flesh, warm blood, a couple of elasticated bandages taped in place, slippery ointment. She lifted her head, and pain banged through her temples. 'Shit.'

She tried looking around. The lights were dim, maybe half-strength. The master alarm lamp was still flashing – its pulsing hurt her eyes – but at least the siren was switched off.

There were starbursts in her eyes, explosions of pain in her head. The colours were washed out; she felt numb, her hearing dulled. She was like a ghost, she thought, only partially here.

Malenfant reached down and removed the loose ties around her waist. She felt herself drifting up from the partition. 'You've been out for fifteen minutes. You were a hazard to shipping so we tied

267

you up. Michael has been nursing you.' He glanced at the boy. 'Good kid, when his head is in one piece.'

'Unlike mine right now. What happened, Malenfant?'

'They shot at us.'

'Who?'

'The squid. The damn squid. They rode a ball of water at us, hit the starboard solar panel. Ripped it clean off.' Which explained the dimmed power. 'Took some work with the attitude thrusters to kill the spin, bring us under control.'

She heard the subdued pride in his voice. It was Malenfant's first deep space emergency, and he'd come through it, and he was proud of himself. Even in the depths of peril there was a little boy buried in there, the boy who had always wanted to be a spaceman, under all the sublimation and rationalization of adulthood.

'So where does that leave us?'

He shrugged. 'Things got more complicated. We can't make it home on one panel and the nuke reactor. Maybe we can get more photovoltaic material from the surface, rig something up –'

'Or maybe not.'

He eyed her. 'Right now we're a long way from home, Emma. Come see the view.'

The boy, Michael, with his sharper eyes, had been the first to see, on Cruithne's surface, the drops of gold.

The habitats were snuggled into the cups of deep craters, squeezed into ridges, lying in shadows and sunlight. It was as if the asteroid's black, dusty surface had been splashed by a spray from some furnace, a spray of heavy, languid, hemispherical drops of gold. And sections of the asteroid were coated in what looked like foil, sheets extending from the droplets that clung to Cruithne's wrinkled surface, or suspended in space from great ramshackle frames.

Malenfant pointed at the Cruithne image. 'I think that must be the original *Nautilus*.' It was a bubble bigger than the rest, more irregularly shaped, nestled into a crater. The droplet's meniscus was bound together by a geodesic netting, and the whole thing was tethered to the asteroid's dusty surface by cables. There was a stack of clumpy machinery near the bubble, abandoned; perhaps that had once been the rest of the ship.

She said, 'I guess those sheets spread over the surface are solar arrays.'

Cornelius nodded. 'Manufactured from asteroid materials.'

'I don't see any connections between the bubbles.'

Malenfant shrugged, distracted. 'Maybe the squid tunnel through the asteroid. Inside the bubbles you'd be radiation-shielded by the water; that wouldn't apply on the surface ... How have they tethered those new bubbles to the regolith? I don't see the netting we used on the *Nautilus*.'

'They don't have any metals,' said Cornelius. 'Because we didn't show them how to extract metals. Only organic products, including plastics. I guess they just found a way to tether without metal cables and pitons.'

They watched the asteroid turn, slowly, a barbecue potato on an invisible spit, bringing more of the bubble habitats into view.

She said, 'There are so *many*.'

'Yes.' Cornelius sounded awed. 'To have covered so much of the asteroid in a few months ... and we don't know how far they've spread through the interior. They must be spreading exponentially.'

'Breeding,' said Malenfant.

'Obviously,' Cornelius snapped impatiently. 'But the point is they must be keeping most of each spawned batch alive. Remember what Dan Ystebo told us about the first generation: the four smart cephalopods among the dozens of dumb ones ...'

'So,' Emma said, 'if most of the squid now are being kept alive –'

'They must be mostly smart.' Cornelius looked frightened.

'No wonder they need to keep building new habitats,' Malenfant said.

'But it isn't enough,' said Cornelius. 'Pretty soon they're going to run out of asteroid.'

'Then what?'

'They are stranded on this rock in the sky. I guess they'll turn on each other. There will be wars.'

'How long?' Malenfant said. 'How long have we got before they eat up the asteroid?'

Cornelius shrugged. 'Months at most.'

Malenfant grunted. 'Then the hell with it. We can stay here for twenty days. If we haven't got what we wanted and got out of here by then, we're going to be dead anyhow.'

In a softscreen, Emma saw, something swam.

It was small, sleek, compact. It slid easily back and forth, its arms stretched before it, its carapace pulsing with languid colours. It had a cruel grace that frightened Emma. Its hide shimmered with patterns, complex, obviously information-packed.

'You're talking to them,' Emma said to Cornelius.

'We're trying.'

Malenfant growled, 'We're going way beyond the squid sign-language translator software Dan gave us. We need Dan himself. But he's two hundred light-seconds away. And nobody is talking to us anyhow.'

Cornelius looked harassed. 'Some of them think we're from Earth. Some don't think Earth even exists. Some think we're here to trick them somehow.'

'You think the squid tried to kill us?'

'No,' Malenfant snapped. 'If they're smart enough to see us coming, to fire water bombs at us, they are smart enough to have destroyed us if they wanted to. They intended to disable us.'

'And they succeeded. But why?'

'Because they want something from us.' Malenfant grinned. 'Why else? And that's our angle. If we have something they want, we can trade.'

Cornelius snapped, 'I can't believe you're seriously suggesting we negotiate.'

Malenfant, drifting in the air, spread his hands. 'We're trying to save our mission. We're trying to save our *lives*. What can we do but talk?'

Emma said, 'Have you figured out what it is they want?'

'That,' said Cornelius, 'is the bad news.'

'Earth,' said Reid Malenfant.

'They know Earth, if it exists, is huge. Giant oceans, lots of room to breed. They want to be shown the way there. They want at least some of them to be released there, to breed, to build.'

Cornelius said tightly, 'We ought to scrape those slugs off the face of this rock. They're in our way.'

'They aren't slugs,' Emma said evenly. 'We put them here. And besides, we didn't come here to fight a war.'

'We can't give them Earth. They breed like an explosion. They already chewed their way through this asteroid, starting from nothing. They'd fill the world's oceans in a decade. And they are *smart*, and getting smarter.'

Malenfant rubbed his eyes, looking tired. 'We may not be able to stop them for long anyhow. Their eyes are better than ours, remember; it won't be hard for them to develop astronomy. And they saw us coming; whatever we tell them, maybe they can track back and figure out where we came from.' He looked at Emma. 'What a mess. I'm starting to think we should have stuck to robots.' He was kneading his temple, evidently thinking hard.

Emma had to smile. Here they were, in a disabled ship, approaching an asteroid occupied by a hostile force – and Reid Malenfant was still looking for the angle.

Malenfant snapped his fingers. 'Okay. We stall them. Cornelius, I take it these guys aren't going anywhere without metalworking technology. They already know how to make rocket fuel. With metal they can achieve electronics, computers maybe. Spaceflight.'

'So –'

'So we trade them metal extraction technology. Trade them that for an unhindered landing and surface operations.'

Cornelius shook his head, the muscles of his neck standing out. 'Malenfant, if you give them metal you set them loose.'

'We deal with that later. If you have a better alternative let's hear it.'

The moment stretched.

Then Cornelius turned to his softscreen. 'I'll see what form of words I can come up with.'

Emma caught Malenfant's arm. 'Do you know what you're doing?'

He grinned. 'When did I ever? But we're still in business, aren't we?'

Whistling, he pulled himself down the fireman's pole to the meatware deck.

Mary Alpher:

> Thank you for visiting my home page.
> I want to use this space to record my dissent at the national gung-ho mood right now. I am dismayed at the sending of troops to the near-Earth asteroid Cruithne.
> I've been writing and editing science fiction most of my working life, and reading the stuff a lot longer than that. And this is *not* turning out to be the future I dreamed about.
> I wouldn't call myself a Utopian. Nevertheless I always

imagined, I think, on some level, that the future was going to be a better place than the present.

> In particular, space. I thought we might leave our guns and hatred and destructiveness down in the murky depths of Earth, where they belong. Neil Armstrong was a civilian when he landed on the Moon. *We came in peace for all mankind.* Remember that?

> I believed it. I believed – still believe – that we are, if not perfectible, at least improvable as a species. And that basic world view, I think, informs much sf.

> Maybe all that was naïve. Nevertheless I never dreamed that only our second expedition beyond the Earth-Moon system should be a gunboat.

> Of course it's not going to work. Anybody who thinks they can divert the course of the river of time with a few gunshots is much more naive than I ever was.

> Thanks for your attention. Purchasing details and a sample chapter of my latest novel, *Black Hole Love*, are available <here> . . .

Emma Stoney:

'. . . That was the thruster burn to null out our approach and cross-range velocities. Now we're free-falling in on gyro lock. GRS is active and feeding to the computer, the radar altimeter is online and slaved to the guidance. Confirmed green board. All that jargon means things are good, people. Should hit the ground at walking speed, no need to worry at all . . .'

To the accompaniment of Malenfant's competent, comforting commentary, with the grudging permission of the squid factions, *O'Neill* was on its final approach.

Cruithne rock slid past the windows of the zero G deck.

They were so close now Emma could see the texture of the surface: shaped by bombardment, crater upon crater, plains cracked open and reassembled, all of it coated with glistening black dust, like a burned-out bombing range. And now when the attitude thrusters pulsed they raised up dust from the surface, dust that drifted off into space or fell back in silent, slow fans.

We are already touching Cruithne, she thought. Disturbing it.

She had no sense of coming in for a landing. The gravitational pull of the asteroid was much too weak for that. The asteroid wasn't *down* but straight ahead of her, a curving wall, pockmarked, wrinkled. It was more like a docking, as if she was riding a small boat towards some immense, dusty, ocean-going liner.

Michael was staring at the asteroid, eyes wide, mouth hanging open. On impulse Emma took his hand and held it tightly.

Cornelius said, 'There go the penetrators.'

Emma saw the penetrators snake out from *O'Neill's* hull. They were miniature spacecraft shaped like golf tees, three or four feet long, trailing steel hawsers. Each had an armoured exterior and a body packed solid with sensors – computers, heating devices, thermometers, seismometers, comms equipment to transmit data along the hawsers to the *O'Neill*. She could see the pulse of the tiny rockets in the penetrators' tails, a spray of exhaust crystals that receded from the asteroid in perfectly straight lines, shining in the sun.

The penetrators hit the asteroid surface at six hundred miles an hour, as hard as an anti-tank round, and disappeared in puffs of black regolith. Soon there were smoke rings, neatly circular, rising from the crater floor, with slack hawsers trailing back to the spacecraft. The penetrators, after suffering a deceleration of maybe ten thousand gee, had come to rest six feet under Cruithne's surface.

Designing a probe that could return precise science data, and yet survive being driven at speed into a rock wall, was quite a feat, a project on which Bootstrap had spent a lot of money. But right now science lay in the future. The penetrators' main purpose was fixing the *O'Neill* to Cruithne's surface, mooring the ship like a smack to a yacht.

Now Emma heard a whirr of winches. Languid vibrations snaked along the cables, and she could see the surface inch closer. One penetrator came loose in a puff of dust; its cable went slack and coiled away, out of sight.

There was the softest of shudders, a brief blur of dust.

Then there was only silence and stillness – and a piece of Cruithne framed in the window.

Malenfant came clambering up the fireman's pole, his face split by a grin. 'The *O'Neill* has landed.' He hugged her; she could see Michael was grinning, responding to Malenfant's vigour and happiness.

'Now,' said Malenfant. 'Now we go to work.'

The chains of fireflies, as they hauled giant loads of regolith like so many metallic dung beetles, were comical and inspiring.

Emma was amazed how quickly the fireflies were able to work in the peculiar environment of Cruithne. Autonomously controlled, with surprising grace and skill, they levered their way across the surface with their tethers and pitons and claws. And the low gravity allowed them to shift large masses with ease.

It was just hours before Emma was able to crawl through a tight fabric tunnel from the *O'Neill* and into the new dome.

She stood up and looked around. She was standing on plastic sheeting which merged seamlessly with the walls. The whole thing was just a fabric bubble thirty feet wide at the base, like an all-in-one plastic tent. The roof above her, ten feet up at its tallest, was a pale translucent yellow, supported by air pressure. The fireflies had thrown a cable net over the roof, and then shovelled regolith over that, to a depth of three feet, for radiation shielding. Equipment, transferred from *O'Neill*, was piled up in the centre of the dome.

The lighting, from yellow tritium bulbs, was utilitarian and harsh. There was a smell of burning, like autumn ash: that was asteroid dust, she knew, leaked into their hab environment despite all their precautions, thin fine stuff that was slowly oxidizing, burning in the air.

She knelt down. Regolith was visible through the floor, blurred lumps of coal-black rock. The crater floor had been scraped smooth by the fireflies before the dome was erected; she could see grooves and ridges where ancient ground had been raked like a flower bed in a suburban garden. She pushed a finger into the sheeting. It was very tough stuff, tougher than it looked; she was only able to make a dent of an inch or so. And as she pushed she felt herself lifting off the floor in reaction; Cruithne's feeble gravity stuck her only gently to the ground.

Michael had crawled after her. He seemed relieved to be out of the ship. He started running around the perimeter of the dome – or rather he tried to run; with every step he went sailing into the air, bounced off the curving roof, and came floating back down again for another pace. After a few paces he started getting the hang of it, and he picked up speed, pacing and pushing against the ceiling confidently.

The shelter was crude. But Emma felt her spirits lift. After ninety days it was a profound relief not to be confined to the cramped metal cans of the *O'Neill*, for a while at least.

It also didn't smell as bad as the *O'Neill*.

That night they had a party in the hab dome, raiding their precious store of candy bars and washing them down with Cruithne water.

The next day the four of them prepared to explore Cruithne.

Huddled together, they stripped naked – after ninety days, all shyness was gone, though Emma did feel unaccountably cold – and, clumsy in the low gravity, they began to help each other don their skinsuits.

Malenfant kept up a running stream of instructions. 'Make sure you get it smoothed out. If the pressure isn't distributed right you'll have blood pooling . . .'

Emma's skinsuit was just a light Spandex coverall, like a cyclist's gear. The material was surprisingly open mesh; if she held up her hand and stretched out her fingers she actually could see her flesh through fine holes in the weave. The Spandex, a pale orange that turned blue around any rips, was used to avoid the outgassing and brittleness suffered by rubber in a vacuum. The suit had a hood and gloves and booties, and the pieces fit together with plastic zippers at her neck, wrists and up her belly to her neck. The only thing she wore inside the suit was a catheter that would lead to a urine collection bag.

The light, comfortable skinsuits had replaced the old pressure garments – giant, stiff, body-shaped inflatable balloons – worn by earlier generations of space travellers. But it was important to have the skinsuit fit properly; the pressurization had to be equal all over her skin.

But this was actually old technology. Burns victims had long needed elasticated dressings which would apply a steady pressure over an extended area of the skin, so that scarring occurred in a way beneficent to the patient. It didn't surprise her to learn that an offshoot of Bootstrap had bought up a medical supply company from Toledo which had specialized in such stuff for decades, and was now making a profit by selling better burns dressings back to the hospitals.

Over the top of the skinsuit came more layers, loose-fitting and light. First there was a thermal protection garment, a lacing of water-bearing tubes running over her flesh to keep her temperature even, and then a loose outer coverall, a micrometeorite protection garment. This actually had her name stitched on the breast, NASA-style: STONEY. She put on her bubble helmet with its gold sun-visor, and her backpack, a neat little battery-powered rucksack with pumps and fans that could cycle the air and water around her suit for as long as twelve hours.

Now I actually look like an astronaut, she thought.

Malenfant made each of them, in turn, sit in their suits and go to vacuum in the hab's small collapsible airlock. He called it the suits' final acceptance test.

Then, the last checks complete, it was time to leave.

They squeezed into the airlock. Emma could feel oxygen blowing across her face, hear the warm hums and whirrs of her backpack.

Michael, beside her in the airlock, clutched her hand. But he showed no fear. He had seemed calm and controlled, in fact, since they had arrived at Cruithne. It was as if, now they had arrived, he knew why they were here, what they would find.

As if he was meant to be here.

Malenfant unzipped the airlock's fabric door, rolled it down, and stepped forward.

Emma glimpsed frozen air sailing away into the vacuum, particles of it glinting in the sunlight, as if this handful of molecules was trying to expand to fill all of infinite space. The last noises disappeared, save for her own breathing, loud in her bubble helmet, and the sounds that carried through her suit: the rustle of fabric, the slither of the skinsuit against her flesh when she moved.

Still gripping Michael's hand, Emma pushed her head out the hatch. The sun's light flooded over her, astoundingly bright after months in the dingy interior of the *O'Neill*. She took a step out of the airlock, and, gentle as a snowflake, settled to the dirt of Cruithne.

Where her blue-booted feet hit the regolith, with dreamy slowness, she kicked up a little coal-black asteroid dirt. It sailed into the air – no, just *upward* – for a few feet, before settling back, following perfect parabolas.

The four of them, huddled together in their glowing white suits, were the brightest objects in the landscape, like snowmen on a pile of coal. But already the clinging black dust of the asteroid had coated their lower legs and thighs.

The ground was coal-black, layered with dust, and very uneven, extensively folded. She could see maybe a hundred yards in any direction before the ground fell away, but the horizon was close and crumpled, as if she was standing on a hill-top. The hab dome was a drab mound of regolith over orange fabric, and it was surrounded

276

by ground that was scarred by firefly tracks. Beyond it she could see a cluster of equipment: the bulky form of the tethered *O'Neill*, and the coiling lines leading to Malenfant's illegal nuclear power plant, now installed somewhere over the horizon of Cruithne.

And the shadows were already shifting under her feet, lengthening as she watched.

When she raised her head and looked into the sky, the sun was almost over her head, its glare steady and fierce, so that she cast only a short shadow. Off to her left she saw a point of light: blue, bright, it was the Earth. But the Moon was invisible, as were the stars, washed out of her vision by the intense brightness of the sun.

Beyond sun and Earth there was *nothing*: above, behind, beyond her, like the depths of the deepest, darkest ocean, but spreading around her in all three dimensions. The sense of scale, of openness, after the enclosure of the ship and the hab dome, was stunning. Watching the sliding shadows, she understood on some gut level that she was indeed clinging to the outside of a rock that was tumbling in space. She swallowed hard; she absolutely did not want to throw up in a spacesuit.

A firefly robot came tumbling past, ignoring them, on some errand of its own. It was a hatbox covered with gleaming solar panels, and with miniature manipulator arms extending before it. It worked its way over the surface with a series of tethers that it fired out before itself, then winched in after it, never less loosely anchored than by two tethers at a time, and little puffs of exhaust vapour escaped from tiny kid's-toy rocket nozzles at the rear. The firefly's case was heavily stained with regolith; there were cute little wiper blades on each of the solar cell panels. The robot moved jerkily, knocked and dragged this way and that by its tethers and tiny rockets, but in the silence and harsh sunlight it was oddly graceful, its purposefulness undeniable.

The firefly disappeared over the close horizon. Emma wondered if it was from the *O'Neill* or the *Nautilus*. Ours or theirs.

She knew, in fact, that the way the firefly had gone was where the blue artefact stood in its excavated pit. A door to the future, a quarter-mile away.

The thought meant nothing. She was immersed, already, in too much strangeness.

And today, there was work to do. She turned back to the others.

e-CNN:

. . . to recap, you are seeing pictures received live from Cruithne, broadcast from the asteroid just minutes ago. As you can see the image is a little nondescript right now, but our experts are telling us that we are seeing a stretch of Cruithne surface known as 'regolith', with the black starry sky in the background, or rather there would be stars but for overloading by the sunlight.

The slave firefly robot seems to be panning right now, under *your* command, and we're trying to make out what we're seeing. It is a little like looking for a black cat in a mine shaft, hah hah.

Just to remind you that *you* can take part in the live online exploration of Cruithne with the Bootstrap bandit astronauts. Just select your preference from the menu at the bottom of the picture and your vote will be polled, with all the others, once a second, and the recommendation passed straight to our camera firefly on Cruithne via our e-controller. *You* control the picture; *you* are on Cruithne right along with the astronauts; *you* can be a Bootstrap bandit, alongside the infamous Reid Malenfant.

Right now the image seems a little static; perhaps you folks are arguing amongst yourselves, hah hah.

There! Did you see that? Bob, can we rerun that – we can't. Well, it looked to me like an astronaut, and it looked to me like he, or she, was waving at us. Maybe it was Reid Malenfant himself. If you folks out there want to start voting to pan back maybe we can get a good look . . .

Maura Della:

This was the Great Basin of Nevada.

Stretches of empty highway roller-coasted over mountain ranges and down into salt flats. The human hold on this land seemed tenuous: she drove past ghost towns, federal prisons, brothels surrounded by barbed wire. The corroded mountainsides were dominated by abandoned gold mines, and the land in between was sagebrush open range. Dust devils danced across the flats, eerie.

Eerie, yes. And, she thought, a kind of sinkhole for American national craziness too. To the south was the infamous Area 51, still a centre of mystery and speculation. To the north-west, in the Black Rock desert, hippies and ageing punks and other fringe meatware had gathered for decades for their Burning Man Festival, an annual orgy of gunplay, punk rock and off-road driving.

Somehow it seemed an entirely appropriate place to site America's largest education and protection centre for the Blues, the strange smart alien children who had sprouted in the midst of humanity.

And Maura Della was on her way to visit little Tom Tybee there.

She stopped for gas in a place called Heston. The guy who came out to serve her was about sixty; he had a beard like Santa Claus, and a red baseball cap with the logo of a helicopter firm. The big plate glass of the gas station window was shattered; there were brutal-looking shards scattered over the forecourt. Santa Claus saw her looking at the glass. She didn't want to ask him how it got there, but he told her anyhow. 'Sonic boom,' he said.

The thing of it was, the conspiracy theorists here had a point. If there was anywhere in the US that was manipulated by remote and mysterious agencies it was Nevada, where ninety per cent of the land was managed by the federal government, a remote and imperial power to the ranchers and miners who lived here. Nevada was America's wasteland, the dumping ground for the rest of the country.

She paid, and got out of there.

At the centre she was met by the principal, Andrea Reeve.

Reeve walked her around the centre. It looked like, well, a grade school: flat-roofed buildings with big bright windows, a yard with climbing frames and play areas and big plastic outdoor toys, a shiny yellow fireman robot patrolling the outer walls. But most schools weren't surrounded by an electrified fence.

Inside, the centre was bright, modern, airy. The rooms weren't set out like the formal classrooms Maura remembered, with rows of desks, a teacher and a blackboard at the front. The furniture was mixed and informal, much of it soft. The walls were covered by e-paintings that cycled every couple of minutes, and other aids like number tables and giant animated alphabet letters, as well as drawings and other pieces of work by the children.

Everything was *low*, Maura noticed. Here was a coat rack no more than four feet from the ground, a canteen where the tables and chairs looked like they were made for dolls. The walls were mostly bare beyond the height a small child could reach.

Reeve saw her looking. 'Most of our children are young,' she said. 'Very few are over nine. It's only a few years ago that the Blue phenomenon became apparent, less time since the systematic searches for the children began. We've brought them here from all over the continental US, and some from overseas. Generally rescue cases, in fact.'

Reeve looked like schoolteachers always had, thought Maura: comfortably round, a little dowdy, hair streaked with grey. Maura found herself responding instinctively, trusting the woman. But, confusingly, this motherly woman was actually about two decades *younger* than Maura herself. Maybe parents feel like this all the time, she thought.

But Reeve looked overtired, a little baffled, evidently disturbed by Maura's presence here.

They both knew Maura had no formal influence here. The truth was she wasn't even sure where she stood, now, on the issue of the children. On the one hand she clung to her promise to oversee Tom Tybee; on the other she was a member of a government responsible for protecting the wider public from danger. Was it possible those two motivations conflicted?

She only knew one way to figure it out, and that was to come see for herself.

And now here were the children themselves. They were scattered through the rooms, working individually or in little groups. The children stood, sat or lay on the floor without self-consciousness. Many of the children wore cordless ear pieces and worked at bright plastic softscreens. There were teachers, but mostly the children seemed to be working with teaching robots, cute, unthreatening little gadgets covered in orange fur or shiny velvet.

'We refer to these rooms as laboratories,' said Reeve. 'The children have differing individual needs, levels of achievement and learning paces. So we use the robots, individually programmed and heuristically adaptable.

'A lot of the work we do is remedial, you might be surprised to know. Some of the children don't even have much speech, and even from here in the US they are often sub-literate. They have tended to be taken out of school, or thrown out, as soon as their special abilities are recognized.' She eyed Maura. 'You do need to understand the difficulties we face. Many of these children display some of the symptoms associated with autism. There is a mild form known as Asperger's Syndrome, or eccentric boffin syndrome. Such a child may be highly intelligent, and driven by an obsession that pushes her to extraordinary achievements. But at the same time she may be extremely clumsy and uncoordinated. Also socially clumsy. You see, we have to protect them from themselves.' She sighed. 'In some cases the disorder may be more severe. Some of the children seem to have only a peripheral response to pleasure and pain. That makes it difficult to control them –'

'Because they don't respond to punishment?'

'Or to hugs,' Reeve said severely. 'We aren't monsters, Representative.'

'I don't see how you can dissociate evidence of a disorder like that from, umm, the bruises left by the handling some of these kids have received.'

'No. And we don't try. You must believe, Ms Della, that we do our best for the children here, as intellectuals, and as children.'

'And once they are past the remedial stage –'

'Once past that, they are very soon beyond *us*,' Reeve sighed. 'All we can do is monitor them, try to ensure their physical needs are met, and give them some elements of a rounded education. And we try to develop social skills.' Reeve eyed Maura. 'Often we have to all but drag them to the games, to the yard, and *teach* them how to play. A child is a child, no matter how gifted.'

'I'm sure you're right.'

'But it isn't made easier by the *experts* who come here,' said Reeve severely. 'Of course we understand, it's part of our charter, that the more advanced children are essentially performing original research, with results that might benefit the broader academic community. And we have to make their results accessible. But to have teams of academics trampling through here, quizzing the children and disrupting their general education, all for the sake of seeking out some new nugget of knowledge that can be written up and published under *their* names –'

Maura half-tuned her out. This was obviously Reeve's particular grievance, her hobbyhorse. What was Reeve really concerned about – the fate of the children here, in this rather sinister place, or the fact that the jackdaw academics clearly didn't credit *her* in their papers and theses?

Each child wore a pale gold coverall, zipped up the front, with a blue circle stitched to the breast.

'Why the uniforms?'

'Everyone asks that. We call them play suits. We had to come up with something, when the blue-circle identifiers became federal law. They're actually very practical. They are made of smart fabric that can keep warm in winter, cool in summer . . . Actually the children seem to find the blue circle logo comforting. We don't know why. Besides, it does help us identify the children if any of them escape.'

Nevada. Barbed wire. Uniforms. *Escape*. This was a school, perhaps, but with a powerful subtext of a cage.

Reeve led her into another laboratory. There was equipment of some kind scattered around the room on lab benches. Some of it was white-box instrumentation, anonymous science lab stuff, unidentifiable to Maura. But there were also some pieces of apparatus more familiar from her own school days, Bunsen burners and big chunky electromagnets and what looked like a Van de Graaff generator.

There were five children here, gathered in a circle, sitting cross-legged on the ground. One of them was Tom Tybee. The children didn't have any tools with them, no softscreens or writing paper. They were simply talking, but so fast Maura could barely make out a word. One of the children was a girl, taller than the rest, her blonde hair plaited neatly on her head. But it wasn't clear that she was in any way leading the discussion.

'We call this our physics lab,' said Reeve softly. 'But much of what the children seem to be exploring is multi-disciplinary, in our terms. And if you can't follow what they're saying, don't worry. If they don't know a word, they will often make up their own. Sometimes we can translate back to English. Sometimes we find there *is* no English word for the referent.'

'Clever kids.'

'Little smart-asses,' said Reeve with a vehemence that startled Maura. 'Of course most of what they do is theoretical. We can't give them very advanced equipment here.'

'If it's a question of budget –'

'Representative Della, they are still children. And you can't put a child, however smart, in charge of a particle accelerator.'

'. . . I suppose not.'

Watching the children talking and working, quietly, purposefully,

Maura felt a frisson of fear, the superstitious, destructive awe she so reviled in others.

The question was, what were they working *towards*? What was their goal, why were they here, how did they know what to do? The questions were unanswerable, deeply disturbing – and that was without being a parent, without having to ask herself the most profound questions of all: *Why my child? Why has she been taken away?*

Perhaps, she thought uneasily, we will all soon find out. And then what?

'. . . Hello, Ms Della.'

Maura looked down. It was Tom Tybee. He was standing before her, straight and solemn in his golden suit. He was clutching an orange football shape.

Maura forced a smile, and bent down to Tom's level. 'Hello, Tom.'

The taller blonde girl had come to stand beside him. She was holding Tom's hand, and was watching Maura with dark, suspicious eyes.

'Look.' Tom held out his toy to her. It was his Heart: an emotion container, a sound-vision recording device which enabled the user to record his favourite experiences. Maura wondered what he found to record here.

'My mom gave it to me.'

'Well, I think it's terrific.'

Reeve said, 'Representative Della, meet Anna. Our oldest student.'

The girl stared at Maura – not hostile, just reserved, wary.

'Can I go?' Tom asked.

Maura felt unaccountably baffled, excluded. 'Yes, Tom. It was nice to see you.'

Tom, his hand still in Anna's, returned to the group and sat down, and the rich flow of their conversation resumed. Anna joined in, but Maura noticed that she kept her grey eyes on herself and Reeve.

'You see?' Reeve said tiredly.

'See what?'

'How they make you *feel*.' Reeve smiled, and pushed grey hair out of her eyes. 'Hello, goodbye. I know they can't help it. But they simply aren't interested in us. It's impossible to feel warmth for them. People, the staff, tend not to stay long.'

'How do you vet your staff?'

'We use parents and relatives where we can. Tom Tybee's father has done some work here, for instance . . . I'll take you through the recruitment procedures.'

'Where is Anna from?'

'The North Territory School.'

'Australia.' The worst in the world, a virtual concentration camp. No wonder she is so wary, Maura thought.

Well, this wasn't a summer camp either, she reminded herself. It was a prison.

But the real bars around these children were intangible, formed by the fear and ignorance and superstition of the society which had given them birth. Until that got better, until some kind of public education worked its way into the mass consciousness to displace the hysterical fear and hostility that surrounded these children, maybe this fortress was the best anybody could do. But she promised to herself that she would watch this place, and the others around the country, and ensure that here at least that things did not get worse for Tom Tybee, and Anna, and the other children here, the Blues.

Some childhood, she thought.

She let Reeve take her to her office, and they began to go through staff profiles.

Reid Malenfant:

Malenfant stood tethered to the surface of Cruithne, waiting.

He was aware how grimy he had become. After a couple of weeks on the asteroid, everything – his suit, the fireflies and habitats, every piece of equipment – had turned to the dismal grey-black colour of Cruithne, coated with coal-dark electrostatically-clinging regolith dust.

A fabric canopy towered over him. Erected by the squid with their waldoes and fireflies, it was rigid, improbably skinny, a tent that could surely never remain upright on Earth; yet here, in Cruithne's vacuum and miniature gravity it could last years, unperturbed, until the fabric itself crumbled under the relentless onslaught of solar radiation.

An automated countdown was proceeding in his headrest. Impatient, he snapped a switch to kill the robot's soft Midwestern female voice. What difference did it make, to know the precise second? This operation wasn't under his control anyhow. This was all cephalopod now, and Malenfant was just an observer. And he was dog tired.

Meanwhile Cruithne turned, as it had for a billion years. Sun and stars wheeled alternately over him. When the raw sunlight hit him he could feel its strength, and the fans and pumps of his backpack whirred, the water in his cooling garment bubbling, as his suit laboured under the fierce hail of photons to keep him cool and alive.

It was, without question, a hell of a place to be.

This operation was the fulfilment of Malenfant's bargain with the squid.

The mining operation here was an order of magnitude more ambitious than the simple regolith-scraping Sheena 5 had initiated when she first landed. The tent-like canopy had been set up over a suitable impact crater – which Emma had named, with her gentle humour, Kimberley. The canopy was just a low-tech way to contain ore thrown out by the robot dust kicker now burrowing its way into Cruithne. When the canopy contained enough ore it would be sealed up and moved to the processing site.

There, mechanical grinders would chew steadily at the ore within a rotating cylinder. The spin would force the grains of crushed ore through a series of sorting screens, and the sorted material dropped onto rotating magnetic drums. The idea was to separate non-magnetic silicate grains from nickel-iron metal granules; every so often the metallic material would be scraped off the drums and recycled through the sorter, until only highly pure metal was left.

It was possible to cast raw asteroid metal directly, but the native metals were heavily polluted with carbon and sulphur and the result would be an inferior product. So the ore would be passed through a solar toaster, as Malenfant thought of it, an inflatable solar collector working at a couple of hundred degrees Centigrade. The toaster was the key to a process called gaseous carbonyl extraction, which allowed the extraction of ultra-pure metals – and, as a bonus, the direct fabrication of ultra-pure iron and nickel products in high-precision moulds via chemical vapour deposition.

The objective of these first tentative steps was just to give the squid access to the most easily extracted metals: nickel and iron in the form of metallic alloy. In fact, locked up in Cruithne there were also troilite, olivine, pyroxene and feldspar, minerals which could also serve as sources of ferrous metals when the nickel-iron was exhausted, even if their extraction was a little more complex.

Besides that, the ore also contained other valuable metals like cobalt and the platinum-group metals, as well as non-metals like sulphur, arsenic, selenium, germanium, phosphorus, carbon . . .

Cornelius Taine had been dead set against pointing the squid towards more advanced processing techniques. In fact, Cornelius had been all for reneging on Malenfant's contract with the squid altogether. Malenfant had insisted on keeping his promise, but had given in to Cornelius on the advanced processing.

Not that it made much difference, he figured; the squid were smart and would surely not take long to figure out how to extract the full potential of these ancient rocks, whether humans showed them what to do or not.

Cornelius was right to have reservations, however. The squid, if they did get out of the resource bottleneck of Cruithne, would be formidable rivals. But they would surely make bad enemies. Maybe it wasn't a good idea to start the relationship of the two species with a grudge.

All three of the adults had spent time out on the surface modifying firefly and miner robots, surveying the asteroid for a suitable crater to serve as a pit head, and operating test and pilot runs of the various processes involved. Cruithne had turned out to be a congenial environment to work in. The gravity here was better than zero G because tools, dust and people tended to stay where you last put them rather than float away. But on the other hand structures did not have to be as strong as under Earth's ferocious pull.

But the work hadn't been easy. Though the skinsuits were a marvellous piece of lightweight engineering, a couple of hours of even the lightest physical work – shovelling crumbling regolith into the hoppers of the test plants, for example – left Malenfant drenched in sweat and with sores chafing at his elbows, knees, armpits, groin. Cornelius had actually suffered worse; a pressure imbalance caused by a rucking of his suit had given him a severe embolism on one leg, an incident which hadn't help improve his mood.

Anyhow it was over now. Malenfant was proud of what they had achieved here. The technological infrastructure they had built here was neat, elegant, simple, low-maintenance.

. . . Earth came into view, a bright blue disclet shadowed by the pallid Moon.

It struck him that it had been the dream of his whole life to come to a place like this: to stand here on the surface of another world, to watch heavy machinery tear into its rock and begin the construction of a living space, to watch the beginnings of the expansion of Earth life beyond the planet, fulfilling the dreams of Tsiolkovski and Goddard and Bernal and O'Neill and so many others.

Well, he'd got himself here, and he ought to be grateful for that. Not only that, his basic plan – using asteroid materials to bootstrap extraterrestrial colonization – was obviously working.

But he hadn't expected it to be like *this* – in the hands of another species.

In a way, a part of him wished it wasn't so: that this had been a simple story of asteroid mines and O'Neill colonies and homesteads in space, that the extraordinary future hadn't intruded. Simple dreams, easily fulfilled. But that had never been an option.

The future, it seemed, was turning out to be one damn thing after another.

He turned away from the canopy, and began to make his way back to the *O'Neill*.

When the squid made their next surprising request Malenfant and the others held a council of war on the *O'Neill*'s meatware deck.

Cornelius Taine, as ever, was hostile to any form of rapprochement with the squid beyond what was absolutely necessary to maintain their base on this asteroid. 'So they want to leave. Good riddance. They shouldn't be here anyhow. They weren't in the plan.'

Emma said severely, 'You mean they should be dead.'

'I mean they shouldn't exist at all. The plan was for one squid to live long enough to bootstrap the operation here, that's all, not this whole new enhanced species we have to contend with. Dan Ystebo should be prosecuted for his irresponsibility –'

'You aren't helping, Cornelius,' said Malenfant.

'Let them split off their chunk of rock and go. We don't need them.'

'The point is, they are asking us *where* they should go. Another NEO, the asteroid belt.'

Cornelius's face worked. 'That ought to remain . . . secure.'

Emma laughed. '*Secure?* Secure against what?'

Cornelius was growing angry. 'We could be remembered as the ultimate suckers. Like the native Americans who sold Manhattan for a handful of beads.'

'The asteroid belt is not Manhattan,' Malenfant said.

'No. It's much more. Vastly more . . .' Cornelius started to list the resources of the Solar System: water, metals, phosphates, carbon, nitrogen, sulphur, rattling through the asteroids and the ice moons of Jupiter and the atmospheres of the giant planets and the Oort Cloud. '. . . Take water. Water is the most fundamental commodity. We think the main-belt asteroids could contribute about half the water available on Earth. And a single ice moon, say Jupiter's Callisto, has around *forty times* as much water as Earth's oceans. Even if you exclude the Oort Cloud the Solar System probably contains something like *three hundred times* Earth's water – and almost all of it locked up in small, low-gravity, accessible bodies.

'The Solar System may be able to sustain – comfortably, conservatively – as many as a *million* times the population of the Earth.' He watched their faces. 'Think about that. A million human beings, for every man, woman and child alive now.'

Emma laughed nervously. 'That's . . . monstrous.'

'Because you can't picture it. Imagine how it would be if the human race reached such numbers. How often does an authentic genius come along, an Einstein, a Beethoven, a Jesus? Once a millennium? We could cut that down to one a *day*.'

'Imagine a million people like me,' growled Malenfant. 'We could have one hell of an argument.'

'Those cephalopods are ferocious predators, and they breed damn fast. If they start propagating through the Solar System they could take it all in a few centuries. And rob us of the future, the human conquest of the universe. The future we *saw*.'

'If the cephalopods are better adapted,' Malenfant said easily, 'and maybe they are, that's why we chose the squid solution in the first place, then maybe that's the way it's supposed to be.'

'No,' Cornelius said, muscles in his cheek working. 'This isn't simple Darwinism. *We created them*.'

'Maybe that will turn out to be our cosmic role,' Emma said dryly. 'Midwives to the master race.'

Malenfant growled, 'Look, let's keep Darwin and God out of it. Cornelius, face the facts. We don't have a real good handle on what the squid are going to do here. They seem to be split into a number of factions. But some of them at least seem to be determined on carving off a chunk of this rock and going *someplace*. Population pressure is ensuring that. If we deceive them – if we try to send them off to freeze in the dark – and they *survive*, they aren't going to be too pleased about it. And if we don't give them any clear guidance –'

Emma nodded. 'Then they'll seek out the one place they know has the water they need.'

Cornelius said, 'We can't let them find Earth.'

'Then,' pressed Malenfant, 'where?'

Cornelius shook his head, pressured, frustrated. 'All right, damn it. Send them to the Trojan asteroids.'

Malenfant looked at him suspiciously. 'Why there?'

'Because the Trojans cluster at Jupiter's Lagrange points. By comparison, the belt asteroids are spread over an orbit wider than that of Mars. So it's easy to travel between the Trojans. And we think they sometimes exchange places with the outer moons of Jupiter. You see? That means that access to Jupiter orbit from the Trojans – energetically speaking – is very cheap. While the asteroids themselves are rich.' Cornelius shook his head. 'My God, what a Faustian bargain . . . We think the asteroid mass available in the Trojans is several times greater than that in the main belt itself. Not only that, they seem to be super-carbonaceous –'

'What does that mean?'

'They're made of the same stuff as C-type asteroids and comet nuclei. Like Cruithne. But in different, more volatile-rich proportions. It was *cold* out there when the planets formed. Cold enough for the lighter stuff to stick.'

Malenfant frowned. 'It sounds a hell of a piece of real estate to give away.'

'That's what I've been trying to tell you,' Cornelius said. 'Some of us think the Trojans might prove to be the richest resource site in the System. So surely even a species as fecund as the squid is going to take some time to consume them all. And even when they're done they may choose to go to Jupiter and its moons rather than come back in to the sun.'

Malenfant growled, 'I see your logic. We're giving them a big territory, enough to occupy them for centuries.'

'Time enough for us to do something about it,' said Cornelius tensely.

Malenfant looked at Emma. 'What do you think?'

She shrugged. 'Geopolitics are beyond me,' she said.

'This is beyond geopolitics,' said Cornelius. 'We're playing games, with an opponent of unknown potential, over the future of the species.'

'We'll tell them to aim for the Trojans,' Malenfant said, relieved the decision was made. 'Cornelius, start working on trajectory information . . .'

It took the emigrant squid only days to build their cephalopod *Mayflower*.

They sent their robots to work levelling the floor of a small crater. Over the crater they built a roughly spherical cage of unprocessed asteroid nickel-iron. Then they began to manufacture the skin of the bubble-ship that would take them to Jupiter's orbit. It was simple enough: modified firefly robots crawled over the floor of the crater, spraying charged molecules onto a substrate, like spray-painting a car, until a skin of the right thickness, and precision of manufacture down to the molecular scale, was built up.

Malenfant observed as much as he could of this. It was a manu-facturing process, called molecular beam epitaxy, which had been piloted on Earth decades before. But nobody had succeeded in developing it to the pitch of sophistication the squid had reached.

Malenfant was somewhat awed: it seemed to him the squid had simply identified their manufacturing problem, immediately devised a *perfect* technology to deal with it, built and applied it. It was a technology that would be worth uncounted billions to Bootstrap, in some unlikely future in which he made it back home and stayed out of jail.

Anyhow, when the fabricators had completed the bubble – a gold-tinted plastic – the squid started to fill it with asteroid water, extracted by simple inflatable solar heaters. A cap of Cruithne substrate rock, sheared off the asteroid and anchored to the metal cage, would serve as feedstock for methane rockets and a source of raw materials for the habitat.

Though the technology was simple, it still seemed something of a miracle to Malenfant to see water bubbling up out of coal-black asteroid rock.

It would be a long, grim journey, Malenfant knew. Under the low acceleration of the methane drive it would take many years for this bubble-ship to reach the cluster of Trojan asteroids, five times Earth's distance from the sun. The current generation of squid – none of whom would live to see the conclusion of the journey – were surely condemning generations of their offspring to a journey through despair and darkness and squalor.

And it might not work. If population controls failed, there would be wars, he thought. Savage. Perhaps the fragment of civilization on this ship would fall so far there would be nobody left alive who knew how to fix the methane rockets, or breaches in the habitat meniscus.

Somehow he didn't think that would come about. Already this miniature colony, here on Cruithne, had survived long enough to show the cephalopods possessed a purpose – a ruthlessness – that far transcended the human.

And at last, the survivors would reach Jupiter's leading Trojan point, a place where the sun would be a point source brighter than any star, and Jupiter itself a gleaming gibbous disc, and in the sky a million asteroids swarmed.

. . . With the gentlest of nudges from spring-loaded latches the droplet parted from its asteroid parent. The moment had come: no countdown, no fuss.

The rise was slow; nothing that big was going to make any sudden moves. It sailed upwards like a hot-air balloon, huge waves rippling softly over the golden structure, the cap of asteroid rock sullenly massive at the base.

When it reached the sunlight a glow exploded from the droplet's interior.

As their great journey began – away from the complexities and politics of the crowded inner worlds, off to the wide open emptiness, the calm and cold precision of the outer System – Malenfant thought he glimpsed the squid themselves, rushing this way and that, peering excitedly from their rising bubble-ship.

But perhaps that was just his imagination.

He watched as the droplet shrank, receding, hoping to see the moment when it was far enough from the asteroid for the methane rockets to be lit in safety. But the flames would be invisible, and he was growing tired.

Malenfant raised his hand in salute. Goodbye, goodbye, he thought. Perhaps your great-great-grandchildren will remember me. Maybe they will even know I was the being responsible for sending their ancestors out here, for giving you this chance.

But they will never know how I envied you today.

It had taken fifteen of their twenty available days, here on Cruithne, to deal with the cephalopods. Now they had five days left, five days to confront the thing that lay on the other side of the asteroid, to confront the alien.

He turned and started to crawl back across Cruithne, and to home.

Bill Tybee:

There was a new assistant at the Nevada centre, started a week ago. A big bull-necked Texan called Wayne Dupree.

Wayne did *not* look like any kind of teacher to Bill – he had the biggest, thickest arms Bill had ever seen on any human being – nor was he a parent or relative of any of the kids. And he had no noticeable skills in teaching or child care. He just supervised the kids in glowering silence as they went about the routine of their lives, occasionally administering a shove or a prod.

Wayne was the first adult Bill saw strike one of the kids here.

Bill complained about that to Principal Reeve. She made a note in a file, and said she'd look into it, but she was sure Wayne wasn't overstepping any mark.

And Bill was sure she didn't do a damn thing about it, because he saw Wayne do it again, a day later.

The turnover of staff here had always been high. Bill had noticed that the professional types soon became discouraged by the kids' baffling opacity and distance. After a few months Bill had become one of the more experienced helpers here; he was even assigned to train new folk.

But recently a new type of person, it seemed to him, had been appointed to work here.

Persons like Wayne.

Despite the shutting down of the Milton Foundation, the Blue kids continued to be the subject of feverish, superstitious awe and fear – a mood whipped up needlessly, in Bill's opinion, by commentators who speculated endlessly about the children's superhuman nature and cosmic role and so forth. There was still protection, of course. In fact security had gotten so tight it was virtually impossible for anybody to pass in or out of the centre outside of an armoured truck.

But it seemed quite possible to Bill that it might be becoming more acceptable to people at large that the Waynes of the world be recruited to 'supervise' the Blue children, that the centres be allowed to evolve from education homes for gifted children to prisons for freaks, guarded by brutes, just like the Milton Schools. It had happened before. As long as it was out of sight, of course.

But none of it mattered, Bill thought doggedly, not as long as he was here with Tom, and could keep him from harm's way.

Bill promised himself that if Wayne ever did raise a hand to his son, he would take on Wayne, despite any consequences, and that was that.

Sooner than Bill had expected, it came to a head.

Tom's group, in their shiny gold uniforms, were working in the physics lab. Wayne and Bill were both on duty, sitting in chairs in opposite corners of the room.

The kids were building something: a cage of wires and electro-magnets and batteries and coils. They'd been working all day, in fact, and Bill and the other assistants had had some trouble making them stop to eat, or even take toilet breaks, let alone do any of their other study programs.

The kids seemed to be growing more purposeful in their activities. They didn't have a written plan, and they didn't even speak to each other much, but they all worked together flawlessly, according to their abilities. The older ones, including Anna, did the heavier work like the bulky construction of the metal frame, and also more dangerous stuff such as soldering. The little ones generally worked inside the cage itself, their fine little fingers doing fiddly, awkward manipulations.

Bill watched Tom clambering around inside the cage like a mon-key, snipping and twisting together bits of wire with flawless accu-racy. As he concentrated his tongue stuck out of his mouth, just as it used to when he made clay soldiers or drew pictures of flowers for his mother.

As the day's end approached the kids seemed to have finished their cage. It was a box that was taller than Tom. Anna made them stand back, threw a few switches, and watched. Nothing happened as far as Bill could see save for a dull humming, a sharp scent of ozone. But Anna nodded, as if satisfied.

Then the kids broke away and, as if going off duty, wandered off around the lab.

Some of them went to the bowls of food Bill and Wayne had put out around the room. They seemed to avoid the dishes Wayne had slyly dipped his fat fingers into. Others, Tom and Anna among them, began playing. They started to throw Tom's electronic Heart around, catching it like a football, kicking it along the ground like a soccer ball. That was okay. The Heart was built for kids and was meant to last a lifetime, and was more than strong enough to take the punishment. The kids were noisy now, calling and yapping and even tussling a little.

As if they were normal.

Bill studied the wire cage, wondering how safe the damn thing was. At the end of each day the inspectors and experts crawled over everything the kids did. If it wasn't self-evidently safe they would shut it down and pull it apart, or maybe amend it to remove the hazard. The next day the kids would just start putting it back the way it was, unless physically restrained from doing so. And so it would go on, like building that bridge in *Apocalypse Now*, a battle of stubbornness between the kids and their adult keepers, until the kids were forced – or sometimes chose – to move on to something else . . .

That was when it happened.

Bill saw that the Heart had rolled between Wayne's feet. The kids were standing in a loose pack in front of Wayne, watching him.

The moment stretched, growing tauter.

Then Wayne looked at the Heart, and the waiting kids. Something like a grin spread over his face, and he lifted his hefty foot and pushed the Heart back along the floor.

A little boy called Petey, no older than Tom, collected the Heart. Petey, shyly, put the Heart back on the ground and rolled it back to Wayne.

Again Wayne returned it.

Back and forth the Heart went, a couple more times. The kids came a little closer to Wayne.

Then Petey picked up the Heart, and threw it at Wayne.

Wayne caught it one-handed, grinned wider, and threw it back to another kid.

Who threw it back again.

The game gradually built up steam. The kids seemed to be warming to this surprising new Wayne, this big bear of a man who was suddenly prepared to play ball with them. They ran around, starting to laugh and call, and threw the Heart to each other and to Wayne. Even Anna, Tom's quiet, reserved honorary sister, was joining in, her thin frame rising like a giraffe's above the rest of the children.

Bill started to relax. If Wayne was playing with the kids, however unimaginatively, at least he wasn't doing them any harm.

Bill kept watching, however.

Now Wayne got hold of the Heart, wrapped it in his huge fist, and lifted it high above his head.

The kids crowded around him, calling. 'Me! Give it to me!' 'No, me!' 'Me, me! Give it to me! My turn!' Bill saw that Tom was at the front of the little crowd, jumping up and down right in front of Wayne, reaching for the Heart.

Wayne looked over the kids, one by one, still grinning, as if selecting. And Bill saw the change in his face, the hardening of his fist around the solid plastic toy.

To Bill it was a nightmare of paralysis. He knew he could never reach Wayne in time.

In slo-mo, down came Wayne's arm, that heavy plastic ball nestled in his fist, the Heart heading straight for Tom's big, fragile skull.

There was a blur of motion. That big arm was knocked sideways, with something clinging to it.

Wayne's meaty forearm brushed Tom, knocking him back, and the boy screamed; but Bill knew in the first instant that he wasn't badly hurt. The other children scattered away, yelling.

Wayne stood up, roaring, his face twisted, lifting his arm high above his head. The girl, Anna, had sunk her teeth deep into the flesh of his bicep. And now she was hanging on by her teeth, her arms and legs dangling, bodily lifted off the ground by Wayne's brute strength.

Bill grabbed Tom and pulled him away.

Wayne shook once, twice; Anna's head was rattled back and forth, but still she wouldn't let go. So Wayne took a pace and slammed his arm against the wall. Bill heard a crack as Anna's skull collided with the smooth plastic there. She came loose of his bicep. She seemed stunned, her limbs loose, and she slid to the floor like a crumpled doll. Her mouth was bloody, like some carnivore's.

Wayne clutched his torn flesh, blood seeping through his fingers, snarling obscenities. Bill saw something white there, embedded in the flesh – one of Anna's teeth, perhaps.

Bill tensed. One leap and he would be on Wayne's back.

. . . And then something came ghosting through the wall. It was a glowing, fizzing bullet: just a point of light, yellow-white, bright as the sun, and it cast shadows as it moved.

Bill, shocked, skidded to a halt.

The light slid smoothly through the air, floating like Tinkerbell, heading downwards and towards the centre of the room.

Wayne, looming over Anna, didn't see it coming.

The light slid neatly into the top of his head. There was a sharp smell of singed hair, burned meat. Wayne convulsed, eyes flickering. The light passed out at the nape of Wayne's neck, following an undeviating straight line, as if the man, two hundred pounds of vindictive muscle, was no more substantial than a mass of mist and shadows.

Wayne, shuddering, toppled backward like a felled tree.

The children were wailing. Bill found Tom clutching his legs; he reached down, lifted up his son, and buried his face in the crying boy's neck. 'It's all right. It's all right –'

'What the hell –'

Bill turned. Principal Reeve and a couple of the other assistants had come in at a run. 'Get the medic,' Bill said.

'What happened?'

He pointed to Anna. 'She's hurt. And her teeth –'

But Reeve was no longer listening to him, it seemed, despite the blood and fallen bodies.

At the centre of the room, something was glowing, yellow-bright. Bill turned. It was the yellow dot, the glowing Tinkerbell. It had come to rest at the heart of the children's wire cage; it bobbed to and fro, following complex paths.

The children were calmer now. A couple of them were with Anna, trying to help her sit up. But the rest had started to cluster around the cage and its imprisoned light point; its brilliance shone over their faces.

Bill followed them, his son still in his arms. Fascinated, Bill reached out a hand towards the cage. He felt something, a ripple, as if a mild electric shock was passing through his system. He reached further –

A hand grabbed his arm, pulling it back. Tom's hand.

Maura Della:

Bill Tybee was pretty distressed, and he had a right to be, Maura thought.

Wayne Dupree had, it turned out, come from an extremist Christian group who believed the Blue children were the spawn of Satan, or somesuch, and so required destruction. He had got himself into the centre on a fake résumé and references from other members of his cult group: credentials which, Maura agreed, the most minimally competent vetting process should have weeded out.

On the other hand, Dupree hadn't succeeded – and not because of the system, or the presence of other adults, even a devoted parent like Bill – but because of the freakish plunging of the Tinkerbell anomaly into his body, just at the right moment.

'... Which I can't believe was a coincidence,' she told Dan Ystebo, as they walked into the centre's physics lab, now crowded with researchers.

He laughed uncomfortably, his big belly wobbling. 'I don't know why you brought me here. This isn't exactly my field. And you have no jurisdiction here.'

'But you spent long enough in the asylum with Reid Malenfant. This is more spooky stuff, Dan. Somebody has to figure out what all this really means. If not us, who?'

'Umm,' he said doubtfully.

In the lab, they confronted the anomaly that had killed Wayne Dupree.

Tinkerbell in a cage, Bill Tybee called it, and that was exactly what it looked like. Just a point of light that glowed brightly, like a captive star, bobbing around in a languid, unpredictable loop inside its ramshackle trap of wire. The anomaly was so bright it actually cast shadows of its wire mesh cage: long shadows that fell on the white-coated scientist types who crawled around the floor, and on their white boxes and probes and softscreens and cameras and tangles of cabling, and even on the primary-colour plastic walls of this schoolroom, which were still coated with kids' stuff, blotchy water-colour paintings and big alphabet letters and posters of the last rhinos in their dome in Zambia.

It was this contradiction, the surreally exotic with the mundane, which made Maura's every contact with these children so eerie.

Dan Ystebo was beside her. 'It looks as if someone found a way to split the atom in the middle of a McDonald's, doesn't it?'

'Tell me what's going on here, Dan.'

He guided her forward through the nest of cabling towards the glowing thing in the cage. There was a protective barrier of white metal, thrown up a yard from the cage itself. He said, 'Hold your hand out.'

She held her palm up to the glow, as if warming it by a fire. 'By golly, I can feel the heat. What makes it glow?'

'The destruction of neutrons, from the atmosphere. Step a little closer.'

She stepped right up to the protective barrier, nervous. This time she felt a ripple in the flesh of her hand, a gentle tugging. When she moved her hand from side to side she felt the wash of some invisible force.

'What's that?'

'Gravity,' said Dan.

'Gravity? From the anomaly?'

'At its surface the gravity pulls about thirty *thousand* G. But it drops off quickly, down to less than one per cent of G a yard away. The anomaly masses about a million tons. Which, if it was water, would be enough to fill a fair-sized swimming pool.'

'All crammed into that little thing?'

'Yup. It's around a sixteenth of an inch across. Right now these guys, the physicists here, don't have a good handle on its shape. It's presumably spherical, but it may be oscillating.'

'So it's pretty dense.'

'A little denser than an atomic nucleus, in fact. So dense it shouldn't even notice normal matter. An anomaly like that should pass right through the Earth like a bullet through a cloud.'

'Then how come it doesn't fall through the floor right now?'

Dan looked uncertain. 'Because of the cage.'

'This contraption the children built?'

'Maura, it seems to generate a very powerful, localized magnetic field. A magnetic bottle that holds up the nugget.'

'How?'

'Hell, we don't know. We *can* do this – we have to build magnetic bottles for fusion experiments – but only with such things as superconducting loops, and at vast expense. How the kids do it with a few yards of copper wire and an old car battery –'

She nodded. 'But this is where the potential is. The technological potential.'

'Yeah. Partly, anyhow. If we could manipulate magnetic fields of that strength, on that scale, so easily, we could build an operational fusion reactor for the first time. Clean energy, Maura. But that's not all.'

'So what is Tinkerbell? Some kind of miniature black hole?'

'Not quite as exotic as that.'

'*Not quite?*'

'It seems to be a nugget of quark matter. The essential difference from ordinary matter is that the individual quark wave functions are delocalized, spread through a macroscopic volume . . .'

It took some time for Maura, cross-examining him, to interpret all this.

In ordinary matter, it seemed, atomic nuclei were made of protons and neutrons, which in turn were made of more fundamental particles called quarks. But the size of a nucleus was limited because protons' positive charges tended to blow overlarge nuclei to bits.

But quarks came in a number of varieties.

The ones inside protons and neutrons were called, obscurely, 'up' and 'down' quarks. If you added another type of quark to the mix, called 'strange' quarks – a geeky term which didn't surprise Maura in the least – then you could keep growing your positive-charge 'nuclei' without limit, because the strange quarks would hold them together. And that was a quark nugget: nothing more than a giant atomic nucleus.

'We've actually had evidence of quark nuggets before – probably much smaller, fast-moving ones – which strike the top of the atmosphere and cause exotic cosmic ray events called Centauro events.'

'So where do the nuggets come from?'

Dan rubbed his nose. 'To make a nugget you need regions of very high density and pressure, because you have to break down the stable configuration of matter. You need a soup of quarks, out of which the nuggets can crystallize. We only know of two places, in nature, where this happens. One place is – was – the Big Bang. And the nuggets baked back there have wandered the universe ever since. The theory predicts we should find Bang nuggets from maybe a thousand tons to a billion. So our nugget is right at the middle of the range.'

'Where else?'

'In the interior of a neutron star. A collapsed supernova remnant: very small, very hot, very dense, the mass of the sun crammed into the volume of a city block. And when the pressure gets high enough quark matter can form. All you need is a tiny part of the core of the star to flip over, and you get a quark matter runaway. The whole star is eaten up. It's spectacular. The star might lose twenty per cent of its radius in a few seconds. Maybe *half* the star's mass – and we're talking about masses comparable to the sun, remember – *half* of it is turned to energy, and blown out in a gale of neutrinos and gamma rays.'

Quark matter runaway. She didn't like the sound of that. 'Which origin are we favouring here?'

'I'd back the Big Bang. I told you our nugget is right in the middle of the mass range the cosmogenic-origin theory predicts. On the other hand we don't have a real good mass spectrum for neutron star nuggets, so that isn't ruled out either. But then there's the slow velocity of our nugget. The nuggets should squirt out of neutron stars at relativistic velocities. That is, a good fraction of lightspeed. But the Big Bang nuggets have been slowed by the expansion of the universe . . .'

Slowed by the expansion of the universe. Good God, she thought. What a phrase. This nugget is a cosmological relic, and it's right here in this plastic schoolroom. And brought here, perhaps, by *children.*

He spread his hands. 'Anyhow that's our best guess. Unless somebody somewhere is manufacturing nuggets. Ha ha.'

'Funny, Dan.' She bent to see closer. 'Tell me again why Tinkerbell shines. Neutrons?'

'It will repel ordinary nuclei, because of the positive charges. But it can drag in free neutrons, which have no charge. A neutron is just a bag of quarks. The nugget pulls them in from the air, releasing energy in the process, and the quarks are converted to the mix it needs . . .'

Converted. Runaway. 'Dan, you said something about a drop of this stuff consuming an entire star. Is there any possibility that this little thing –'

'Could eat the Earth?'

She'd tried to keep her tone light, but her fear, she found as she voiced the notion, was real. Was this the beginning of the Carter catastrophe, this little glowing hole in the fabric of matter? . . .

'Actually, no,' said Dan. 'At least we don't think so. It's because of that positive charge; it keeps normal nuclei matter away. In fact the larger it grows the more it repels normal matter. But if it was negatively charged –' He waved his fingers, miming an explosion. '*Ka-boom.* Maybe.'

'Maybe?'

'Listen, Ms Della, there are opportunities as well as threats here. If you feed a nugget neutrons or light ions it will eat them, giving off energy in the process. You could conceivably throw in radioactive waste. Tritium, for instance. Then, when the nugget is fat enough, you could bombard it with heavy ions to split it. Two nuggets. Then four, then eight . . . A safe, efficient, clean energy source. *Extremely* valuable. And –'

'Yes?'

'I don't have to outline the weapons potential. More than half the researchers here are from military labs.'

'Okay. And I take it the children won't tell you how they managed all this.'

'No . . .'

So, Maura thought, Tinkerbell was at once a great possible boon to mankind, and at the same time a great possible threat. Both carrot and stick. Almost as if the children planned it that way.

These Blue children, it seemed, had upped the stakes. For the first time a group of children had moved beyond eerie behaviour and startling intellectual stunts to the physical, to something approaching superhuman powers.

Already we were terrified of them, she thought. But if, when, this news gets out . . .

'Okay, Dan. What now?'

'The children want to talk to you.'

'Me? I have no power here.'

'But the children know you. At least, Tom Tybee does.'

She closed her eyes, took a breath. But who am I negotiating with, exactly? And on behalf of whom? It seemed mankind's relationship with its strange Blue offspring was about to reach a new crisis.

Dan grinned. 'It's take-me-to-your-leader time, Representative.'

'Let's do it.'

They walked out of the lab room. Her shadow, cast by the trapped cosmological glow, streamed ahead of her.

Anna was waiting for her in the Principal's office. Maura walked in with Reeve and Dan Ystebo.

When they entered, Anna backed away against the wall. Maura could see bruises on her neck, and when she opened her mouth she was missing a lower front tooth. 'Just you,' Anna said to Maura. Her voice had the faintest trace of Aussie twang.

Principal Reeve said, 'Now, Anna –'

Maura held up her hand.

'Just you,' said Anna. 'That was the deal.'

Maura nodded. 'If you say so. But I need your help. I'd like Dan here –' Maura indicated him '– to stay with me. I don't understand as much of the technical stuff as I ought to.' She forced a smile. 'Without Dan to interpret, it will take me a lot longer to figure out what you want. I guarantee, positively guarantee, he's no threat to you. But if you want him to leave, he leaves.'

Anna's cool grey eyes flickered. 'He can stay. Not *her*.'

Reeve was visibly tired, stressed-out, baffled, angry. 'Representative, she's a *child*. And you're letting her give you orders.'

'We nearly allowed her to be killed, Principal,' Maura said gently. 'I think she has a right to a little control over the situation. Don't you?'

Reeve shook her head, furious. But she left, slamming the door behind her.

Anna showed no reaction.

Maura said, 'We're going to sit down, Anna. All right? In these two chairs, on this side of the desk. You can sit, or stand, whatever you want.'

Anna nodded, and Dan and Maura sat down.

Anna said, 'Would you like a drink?'

Maura was surprised. 'I – yes. Yes, please.'

Anna crossed to the water cooler, neatly extracted two paper cups, walked gracefully around the table and handed them to Dan and Maura.

'Thank you,' Maura said, sipping the water. It was warm, a little stale. 'Now, Anna. Tell me what it is you want.'

Anna dug her hand in a pocket of her gold jump-suit, pulled out a crumpled piece of paper, and pressed it on the desk. She pushed it across to Maura.

The paper looked like a page torn out of an exercise book. It contained a list written out in a childish hand, complete with errors, a couple of the longer words even phonetically spelled.

She passed it to Dan Ystebo. 'Deuterium,' he read. 'A linear electrostatic decelerator . . . Maura, I think they want to grow Tinkerbell. Maybe even make her some companions.'

Anna said, 'We will give you the Tinkerbell. And others.' She frowned with the effort of speaking, as if English was becoming unfamiliar. 'They could light cities, drive starships.' She looked at Maura. 'Do you understand?'

'So far,' said Maura dryly.

'We have other gifts to offer,' said Anna. 'In the future.'

'More technology?'

Anna was concentrating, a crease appearing in the middle of her perfect forehead. 'We are still learning, here at this centre. And elsewhere.'

Dan leaned forward. 'Are you in touch with the others? The other children, like you? In the other centres? How?'

She returned his gaze, calmly. 'We have suggestions. Ways of making food. Ways to make medicine, to make ill people well, to make them –' that pause, the struggle with the language again '– not grow old. And we have better ways for people to be together.'

Dan frowned. 'What do you mean? Politics? Ethics?'

'I don't know those words.'

Maura said, 'Better ways for people like me to run things.'

'. . . Yes. But nobody should have to run things.'

Dan laughed out loud. 'She gotcha there, Representative.'

'We have to work all this out,' said Anna.

'I understand,' Maura said evenly. *But the promise is there.* 'And you will give us all this?'

'In return.'

'In return for what?'

'No harm.'

Maura nodded. 'You must understand I can't promise you anything. Those in charge here have a wider duty, to protect people. Do you understand that people are frightened of you?'

Anna returned her gaze, and Maura felt chilled.

'This is an important time,' said Anna suddenly. 'Everything we do now is very important. Because everything comes out of here.'

'Out of the here and now,' Dan said. 'The future flows from this moment. We cast long shadows. Is that what you mean?'

Anna didn't reply. She seemed to be withdrawing.

Dan was frustrated. '*Why are you here?* To help us avoid the Carter catastrophe? *Are you from the future,* Anna?'

There was no reply, and Maura put her hand on Dan's arm to silence him.

The sunlight outside the centre buildings was hot, flat, glaring.

Tinkerbell in a cage.

Everything Maura had seen seemed unreal, remote, as if swimming away into space after Reid Malenfant.

'. . . Quite a prospectus those kids offer,' Dan was saying.

'Yes.'

'New technologies, new medicine, new clean power. What sounded like a utopian political and ethical framework. Peace and prosperity for all.'

'Absolutely,' Maura said.

'So, you think anyone will listen?'

'Not a hope in hell.'

Dan sighed. 'But we'll want the goodies even so, won't we?'

'You bet. You think we can afford to give them what they want? The deuterium, the decelerator –'

'Representative, I'm not sure if we can afford *not* to.' Dan glanced around to be sure nobody else could overhear them. 'So here we have these children building their magic cage *just in time* for this quark nugget – which has been wandering the universe since the Big Bang – to come floating in, ripe to be captured. And not only that, it arrives in the nick of time to save Anna from the evil clutches of wacko Wayne Dupree. And on exactly the right trajectory too.'

'Coincidence?'

'What do you think?'

She said, 'Not in a million years.'

Ystebo scratched his belly. 'I'd offer you longer odds than that . . . I think we're dealing with another of those damn causal loops. Somebody, far enough downstream, has the technology to reach into the past to deflect the path of a quark nugget *just so*, to make it arrive right on cue to save the day. It may have been travelling a billion years, just to get here, and play its part. The ultimate *deus ex machina*.'

'And that makes you feel –'

'Awed. Terrified.'

'Dan, are they threatening us?'

'Not directly. But – look: if we *don't* co-operate, the children will know in the future, when they grow up, when they get downstream – I mean, they'll *remember* what we did – and they'll send more quark nuggets from the Big Bang and get what they want anyhow, maybe causing a lot more damage.' He seemed to be shivering, despite the heavy warmth of the sun. 'If you think about it, it could happen any moment, depending on the decisions we make. It won't even be necessary to wait for consequent actions to flow; the children will *know*. Representative, we can't be sure what we're dealing with here. A multi-headed monster spanning past, present and future. The children have, effectively, unlimited power . . .'

The thought of children, their grown versions, in the future – in the far downstream, with much enhanced powers – reaching back with some kind of time-manipulation technology to right the wrongs they suffered here was startling. Children have been victims throughout history, she thought bleakly; maybe all children should have such power, and we would treat them with respect.

. . . But then she found herself thinking like a politician, as someone responsible for her nation's destiny:

Now – assuming this threat from the downstream children is real – how would you go about eliminating it?

Why, by making sure the children never reach the downstream. Of course.

Immediately she filed that ugly logic, its foul conclusion, in the back of her mind.

But she knew it would be with her, part of her calculation, from now on; and she hated herself for it.

'So,' Dan said. 'What do we do now?'

'The same as always,' said Maura briskly. 'We try not to do too much damage while we wait to see what happens next. Oh – is there any way we can contact the mother? Tom Tybee's mother?'

Dan laughed. 'Don't you know where she is right now? . . .'

They walked on towards the security fence, where their car was waiting.

June Tybee:

The throwing-up had started when *Bucephalus* was still on the ground.

That was nerves rather than space sickness. But it began in earnest once the injection to Earth orbit was complete, and the crew were put through the complexity of docking with the pre-orbited tanks of fuel required to reach Cruithne. Then – when the diarrhoea cut in – the recycled air filled with a stench so powerful June knew they would be living with it for the rest of the trip.

And you couldn't open the windows, not once.

June suffered herself. Most of the troopers did. But she got over it four, five days out.

Not everybody adapted so well, however. Eight troopers – sixteen per cent of the total – just kept barfing and shitting and getting weaker and weaker, unable even to hold down a morsel of food. So they had been allocated a corner of one of the decks, screened off from the rest, and were basically treated as casualties, non-functional for the duration of the voyage, all the way out to Cruithne and back.

The rest of the troopers endured tough exercise regimes: three or more hours a day on treadmills, elasticated ropes to stretch against, and so forth. Even so, the medics said, they would likely suffer some longer-term physiological damage, bone calcium depletion and other shit. But that could be treated later, when they got back to Earth. On their return in glory, after the medals and the handshakes from the Prez, they would all be retired on fat pensions, with a full entitlement to sell their stories to the highest bidders. Plenty of time to put right a little calcium loss then.

What was more important *now* was to get through the mission in one piece, so June could get back to Bill and Tom and Billie and the rest of her life.

A week out, the troopers dismantled the interior of this big five-deck troop module, opening up a giant cylindrical space like a huge oil can, and they began their zero G exercises in earnest.

At first her head felt like a bag of fluid that just sloshed about every time she moved. But that passed, and she soon found herself ricocheting back and forth across the oil can, practising landing, deploying the pitons and tethers that would hold her to the asteroid's surface, readying her weapons, smoothly working up to a fully suited drill. All of these manoeuvres were basically impossible on Earth, despite the efforts at simulation in the big NASA flotation-tank facilities.

June found, in fact, that once she was over her sickness she revelled in the freedom of zero G – to be able to fly through the air, free to move in three dimensions, without the clinging resistance of water.

Some of the troopers groused when, three weeks out from home, they started exercises sealed up in their full spacesuits. But June welcomed it. Sealed off from the rest of the troopers, she only had to smell herself – a sour stink of sweat and determination.

Despite the distraction of the training, the long journey out soon became pretty hellish. She was out in the middle of interplanetary space, after all; she really hadn't expected this sense of confinement, even claustrophobia.

And the tedium of life aboard a spacecraft was dismaying: the hours she had to spend every day on the dull repetitive exercises – or, worse, clean-up duties, scraping algae off of the walls, fixing water recycling systems that had proven balky since they left Earth, and so on, a *lot* of such work in this thrown-together, gremlin-ridden ship.

The troopers' spare time, what there was of it, was taken up with what you'd expect. TV, card games (Velcro strips on the back), and a surprising amount of casual sex: hetero, homo, bi, solo, couples and larger groups, much of it exploring the possibilities of the zero G regime. June had avoided all of that, and nobody had bothered her; the fifty-fifty male-female ratio saw to that.

Instead, she spent a lot of her time reading.

The accounts of the early astronauts, for instance. Not the flash-bang glory of Apollo and the rest of the early US program, but the Russians: dogged cosmonauts with names like Dobrovolsky, Patsayev, Volkov, Lazarev, Makorov, Popovich . . . From as early as 1971 the cosmonauts had endured hundreds of days in low Earth orbit in Soviet space stations, the Salyuts and the Mir, just boring a hole in the sky, nowhere to go, trying to keep themselves alive and sane. Some of those old guys had travelled further and longer than she had – if not in a straight line – and *they* had only dubious tractor-factory technology to rely on. And some of the cosmonauts hadn't come home.

Reading their accounts somehow made the *Bucephalus* less of a prison, for her.

That and thinking about Tom and Billie.

Faster than Reid Malenfant, the *Bucephalus* streaked across space towards Cruithne.

Maura Della:

Open journal. March 3 2012.

It was, of course, the extraordinary incident at Nevada that led to the decision – the right one, I think – to shut down the Blue education centres. The idea was to try to liquidate the threat, eliminate the unknowns, represented by the Blue children. Those responsible for the safety of the nation had no other choice.

The media images of cold-eyed childcare professionals, backed up by heavily armed troops, going into the centres and bundling bewildered, unresisting kids out of their beds, are offensive to anyone with a soul. However strange these children might be they are still just kids. But it had to be done.

Anyway I know that what offends people about those images is not so much the handling of the children itself but the way we were made to confront our own hypocrisy. Everybody has always known, in their hearts, that the true purpose of the centres was containment. Everybody is complicit. Guilty, ashamed – but still afraid – we turned away.

Now the children, separated from their fellows, have disappeared into secure environments, mostly military, all across the country. Out of sight they will be forgotten; separated, they will be contained. That's the idea anyhow.

It isn't particularly palatable. But the problem did appear to be approaching a resolution.

Except at Nevada itself.

The wisest thing for me to do would have been to keep out of it; no matter what the resolution to the situation, there was absolutely nothing to gain for me. But staying away just wasn't an option. My damnable conscience, a true handicap for a politician, saw to that.

Which is how I came to be at the centre when the climax came . . .

Dan Ystebo was waiting at the security gate when Maura got back to the centre.

A week after the quark nugget incident, the grade-school façade of the place had been stripped away. Most of the staff, including Principal Reeve, were gone. Security was tighter than ever, with what looked to Maura like a substantial military force deployed around the perimeter fence and across the compound. Guys with guns, in heavy body armour.

Dan walked her briskly to the heart of the compound. He looked fat and flustered, but she suspected he was relishing his informality and sloppiness compared to the stiff military types who now ran the place. Many of the rooms had been cleared out and given over to military functions – weapons storage, surveillance, a command post – with here and there a discarded toy or the dangling corner of some child's painting, deeply incongruous, reminders of the life and youth that had, if briefly and under restraint, come to this corner of the Nevada desert.

'. . . I prepared you a written report,' Dan was saying. 'I can download it to –'

'Just summarise.'

'The first stage of the clearance operation went to plan. In as much as these goons had a plan at all . . .'

Most of the children, Dan said, had been cleared out of the centre on the first sweep. But a hard core of a dozen or so had barricaded themselves in one of the lab rooms, and wouldn't be moved. And one of the children was – had to be, of course – little Tom Tybee.

After two days it had been obvious the situation was turning into a siege. The commanders were seeking sanction to use greater force, and the whole thing threatened to become a horrible mess.

They came to a room Maura recognized. It was the physics lab. But much had changed.

It was much bigger than she remembered; evidently two or three of the centre's rooms had been knocked together. And it was brighter; the ceiling was coated with big fluorescent strips, which dumped hard flat colourless light over everything, creating a shadowless, pearly glow.

The room was ringed by soldiers and white-coated staff, monitoring, recording. There was a sharp stink of ozone, and a sour compound of sweat and faeces and urine.

And, replacing the high-school type science instruments she had seen in here before, there was now a much more substantial array of gear. There were instruments of all kinds, mostly unrecognizable to her, all over the lab. Ducts and cables ran everywhere over the floor, taped together.

The main item was some kind of torus, a fat ring of metal tightly wrapped with wire coils, maybe fifteen feet across; it sat on a series of wooden trestles. Tubes led off to other assemblies of gear, one of them the crude Tinkerbell containment cage that Maura remembered from her last visit. And there was a new cage, a mass of wire and metal rods, growing out of the middle of the torus.

Suffusing everything was the bright glow of the object in the original wire cage: the Tinkerbell anomaly, still dipping and darting through the air. Its light was unearthly, easily casting shadows that could not be dispersed even by the powerful fluorescents above.

And, through the little jungle of equipment, the children moved.

They stepped carefully, carrying bits of gear to and fro, their childish gait uncertain. Three of them sat on the floor, surrounded by white equipment boxes, eating what looked like hamburgers. In a corner, a couple of kids were sleeping, curled up together. One, a dark little girl, had her thumb in her mouth. All the kids were wearing what looked like night clothes, loose tunics and trousers, no shoes or socks. The pyjamas were grubby, sometimes torn, but neatly stitched with blue circles.

The children looked ill to Maura, but maybe that was an artefact of the hard fluorescent light.

She said to Dan, 'I take it we gave them what they wanted, what Anna demanded.'

'The equipment was here in twenty-four hours, up and working twelve hours later.'

'Tell me what it's for.'

'It's a factory. As we thought. It makes quark nuggets, droplets of quark matter. The children are growing positively charged nuggets through neutron capture.' He pointed to the original cage, the darting Tinkerbell light. 'Small nuggets bud off the big mother in there. We don't know how that happens, incidentally; we thought that to make quark nuggets you would need to slam heavy ions together at near lightspeed in a particle accelerator.'

'Evidently not,' Maura said. 'How small is small?'

'The size of an atomic nucleus. The nuggets come spraying out of the cage and pass through the magnetic spectrometer – that box over there – where a magnetic field separates them out from other products. We have Cerenkov radiation detectors and time-of-flight detectors to identify the nuggets. Then the nuggets pass through *that* device –' a long boxy tube '– which is a linear electrostatic decelerator. At least we think it is. The children modified it. The quark nuggets emerge from the cage at relativistic velocities, and the decelerator –'

'Slows them down.'

'Right. Then the nuggets enter the torus, the big doughnut over there. That contains heavy water, which is water laced with deuterium, heavy hydrogen. The quark nuggets are fed protons to make sure they have a positive charge. That's important because a negatively charged nugget would –'

'Cause a runaway. I remember.'

'The quark nuggets go on to another magnetic bottle, at the end of the line there, and they are allowed to grow by absorbing neutrons. In the process energy is released, as gamma rays.'

'And that's how a power plant would be built.'

'Maura, this apparatus is *already* producing power, but not at useful levels yet.'

A taller girl walked through the room, giraffe-thin. She turned, unexpectedly, and looked at Maura.

'Anna,' said Maura to Dan.

'Yeah. And there's Tommy Tybee.' He was one of the three eating.

'We're feeding them?'

Dan eyed her. 'Of course we are. We haven't yet reached the point where we are prepared to starve out children. Anyhow it's siege psychology. The trick-cyclist types here are trying to keep up a line of dialogue with the kids; the food, three or four times a day, is one way. And the kids get what they want. Junk food, soda, candy.'

'Not so healthy.'

'Not a green vegetable in sight. But I think the consensus is we'll fix their health later.' He pointed. 'The troopers even brought in a Portaloo. The kids don't wash much, though. And not a damn one of them will clean her teeth . . . Here's the deal. We don't get to cross this perimeter.' A blue line, crudely sketched in chalk, ran across the polished floor. It looked to Maura like a complete ring, running all the way around the equipment and the children's encampment. 'We put food and stuff outside the line. Anna, or one of the others, collects it.'

'What happens if we cross the line?'

'We don't know. The goons haven't tried yet. They know what happened to that care worker. The bullet from the future.'

'The kids must sleep –'

'In shifts.' He pointed to the little huddle of sleeping forms. 'Even now. They always have lookouts. And they move in clusters. It wouldn't be possible to snatch one without others seeing, being close enough to react.' He scratched his beard thoughtfully. 'There are some military college types analysing the patterns of the kids' behaviour. Turns out it's very sophisticated. They work as if they are a single unit – but you don't hear any of them giving commands or directing the others.'

'Then how? Telepathy?'

Dan shrugged. 'They are all super-smart. Maybe they can all figure out the solution to this dynamic tactical problem. Maybe they just *know*.' He paused. 'But it's eerie to watch, Ms Della. You can see the collective way they move. Like a pack.'

'Not human.'

'I guess not.'

The atmosphere here was one of tension and suspicion. An image came into her mind: of *Homo Sap* children sitting around a fire, talking fast and fluidly, making fine tools and bows and

311

arrows, surrounded by a circle of baffled and wary Neanderthal adults . . .

There was a sudden commotion on the other side of the lab: a brief scuffle, voices raised.

Somebody, an adult civilian, had stepped inside the blue chalk perimeter of the children's domain. A couple of soldiers were reaching for him, weapons at their waist, but the intruder was out of reach.

'Oh, Christ,' said Maura.

It was Bill Tybee.

Little Tom came running out of the group of burger-munching kids, thin legs flashing. He ran straight to his father and clung to his legs, as if that was all that mattered, as if he was just some ordinary kid, and here was his father home from a day's work.

Bill kneeled down. 'You've got to come with me now, Tom. It's over now. We'll go back home, and wait for mommy . . .'

As his father gently coaxed, Tom, clinging, was weeping loudly.

All around the room, Maura saw, weapons were being primed.

The girl Anna came forward now. Bill tensed, but let her approach the boy. Anna laid her own thin hand on Tom's head. 'Tom? You can go with your father if you want. You know that.'

Tom's eyes were brimming pools of tears. His head tipped up, he looked from Anna to his father and back again. 'I don't want you to go, dad.'

'But we both have to go.' Maura heard the effort Bill was making to keep his voice level. 'Don't you see? Everything will be fine. Your room is still there, just the way you left it . . .'

'No. Stay here.'

'I can't.' Bill's voice was breaking. 'They are sending me away. The soldiers. I have to go now. And you have to come with me.'

'No –'

The girl stepped back. 'Let him go, Mr Tybee.'

Maura knew what was coming. Dread gathering blackly, she pushed forward; she got to the perimeter chalk line before she was stopped by a burly trooper. She called, 'Bill. Come out of there.'

Bill grabbed the boy and straightened up, clutching Tom against his chest. 'He's my son. I can't stand any more of this. Jesus, don't any of you understand that?'

Maura said, as harshly as she could, 'You *have* to let him go, Bill.'

'No . . .' It was barely a word, more a roar of anger and pain. Holding Tom, Bill pulled away from Anna and tried to step out of the circle.

There was a flash.

Bill fell, screaming, grabbing at his leg.

Tom, released, tumbled; two children caught him and hauled him back to the centre of the lab, out of reach.

Bill was on the ground, his lower right leg reduced to a mass of smashed flesh, shards of bone, a few tatters of cloth. A burly trooper in heavy body armour took a step forward, over the chalk line. He grabbed Bill around the waist – Maura heard the whirr of hydraulics – and he hauled Bill bodily out of the blue circle, out of the room.

A trooper jumped on a table – a sergeant, Maura realized. 'Let's clear the room now, people. Let's keep it orderly . . .'

'My God,' said Dan Ystebo.

Maura said, 'Another bullet from the future?'

'The flash came from the bottle.' He pointed at the magnetic bottle at the end of the quark nugget production line. 'They shot him with a quark nugget.' He laughed, his voice strained. 'They don't need help from downstream any more.'

A trooper approached; they were hustled out of the room. But as she left, Maura couldn't shut out of her head the sound of two people screaming: Bill Tybee, in the care of the paramedics, fighting to stay conscious; and his son, Tom, torn between warm past and chill future, a future he already knew his father couldn't share.

And she knew, now, there were few options left.

Maura and Dan were restricted to a bunker a couple of miles from the centre itself.

It was comfortable here: air-conditioned, clean, orderlies to serve coffee to the Representative and her companion. But in the big central command, control and communications room – C-cubed, as the military types called it, filled with gleaming softscreens and the subdued murmurs of the staff – there was an air of tension.

. . . Even though the target, monitored from a hundred angles, was just a group of eleven children, still confined to their blue chalk circle. Just children: working, sleeping, eating, even playing. Eleven spindly, unwashed kids.

The first counter-measure was invisible.

When it was initiated some of the children – Maura counted them, four, five, six – fell down immediately. Maura could see them vomiting, and one little girl had a dark stain spreading over her backside as her bowels loosened. They were clutching their stomachs and crying – *zoom in on twisted faces*.

Anna hauled the little ones into the big new cage they had built at the centre of the heavy water torus. As soon as they were inside the cage the children's retching seemed to stop, and they immediately calmed. Anna sat the smallest girl on her lap and stroked her sweat-tangled hair.

Soon all the children were inside the cage, sitting or standing or lying. Anna led them in singing, what sounded like a nursery rhyme.

'So much for that,' said Dan.

'What was it?'

'Deer-savers,' he said. 'Like on the hood of your car. Infrasound, very low frequency stuff. If you tune it right you can cause disorientation, nausea, even diarrhoea. The FBI have been using it for years.'

'Good God almighty.'

'Every conspiracy nut knows about it. It was the best hope, in my opinion.'

'Hope of what?'

'Of a peaceful conclusion to this mess. But it didn't work. Look at them. As soon as they got inside that cage of theirs they were immune. The cage is a barrier against infrasound.'

'Yes, and what else does it do?'

'I have a feeling we'll find out. So what next?'

Next turned out to be an invasion.

They kept the infrasound turned on for twelve hours. At least that kept the children trapped in their cage of steel and wire. Some of the kids managed to sleep, but there was no food in there, no water, no sanitation.

Then the troopers went in, eleven of them in their exo-suits: strictly SIPEs, for Soldier Integrated Protective Ensemble. They walked with a stiff, unnatural precision. Over each trooper's head was a complex, insectile mask, a totally contained respiratory system, night-vision goggles and a heads-up display, even cute little sensors that would aim weapons the way the soldier happened to be looking.

Eleven super-soldiers, one for each super-kid, stomping through grade-school corridors. Maura wondered what the troopers were feeling, how they had been briefed – how they were supposed to deal with this personally, even supposing they were successful.

In the event they didn't even reach the lab.

Maura actually saw the quark nugget bullets come flying out through the walls of the compound, then falling into the body of the Earth.

Then the retreat began.

Three troopers had died. Two more were injured and had to be carried out by their companions. One came out with her SIPE half-disabled, one leg dragging crazily.

The children, fragile-looking stick figures in their tent of wire, didn't seem to have moved.

Dan Ystebo grunted. 'One option left, then.'

It took another ten hours for the final approval to be obtained.

Far beyond her jurisdiction, Maura Della was nevertheless consulted by Administration officials. She was invited to take part by e-presence at security meetings in the White House family theatre. The attention was flattering, the weight of the decision overwhelming.

Before she made her final recommendation she took time out, went and sought out a shower room, stood in the jet for long minutes with the dial turned to its hottest, and the air filled up with sauna steam.

She hadn't slept for maybe thirty-six hours. She couldn't remember the last time she had sat down to eat. She had no idea how well her mind was functioning.

But this was, it seemed, a battlefield. The front line. And you don't get much sleep on the battlefield.

Open journal. March 8.

It's clear that whether she meant it or not, Anna's briefly sketched prospectus – a new social order, devised by the Blue children – has finally crystallized hostility to them, even more than the physical threat they represent. Nobody is about to submit to an ideology drawn up by a bunch of swivel-eyed kids. And underlying that is an inchoate fear that even considering the proposals will somehow lead to a transfer of actual control to the children.

After all, what were Nazi Germany and the Soviet Union but triumphs of a centralized, planning, 'scientific' élite? It seems to me that the human race simply isn't advanced enough yet to be able to trust any subset of itself with the power to run the lives of the rest.

That isn't to say that in all parts of the planet the response will be the same. Maybe some deranged totalitarian asshole is trying to recruit local Blue kids to prop up his lousy regime even now. And even some politically advanced parts of the world might not find the children's proposals quite as instinctively repelling as Americans. The French, for example, have an instinct for centralization that dates back to Colbert in the seventeenth century. As a visiting American I have been bemused to observe how their senior people work, top managers trained in the *grandes écoles* gliding between positions as ministerial advisers and captains of industry . . .

Not in America, though. America was after all built on the belief that centralized control is in principle a bad thing. And what about democracy? In fact I would be deeply suspicious of anybody, any stern utopian, who advocated handing over power to any élite, however benevolent.

But I suspect there is a still deeper fear, even an instinct, that lies buried under the layers of rationalization. Even in my own heart.

It may be that these children *are* in some sense superior to the *Homo Sapiens* stock from which they had emerged. Maybe they could run the world better than any human; maybe a world full of Blues would be an infinitely better place, a step up.

Maybe. But as I was elected to serve the interests of a large number of *H Sap* – and as a proud *H Sap* myself – I'm not about to sit around and let these Blues take my planet away.

If this final solution is turned down now, presumably further military options will be discussed, rehearsed, tried out, in escalating severity. Maybe we will, in the end, come back to this point again, the unleashing of the fire. But by then it could be too late.

Time is the key.

But all this is rationalization. I have to decide whether to destroy eleven American children. That is the bottom line.

I did not enter politics to be involved in this kind of operation. But who did? And I have learned that leadership is, more often than not, the art of choosing the least worst among evils.

Always assuming we still have a choice.

Learning to live with myself after this is going to be interesting.

She turned off her shower. The steam dispersed, the air cleared, and she was instantly cold.

Once again she stood with Dan Ystebo in the C-Cubed centre. But the place was silent now, save for the soft hiss of the air-conditioning, the whirr of the cooling fans of the equipment.

The various instruments monitoring the children's physical state, their heartbeat and respiration and temperature, and measuring the temperature and air composition, and the electromagnetic fields and particles criss-crossing the rebuilt physics lab – all of this was ignored. Everybody was watching the softscreens, the visual images of the centre's exterior, the children in their cage.

. . . And the moment came unexpectedly, softly.

There was an instant of blinding light.

Then it was as if a giant metal ball had dropped out of the sky. The centre – the buildings, the drab dormitory, the fence, a few abandoned vehicles – seemed to blossom, flying apart, before they vanished, their form only a memory. A wave passed through the ground, neat concentric pulses of dirt billowing up, and it seemed to Maura that the air rippled as a monstrous ball of plasma, the air itself torn apart, began to rise.

The sensor burned out. The screen image turned to hash, and the bunker turned into an electronic cave, sealed from the world.

The bunker was well-protected. She barely felt the waves, of heat and sound and light and shattered air, that washed over it.

'A backpack nuke,' she said to Dan Ystebo.

'Cute name.'

'About a kiloton. They buried it in the foundations, weeks ago . . .'

A wall-mounted softscreen came back on-line, relaying a scratchy picture.

It was an image of the centre. Or rather, of the hole in the ground where the centre had been. A cliché image, the stalk of a mushroom cloud . . .

The camera zoomed in. There was something emerging from the base of the cloud. It was hard, round, silvery, reflective, like a droplet of mercury. It was impossible to estimate its size.

There was utter silence in the bunker, the silver light of the droplet reflected in a hundred staring eyes.

The droplet seemed to hover, for a heartbeat, two. And then it shot skyward, a blur of silver, too rapidly for the camera to follow.

'I wonder where they are going,' Dan said.

'The downstream, of course,' she said. 'I hope –'

'Yes?'

'I hope they'll understand.'

The mushroom cloud swept over the sun.

Emma Stoney:

. . . And on Cruithne, Emma prepared to explore an alien artefact.

The continual shifting of the light, the slow wheel of the stars and the shrinking of her shadow, lent the place an air of surreality. Nothing seemed to stay fixed; it was as if craters and dust and people were swimming back and forth, toward her and away from her, as if distance and time were dissolving.

Somehow, standing here on the asteroid's complex surface, it didn't seem so strange at all that the 'empty' space around her was awash with trillions of neutrinos – invisible, all but intangible, sleeting through her like a ghost rain. If she was going to hear echoes from the future anywhere, she thought, it would be *here*.

But nothing seemed *real*. It seemed wrong that she should be here, now; she felt like a shadow cast by the genuine, solid Emma Stoney, who was probably sitting in some office in New York or Vegas or Washington, still struggling to salvage something of Bootstrap's tangled affairs.

But here was Malenfant's voice crackling in her headset, barking orders in his practical way: 'Make sure you're attached to at least two tethers at all times. Do you all understand? Cornelius, Emma, Michael?'

One by one they answered – even Michael, in his eerie translated voice. *Yes. I won't fall off.*

'Let's get on with it,' Cornelius murmured.

Malenfant led them to a pair of guide cables. They were made of yellow nylon, and had been pinned to the dirt by the fireflies. Looking ahead, Emma saw how the tethers snaked away over the asteroid's tight, broken horizon. Malenfant said, 'Clip yourself to the guide cables. We've practised with the jaw clips; you know how to handle them. Then unhook yourself from your tether from the dome. Remember, always keep a hold of at least two cables . . .'

Emma lifted herself with her toes, tilted, and let herself fall gently forward. It was like falling through syrup. The complex, textured surface of the asteroid approached her faceplate; reflections skimmed across her gold visor.

She let her gloved hands sink into the regolith. She heard a soft squeaking, like crushed snow, as her gloves pushed into the dust.

This was the closest she had come to Cruithne.

On impulse, she unclipped her outer glove, exposing her skinsuited hand. She could actually see her skin, little circles of it amid the orange Spandex, exposed to vacuum, forty million miles from Earth. Her hand seemed to prickle, probably more from the effects of raw sunlight than the vacuum itself.

She pushed her half-bare hand into the asteroid ground. The surface was sun-hot, but the regolith beneath was cold and dry. She felt grains, sharp, shattered, very small, like powder. But the dust was very loose, easily compacted; it seemed to collapse under her gentle pressure, and soft clouds of it gushed away from her fingers.

When she had pushed her hand in maybe six inches the dust started to resist her motion, as if compacting. But her probing fingers found something small and hard. A pebble. She closed her hands around it and pulled it out. It was complex, irregularly shaped, the size of her thumb joint. It was made of a number of different rock types, she could see, smashed and jammed together. It was a breccia, regolith compacted so the grains stuck together, analogous to sandstone on Earth.

She rolled the pebble in her fingers, letting dust flake off on her skin, relishing the raw physical contact, a window to reality.

She tucked the pebble back in its hole. She rubbed her fingers over each other to scrape off a little of the dust that clung to her skinsuit glove, and put back her outer glove. Snug in its layers of cooling and meteorite protection gear, her hand tingled after its adventure.

When they were done, clipped to the cables in a line, Malenfant stood briefly to inspect them, then let himself fall back to the surface. 'Here we go.' And he crawled away, towards the horizon.

Emma dug her gloved hands into the regolith, and pulled herself along the ground. She could see the feet of Michael ahead, was aware of Cornelius bringing up the rear behind her. It was like skimming along the floor of a swimming pool; she just paddled at the regolith with one hand, occasionally pushing at the ground to keep up.

They covered the ground rapidly. Fireflies ghosted alongside them, scrabbling over the surface in a blur of pitons and tethers, making this an expedition of scrambling humans and spider-like robots.

. . . Her perspective seemed to swivel around, so that she no longer felt as if she was sailing over a sea-bottom floor but climbing, scrambling up the face of some dusty cliff. But this cliff bulged outward at her, and there was nothing beneath her to catch her.

. . . And now the world seemed to swivel again, and here she was clinging to a ceiling like a fly. She found herself digging her gloves deep into the regolith. But she couldn't support her weight here, let alone keep herself pinned flat against the roof. Her heart thumped, so loud in her ears it was painful.

A hand grabbed her shoulder.

It was dark, she realized. Without noticing she'd sailed into the shadow of the asteroid. She flipped up her gold visor, and now Malenfant loomed, a fat, ghostly snowman. There were stars all around his head. 'You okay?'

She took stock. Her stomach seemed to have calmed, the thumping of her heart slowing. 'Maybe moving around this damn rock is harder than I expected.'

She looked back. Cornelius came clambering along the guide ropes after her, paddling at the regolith like a clumsy fish. Despite the darkness of the asteroid's short 'night', Cornelius wouldn't lift his sun visor.

Malenfant grinned at Emma and made a starfish sign in front of his face, a private joke from their marriage. *The poor sap has barfed in his suit.*

Somehow that made Emma feel a whole lot better.

'Anyhow it's over.'

'It is?'

Malenfant helped her to her feet. 'We're here.'

And she found herself facing the artefact.

It was just a hoop of sky-blue, protruding from the asteroid ground, rimmed by stars. It sat in a neat crater-like depression maybe fifty yards across.

She could see the marks of firefly pitons and tethers, the regular grooves made by their scoops as the robots had dug out this anomaly from the eroded hulk of Cruithne. The fireflies had fixed a network of tethers and guide ropes around the artefact. They looked, bizarrely, like queuing ropes around some historic relic.

Malenfant, tethered to the dirt, stood before the artefact, facing it boldly. Cornelius and Michael were clambering along more tethers toward him, ghosts in the pale starlight, just outlines against a background of black dirt and wheeling stars and alien blue.

Emma approached the artefact. It was perfectly circular, as far as she could see, like a sculpture. A small arc, at the base, was buried in the dirt of Cruithne. There were stars all around the ring, in the night sky – but not within its hoop, she noticed now. The disc of space cut out by the hoop was black, blacker than the sky itself, blacker than the inside of her skull.

It was obviously artificial. A made thing, in a place no human had been before.

And it was *glowing*, here in the asteroid night. She glanced down at herself. There was blue artefact light on her too, highlighting from the folds of her meteorite protection oversuit.

Malenfant said, 'Let's not freak out. It's not going to bite us. We're not going to slacken up on our tether drill, and we're going to watch our consumables every second of the stay here. Is that understood? Okay, then.'

Clipping themselves to the guide ropes, Emma firmly gripping Michael's hand, the four humans moved in on the artefact.

Reid Malenfant:

Malenfant got to maybe six feet of the base of the hoop, where it slid into the regolith. The hoop towered over him. That interior looked jet black, not reflecting a single photon cast by his helmet lamp.

He glared into the disc of darkness. What are you for? Why are you here?

There was, of course, no reply.

First things first. Let's do a little science here, Malenfant.

Sliding his tether clips along the guide ropes, he paced out the diameter of the hoop. Thirty feet, give or take. He approached the hoop itself. It was electric blue, glowing as if from within, a wafer-thin band the width of his palm. He could see no seams, no granularity.

He reached out a gloved hand, fabric encasing monkey fingers, and tried to touch the hoop.

Something invisible made his hand slide away, sideways.

No matter how hard he pushed, how he braced himself against the regolith, he could get his glove no closer than an eighth of an inch or so to the material. And always that insidious, soapy feeling of being pushed sideways.

He reported this to Cornelius, who grunted. 'Run your hand up and down, along the hoop.'

Malenfant did so. 'There are – ripples.'

'Tidal effects. I thought so.'

'Tidal?'

'Malenfant, that hoop may not be material.'

'If it ain't material, what is it?'

Folded time.

That was Michael, skimming easily around the artefact, as if he'd been born in this tiny gravity.

Malenfant snapped, 'What the hell does that mean?'

Cornelius said, 'He's saying this thing might be an artefact of spacetime.' He laboured at the instruments the fireflies were deploying. The instruments, sleek anonymous boxes, were connected to each other and to a central data collection point by plastic-coated cables, light pipes and diagnostic leads. The cluster of instruments was powered by a small radiothermal isotope power generator. The cables refused to uncoil properly and lie flat. Cornelius stared at chattering data, avoiding the stern mystery of the thing itself. 'I have a gravity gradiometer here. I'm picking up some strange distortions to the local gravity field which . . . I need to figure out some kind of gravity stress gauge which will tell me more.' Mumbling on, he tapped at his softscreen with clumsy gloved fingers.

Malenfant understood not a damn word. He had the feeling Cornelius wouldn't be much help here.

He walked back to the centre of the hoop. That sheet of silent darkness faced him, challenging.

Abruptly the sun emerged from behind a hill to his left, as Cruithne's fifteen-minute day rolled them all into light once more. His shadow stretched off, to his right, over the crumbled, glistening ground, shrinking as he watched.

The sunlight dimmed the eerie blue glow of the hoop. But where the light struck the hoop's dark interior, it returned nothing: not a highlight, not a speckle of reflection.

He reached out a hand, palm up, to the dark surface.

No.

Michael was beside him. The kid reached up and grabbed Malenfant's arm, trying to pull it back. But Michael was too light; his feet were dangling above the regolith, tethers snaking languidly around him.

Malenfant lowered him carefully.

Michael bent and rummaged in the asteroid dirt. He straightened up, hands and sleeves soiled, holding a pebble, an irregular chunk of breccia the size and shape of a walnut. He threw the stone, underarm, into the hoop.

It sailed in a straight line, virtually undisturbed by Cruithne's feeble gravity.

Then the stone seemed to slow. It dimmed, and it seemed to Malenfant that it became reddish, as if illuminated by a light that was burning out.

The stone disappeared.

Michael was looking up at him, grinning.

Malenfant patted his helmeted head. 'You're a scientist after my own heart, kid. Hands on. Let's go find that rock.' He started to work his way around the artefact to the far side. The ropes were awkward, and clipping and unclipping the tethers took time.

Michael stared around at the ground beneath the hoop. He was still grinning, the happiest he'd been since he had left Earth. *My stone is not here.*

'Dear God,' Emma said. 'Just as we saw when the firefly went through.'

'Yeah. But seeing it for real is kind of spooky. I mean, where is that stone now?'

Michael found another stone, dug out of the dirt, and he threw it into the black surface. The stone slowed, turned red, winked out. This time it looked to Malenfant as if it had *flattened* as it approached the surface . . .

'Malenfant.'

He turned. Emma was pointing.

The surface was churned up, pitted and cratered – but then, so was the surface all over the asteroid. What made this different was what lay in the craters.

Scraps of flesh. Dead squid, bodies crushed and broken, disrupted by vacuum, desiccated, life-giving fluids lost to space.

He loosened his tether and tried to get closer to her.

'There was a war here,' said Emma.

'Or an execution. Or –'

'Or suicide.' He felt Emma's hand creep into his. 'It's just like home.'

'What do you mean?'

'Maybe these are the ones who explored the artefact. The Sheenas. Or maybe some of them were touched by the downstream signal.'

'Like Michael, and the other children.'

323

'Yes. And the others feared them, feared what they had become, and killed them.'

Or maybe, Malenfant thought, the smart ones won. He wasn't sure which was the scarier prospect.

'What have we got here, Cornelius?'

'Ask the boy,' snapped Cornelius. 'He's the intuitive genius. I'm just a mathematician. Right now I'm trying to gather data.'

Malenfant said patiently, 'Tell me about your data, then.'

'I didn't know what to measure here. So I brought everything I could think of. I have photodetectors so I can measure the light that's reflecting off that thing, and the light it emits, at a variety of energies. I have a gravity gradiometer, six rotating pairs of accelerometers, that they use in nuclear submarines to detect underwater ridges and mountains from variations in the gravity pull, nice ploughshare stuff . . . There's a powerful magnetic field threading the artefact. Did I tell you that? Oh, and I have particle detectors. Solid state, slabs of silicon which record electrical impulses set off by particles as they pass through. Nothing very elaborate. I even have a lashed-up neutrino detector which is showing some results; Malenfant, that thing seems to be a powerful neutrino source –'

Cornelius was talking too much. Spooked, Malenfant thought. Handling this less well than the kid, in fact. 'What is an artefact of spacetime?'

Cornelius hesitated. 'I shouldn't have said that. I'm speculating.'

Malenfant waited.

Cornelius straightened up stiffly. 'Malenfant, I feel like an ancient Greek philosopher, Pythagoras maybe, confronted by an electronic calculator. If we experiment we can make some guess about its function, but –'

And Emma was yelling. '*Michael!*'

Michael had taken off all his tethers. He looked back at Emma, waved, and then made a standing jump. In the low gravity he just sailed forward, tumbling slightly.

Emma grabbed for him, but he had gone much too far to reach.

He hit the black surface, square at the centre, just as he'd clearly intended. He seemed to Malenfant to flatten – his image became tinged with red – and then he shot away, as if being dragged into some immense tunnel.

. . . There was a screech in Malenfant's headset, a howl of white noise, loud enough to hurt his ears. He saw Emma and Cornelius clap their hands to their helmets, in a vain attempt to block out the noise.

After a couple of seconds, mercifully, it ceased.

But Michael was gone.

Emma was standing before the artefact. 'Michael!' The burnished hoop was gleaming in her gold faceplate. Malenfant couldn't see her face. But he knew that tightness in her voice.

He looked for something practical to do. Emma was untethered, he saw. He bent and picked up loose tethers and clipped them to her belt.

She turned to him. 'So,' she said. 'What do we do now?'

'Malenfant.' It was Cornelius. 'Listen to this.' He tapped at his softscreen, and a recording played in Malenfant's headset. Words, too soft to make out.

'It's the screech,' said Cornelius. 'It came from the artefact, a broad-spectrum radio pulse which –'

'Turn up the volume, damn it.'

Cornelius complied.

It was, of course, Michael – or rather, his translated voice.

I found my stone.

Emma Stoney:

The three of them beat a hasty retreat back to the dome.

Cornelius dragged off his suit, went straight to his softscreens and started working through the data.

Malenfant patiently gathered up the discarded equipment. He hooked up their backpacks to recharge units. And then he got a small vacuum cleaner to suck up the loose dust.

Emma grabbed his arm. 'I can't believe you're doing this.'

'We'll all be finished if we forget the routines, the drills, our procedures –'

'*We lost Michael.* We all but kidnapped him, brought him all the way to this damn asteroid, and now we lost him. His oxygen will expire in –' she checked '– ten more hours.'

'I know that.'

'So *what are you going to do?*'

He looked exhausted. He let go of the cleaner; it drifted to the floor. 'I told Cornelius he has one hour, one of those ten, to figure out what we're dealing with here.'

'And then what?'

He shrugged. 'Then I suit up and go in after the boy.'

Emma shook her head. 'I never imagined it would come to this.'

'Then,' Cornelius said coldly, 'you didn't think very far ahead.'

'Your language is inhuman,' said Emma.

Cornelius looked startled. 'Perhaps it is. But to tell you the truth, I'm not sure Michael *is* fully human. He's been one step ahead of us since we arrived here. It may be he knew exactly what he was doing when he walked through that portal, where he was going. It was his choice. Have you thought of that? . . .'

An air circulation pump clattered to a stop.

Malenfant and Emma stared at each other. After so many weeks in the *O'Neill* and the hab bubble, she'd gotten to know every mechanical bang and whirr and clunk of the systems that kept her alive. And she knew immediately that something was wrong.

She followed Malenfant to Cornelius, who was sitting on a T-chair by the hab's mocked-up control board. The softscreen display panels were a mess of red indicators; some of them were showing nothing but a mush of static.

'What's happened?'

Cornelius turned to Malenfant, the muscles around his eyes tight with strain. 'It looks like something fried our electronics.'

'Like what? A solar flare?'

'I doubt it.'

Malenfant tapped at a softscreen. 'We're not in any immediate danger. The surface systems seem to have gone down uniformly, but a lot of the hab systems are too stupid to fail.'

Emma said, 'Have we taken a radiation dose?'

'Maybe. Depending what the cause of this is.'

'. . . My God.'

Cornelius had produced an image on the softscreen.

It was a star field. But something, an immense shape, was occluding the stars, one by one. In the middle of the black cut-out form, a light winked.

'*That's a ship*,' said Malenfant. 'But who –'

With a mechanical rattle, all the hab's systems stopped working, and silence fell.

Cornelius turned to Malenfant. 'Too stupid to fail?'

Emma felt hot, stuffy, and her chest ached. Without the air circulation and revitalization provided by the loop systems, the

326

carbon dioxide produced by her own lungs would cluster around her face, gradually choking her –

She waved at the air before her mouth, making a breeze, fighting off panic.

The softscreen image, relayed by some surface camera, fritzed out.

'I think we'd better suit up again,' said Malenfant.

June Tybee:

June lay loosely strapped into her couch. She was one of ten troopers in this big circular cabin, which was one of five stacked up at the heart of *Bucephalus*. The troopers in their armour looked like a row of giant beetles.

Her suit, after weeks of practice, felt like part of her body, even the bulky helmet with its thick connectors. The suit was coloured charcoal grey, nearly black. Asteroid camouflage. It had been a relief for June when the order had come, just before the brilliant flash of the EMP bomb, to close up her visor. The troopers ought to be rad-shielded, here at the heart of the ship. But it didn't do any harm to be wrapped in the suit's extra shielding.

Now the covers on the cabin windows snapped open. The windows were just little round punctures in the insulated, padded walls. But they were enough to show her the stars.

. . . And something else: a shape, charcoal black and massive, that came swimming into her field of view. It looked like a barbecue brick that somebody had been taking pot shots at. But there were structures on the surface, she saw: little gold domes, what looked like a spacecraft, a glimmer of electric blue.

There were whoops and shouts, and June felt her heart thump with anticipation.

It was Cruithne. They had arrived.

But then a series of bangs hammered at the hull of the carrier. She knew from experience what that was: blips of the attitude control thrusters. But such a prolonged firing was unusual.

She felt a ghostly shove sideways. It took a while for a ship the mass of *Bucephalus* to change course. But right now it was trying mighty hard.

And something new came sailing past the window. It was a golden sphere, rippling and shimmering. It was inexplicable: beautiful, even graceful, but utterly strange, a golden jellyfish swimming up at her out of the darkness.

Suddenly it came to June where she was, what she was doing, how far she was from home. The *Bucephalus* suddenly seemed very fragile. Fear clutched at her chest, deep and primitive.

Emma Stoney:

'Jeez,' said Malenfant, his radio-transmitted voice crackling in her ear. 'It's the man.'

Emma was out in the open, locked into her suit, staring at the sky.

The ship was like nothing she had seen before.

It was a squat cylinder with a rounded snub nose. She could see no rocket nozzles at its flaring base. It had two giant fin-like wings, on which were marked the letters 'USA' and a USASF roundel and a Stars and Stripes painted close to the base. There were complex assemblies mounted on some parts of the hull: an antenna cluster, what looked like a giant swivel-mounted searchlight. The hull was swathed with thick layers of insulation blankets, pocked and yellowed by weeks in space.

Somehow it disturbed Emma to see that huge mass hanging over her in the Cruithne sky: a sky she had become accustomed to think of as empty, save for the stars, the gleam of Earth, the lurid disc of the sun.

A few yards ahead of her a firefly robot was manoeuvring, working its pitons and tethers, in a tight, neat circle, over and over, its carapace scuffed and blackened with dust. It was scrambled, like the equipment in the hab module.

But their suits were working fine. Malenfant had gotten into the habit of burying the suits under a few feet of loosely packed regolith. *Just a little more protection*, he always said. Now Emma was starting to see the wisdom of that.

'He's coming down over the pole,' Malenfant murmured now, watching the ship. 'Looks like an SSTO design. See the aerospike assembly at the base there? The base would serve as the heatshield on re-entry. It's one big mother. How could they assemble it, fly it so quickly, chase us out here?'

Cornelius shrugged, clumsy in his suit. 'Shows how seriously they take you. Anyway now we know what happened to the electronics.'

'Oh,' said Malenfant. 'An EMP.'

Emma asked, 'EMP?'

'Electromagnetic pulse,' said Cornelius. 'They set off a small nuclear weapon above the asteroid. Flooded our electronics with radiation.'

'My God,' said Emma. 'How much of a dose did *we* take?'

They had no dosimeters, no way to answer the question. Emma felt her flesh crawl under her skinsuit, as if she could feel the sleet of hard radiation coursing through her body.

'Anyhow it was seriously dumb,' said Malenfant. 'It's made it impossible for us to talk with them.'

Cornelius said, 'Maybe they thought they had no choice. They didn't know what they were flying into here, after all –'

And then Emma saw something new: a sac of water, encased in rippling gold fabric, sailing up from the surface of Cruithne towards the intruder.

Malenfant clenched a fist. 'God damn, it's the squid. The ones who stayed. They're fighting back.'

Emma's heart sank. They were doomed, it seemed, to a battle, whether they wanted it or not.

Sparks burst from complex little clusters along the hull of the ship. The great ship began to roll, deflecting ponderously. But it wasn't going to be enough.

The converging of the two giant masses, in utter silence, was oddly soothing to watch, despite her understanding of the great and deadly forces involved: they were like clouds, she thought, complex clouds of metal and water and fabric.

The water bomb's membrane snagged on some projection on the ship's hull. The water within gushed out, blossoming to vapour in a giant, slow explosion. The ship was set tumbling erratically, nose over tail, and the membrane, crumpled, fell away. Emma could see more sparks now as the pilots blipped their attitude thrusters, struggling to bring their craft under control.

'Not enough,' Cornelius said.

'What do you mean?' Emma said.

'If the collision had been head on the squid missile would have wrecked that thing. Cracked it open like an egg. But that sideswipe is just going to inconvenience them.'

'You mean,' said Malenfant, 'it will make them mad.'

Now little hatches in the ship's hull slid back, and tiny, complex toys squirted out into space. They swivelled this way and that, tight and neat, and then squirted in dead straight lines over the horizons.

'Comsats,' said Malenfant. 'For command, communications, control. So they can see all the way around the rock when they begin their operations.'

Emma asked, 'What operations?'

'Taking Cruithne. What else?'

And then the ground shook.

They were all floating a little way upwards, she saw, like water drops shaken off by a dog. When they landed they staggered. Emma thought she could feel huge slow waves working through the dust-laden ground.

Malenfant snapped, 'What the hell now?'

Cornelius was pointing to the horizon.

From beyond Cruithne's dusty shoulder, an ice fountain was bursting upwards. Droplets fanned out in perfectly straight lines, gleaming like miniature stars, unperturbed by Cruithne's feeble gravity.

'They're hitting the squid,' she said. 'Their domes –'

'Yeah,' Malenfant growled.

'How did they do that?' asked Emma. 'How do you fight a space war?'

Malenfant said, 'Maybe they fired a projectile. Like an anti-satellite missile.'

'No.' Cornelius pointed to the searchlight-type mount on the hull of the ship. 'That looks like a laser beam director to me. Probably a chemical laser, several megawatts of power, a mirror a few feet across.'

Emma asked, 'Could they fire it again?'

'You bet,' said Malenfant. 'The babies they developed for Star Wars back in the '80s were designed for thousands of shots.'

Already the ice fountain was dying.

Emma was glad some of the squid, at least, had been spared this, that they were on their way to the Jupiter-orbit Trojans, where they would be far beyond the reach of this heavy-handed military intervention.

Unlike herself.

'They'll take out our habitat next,' Cornelius said. 'Then trash the *O'Neill*.'

'They wouldn't do that,' Emma said. 'That would kill us.'

'They don't know who's firing at them. They're going to shoot first –'

'– and let Saint Peter sort us out,' Malenfant said grimly. 'Hell, it's what I'd do.'

Emma said, 'Without the habitat, without *O'Neill*, we'll be dead when the suits expire. Ten, twelve hours.'

Cornelius said tightly, 'I think we know that.'

More hatches opened and tiny rockets hurtled out, trailing cables. The rockets fell over Cruithne's tight horizon, and Emma saw sprays of regolith dust. The cables went taut, and the ship began to turn, grandly, like a liner towed by tugboats.

'He's harpooned us,' said Malenfant. 'And now he's winching himself in.'

Another hatch was opening in the ship's belly. She saw a rectangle of pale grey light, the figure of a person – a soldier – heavily armoured. The soldier looked ant-sized. For the first time she realized how big the ship really was.

Cornelius moved. 'We have to get away. Come on.' He dragged his tethers out of the regolith, lay down flat, and began pulling himself by his fingertips over the surface. He wasn't even bothering to anchor himself, Emma saw.

'Cornelius is in kind of a hurry,' she said.

Malenfant said grimly, 'I suspect he knows something we don't. We'd better follow him.'

Emma fell forward. Cruithne dust billowed around her, and she began to float-crawl forward, after the fleeing Cornelius.

June Tybee:

June was ready by the closed hatch. Her harness, slung loosely about her suit, was attached to a guide rope that coiled loosely above her head.

Just like taking a parachute drop, she thought.

Except, of course, it wasn't.

The hatch slid open.

Cruithne was framed in the hatchway: dark as soot, dimpled with craters of all sizes, here and there glistening blue or red. She could see the guide rope snaking, coils frozen in zero G, to a piton-tipped rocket buried in the dirt. There was no sense of gravity. It was like looking straight ahead at a wall, rather than down to a ground.

Such had been her proficiency in the zero G drills she had been selected in the first wave. And so here she was in the hatchway of a spacecraft, and she was facing an asteroid.

Oh Christ oh Christ . . .

Someone slapped her on the back. She didn't allow herself to hesitate. She gave her harness one last tug, floated forward, and pushed, hard, out the hatch.

She was floating between two vertical walls, as if crossing between two buildings, following the coiling cable. And when she looked down –

She looked down, and saw stars.

To left and right, above, more stars. Space, above her and below her and all around her. The confinement of her months inside *Bucephalus* fell away, and the scale of the universe opened out from a few feet to infinity. She felt her stomach churn. Nothing, no amount of training or simulation, *nothing* had prepared her for the reality of this, of drifting in space.

They should have tried, though, she thought.

She clutched her weapon to her chest, focused on it to the exclusion of all else. Such weapons were her speciality – in fact she had trained others in their use. The gun was distorted in her view by her curved, tinted faceplate. It was a combination laser rifle and projectile weapon – ordinary bullets, the clips and barrels modified to take account of the vacuum. Big trigger for gloved fingers. A fancy graphite lubricant that wouldn't seize in the vacuum. Big modular parts for easy repair. LED display to show her the laser's power – right now, of course, it was fully charged . . .

The transfer could only have taken a minute. It seemed much longer.

Here came the asteroid at last, its detail exploding, filling her faceplate. She saw how its surface was sculpted by craters, circles on circles, like the beach after the rain, like that day in Florida with Tom. But this beach was black as coal, not golden, and the sky was black too, not washed-out blue, and she was a long way from Florida.

Her radar pinged in her ear, warning her she was close.

She spread out her arms and legs, starfishing, as she'd been trained. She couldn't tell from looking how far she was from the surface; the closer she got, the more craters and ragged holes she could see, so the surface texture was the same on every scale – what was the word, fractal?

It came as a shock when her hands pressed against soft, crumbling dirt.

She felt herself tipping. Then her knees and toes hit together. It felt as if she was clinging to a wall – and, oh shit, she was bouncing, floating back into space. She scrabbled at the asteroid.

She was panicking.

She shut her eyes and took a deep breath.

She opened her eyes, reached for the pitons dangling from her belt, dug one into the surface, then a second, a third. Rapidly, efficiently now, she hooked her tethers to the ropes, tested them with quick tugs, and then – another deep breath, a moment of concentration – she ripped her harness clear of the guide rope, and she was no longer connected to *Bucephalus*.

She dug her piton out of the ground, moved her tether, crawled forward. And here she was, mountaineering up the face of an asteroid. The belly, arms and legs of her suit were already streaked and stained black, and she had to stop every few minutes to wipe the shit off her faceplate. It was like crawling over a broad, soot-strewn hill, as if after some immense forest fire.

She could see the *Bucephalus*, hanging in the sky like some complex metal sun. More troopers were coming down to Cruithne, sliding down the wire in absolute silence.

Holy cow, she thought. I made it. Her spirits lifted. Tommy, Billie, this will make a hell of a story for you and your kids. I hope somebody is recording this.

She saw a sub-satellite sailing over her head, a little metal spider with glistening solar panels, filmy antennae. It spun and jerked, angling down in a straight line towards the horizon, until it passed out of her sight. The gravity of Cruithne was too weak for useful orbits, so the sub-sats were using small thrusters to rocket their way around the asteroid. The lifetime of the sats was only a few hours, limited by their fuel, but that ought to be enough; if the asteroid wasn't secured by then they would all be in trouble anyhow.

When she looked back *Bucephalus* was already hidden behind the close horizon. It was as if she was alone here.

She ought to wait. The orders, for now, were just to spread out over the first few hundred yards, and then to move steadily over the asteroid, keeping line of sight contact on a buddy basis. Then they would converge on the various installations.

333

Clinging to the dirt she sucked orange juice, sharp and cold, from the nipple dispenser inside her helmet, and found a fruit bar in there and crunched it; when she pulled away a little more of the bar slid out towards her mouth.

She was in shadow right now, out of the sun, and she could see stars. The spin of the asteroid was becoming more apparent; she could see how the stars were wheeling slowly over her. And now here came Earth, fat and beautiful and blue, heavy with light, the most colourful thing she could see. It was just a mote in the sky; it was hard to believe that everything she had known before climbing aboard *Bucephalus* – the kids, Bill, her family, all the places she had lived, everywhere she had visited – all of it was contained in that pinprick of light.

Something sailed over her head, brilliant white in the sun. Another sub-satellite?

But the thing she saw was wriggling. It had arms and legs. And some kind of cloud spreading around it, spherical, misty. Gradually the wriggling stopped. Like a stranded fish, she thought, numbly.

Something had gone wrong.

Then the asteroid shuddered and shook her loose, and she sailed upward into space.

There was a flash, ahead of her, in the direction of *Bucephalus*.

Now more objects came hailing over the horizon, complex, glittering, turning, moving in dead straight lines, all in utter silence. Pieces of wreckage.

In that moment she knew she wasn't going home again.

Emma Stoney:

The three of them were back at the artefact.

There was a shudder, hard enough to make Emma cling to her tether. Little sprays of impact-smashed asteroid dust shot up from the ground.

Cornelius looked at his watch, a big mechanical dial strapped to his wrist. He made a clenched-fist, grabbing gesture. 'Right on time.'

The tremor, or whatever it was, subsided. Emma looked around. Nothing seemed to have changed. The sun was wheeling slowly over her head. The blue circle protruded from the dust as if it had been there for a billion years, oblivious to the affairs of the humans who squabbled over the asteroid's battered surface.

Malenfant said, 'What have you done, Cornelius?'

'An X-ray laser.' Emma could hear the exultation in Cornelius's voice. 'A little Star Wars toy of my own. Small nuke as the power source . . . Well. It worked. And we felt it, all the way around the asteroid to here, through three miles of rock.'

Emma snapped, 'How many people have you killed?'

Cornelius, clinging to his tether, turned to face her. 'They would have killed *us*. It was us or them. And we couldn't give them access to the portal.'

'Why not? My God, they represent the government. And besides, there were troopers coming down off that ship. Sliding down a wire to the surface. I *saw* them. Do you really think you'll have killed them all?'

'Take it easy,' Malenfant said. 'First we have to figure what's happened. Did they have time to trash our hab, the *O'Neill*? If not, that's the only place on the asteroid to survive, the only way any of us can get home.'

'You're suggesting we can make some kind of deal?' Emma asked, incredulous.

'Emma, you know me. I spent my life making deals –'

And that was when somebody shot her.

June Tybee:

June coughed and found she had vomited, orange juice and fruit bar and other shit spraying over the inside of her faceplate.

She was dangling from a single tether, as if the asteroid had turned to a roof over her head. Another couple of tethers curled around her, ripped free of the regolith. There was only space below her, an infinite place she could fall down into forever.

The ship wasn't there any more. It looked like it had burst like a balloon. There was just a cloud, slowly dispersing, of fragments, metal and plastic and ripped-off insulation blanket.

There were bodies, of course, fragments in the cloud. Some of them were unsuited, just shirtsleeved: those invalided troopers, maybe the pilots. They had never had a chance.

For some reason *that*, the merciless killing of those helpless people, made her more angry than anything else, more even than the fact of her own stranding here, the fact that she would never see Tom or Billie again.

She had to get back to the asteroid before her last tether gave way. Cautiously, hand over hand, she pulled herself along the curling rope.

When she had got close enough to touch the regolith, she pounded more pitons into the surface.

She broke radio silence, and tried calling. The sub-satellites still squirted over her head, darting this way and that like busy metal gnats, unable to comprehend the fact that the giant ship that had brought them here was gone.

No reply.

She had been the furthest from the ship at the moment of the explosion; maybe that was why she was spared. There might be others, disabled somehow. If that was so there wasn't a damn thing she could do about it.

Before she'd left the ship they'd been shown the position of the main squid habitats – since destroyed by the chemical laser – and the humans here, Malenfant and his associates. They had been heading for the far side of the asteroid.

That was where she must go.

The asteroid was a small place. She would surely find the enemy before her consumables expired. Even if not, she must leave enough margin to get back to their ship. If she wasn't going home, neither were they.

She pulled out her tethers and began working her way once more around the asteroid. She had a positioning system built into a heads-up display in her faceplate, coordinates fed to her by the surviving sub-sats.

It wasn't so hard.

She came through the wreckage of a squid bubble habitat.

There was little to see here. The habitat membrane had simply been burst open. Only a few shreds of fabric, a cluster of anonymous machinery, was left here. No squid. Presumably they had all been sent sailing off into space, when their world ended, as had her own buddies.

Good. She only hoped the squid had been smart enough to understand death.

A little after that, she found herself coming into view of the blue circle. She pressed herself against the regolith. Such was the tight

336

curvature of the asteroid, the claustrophobic nearness of its horizon, she was uncomfortably close.

Three figures were standing near the artefact, loosely tethered. They moved to and fro in her sights, gesticulating, talking.

As she'd been trained, she braced her toes in the regolith and fixed her tethers tighter, before she raised her weapon. Otherwise the recoil might blow her clean off Cruithne. She aimed. Unlike on Earth, the slug would travel in a dead straight line, not significantly perturbed by Cruithne's miniature gravity. She'd trained others for this; now they would never have a chance to put those skills to use.

She fired. And again.

Reid Malenfant:

The invisible slug hit Emma, hard, in the leg. She was knocked off the surface. The tether attached to her waist reached its full extent, and jerked taut, and pulled her back. She came slamming down to the surface, landing on her back. And then she bounced, drifting upward and back along the length of the tether.

'Emma? *Emma!*' Clumsily, ignoring his own tether drill, Malenfant hurried to her. He hauled her in by her tether, like landing a fish, and picked her up. Her thigh was a bloody ruin. Malenfant could see blood boiling and popping. 'We need a tourniquet.'

Regolith splashed at his feet.

Cornelius grabbed his arm. 'No time,' he said. 'They're coming for us.'

Malenfant looked around at the pocked landscape. He could see nobody. There wasn't even any sound to help him tell where the shots were coming from.

Another splash, another new crater.

There was no shelter, anywhere.

The blue circle towered over Malenfant, framing darkness. 'This way,' he said. 'Into the portal.'

Cornelius pulled back. 'It's one way. *We won't be able to get back.*'

'I know.' Malenfant studied Cornelius, wishing he could see his face. 'But we'll be alive. And something might turn up.'

'Like what?'

'Trust me,' said Malenfant.

And, clutching Emma in his arms, he loosed his tethers, braced against the regolith and jumped.

There was a blue flash, an instant of astonishing pain –

4

MANIFOLD

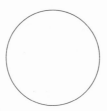

The illimitable, silent, never-resting thing called Time, rolling, rushing on, swift, silent, like an all-embracing ocean-tide, on which we and all the Universe swim like exhalations . . .

– THOMAS CARLYLE

Maura Della:

Open journal. April 14 2012.

Maybe I'm just getting too old.

I should have expected this, this brush fire of panic that has swept the planet, after every TV news channel and net site carried the pictures of the Blue kids sailing out of a nuclear explosion. After the confusing messages and visions from the sky, a consensus seems to have emerged: that we were shown a false future, that the Carter prophecy is real, that we have just two centuries.

To some extent the human race today seems to react as a single organism to great events. After all, we live in a wired world. Memes – information, ideas, fears and hopes – spread around the media and online information channels literally at lightspeed.

It may be that this mass reaction is the greatest single danger facing us.

Anyhow I guess this is what happens when the lead story – all over the TV and radio channels and info nets of a wired-up mankind – is doomsday . . .

Atal Vajpayjee:

Atal lay in the undergrowth and focused his binocular corneal implants.

The Pakistani soldiers who guarded this place walked back and forth, weapons on their shoulders, oblivious in the dense sunshine. It gave him a pleasing sense of power to be able to see those soldiers, and yet to know they could not see him.

He had found his spotting position without disturbance. He had followed the Grand Trunk Road between Rawalpindi and Peshawar, until he reached a modest track that led into these wooded hills. From here, the buildings of the Topi scientific research institute were clearly visible.

Topi was the place where scientists had developed Pakistan's nuclear weapons.

Now he need only wait for the command to come through.

The day was hot. He wiped his forehead, and his fingers came away stained with camouflage paint. He wondered if the boy who had come home that day, more than ten years ago, would recognize him now.

Atal had been just eighteen years old.

He had grown up knowing that Kashmir was India's most troubled province. Still, he had been happy, his father a prosperous cloth merchant in Srinagar. Even the crackle of gunfire at night, off in the hills, did not disturb him.

Everything changed on the day he came home from his studies – he would have been a doctor – to find his mother crumpled on the step, crying, wailing. And in the house he had found the remains of his father.

Remains. A cold, neutral word. Only the lower half of the body had been identifiable as human at all. His mother had been able to identify it only by a scar on the left foot. The authorities were able to provide no comfort, to produce no suspects.

Atal soon learned the truth.

His father had worked for many years as an agent of the central Indian government. He had striven to maintain the precarious stability of this troubled place. And in the end that cause cost him his life.

Since then, Atal had worked for revenge.

The war had already begun, with skirmishes between troops in the hills, border raids by Pakistani jets, the firing of India's Agni missiles against military targets.

It was a war that was inevitable, because it was a war that everybody wanted. If the strange predictions of the Western scientists were true – if the world really was doomed, if superhuman children had defeated the US Army in the desert and flown to the Moon – then it was important that ancient wrongs should be righted, before the darkness fell.

He knew he would probably not live through the day. But that did not matter. There would be no future, no world for his children. There was only *this*, the goal, the taste of victory before the failing of the light.

. . . The radio screeched. Grunting, he gouged the little device out of his ear. It lay on the grass, squealing like an insect.

Electromagnetic pulse.

He looked over his shoulder. Contrails: four, five, six of them, streaking from the east. Ghauri missiles, nuclear-tipped. Bombay, Delhi, Calcutta had only minutes to live.

But the returning fire from India was assured.

It was the day, at last. He stood, raised his weapon, roared in defiance.

A movement to his right.

An explosion in his head. Light, sound, smell, became confused, whirling.

He was lying on his side. Darkness fell.

Xiaohu Jiang:

Xiaohu opened her window, and gazed out at the Beijing night. This tower block was one of a series, well-maintained but utterly cheerless, marching like tombstones around the perimeter of the old city. Her mother had told her that the Beijing sky, at this time of year, used to be famous for its clarity. Now, even the sun at noon was sometimes obscured.

Xiaohu was particularly tired this night.

Her work, at the state-run municipal waste processing plant, was as ever grim and demanding. And – notwithstanding the strange news from America, the bright new spark everyone could see on the face of the Moon – she had no choice but to attend the *xuexi hui*, the weekly political study session, in the large communal area at the base of the building.

Still, somewhat to her surprise, the materials distributed this week had actually been interesting.

Here, for example, was a new edition of an old pamphlet, *An Outline of Certain Questions About Socialism*, which dealt with the official Party response to the Carter prediction. It had surprised her. If Carter was correct, the pamphlet claimed, then only misery lay ahead for future generations. If a child never existed, it could not suffer. Therefore the moral thing was to stop producing children, to spare them pain.

The new doctrine was surely designed as a buttress for the Party's long-standing attempts to control the national population. Everyone was used to official manipulations of the truth – to *zhilu weima*, to point at a deer and call it a horse, as the expression went.

But still, this resonated in Xiaohu's tired mind. There *was* truth here, she thought. Genuine wisdom. But what did it mean for her?

She closed the window and stepped silently into her bedroom. Here was her daughter, Chai, sleeping silently in her cot, her face itself like a tiny round moon, her bud mouth parted.

Chai was not legitimate. Few people knew of her existence, not even her father. Xiaohu had been hatching elaborate plans to provide Chai with a life, an artificial background, a means to achieve respectability, education, a way of life.

Or rather, Xiaohu thought bleakly, a way to get through her life with the minimum pain. But now, the American predictions had made that impossible.

Negative utilitarianism, Xiaohu told herself, reducing evil rather than maximizing good. Perhaps that was all that had ever been possible in this flawed world. She felt enormously tired.

Xiaohu kissed her daughter. Then she took a pillow and set it gently on the child's placid face.

Bob David:

He had always been good with his hands. By the age of seven or eight he had been stripping down truck engines with his father. By twelve he was building his own stock car from scrap.

The thing he was building now – here in his basement in this draughty tenement block in downtown Cambridge, Massachusetts – was simpler than that.

The key to it was a fancy new stuff called red mercury: a compound of antimony and mercury baked in a nuclear reactor, capable of releasing hundreds of times the energy contained in the same mass of TNT. Thanks to red mercury he would be able to fit his bomb into a briefcase.

Bob had grown up here, in Cambridge. He had spent his whole life resenting the asshole nerds who passed him by in class; even as a little kid he'd known that the future was theirs, not his. He'd learned the hard way that there weren't too many places in the world for a guy who was only good with his hands.

He was glad when they started passing the Blue laws and hauling off the smart little assholes to those prison schools in Nevada and New York.

Ironically the only paying, legal job Bob had ever got in his life had been at MIT, the nest of the killer nerds. At the Massachusetts Institute of Technology, even the walls bore the names of scientific gods, Archimedes and Darwin and Newton and Faraday and Pasteur and Lavoisier.

Bob worked in the kitchens, just a slop-out hand.

Even so, despite his resentment, he probably wouldn't have come up with his plan if not for the end-of-the-world news.

He'd listened to what the President had to say. That the doom-soon news was only a prediction, a piece of math. That the Blue children were just children, no matter how strange they seemed. That they mustn't react negatively; they mustn't resort to despair and destruction.

Bob had thought about that.

He'd seen the TV shows and followed the chat groups. For sure the world was going to end, it seemed, even if nobody knew how. But there was a whole host of possibilities, from nuclear war to the air going sour to these genetic mutants, the Blues in their silver base on the Moon, taking over the planet.

And every one of these horrors, it seemed to Bob, was caused by science.

After that Bob had known what he had to do.

He had thought it would be hard to get hold of the raw materials. But that hadn't been hard at all, as it turned out. Just as it hadn't been hard for him to assemble the clean, beautiful machine that was birthing in his cellar.

Patiently he assembled his machine, testing each part before he added it, whistling.

Maura Della:

In western Europe the birth rate had dropped dramatically, as, it seemed, people tried to spare their unborn children the horror of existence. Conversely, the Japanese seemed to be descending into hedonistic excess. *The unborn, who do not yet exist, have no rights; and therefore we are entitled to burn up the world . . .*

And all over the world, old scores were being settled. There had been border conflicts all over the planet, including three limited nuclear exchanges. In southern Africa there had been outbreaks of Rift Valley fever, an ethnic-specific disease which killed ten times as many whites as blacks. Some people were turning to religion. Others were turning *against* it: there had been several assassination attempts on the Pope, and something like a jihad seemed to be raging in Algeria. In the Mid East, a major Islam–Christianity conflict was looming, with some Muslim commentators arguing that the Christians were trying to accelerate the apocalypse of their Gospels.

America wasn't spared, of course. Science labs and technology institutes and corporations all over the country had been subject to attack, with the destruction of MIT being the worst single incident. As for the remnant Blue children, they had already long been targets; now there were commentators – even on network TV – describing the helpless kids as Angels of the Apocalypse . . .

And so it went.

Amidst all this, the business of government went on; and as ever it was just one damn thing after another, as Maura and others strove to contain the damage.

The Cruithne issue was containable.

There had been more probes to the asteroid, endlessly photographing and measuring the wreckage, to no damn purpose as far as she could see. There was talk of sending more humans, volunteers to pass through the artefact. Maura doubted such missions would be approved. What was the purpose, if no data could be sent back?

Personally, she backed the USASF suggestion: to irradiate the surface of Cruithne, make it uninhabitable for a thousand years, and let the future, the damn downstreamers themselves, deal with it.

Notwithstanding Malenfant's illegal launch – the strange artefact he had encountered, the failure of the military task force sent after him, the apparent deaths of all concerned, the exodus of the enhanced squid – all of that had taken place on a rock off in space somewhere. The Cruithne picture show was just too far away, too abstract, too removed from people's experience to deliver any real sense of threat, and already fading in the memory.

There were even rumours that the whole thing had been faked: mocked-up images beamed down from some satellite by the FBI, the United Nations, rogue Third World powers, or some other enemy intent on destabilization, or mind control, or whatever else sprouted from the imagination of the conspiracy theorists. (And of course, as Maura knew well, there was a small department of the FBI set up to invent and encourage such false rumours.)

But the Blue children were different.

Maura had been startled by the fact that people, on the whole, seemed to applaud the use of the nuke. What was causing the current wave of panic was the fact that the attempt – the last resort, the source of all power in the Western mind – had failed.

And then – spectacularly, inexplicably – the children had flown to the Moon. Their escape in that damned silver bubble had been tracked live on TV, as was their subsequent three-day flight to the Moon, and their feather-gentle landing in Tycho, one of the brightest craters on the Moon's near side.

The remaining children were viewed with awe or terror or greed. In some parts of the world they were being used as weapons. Elsewhere they were seen as gods, or devils; already cities had burned over this issue.

In some places the children were simply killed.

Americans, of course, had responded with science. In America, kids were now studied and probed endlessly, even before they were born. If evidence of Blue super-abilities was found, or even suspected, the children were taken away from their parents: isolated, restricted, given no opportunity to manipulate their environment, granted no contact with other children, Blue or otherwise.

There were even, in remote labs, experiments going on to delete, surgically, the source of the Blues' abilities. Lobotomies, by another name. None of it was successful, except destructively.

The purpose of all this was control, Maura realized: people were trying, by these different stratagems, to regain control over their children, the destiny of the species, of their future.

But it was futile. Because up there, she thought, in that silver speck sitting in the lunar dust, *there* is where the future will be decided . . .

And meanwhile the Moon hung up there night after night, colonized somehow by *American children*, and the constantly-circulating space telescope pictures of that strange silver dome on the lunar surface, like a mercury droplet, anonymous and sinister, served as inescapable symbols of the failure of the Administration – of America – to cope.

And yet, Maura thought, cope she must; and she laboured to focus on her mounting responsibilities.

After all, even in the worst case, we still have two centuries to get through.

Reid Malenfant:

. . . fell into light, searing white, brighter than sunlight, that blasted into his helmet. He jammed his eyes shut but could still see the glow shining pink-white through his closed lids, as if he had been thrown into a fire. There was no solid surface under him. He was falling, suspended in space. Maybe he had pushed himself away from Cruithne.

Emma, squirming, slipped out of his grasp. He reached for her, floundering in this bath of dazzling light, but she was gone.

He felt panic settling on his chest. His breathing grew ragged, his muscles stiffening up. He'd lost Emma, he had no idea where Cornelius was, he had no surface to cling to, no point of reference outside his suit.

And all of this was taking place in utter silence.

Something was wrong. Badly wrong. How come they hadn't followed Sheena to her stately vision of the far-future Galaxy? Where was Michael? Where was *he*?

Do something, Malenfant.

The suit radio.

'Emma? Cornelius? If you copy, if you're there, respond. Emma –' He kept calling, and, fumbling for the control, turned up the gain on his headset. Nothing but static.

He tried opening his eyes a crack. Nothing but the blinding glare. Was it a little dimmer, a little yellower, than before? . . . Or was it just that his eyes were burning out, that this dimming would proceed all the way to a permanent darkness?

Don't grab at the worst case, Malenfant.

But what's the best case?

He tried to calm his breathing, relax his muscles. He had to avoid burning up the suit's resources. He reached for the helmet's nipple dispenser, took a draught of orange juice. It was so hot it burned his tongue, but he held it in his mouth until it cooled, and swallowed it anyhow.

There was a noise in his ear, so loud it made him start.

'. . . Emma?'

But it was just the suit's master alarm, an insistent repetitive buzz. He risked a momentary glimpse again – that flood of yellow-white light, maybe a fraction less ferocious – and saw there were red lights all over the heads-up display on his faceplate. He felt for the touchpad on his chest – Christ, he could feel how hot it was even through his gloved fingers – and turned off the alarm.

He didn't need to be told what was wrong. He was immersed in this light and heat, coming from all around him. So there were no shadows, no place for the suit to dump its excess heat.

He could smell a sharp burning, like in a dry sauna. The oxygen blowing over his face was like a desert wind. But, of course, he must breathe; he dragged the air into his lungs, trying not to think about the pain in his throat and lungs. Christ, even the sweat that clung to his forehead in great microgravity drops felt as if it was about to boil; he shook his head, trying to rattle it off.

The master alarm sounded again; he killed it again.

So what are you going to do, Malenfant? Hang around here like a chicken in a microwave? Wish you had taken a bullet in the head from that trooper on Cruithne?

Try something. Anything.

The tethers.

He fumbled at his waist. His surface-operations harness, the trailing tethers, were still there. He pulled in one tether until he got to the piton at the end – and snatched his hand away from the glowing heat of the metal.

He started to whirl the piton around his head, like a lasso, slowly.

Maybe he would hit Cruithne, or one of the others. The chances were slim, he supposed. But it was better than nothing.

It would help if he could see what he was aiming for. He risked another glimpse.

The light was definitely more yellow, but it was still dazzling, too bright to open his eyes fully.

Concentrate on the feel of the tether in your hands. Pay out a little more, extend the reach.

The master alarm again clamoured in his ear. He let it buzz, concentrated on paying out his fishing line, hand over hand, taking little short panting breaths through a drying mouth, shutting out the heat. He had a lot of spare line at his waist, maybe a hundred feet of the fine, strong lightweight nylon rope, and he could reach a long way with it before he was done.

He didn't feel quite so bad as before, he realized. At least he was doing something constructive, planning ahead beyond sucking in the next breath. And, of course, it helped that he wasn't being cooked quite so vigorously.

The buzzing shut itself off.

He risked another glimpse. Beyond the winking red lights of his HUD, the white glare was turning to yellow, the yellow to orange: still bright as hell, like a sun just starting its dip towards a smoky horizon, not something you'd choose to gaze into for long – but, maybe, bearable.

A couple of the HUD's red lights turned to yellow, then green. The air blowing over his face started to feel cooler.

Still working his tether, he turned his head this way and that, peering out of his helmet. He looked down beneath his feet, up above his head, tried to twist around. He peered into the dimming yellow-orange glow. It was like staring into a neon tube. He had no sense of scale, of orientation, of space or time.

. . . He saw something. An orange-white blob, a little darker than the background glow, down below his feet. It was moving.

Waving arms and legs.

Suddenly his sense of scale cut in. It was a person, Emma or Cornelius or even Michael, suspended in space just as he was, forty, fifty feet away. Still alive, by God. Malenfant imagined the three of them tumbling out of the blue-circle portal, falling into this empty three-dimensional space, drifting slowly apart. Hope, unreasonably, pumped in his breast.

But it couldn't be Emma, he realized abruptly. There was no way she could kick with that damaged leg of hers.

Cornelius, then. He was making a gesture with his hands, tracing out some kind of round shape, a circle.

Malenfant was whirling his tether above his head; he would have to change the plane of rotation. That took a little skill and patience, but now he could actually see the heavy piton at the cable's end against the orange-yellow glow, and soon he had the tether snaking out towards Cornelius.

Malenfant tried calling again, but there was no reply, from either Cornelius or Emma. He felt his own body rock to and fro in reaction to the tether's swinging mass. The tether was swinging closer to Cornelius now, close enough surely for him to see it. But Cornelius, drifting, spinning, slowly receding, showed no awareness of what

Malenfant was doing; he just kept repeating his circle gesture, over and over.

At last the tether snagged on Cornelius.

Cornelius reacted to the touch of the tether with a start. He twisted and reached out to his side with jerky, panicky gestures. And, to Malenfant's immense relief, he grabbed the line, wrapped it around his waist a couple of times and tied it off. Then he pulled on it gingerly, and started to haul himself along it.

Huge waves oscillated up and down the line. Malenfant felt his own motion change, gentle, complex tugs this way and that.

Meanwhile the glow continued to dim, noticeably, the yellow increasingly tinged with orange rather than white. It was like being inside a giant iron sphere, heated to white hot, now cooling fast.

The tether to Cornelius provided an anchor, of sorts, and Malenfant was able to pull himself around it. Like a damn trapeze artist, he thought. He twisted, trying to search all of this cooling three-dimensional space, looking for Emma.

And there she was: in fact closer than Cornelius, no more than ten or fifteen feet away. She was directly above him, drifting, inert, her limbs starfished, her gold sun visor down. The blood was still leaking from her shattered leg, little droplets of it pumping out. She was slowly turning, as if her wound was a rocket, a miniature attitude thruster fuelled by blood.

Malenfant got hold of another tether, checked its piton was secure, and started swinging it around his head.

He managed to get the tether to brush over Emma's chest, but, unlike Cornelius, she made no attempt to grab at it. He was going to have to hook her without her co-operation. He aimed for her good leg, playing out more line. If he could get the tether to hit her leg the momentum of the piton might make it wrap around her ankle a couple of times.

He tried once, missed. Tried again, missed.

It was getting increasingly difficult to aim, as Cornelius clambered closer. In fact, Malenfant realized belatedly, Cornelius was actually dragging Malenfant *away* from Emma, towards their joint centre of gravity. Malenfant glared down, across the twenty feet or so that still separated him from the doggedly working Cornelius. 'Cornelius, hold it a minute. Can't you see what I'm doing here? Cut me a little slack . . .' Cornelius didn't respond. Malenfant tried waving at him, miming that he should back off. But Cornelius didn't seem aware of that either.

Swearing under his breath, Malenfant continued to work.

It took a couple more swings, a couple more agonizing near-misses, before Malenfant at last managed to hook his line around Emma's foot. The tether immediately started to unravel, so Malenfant risked everything and gave the tether a hard yank.

The tether came loose.

But it had been enough, he saw with an immense relief; still starfished, passive, spinning, she was drifting towards him. He rolled up the tether hastily and slung it over his arm.

She came sliding past him, like a figure in a dream, not two feet away. He reached up and grabbed her good leg. He pulled her down to him until he had her in his arms once more. Under his gloved hand something crumbled away from Emma's suit. It was a fine layer of white soot.

Clumsily he pushed up her gold visor. There was her face, lit by the still-brilliant orange glow of the sky. Her eyes were closed, the fringe of hair that poked out of her Snoopy hat plastered against her forehead by big, unearthly beads of sweat. It was hard to judge her colour, but it looked to him as if her face was pink, burned, even blistered in a few places, on her cheekbones and chin. He reached out without thinking, meaning to touch her face, but of course his gloved hand just bumped against the glass of her faceplate.

. . . Enough. He was still in the business of survival, here. He got a tether rope and knotted it around his waist and Emma's, making sure they couldn't drift apart again.

What next?

Emma's leg. It was still bleeding, pumping blood. A tourniquet, then. He grabbed a loop of tether rope.

But now somebody was clambering over his back. It was Cornelius, of course, pulling himself along with big clumsy grabs. Malenfant felt a thump at the back of his helmet, and heard a muffled shouting that carried through the fabric of Cornelius's helmet, his own.

'. . . that you? Malenfant? Is that . . .'

Malenfant yelled back, as loudly as he could. 'Yes, it's me.'

'. . . portal. Have you tethered us to the portal?' The words were very muffled, like somebody shouting through a wall. 'The portal. Can you see it? Malenfant . . .'

The portal. That's what Cornelius had been signalling, even as he drifted away into space, with his circle gestures. The portal. The most important object in the world right now, because it was their only way out of this place.

And it hadn't even occurred to Malenfant to think about it.

'. . . Malenfant, I'm blind. All this light. I can't see . . . The portal, Malenfant. Get us back to the portal.'

So, adrift in this featureless universe, he had another tough call. The portal, or Emma's tourniquet.

He shouted back to Cornelius. 'I have Emma. I'll find the portal. But she needs a tourniquet. Do you understand? A tourniquet.'

'. . . tourniquet. The trooper. I remember . . .'

Malenfant reached down and guided Cornelius's hands to Emma's damaged leg. As he touched Cornelius's suit he kicked up another cloud of ash particles. He showed Cornelius by touch where the wound was, gave him a length of tether.

Tentatively at first, then with more confidence, Cornelius began to work, pulling the rope around the damaged leg. Malenfant watched until he was sure Cornelius was, at least, going to do no more harm.

Then Malenfant clambered over Cornelius's back, turning this way and that, looking for the portal.

. . . *There.* It was an electric-blue circle, containing its disc of inky darkness, its colour a painful contrast with the dimming, orange-red background of the sky. But it was drifting away fast. And when the portal was out of reach, it would be gone forever, and this little island of humanity would be stuck here for good.

Hastily Malenfant prepared his tether, weighted with a piton to which asteroid dust still clung. Anchoring himself against Cornelius's back, he whipped it around his head and flung it towards the portal. The tether was drifting well wide of the portal. Malenfant dragged it back, tried again, paying out the tether hastily. He tried again, and again.

If he had been blinded, Cornelius had had it so much worse. But even so he had been *thinking*; he knew immediately how important it was to grab hold of the portal, and – alone, blinded, overheating – he had even tried to signal the fact, to whoever might be watching.

Cornelius was one smart man.

On the fifth or sixth time, the piton sailed neatly through the black mouth of the portal, dragging the uncoiling tether after it. He let it drift on. It was, in fact, a little eerie. He could see that the piton had just disappeared when it hit the portal surface, and now the tether, too, was vanishing as it snaked into the darkness.

353

He began to pull the tether back, cautiously, hardly daring to breathe.

My God, he thought. Here I am fishing for a spacetime wormhole. On any other day this would seem unusual.

The tether grew taut.

He pulled, hand over hand, gently. He felt the combined inertia of the three of them, a stiff resistance to movement. But he was patient; he kept the pressure on the tether light and even.

'. . . WE'RE MOVING . . .'

Cornelius's voice, radio-transmitted, had blared in his ear. Malenfant winced and tapped at the touchpad on his chest.

'Cornelius? Can you hear me?'

Cornelius's voice was heavily laden with static, as if he was shouting into a conch shell, but he was comprehensible. 'Are we moving? Did you –'

'Yes, I got hold of the portal.' He added reflexively, 'I think we'll be okay now.'

Cornelius managed a croaky laugh. 'I doubt that very much, Malenfant. But at least the story goes on a little longer. What about Emma?'

'She hasn't woken up yet. You know, Cornelius, sometimes eyes recover. A few days, a week –'

Cornelius drifted alongside him, sullen, silent.

Let it pass, Malenfant.

They reached the portal. It loomed over Malenfant, huge and blue and enigmatic, brilliant against the reddening sky. Malenfant touched the surface, tried to figure a way to attach a tether or a piton to it.

He discussed the problem with Cornelius.

'Just hold onto it, Malenfant,' he said, and he had Malenfant pull him around until he was doing just that, his hands loosely wrapped over the portal's blade-sharp rim.

Malenfant turned to Emma. She was still unconscious, but she seemed to be sleeping peacefully now. He saw a soft mist on her faceplate close to her mouth. 'I wish I could get this damn suit off of her, give her a drink.'

Cornelius turned blindly. 'Maybe something will come along, Malenfant. That's what you always say, isn't it?'

'Yeah. Yeah, that's what I always say. How's your suit?'

'I'm out of orange juice. And I think my diaper is full . . . Malenfant, what colour is the sky?'

'Red.' Malenfant lifted up his gold visor. It was still bright, just a uniform glow, but it was not so bright he couldn't look at it with his unprotected eyes. 'Like hot coals,' he said.

'That makes sense,' said Cornelius. 'After all our radios work again. So this universe must have become transparent to electro-magnetic radiation. Radio waves –'

This universe. 'What are you talking about, Cornelius?'

'Malenfant – where do you think we are?'

Malenfant looked around at the sky's uniform glow. 'In some kind of gas cloud.' He tried to think out of the box. 'Maybe we're in the outer layers of a red giant star.'

'Umm. If that's so, why was the sky white-hot when we got here? Why is it cooling down so fast?'

'I don't know. Maybe the cloud is expanding –'

'Can you see a source? A centre? Any kind of non-uniformity in the glow?'

'It looks the same to me every which way. Come on, Cornelius. Time's a little short for riddles.'

'I think we fell into another universe.'

'*What* other universe? How?'

Cornelius managed a laugh, his voice like a dry, crumpling leaf. 'You know, Malenfant, you always have trouble with the big picture. You didn't seem disturbed philosophically by the idea of a gateway that takes you instantaneously to another time. Well, now the portal has just taken us to another spacetime point, instantaneously, like before. It's just that *this* time that point is in another universe, somewhere else in the manifold.'

'The manifold?'

'The set of all possible universes. Probably one related to ours.'

'*Related?* . . . How can universes be related? Never mind.'

Cornelius turned blindly. 'Damn it, I wish I could see. There's no reason why this universe should be exactly like ours, Malenfant. Most universes will be short-lived, probably on the scale of the Planck time.'

'How long is that?'

'Ten to power minus forty-three of a second.'

'Not even time to make a coffee, huh.'

'I think this universe is only a few hours old. I think it just expanded out of its Big Bang. Think of it. Around us the vacuum itself is changing phase, like steam condensing to water, releasing energy to fuel this grand expansion.'

'So what's the glow we see?'

'The background radiation.' Cornelius, drifting in red emptiness, huddled over on himself, wrapping his suited arms around his torso, as if he was growing cold.

'How can universes be different?'

'If they have different physical laws. Or if the constants that govern those laws are different . . .'

'If we fell into a Big Bang, it occurs to me we were lucky not to be fried.'

'I think the portal is designed to protect us. To some extent anyhow.'

'You mean if we had been smart enough to come through with such luxuries as air and water and food, we might live through all this?'

'It's possible.'

'*Then where did Michael go?*'

Cornelius sighed. 'I don't know.'

'The Sheena squid came through the portal, and she found herself in the future. Seventy-five million years downstream. Staring at the Galaxy.'

'I do remember, Malenfant,' Cornelius said dryly.

'So how come we didn't follow her?'

'I think it was the Feynman radios. The crude one we built at Fermilab. Whatever was put into the heads of the Blue kids, Michael and the others. The messages from the future changed the past. That is, our future. Yes. The river of time took a different course.'

'If this isn't the future –'

'I think it's the past,' Cornelius whispered. 'The deepest past.'

'I don't understand.'

'Of course not, Malenfant. Why should you?'

'. . . Cornelius. I think the sky is getting brighter.'

It was true; the reddening seemed to have bottomed out, and a strengthening orange was creeping back into the sky.

Malenfant said, 'That's bad, right? We're heading for a Big Crunch. We just lived through a Big Bang, and now we're facing a Crunch. One damn thing after another.'

'We can't stay here,' Cornelius whispered.

Malenfant looked around at the glowing sky, tried to imagine it contracting around him, the radiation that filled it compressing, rattling around the walls of the universe like gas in a piston, growing hotter and hotter . . . 'Cornelius, will there be life here? Intelligence?'

'Unlikely,' Cornelius whispered. 'Our universe was a big, roomy, long-lived place. Lots of room for structure to self-organize, atoms and stars and galaxies and people. Here, even the atoms will exist for just a few hours.'

'Then – what's the point? An empty universe, no life, no mind, over in a few hours? Why?'

Cornelius coughed. 'You're asking the wrong person.'

Malenfant gathered the others – Cornelius curled into a foetal ball, Emma sleeping, starfished, the tether length on her leg dangling – and he faced the portal.

The sky was getting brighter, hotter, climbing the spectral scale through orange towards yellow. 'Visors down.'

Cornelius dropped his own gold sun visor into place, reached over, and did the same for Emma, by touch.

Malenfant wrapped his suited arm around Emma's waist, and grasped Cornelius firmly by the hand. He turned his back on the collapsing, featureless sky without regret, and pulled them both into the portal.

Maura Della:

Houston was hot, muggy, fractious. The air settled on her like a blanket every time she hurried between airport terminal and car, or car and hotel, as if it was no longer a place adapted for humanity.

She booked into her hotel, showered and changed, and had her car take her out to JSC, the NASA Johnson Space Center. The car pulled into the JSC compound off NASA Road One, and she drove past gleaming, antiquated Moon rockets: freshly restored, spectacularly useless, heavily guarded from the new breed of anti-science wackos.

She was dismayed by the depression and surliness of the staff who processed her at the NASA security lodge. The mood in Houston seemed generally sour, the people she encountered overheated, irritable. She knew Houston had special problems. The local economy relied heavily on oil and chemicals, and was taking a particular beating as the markets fluctuated and dived over rumours of the super-technology that the Blue children had been cooking up, stuff

357

that would make fossil fuel technology obsolete overnight. But she had come here with a vague hope that at least at NASA – where they were all rocket scientists, for God's sake – there might be a more mature reaction to what was going on in the world. But the national mood of fear and uncertainty seemed to be percolating even here.

Dan Ystebo came to collect her. He led her across the compound, past blocky black-and-white buildings and yellowing lawns, the heat steamy and intense. Dan seemed impatient, irritable, his shirt soaked with the sweat of his bulky body. He had spent a week here at her behest, crawling over plans and mock-ups and design documents and budgets, in order to brief her.

Maura had been coopted onto the UN-led international task force which was seeking to investigate and manage all aspects of the Blue children phenomenon. And she, in turn, had coopted Dan Ystebo, much against his will.

Dan took her to Building 241, where, it turned out, NASA had been running life support experiments for decades. Now the building was the focus of NASA's response to the government's call to return to the Moon, to establish a presence on the Moon alongside the children.

Dan was saying, 'It isn't ambitious – not much beyond Space Station technology. The modules would be launched to lunar orbit separately, linked together and then lowered as a piece to the Moon's surface, as close as you like to the kids' dome. A couple of robot bulldozers to shovel regolith over the top to protect you from radiation and stuff, and there you are, instant Moon base . . .'

Dan walked her through mocked-up shelters, tipped-over cylinders with bunks and softscreens and simple galleys and bathrooms. Most of the equipment here was thrown together from painted wood panels, but at least Maura got a sense of the scale and layout. She had to get from one shelter to another by crawling along flexible tubes – difficult, but presumably that would be easier in the Moon's one-sixth gravity. All of this was set out in a huge hangar-like room; fixed cranes ran along the ceiling, and there was a lot of litter on the floor: wood and metal shavings, piled-up plans, hard hats. The sense of rush, of improvisation, was tangible.

'Feels like a mobile home park,' she said.

'Yeah,' Dan said. He was puffing from the exertion of crawling through the tubes. 'Except it will be an even worse place to stay. Remember you'll never be able to open a window . . . The power will come from solar cells. The engineers are looking at simple roll-up sheets you could spread across acres of the lunar surface, or drape from a crater wall, whatever. It should be possible to move them around as the lunar day progresses. To survive the two-week nights they say they will need radioisotope thermonuclear generators.'

'More nukes, Dan?'

He shrugged. 'In the short term there isn't much choice. We're constrained by where the kids came down – in Tycho, one of the roughest places on the Moon. The old NASA plans always showed astronauts colonizing a polar crater, somewhere you could catch the sun all lunar day, and where there would be ice to mine. As it is we're going to have to haul up everything, every ounce of consumable. Initially, anyhow.'

He led her into the next hangar-like room. Here there was a single construction: a dome of some orange fabric, inflated, with fat tubes running around its exterior. It was maybe eight feet across, five high. Maura saw a small camera-laden robot working its way into the dome through what looked like an extendable airlock.

'This is stage two,' Dan said, 'a Constructable Habitat Concept Design. You have your dome, inflated from the inside, with self-deploying columns for strength, with a spiral staircase down the centre.'

'What's the fabric?'

'Beta cloth. What they've been making spacesuits out of since Apollo 11. NASA is a somewhat conservative organization. This dome will contain a partially self-contained ecology based on algae. The medics here are looking at electrical muscle and bone stimulation to counteract the low gravity effects. And regolith mining will get underway. The Moon isn't as rich as Malenfant's C-type asteroid, and it is mostly as dry as a bone. But you can make a reasonable concrete from the dust. And the rocks are forty per cent oxygen by weight, and there is silicon to make glass, fibreglass and polymers, aluminium, magnesium and titanium for reflective coatings and machinery and cabling, chromium and manganese for alloys –'

'Living off the land, on the Moon.'

'That's the idea. They are working to stay a long time, Maura.'

He led her to a coffee machine. The sludge-brown drink was free, but bad. The lack of fresh coffee was one of the consequences of the world trade mini-collapse: something small but annoying, the removal of something she had always taken for granted, a sign of more bad news to come.

359

Maura asked him how come the NASA people were reacting so badly. 'If anybody on the planet is trained to think about cosmic issues, to think out of the box of the here and now, it's surely NASA.'

'Hell, Maura, it's not as simple as that. NASA has lacked self-confidence for decades anyhow. Reid Malenfant drove them all crazy. Here was a guy who NASA wouldn't even hire, for God's sake, and he just went out there and did it ahead of them. Look at this.' He dug into a pocket and pulled out a cartoon printed off some online source: bubble-helmeted NASA astronauts in a giant, glittering spacecraft being beaten to the Moon by a bunch of ragged-ass kids in a wooden cart. *What's the big deal, guys?*

Dan was grinning.

'You shouldn't look like you enjoy it so much, Dan. Bad for relations.'

'Sorry.'

'So is that it? Hurt pride?'

'Maybe that's a rational response,' Dan said. 'The Blue kids, after all, have to operate within the laws of physics. So the solution *they* found to space travel must be out there somewhere. How come they got so smart, just sailing up to the Moon like that out of a nuclear explosion, for God's sake, while we stayed dumb, still flying our Nazi-scientist rockets after decades and terabucks? And besides –'

'What?'

'Rocket scientists or not, the people here are only human, Maura. Some of them have Blue kids too . . . The good thing is that these NASA types have been dreaming of this, running experiments and pilot plans and paper studies, for decades now. When the call did come they hit the ground running. And they are preparing to be up there a long time.' He eyed her. 'That's the plan, isn't it, Maura?'

'It's possible. Nobody knows. We don't know what needs the children have. They may be genius prodigies at physics and math, but what do they know about keeping themselves alive on the Moon? Our best option may be to offer help.'

Dan looked sceptical. 'So that's our strategy? We imprison them, we nuke them, and now we offer them green vegetables?'

'We have to try to establish some kind of relationship. A dialogue. All we can do is wait it out.'

'As long as it takes?'

'As long as it takes.'

'Is it true they're sending messages? The children, I mean.'

Maura kept stony-faced.

'Okay, okay,' Dan said, irritated, and he walked on, bulky, sweating.

They walked on to other test sites and seminar rooms and training stations, more elements of this slowly converging lunar outpost, inspecting, planning, questioning.

Reid Malenfant:

There was an instant of blue electric light, a moment of exquisite, nerve-rending pain. Malenfant kept his grip on Emma and Cornelius, focused on the hard physical reality of their suited flesh.

The blue faded.

And there was a burst of light, a wash that diminished from white to yellow to orange to dull red – a pause, as if recovering breath – and then a new glissando back up the spectrum to glaring hot yellow-white.

Then it happened again, a soundless pulse of white light that diminished to orange-red, then clambered back to brilliance once more.

And again, faster this time – and again and again, the flapping wings of light now battering at Malenfant so rapidly they merged into a strobe-effect blizzard.

The warning indicators on his suit HUD started to turn amber, then red. 'Hold Emma.' He pulled Emma and Cornelius closer to him, gathered them in a circle so their faceplates were almost touching, their backs turned to the brutal waves of brilliance, the flickering light shimmering from their visors.

'Cornelius.' Malenfant found himself shouting, though the light storm was utterly silent. 'Can you hear me?'

'Tell me what you see.'

Malenfant tried to describe the pulsating sky. As he did so the clatter of white-red-white pulses slowed, briefly, and the pumping of the sky became almost languid, each cycle lasting maybe three or four seconds. But then, without warning, the cycling accelerated again, and the dying skies blurred into a wash of fierce light.

'Cosmologies,' Cornelius whispered. 'Phoenix universes, each one rebounding into another, which expands and collapses in turn. Each one destroyed so that the next one, its single progeny, can be born. And the laws of physics get shaken around every time we come out of a unified-force singularity.'

'A what?'

'A Big Bang. Or the singularity at the heart of a black hole. The two ways a universe can give birth to another . . . Black holes are the key, Malenfant. A universe which cannot make black holes can have only one daughter, produced by a Crunch. A universe which *can* make black holes, like ours, can have many daughters, baby universes connected to the mother by spacetime umbilicals through the singularities at the centre of black holes. Like a miniature Big Crunch at the centre of every hole. And that's where cosmic evolution really takes off . . . We're privileged, Malenfant.'

Malenfant shouted, 'Privileged? Are you kidding?'

'We're watching the evolution of universes. Or rather, *you* are. A spectacle beyond comparison.'

The pulsing cosmic collapses accelerated once more; the waves of light that washed down from the sky came so fast, one after the other, that it was as if they were caught inside some giant strobe machine. The three of them hung here, framed by the patient blue ring, their battered dust-stained suits bathed in the light of creation and extinction.

Could it be true? – *universes*, born and dying in a time shorter than it took him to draw a breath, as if he was some immense, patient god?

He turned to Emma.

She was still starfished, silent. He tapped her suit's chest control panel, but that only told him about the condition of her suit – labouring, damaged, complaining about the loss of fluids from the ruptured leg. He couldn't see her face, as he did not dare lift her gold visor; it glared in the light of dying cosmoses.

Cornelius was curling into a ball. Maybe he was descending into some kind of shock. It wouldn't be so surprising, after all.

And how come *your* head is still working, Malenfant? If Cornelius wants to curl up and hide, why don't you?

Maybe, he thought, it was because he was too dumb to understand. Maybe if he did understand, like Cornelius, the knowledge would crush him.

Being dumb was sometimes an evolutionary advantage.

'Cornelius. How are you feeling?'

'I'm heating up. These universes aren't long-lived enough to allow our suits to dump their excess heat.'

Malenfant forced a laugh. 'I bet that's one situation that isn't covered by the manufacturers' warranty.'

Cornelius, folded over into a foetal ball, whispered: 'Let me tell you my plan . . .'

The intensity of the light storm increased. Malenfant closed his eyes and huddled over Emma, trying to protect her a few seconds longer.

The suit alarm sounded.

And shut itself off.

And the light storm died.

Malenfant grunted. He opened his eyes and looked around.

The sky was cooling in a soundless explosion of light, dimming as if exhausted from yellow to orange to red, to a dull ember-like glow that was soon so faint he had trouble distinguishing it with his creation-dazzled eyes.

He felt a huge relief, as if he had stepped out of a rainstorm.

Cornelius whispered fretfully, 'Not every universe will make stars, Malenfant. There may not even be atomic structure here. In our universe the various atomic forces are balanced so precisely you can have more than a hundred different types of stable nuclei. Hence, the richness of the matter in our world. But it didn't have to be like that. Everything is contingent, Malenfant. Even the structure of matter . . .'

The sky had become uniformly dark now, and the light, as far as he could see the *only* light in the whole of this universe, was the cold blue glow of the patient, unmarked portal.

Malenfant hugged Emma to him. Her face was peaceful, as if she was immersed in a deep, untroubled sleep. But she looked cold. He thought he could see a frost forming on the inside of her faceplate.

He sensed the growing universe around him, its huge, meaninglessly expanding emptiness. And, it seemed, in all of this baby universe the only clump of matter and energy and light was *here*, the only eyes to see this his own. If he closed his eyes – if he died, here and now – would this cosmos even continue to exist?

A hell of a thought. Therefore, don't think it.

'It's damn cold,' he said.

'You're never satisfied, are you, Malenfant?' Cornelius, still hunched over, was fiddling with the controls on his chest, tapping at them.

'What the hell are you doing there, Cornelius?'

'Sending a message.'

'Via the portal. Like the firefly we sent through. Radio waves into neutrino pulses.'

'Yes.'

'You think somebody is going to be able to come help us?'

'I doubt it.'

'Then what?'

'Turn to band six.'

Malenfant changed the tuning of his suit radio, and there it was: a wash of static, broken up by Cornelius's tapping. He was sending out a series of pulses, crudely controlled by the touchpad.

He remembered where he'd seen a signal like this before.

'3753, 1986. 3753, 1986. That's what you're sending, isn't it, Cornelius? The message we picked up at Fermilab. *You're sending the Feynman radio message back to yourself.*'

Malenfant could hear a smile in Cornelius's voice. 'I always wanted to try something like this.'

'And you're not afraid of breaking causality? That, umm, the universe won't explode or some damn thing to stop you?'

'A little late for that, Malenfant.'

'But how do you know what to send?'

'You were there. I know what to send because I remember what I received. And since we did receive the message, we came here, and we can send it. So it's all perfectly consistent, Malenfant. Just –'

'Backward.'

'I would have said *looped.* And the universe has reconstructed itself, knitting itself together quantum transaction by quantum transaction, around this central causal loop.'

'So where did the message come from in the first place? The information in it, I mean. If you're just copying what you received –'

Cornelius stopped tapping, and sighed. 'That's a deeper question, Malenfant. At any point in spacetime, at any *now,* there are an infinite number of pasts that could have led to the present state, and an infinite number of possible futures which flow from it. This is called the solution space of the universal wave function. Somewhere out in that solution space some equivalent of me figured out and wrote down the message, and sent it back with a Feynman radio.'

'Even if I understood that,' growled Malenfant, 'I wouldn't like it. Information coming out of nothing.'

'Then don't accept it. Maybe the message just appeared, spontaneously.'

'That's impossible.'

'How do you know? We don't have a conservation law for knowledge.' And he carried on with his patient tapping.

The cold, the endless chill of this meaningless, empty cosmos, seemed to sink deeper into Malenfant's bones. 'We're going to freeze to death if we stay here,' he said.

'Our suits aren't made for extremes,' Cornelius whispered. 'Not for extended periods of heat and cold, or for extremes of temperature. But this won't last forever.'

'Another Crunch?'

'Yes. But it may not be for a while –'

And there was no time to say any more, for there was a howl of radio static, a burst of sodium light that washed over them.

Malenfant, grunting with shock, cradling Emma, tried to turn.

Something came erupting out of the portal: complex, spinning, dazzling light flaring. It was a human. Dressed in a heavy black spacesuit, face hidden behind a gold visor. Spinning about its waist – crazily, not under control.

The spacesuited figure carried a gun, a snub-nosed pistol, raised towards Malenfant.

Malenfant struggled to turn, to shield Emma with his body, but his suit, the tether, impeded him.

The trooper was wearing a backpack, much bulkier than Malenfant's. It had small bronze nozzles and big wraparound arm units with what looked like joysticks. Maybe it was some kind of MMU, a manned manoeuvring unit. Sodium light was flaring from lamps. The suit looked as if it had once been as black as coal, but now it was badly charred, the surface flaking off, so as the figure spun it gave off a shower of scorched flakes like a Catherine wheel.

Malenfant called, 'Wait. Can you hear me? You followed us all the way here, through a thousand universes. I can't believe you want to kill us –'

Cornelius was moving. He had dragged at a tether and launched himself across space, directly at the trooper.

'*Cornelius!*'

The trooper, still spinning, swivelled and fired at Cornelius.

Malenfant saw the gun spark, once, twice, in complete silence. Cornelius crumpled about his middle. But he was still moving, still floating through space, his limbs still working, reaching.

His belly hit the trooper's legs. He clung on, groping at the trooper's suit.

Meanwhile the trooper continued to fire; Malenfant saw at least one more shot slice through Cornelius's legs. But now Cornelius, clambering behind the trooper, was out of reach. The momentum of their combined bodies turned their motion into a clumsy, unco-ordinated, complex roll.

The trooper squirmed, trying to get hold of Cornelius. But Cornelius, labouring, had managed to reach down between the backpack and the trooper's suit. He yanked loose a hose. Vapour vented into space, immediately freezing into crystals.

The trooper's motions became scrambled, panicky. Legs kicked helplessly, and gloved hands scrabbled at the helmet as if striving to pull it off.

It took only a minute for the trooper's struggles to diminish, a few last kicks, desperate scrabbles at helmet, chest panel, back pack.

And then, stillness.

Even before that, Cornelius was still too.

There was blood inside Cornelius's helmet. It had stuck to the visor and was drying there. Droplets of it seemed to be orbiting inside the helmet itself. Malenfant couldn't see Cornelius's face, and he was grateful for that.

I'm going to miss you, he thought. Cornelius, the man who under-stood the future, even other universes. I wonder if you understand the place you have gone to now.

The trooper turned out to be a woman. There was some kind of liquid over the interior of her depressurized helmet, and Malenfant didn't look too closely. He did find a name tag sewn to the fabric of her suit. TYBEE J.

He couldn't find the gun.

With loose loops of tether he tied together the bodies of Cornelius and the trooper.

I ought to say something, he thought.

Who for? For the corpses? They weren't around to hear any more, and Emma was unconscious. Then who? Did this universe have its own blind, stupid God, a God whose grasp of the possibilities of creation had reached only as far as this dull, expanding box?

Not for God. For himself, of course.

He said, 'This is a universe that has never known life. But now it knows pain, and fear, and death. You couldn't get much further from home. And I guess it's right that you should stay here, together. That's all.'

Then, bracing himself against the portal, he shoved them gently. There was only the blue glow of the portal, which diminished quickly, and they were soon fading from sight.

He wondered how long the bodies would last here. Would they have time to rot, mummify, their substance evaporate? Would the different physical laws of this universe penetrate them, making their very atomic nuclei decay? Or would they be caught up, destroyed at last, in the Big Crunch which Cornelius had promised would destroy this universe, as it had the others?

The bodies drifted away slowly, tumbling slightly, the two of them reaching the limit of the tether and then coming back together, colliding softly once more, as if their conflict had continued, in this attenuated form, beyond death itself. As, perhaps, it would; their ghosts, trapped in a universe that wasn't their own, had only each other to haunt.

It doesn't matter, Malenfant. Time to move on.

The trooper's MMU backpack, evidently built to mil spec, was considerably more advanced than Bootstrap hardware.

There was a power source – lightweight batteries – which would long outlast Malenfant's own, a significant supply of compressed air, a simple water recycler, and food pods that looked as if they were meant to plug into slots in the trooper's helmet. And there was a med pack, simple field-medicine stuff. The MMU even contained a lightweight emergency shelter, a fabric zip-up bubble.

Suddenly life was extended – not indefinitely, but through a few more hours at least. He was startled how much that meant to him.

Malenfant pulled himself and Emma into the shelter and assembled it around them. It was just big enough for him to stretch out at full length. The fabric, self-heating, was a thin translucent orange, but a small interior light made the walls seem solid. Malenfant felt enormously relieved when he had shut out the purposeless expansion outside, as if this flimsy fabric emergency tent could shelter him from the universes that flapped and collapsed beyond its walls.

When the pressure was right, the temperature acceptable, he cracked his own helmet and sniffed the air. It was metallic, but fine.

He pulled off his gloves. He turned to Emma, opened up her helmet and lifted it off carefully, let it drift away. Emma's burned-red cheek was cold to his touch, but he could feel a pulse, see breath mist softly around her mouth.

He took time to kiss her, softly. Then he used his own helmet nipple to give her a drink of orange juice.

He tried to treat Emma's wounded leg. He didn't like the look of what he saw below the improvised tether tourniquet. The blood and flesh, exposed to vacuum, was frozen, the undamaged skin glassy. But at least she hadn't bled to death, he thought, and she didn't seem to be in any pain. He cleaned up the wound as best he could.

'. . . Malenfant?'

The sound, completely unexpected, made him gasp, turn.

She was awake, and looking at him.

Maura Della:

Life on the Hill had gotten a lot harder, even without the protestors. And the chanting of the protestors, cult groups and other disaffected citizens in the streets outside, always an irritant, had become a constant distraction. There were times – even here, behind the layers of toughened glass – when she could hear the cries of pain, the smash of glass, the smoky crackle of small arms fire, the slap and crash of grenade launchers.

Maura believed there was something deep and troubling going on in the collective American psyche right now. She'd always worked on the belief that Americans liked to imagine themselves elevated from the general human fray, if only a little. Americans had the most robust political system, the best technology, the strongest economy, the finest national character and spirit. Of course it was mostly myth, but it wasn't a bad myth as national fever-dreams went, and Maura knew that Americans' faith in themselves had, historically, tended to turn them into a positive force in the world.

But there was a downside. Whenever things went bad, whenever the myth of superiority and competence was challenged, Americans would look outside, for somebody or something to blame for their troubles. And, whatever went wrong with the world, there was always an element who would blame the government.

Fair enough. But how the hell was she supposed to concentrate with all that going on?

But, of course, she had to.

Just as she had to ignore the other inconveniences of the post-Nevada world. Such as the fact that she wasn't allowed to use e-mail, photocopiers, scanners or even manual typewriters and carbon paper. All government business relating to Bootstrap and the Blue children was now conducted by hand-written note: one copy only, to be destroyed by the recipient after use.

Even her private diary was, strictly speaking, illegal now.

Depressed, she turned to the first fat report on her desk. It was set out in a clear, almost childish hand, presumably that of some baffled, sworn-to-silence secretary. She skimmed through a preface consisting of academic ass-covering bull: ... *able to offer no assurances as to the accuracy of this preliminary interpretation which has been produced, according to this group's mandate, as a guide for further decision-making and* . . .

It was from the team of academics at Princeton who were trying to translate the messages the children had been sending to Earth. (She remembered Dan Ystebo's apparently informed speculations on the subject, and she made a mental note to have one of the FBI plumbers dig out who was leaking this time.)

The sporadic signals were in the form of ultra-violet laser light targeted on an antiquated astronomy satellite in Earth orbit. Why they chose that means of transmission, nobody knew, nor how they had gotten hold of or built a laser, nor why they felt impelled to transmit messages at all. Perhaps all that would come after the greybeard academic types at Princeton and elsewhere had figured out *what* the hell the kids were talking about here.

The message itself was text, encoded in a mixture of ASCII, English, other natural languages and mathematics. But the natural-language stuff didn't seem to bear much relation to the math, which itself was full of symbologies and referents whose meanings the academics were having to guess at.

The math appeared to be some kind of diatribe on fundamental physics.

Maura knew that for a century the theoreticians had been struggling to reconcile the two great pillars of physics: relativity, Einstein's theory of gravity, and quantum mechanics, the theory of the sub-microscopic world. The two theories were thought to be limited facets of a deeper understanding the academics called quantum gravity . . . *It is impossible to delimit a theory which does not yet exist,* the report writers noted pompously. *Nevertheless most theorists had expected to find the quantum paradigm more fundamental that the relativistic. The speculations of the children contradict this, however . . .*

Maura skimmed on. Perhaps – the children seemed to be suggesting – fundamental particles, electrons and quarks and such, were actually spacetime defects, kinks in the fabric. For instance, a positive charge could be the mouth of a tiny wormhole threaded by an electric field, with a negative charge the other mouth, the flow of the field through the wormhole looking, from the outside, like a source and sink of charge. Einstein himself had speculated on these lines a century ago, but hadn't been able to prove it or develop the theory to his satisfaction.

Anyhow, it seemed, Einstein hadn't thought far enough. The children seemed to be saying that the key was to regard particles – not just as loops or folds in space – but as folds in time as well. *Such a fold necessarily creates a closed timelike curve . . .*

So every electron was a miniature time machine.

. . . This has clear implications for causality. The properties of a fundamental particle would be determined by measurements that can be made on it only in the future. That is, there is a boundary condition which is in principle unobservable in the present . . . Imagine a skipping rope, some dusty academic had dictated, struggling to make herself understood. *If a handle is jiggled, the shape of the wave created depends not just on what is happening at the perturbed end but what happens at the other handle . . .*

In this world-view it was this breach of causality that provided uncertainty, the famous multivalued fuzziness of the quantum world.

And so on, at baffling and tedious length.

She sat in her chair, struggling with the concepts.

So the world around her, the familiar solid world of atoms and people and trees and stars, even the components of her own ageing body, was made up of nothing more than defects in spacetime. There was *nothing* but space and time, knotted up and folded over on itself. If that's so, she thought, maybe we shouldn't be surprised at the irruption of all this acausal strangeness. It was there all along, just too low level for us to see, too obscure for us to understand.

But was it possible? . . .

Just accept it, Maura. The important thing, of course, is *why* the children are trying to communicate this to us.

*. . . The children may be attempting to bridge the chasm in under-
standing between our patiently constructed but partial theories and
their own apparently instinctive, or paradox-prescient, knowledge
of the world's structure. It may be they wish us to understand on
a deeper level what has happened to us so far – or, possibly, what
is to happen to us in the future . . .*

A prediction, then.

Or a threat.

Maura shivered, despite the clammy warmth of her office.

Maura, skimming the transcript, found scraps of plain language
interspersed with all this heavy stuff: . . . *We're all right here,
please tell our parents, we aren't hot or cold or hungry but just
right, and it's a lot of fun bouncing around on the Moon, like a
big trampoline . . . You shouldn't have done what you did when
you dropped that big bomb on us and it just made us mad is
all and some of us wanted to come back and hurt you the same
but Anna said we mustn't and it wasn't really your fault that you
cared for us underneath even if you didn't know how to show it
and . . .*

A kid's report from summer camp, beamed down by ultra-violet
laser from the Moon, interspersed with theoretical physics so heavy-
duty a gaggle of Nobel Prize winners couldn't make sense of it. She
felt her heart break a little more.

Even while it scared the life out of her.

She closed the report and dropped it into the high-temperature
incinerator that hummed softly under her desk.

The last report in her tray was colour-coded – by hand, with a
marker pen – as the highest category of secure. It was about how
the new NASA lunar outpost at Tycho would be used as a base for
infiltrating the children's mysterious encampment.

The Trojan-horse children had been selected from birth, screened
for the Blue syndrome from before they could talk or walk. There
were more than a hundred candidate kids at this point, all of them
infants or pre-schoolers. And now their education was being shaped
with a single purpose: loyalty to Earth, to home, to parents. There
was training, discipline, ties of affection, every kind of behavioural
conditioning the psychologists could dream up, mental and physical.
They'd even brought in advertising executives.

Nobody knew what was going to work on these kids – who
would, after all, eventually be smarter than any of the people who
were working on their heads. Eventually, when they got old enough,

the conditioning would be tested, sample candidates put through a variety of simulated experiences.

Little human lab rats, Maura thought, being given mazes to run, with walls of loyalty and coercion and fear.

The objective was to have selected a final cohort of seven or eight individuals by the time the children had reached the age of five or six, and then to ship them to the Moon and offer them to the Blues up there. And then to have the Blues' new friends betray them.

She came to a list of candidate infants. One of them was Billie Tybee: daughter of Bill Tybee, who, a thousand years ago, had turned to Maura for help, and June Tybee, who had died during the failed assault on Cruithne, and the sibling of Tom, one of the children who had gone to the Moon, lost forever to his grieving father.

As if we haven't done enough to that family.

Maura hadn't yet worn her conscience completely smooth. This is, she thought, a war against our own children. And we're using every dirty method on them that we dreamed up in a million years of waging war against ourselves.

But she knew she had to put her conscience aside, once again.

The children on the Moon, whatever they were doing up there, had to be understood, controlled, stopped.

By any means necessary.

Anyhow, if these really are the dying days of mankind, at least we're going out true to ourselves. God help us all, she thought, as she pushed the report into the incinerator.

Reid Malenfant:

Malenfant cradled Emma, gently helped her eat, drink, let her sleep, tried to answer her questions. But she seemed less interested in the fate of the multiple universes through which she'd travelled, unconscious, than in Cornelius and Michael.

'Poor Cornelius,' she said. 'I wonder if he found what he wanted, in the end.'

'I doubt it. But he gave his life for us.'

'But only because he knew immediately there was no other choice. That the trooper would otherwise have killed all three of us. He knew he was going to die, one way or the other.'

'It didn't have to be that way,' said Malenfant.

'Oh, it did.' Her voice was steady, but weak. 'Cornelius was dead from the moment he destroyed that troop carrier. As long as he left one trooper alive, one who knew she or he wouldn't be going home again . . .'

'But for the trooper to follow us through the portal, through those multiple universes –'

'There is a human logic that transcends all of *this*.' She waved a hand. 'All the incomprehensible cosmological stuff. And that's what killed Cornelius.'

'Human logic,' he said. 'You think there's a logic that has brought the two of us here? Wherever the hell *here* is.'

'The only two souls in a universe,' she said weakly. 'It would sound romantic if –'

'I know.'

She was silent a while. Then: 'Malenfant –'

'Yeah?'

'You think we can find a way back home?'

He sighed. 'I don't know, babe. But we can try.'

'Yes,' she said, and she snuggled closer to his spacesuited form, seeking warmth. 'We can try, can't we?' She closed her eyes.

He let her rest for six hours.

Then he sealed up their suits, collapsed the bubble, checked their tethers, attached trooper Tybee's backpack to his waist.

Then, hand in hand, Malenfant and Emma slid through the blue-circle portal, steps of just a few feet taking them gliding between realities.

Universe after universe after universe.

Sometimes they encountered more chains of fast-collapsing phoenixes, imploding skies that washed them with a transient light, and they huddled in the portal as if escaping the rain. But most of the cosmoses they encountered now were long past their first expansion, far from their final collapse, and were empty even of the diseased light of creation or destruction.

Nowhere was there was any sign of life: nothing but the empty logic of physical law.

Sometimes Emma slept inside her suit, allowing Malenfant to haul her back and forth through the portal, whole universes going by without waking her: not even looking, even though they might be, he supposed, the only conscious entities ever to visit these places, these starless deserts.

An immense depression settled on Malenfant. This desolate parade of universe after universe – spacetime geometries utterly empty of warmth and mind and life save for himself and Emma – seemed to have been arranged to demonstrate to him that even the existence of a place in which structure and life could evolve was an unlikely accident. All his adult life he had fought for the future of the species. What was his ambition now? – that squads of humans should follow him through these portals and settle these dead places, wrestle with space and time and the physical laws to make another place to live?

He came to a place which was, at least, different. The sky was huge, black, without stars or galaxies. But there was *something*: a texture to the sky, a swathe of redness, just at the limit of his vision. In trooper Tybee's backpack he had found a visor attachment with a night vision setting. He wrapped the attachment over his helmet; it fit like huge goggles.

He peered around. His own body and Emma's shone like false-colour stars, the brightest objects in the universe.

The sky itself showed a dull red glow, the relic Big Bang radiation of this pocket universe. And there were clouds – diffuse, without structure – which covered much of the sky. The clouds showed up as thin grey-white in Malenfant's enhanced vision, something like high cirrus. 'Almost like home,' he murmured. Actually, not. But it was better than bland nothingness.

'Malenfant.'

He looked into Emma's helmet. She was awake, smiling at him. 'Did you dream?'

'No,' she said. 'I wish that fancy backpack had a coffee spigot.'

'And I wish I could say it's a pretty view.'

'I suppose it is, in its way,' said Emma. 'At least there's *something*.'

'I wonder why there are no stars. There's clearly some kind of matter out there, and it's clumpy. But it hasn't made stars.'

'Maybe the clumps aren't the right size here,' she said.

'What difference would that make?'

'I don't know.'

'It might be something more bizarre,' he said. He told her about Cornelius's speculations on how physical laws, shaken up by each emergence from the Crunch-Bang cycle, might deliver different forms of matter. 'For instance, those clouds might not even be hydrogen.'

She sighed. 'I don't think it makes a lot of difference, Malenfant. All that matters is that this isn't home. Do you think we're getting any nearer?'

'I don't even know what "nearer" means.' He checked his wristwatch. They had been travelling for hours – through how many universes, dozens, a hundred?

'If not for the resources of this trooper's backpack,' said Emma, 'we'd be dead by now. Wouldn't we, Malenfant?' Her voice was an insect whisper. 'I wonder if Cornelius knew that, if he figured that we would need the backpack to survive.'

'To kill for a backpack –'

'Cornelius was the coldest, most calculating human being I ever knew. It was exactly the kind of thing he would do.' She closed her eyes. 'I think I want to sleep now.'

He let her rest for an hour. Then they moved on.

They passed through more glowing-cloud universes. Sometimes the clouds would be sparser or denser, showing more or less structure. But they did not find galaxies or stars, nothing resembling the familiar structures of home.

Then they came to something new. They stopped, drifting in the unchanging blue light of the portal.

It was another red-sky universe. But this time it seemed as if the sparse clouds had been gathered up like cotton wool and wadded together, into a single roseate mass that dominated half the sky. There was a single point of light at the centre of it all, easily bright enough to be visible with the naked eye. Two splinters of light seemed to be protruding from the point, like lens flares, or poles from a toy globe. Malenfant thought he could trace structure in the cloud that surrounded the central point: a tight spiral knot at the centre, glowing a brighter red than its surroundings, and further out streamers and elongated bubbles, all of it swirling around the centre. It was actually beautiful, in a cold, austere way, like a watercolour done in white, grey, red.

Beautiful, and familiar.

'My God,' said Malenfant. 'It's a black hole. A giant black hole. Remember what we saw –'

'Yes. But black holes are made by stars. How can it be *here*, if there are no stars?'

He shrugged. 'Maybe the matter here didn't form stars, but just imploded into – that. Do you think it's a good sign?'

'I don't know. I never was much of a tourist, Malenfant. Tell me what Cornelius told you, about black holes. That universes can be born out of them. That what goes on in a black hole's centre is like a miniature Big Crunch . . .'

'Something like that.'

'Then,' she said laboriously, 'this universe could have *two* daughters. One born out of the black hole, one from the final Crunch.'

He frowned. 'So what?'

'Don't you get it, Malenfant? If universes with black holes have more babies, after a few generations there will be a lot more universes *with* black holes than without. Because they can multiply.'

'We're talking about universes, Emma. What does it mean to say one type of universe *outnumbers* another?'

'Perhaps it's all too simple for you to understand, Malenfant.'

'You mean too complex.'

'No. Too simple. Let's go on.'

'Are you sure you're ready?'

'What choice do I have?' And, feebly, she began to tug herself along the tether that joined them.

They passed on through the gallery of universes, barely noticing, comprehending little. Maybe Emma was right. Maybe they were working their way up a branching tree of universes – new baby cosmoses twigging off through every black hole. If that was so, how were the two of them being guided in their journey? By whom? Why?

Anyhow, on they went.

Even at the rate they travelled – a whole new universe, after all, every couple of minutes – the rate of cosmological evolution seemed damnably slow to Malenfant, a dim, undirected groping for complexity.

At first there were more red-sky universes. Most of them were adorned by black hole roses. Sometimes there was one all-consuming monster, sometimes an array of them, studded randomly around the sky.

Once they were so close to a hole centre that its glare, seen through a dense mass of cloud, was dazzling, and Malenfant was sure he could see movement in the nearer clumps of gas, shadows thousands of light years long turning like clock hands. Perhaps the portal itself was being dragged inwards to the hole. He wondered what would happen then. Could even the portal survive falling into an immense black hole? Or did someone – some unimaginable agency of the downstreamers who built this chain – monitor the portals across the universes, repair them after cosmological accidents?

Then – fifty or a hundred cosmoses (they weren't counting) from the first black hole rose – they came to something new. No infra-red clouds, no black holes. But there was structure.

Malenfant pushed himself away from the portal. He drifted to the end of the tether, rebounding slightly. He shielded his eyes, trying to shut out the blue glow of the portal.

There were wheel shapes in the sky: rimless, but with regular spokes, of the palest yellow light. It seemed to him there was a nesting here, structure on structure, the wheel shapes themselves gathered into greater, loosely-defined discs, just as stars combined into galaxies, which gathered in turn in clusters and superclusters.

There was a length of tether which stretched beyond him, further from the portal by six or seven yards. It just hung in space, coiled loosely. But there was a fine blue mist at its terminus.

Malenfant worked his way along the tether. The mist was made up of very small particles, fine almost to the limit of visibility. At first he thought they must be flaking away from the tether, somehow; but it looked as if they were just condensing out of the vacuum. The mist was everywhere –

Except right in front of him. There was a rough disc shape, directly ahead of him, where no mist was forming. Puzzled, he lifted his arm out to his left. The empty disc shape extended that way. It was a diffuse shadow of himself.

'I think it's something to do with the portal light. There's no mist here, where I block it out. Maybe the light is –' He waved his hands. 'Condensing.'

'How is that possible, Malenfant?'

'Hell, I don't know.' He reached along the tether, meaning to pull himself further.

'No, Malenfant. Look at the tether.'

He let his gaze follow the rope to its end, a few yards ahead.

The tether was disappearing. It looked as if it was being burned away by some invisible, high-intensity ray. Occasionally he saw a flash of green light.

He pulled the tether back. The burning-off stopped. He was able to touch the end of the rope. It had been cut clean through. But the blue mist was still sparkling into existence, right where it had been before.

'There's a limit out there, Emma. A barrier.' He looked around,

377

but there was only the strangely structured sky. 'Maybe the portal is protecting us. Like a shield.'

'A *shield*, Malenfant? You always did watch too much '70s TV.'

'Then you explain it,' he said testily.

'Why does everything have to have an explanation? *This is a different universe.* Maybe the stuff from *our* universe is changing when it goes out there, past the portal's influence.'

'Changing how?'

'The mass of the tether is disappearing. So maybe it's being converted into something else. Light, maybe. And the mist –'

'– is the light from the portal. Condensing. Turning into some kind of matter. So,' he said, 'how can light and matter swap over? . . . Cornelius would have known.'

'Yes. This is a strange place, isn't it, Malenfant?'

'There's nothing for us here.'

He turned away from the wheels, the blue mist, and pulled himself back to the portal.

So they passed on, on down the corridor of universes.

. . . Until they came, at last, to a sky full of stars.

Malenfant let himself drift away from the portal. 'At least I think they are stars.'

The sky was uniformly speckled with points of light, all around them, above and below. No glowing clouds, no black hole roses. It might have been a starry night on Earth.

But there was something wrong. 'They look *old*,' Malenfant said. It was true: a handful of the stars were as bright as orange, one even seemed to be sparking fitfully yellow, but the rest were a dim red. When he donned the night vision goggles, he made out many more star-like points, a field of them stretching beyond the visible. But they were dim and red.

'. . . We've been expecting stars,' Emma said.

'We have?'

'Sure. Think about it. If the key to breeding universes is black holes, you need to come up with the best way there is of making black holes. Which is stars.'

'What about those giant black holes we saw in the rose universes?'

'But they looked like they had ripped up half of creation. Stars have *got* to be more efficient than that. How many black holes were there in our universe?'

'A billion billion. Round numbers,' said Malenfant.

'We're going to see more universes full of stars now. Universes that are star factories, and so black hole factories . . .'

He gathered up the tethers.

More universes, many and strange. Most of them now contained stars of some kind, but they were generally dim, scattered, unimpressive if not dying or dead. And nowhere did they see anything to match the splendour and complexity of their home Galaxy, and nowhere did they see any evidence of life and organization.

Malenfant grunted. 'I feel like I'm trapped in God's art gallery.'

Emma laughed weakly. 'Malenfant, how can you be bored? You're being transported between universes. Not only that, you only have a few hours to live. What do you want, dancing girls? And what difference does it make? We're surely going to die soon anyhow, in some chunk of emptiness or other. I don't think you're destined to die in your own bed, Malenfant.'

'I don't own a bed. But I'd rather die in my own fucking universe.'

'Even a million light years from home?'

'Yeah. Wouldn't you?'

'You do take things personally, don't you, Malenfant? As if all of this, the manifold of universes, is picking on *you*.'

He fixed their tethers and faced the portal, its blank central expanse open, empty, somehow reassuring, a way onwards. 'Hell, yes,' he said. 'What other enemy is there?'

So, holding onto each other, they moved on to another reality, then another.

More skies. More stars, mostly small and unspectacular.

At last they came to a place with a galaxy. But it was small and knot-like, populated by stars that looked dull, uniform and ageing; it seemed to have none of the reef-like complexity of their own Galaxy.

They passed on.

Universe after universe, all but identical to Malenfant's eye: small and uninspiring stars, untidy galaxies, skies littered with the corpses of red, dying stars.

'I wonder why the stars are all so small,' he said. 'And why there are so few. And why they all got so old so quickly.'

'Because there's no giant galaxy to make new ones,' Emma said.

379

'We saw it, Malenfant. The reef Galaxy. All those feedback loops. A way to make stars, and keep on making them, over and over.'

Maybe she was right. If the key goal was to make lots of black holes – and if black holes were best made in giant stars – then you wanted machines to make lots of giant stars, and reef galaxies were the best way they had yet seen.

But evidently it wasn't so easy to make reef galaxies – or rather, to *evolve* them. Malenfant looked around another dull, uninteresting sky. He wondered what was missing, if there was some simple, key ingredient. Carbon, perhaps, or some other element essential to the great star-spawning gas clouds.

Malenfant paused again when they came to a new, different universe. But this time some of the galaxies were broken up, their outlying stars scattered, and their central masses were collapsing into what Malenfant was coming to recognize as the signatures of black holes. And there were patches of glowing gas marring the sky, as if some of the nearer stars had exploded.

Beyond the stars the sky was glowing. It was like one of the early phoenix universes he had seen, born only to die within seconds or hours or days or years. But it wasn't a uniform glow, he saw.

There seemed to be hot spots, one directly above his head and one below his feet, like poles in the sky. And there was a cold band around the equator of the sky, a plane running through his midriff. There were two points on the equator, in fact – once again on opposite sides of the sky – which seemed to be significantly cooler than the average.

He described the sky to Emma. 'It's a collapsing universe. But the collapse doesn't seem to be symmetrical. It's coming in over our heads, flattening out at the sides.'

'Is that possible?'

'Maybe this universe is oscillating,' he said. 'Like a soap bubble, before it bursts. Not collapsing evenly. Going from a sphere to a stretched-out ellipse shape to a flattened disc shape . . . You know, Cornelius said it might be possible to survive a Big Crunch in a universe like that. You have to take control of the universe. And then you manipulate it, mass and energy and gravity fields, to control the oscillations. If you milk them just right you can extract enough energy to live forever.'

'That sounds like Cornelius,' she said dryly. 'Malenfant, does it *look* like life forms are manipulating the universe here?'

'. . . No.'

380

So they went on.

Emma slept again. Trying not to wake her, he drifted on to the next universe, and the next.

Until – without warning, after another routine transition – he landed on Cruithne.

At least, for a few seconds, he thought it was Cruithne.

He and Emma were floating above a grey, dusty surface, dropping through ghostly microgravity. The portal was embedded in the plain, jutting out of it upright, just as it had before. There was a hiss of static in his headset.

His feet settled to the surface. There was the gentlest of crunches, transmitted through his suit fabric, as his boots crushed the regolith of this place. The dust seemed soft, easily compressed.

Standing straight, he grinned fiercely. The touch of gravity was feather-light, but even so it was pleasing to feel solid ground under his feet.

He laid Emma down carefully. The soft, loose dust billowed up around her, falling back slowly in the feather-soft gravity.

Of course, it wasn't Cruithne.

He'd seen more exciting skies. There was a single star, small, spitting light. Its colour was elusive, a blue-green. That was all: there was nothing else to be seen, anywhere in the sky.

He stepped forward. The surface was covered in smooth, flowing dust, like a folded-over sand dune. There were low hills, even what might have been the faded-out remnants of very ancient, very large craters, palimpsests. The dust wasn't the charcoal black of Cruithne, but a bluish silver-grey. Malenfant dug his gloved hand into the dust. It was very fine, like talc, with none of the little knotty clumps he remembered from Cruithne itself. He scraped out a small pit. He thought he could detect a subtle flow, as the dust poured gently back into his hole, filling it in and smoothing it over.

He straightened up, slapped the dust off his hands, and bent over to brush it off his legs. Except that there was no dust there; it seemed to have fallen away from his suit fabric. In fact he could see, where Cruithne II dust was peeling away, lingering traces of coal-dark Cruithne I, still stuck there after so long, after all the exotic cosmoses he had seen.

Dust on Cruithne I stuck to suit fabric because it was electro-statically charged by the action of the sun. So how come this stuff didn't act the same? No electrostatics? Maybe matter here wasn't capable of holding a sizeable electric charge . . .

Why would that be, and what difference would it make?

He had, of course, absolutely no idea.

'. . . This dust is soft, Malenfant. Like the finest feather bed you ever heard of. You remember the story about the princess and the pea?'

'I remember.'

'But I didn't dream. I haven't dreamed once since we went through the portal.' Her voice was a rustle. 'Isn't that strange? Maybe you have to be at home to dream. I think I finished my orange juice.'

'I'll put up the habitat.'

'No . . . *Ungh*.' Behind her visor, her face twisted with pain.

He rummaged in the trooper backpack's medical kit, and found an ampoule of a morphine derivative. In the dim light of the green star he had to squint to read the instructions. Then he pressed it against a valve at Emma's neck.

He watched her face. Her self-control was steely, as it always had been. But he thought he detected relief there.

'Now you made me a junkie,' she said.

'So sue me.' He bent and picked her up.

'I can hardly hear you. That static. Is there something wrong with the radio?'

'I don't think so,' he said dryly. 'The universe is broken, not the radio.'

Then, the mil spec backpack trailing behind him, he stepped a giant microgravity step through the portal.

As their consumables dwindled, Malenfant hurried through universes, dismissing billions of years of unique cosmic evolution with a glance, not bothering to try to figure out *why* this universe should be this way or that, subtly different, subtly wrong. The waste, the emptiness of these cosmoses where there were no eyes to see, oppressed him.

Sometimes Malenfant found himself landing on a Cruithne, more or less like his own Cruithne, sometimes not. Sometimes the stars shone bright and white, but they seemed oddly uniform. Sometimes he found himself in a dying, darkling universe where the stars seemed already to have burned themselves out, a sky littered with diminishing points of orange and red.

Once there was a galaxy over his head, a roof of light, star clusters scattered around it like attending angels. And when he lifted his sun visor, he could see its complex light reflecting from his own cheekbones and nose, the bony frame of his face.

. . . But it wasn't right. Not quite.

There was the core, glowing bright, the broad disc, even a hint of spiral structure. But only a hint. There were none of the massive blue-white sparks he'd been able to see in the images their firefly had returned, none of the great supernova blisters, holes blasted into the big molecular clouds by the deaths of giant stars.

Not quite right.

Malenfant hurried on.

Meanwhile Emma grew weaker. She spent longer asleep, and her waking intervals grew shorter. It was as if she was hoarding her energy, hibernating like the black hole farmers of the far downstream. But parsimony hadn't worked out for the downstreamers. And it wasn't going to work for Emma.

It got to the point where he didn't even look up at the sky any more, as he blundered back and forth. The human mind had evolved for just one universe, he thought. How much of this crap was he supposed to take? He felt exhausted, resentful, bewildered.

'. . . Wait.'

He paused. He had loped out of the portal onto another stretch of scuffed, anonymous regolith. She was lying in his arms, her weight barely registering. He looked down into her face, and pushed up her gold sun visor.

'Emma?'

She licked her lips. '*Look.* Up there.'

No galaxy visible, but a starry sky. The stars looked, well, normal. But he'd learned that meant little. 'So what?'

Emma was lifting her arm, pointing. He saw three stars, dull white points, in a row. And there was a rough rectangle of stars around them – one of them a distinctive red – and what looked like a galaxy disc, or maybe just a nebula, beneath . . .

'Holy shit,' he said.

She whispered, 'There must be lots of universes like ours. But, surely to God, there is only one Orion.'

And then light, dazzling, unbearably brilliant, came stabbing over the close horizon.

It was a sunrise. He could actually feel its heat through the layers of his suit.

He looked down at the ground at his feet. The rising light cast strong shadows, sharply illuminating the miniature crevices and craters there. And here was a 'crater' that was elongated, and neatly ribbed.

It was a footprint.

He stepped forward, lifted his foot, and set it down in the print. It fit neatly. When he lifted his foot away the cleats of his boot hadn't so much as disturbed a regolith grain.

It was his own footprint. Good grief. After hundreds of universes of silence and remoteness and darkness, universes of dim light and shadows, he was right back where he started.

He looked down at Emma. But, as the sunlight played over her face, she had already closed her eyes. Gently he flipped down her gold visor. The light dazzled from it, evoking rich colours.

Maura Della:

The robot bus snaked across the folded floor of Tycho.

Maura gazed out, stunned, at grey-brown ground, black starless sky, a bright blue Earth, full and round like a blue marbled bowling ball. In the valleys, smooth rocky walls rose around her, hiding the Earth and the details of the land. As the shadows fell on the bus it cooled rapidly, and she heard its hull tick as it contracted, fans somewhere banging into life to keep the air warm for her. But there was light here, even at the bottom of the angular lunar chasms: not diffused by the air, for there was no air, but reflected from the rock walls at the top of the valleys.

The Plexiglas blister window was very clear, cleaned of Moon dust and demisted, and she felt as if she was outside the bus, suspended over the lunar ground. She saw dust, heavily indented by bus tracks, which the bus was now following once more with religious precision. The dust was loose, fragile-looking, flecked with tiny craters, with here and there the glint of glass. It was lunar soil, dead, processed by patient, airless erosion, passing beneath her feet like foam on a rocky sea. She longed to reach down, through the window, and run her fingers through that sharp-grained dirt.

But that was impossible.

When she had arrived at the dull, cramped, sour-smelling NASA base, dug into the regolith miles from the children's encampment, she had been told that civilian types like herself weren't expected to

'EVA', as they called it, to walk outside onto the surface of the Moon. Not once, not one footstep; she would pass over the Moon through an interconnected series of air-conditioned rooms and vehicles, as if the whole Moon was one giant airport terminal.

There were a dozen people in the bus.

Most of them were soldiers: hard-faced, bored men and women, their pressure suit helmets the pale blue of the United Nations. They carried heavy weaponry, rifles and hand guns adapted for use either in the vacuum or in atmosphere, and Maura knew there were more weapons, heavier stuff, strapped to the bus's hull. The sole purpose of this squad was to protect, or perhaps control, Maura. Nobody went to Never-Never Land unarmed or unescorted – not even someone as senior in this UN operation as, five years after Nevada, Maura had become.

Bill Tybee came to stand with her at the window. He was limping, and his silver med-alert lapel brooch glinted in the bus's lights. He held a bulb of coffee in a polystyrene holder; she accepted it gratefully.

'Umm. Not too hot.'

'Sorry,' he said. 'Nothing gets too hot here.'

The low pressure, she thought. An old NASA-type cliché, but true nonetheless.

'Never would have put you down as an astronaut, Ms Della.'

'Call me Maura. You're hardly Flash Gordon yourself.'

'Yeah. But what the heck.' Bill Tybee had been brought to the Moon, along with other parents, to work, in his inexpert way, on the interpretation of the Blues' activities – and, of course, to be with his kids, as best he could. Anything that might work, help get a handle on the kids.

'Bill – why Tycho? Why did the children run *here*, from Nevada? I heard the NASA people complaining. We're away from the lunar equator, so you eat a lot of fuel getting here. And the ground is so rugged it was difficult to make the first landings.'

He grunted. 'Those NASA guys have their heads up their asses. You have to remember, Ms Della – Maura. They're *children*. At least they were when they flew up here. So where would a kid pick to go live? How about the most famous crater on the Moon?'

It was as good an answer as she'd heard. '. . . Don't you think they are children any more?'

'Hell, I don't know what they are,' he muttered. '*Look* at that.'

The bus climbed a crest, and once more the landscape was set out before her, the blue of Earth garish against the subtle autumn colours of the Moon. The ground was folded and distorted; she could actually see frozen waves in the rock, ripples from the aftermath of the great impact which had punched the Tycho complex into the hide of the Moon. But the sheets of rock were themselves punctured with craters, small and large, and strewn with rubble.

Tycho was young for the Moon, but unimaginably old by the standards of Earth.

The ride, on the bus's big mesh wheels, was dreamy; the bus tipped and rolled, languid, as it crawled across the broken ground. She felt light, blown this way and that. It was indeed a remarkable experience.

There were rings of security around Never-Never Land, concentric like the rocky terraces that lined the walls of Tycho.

The bus rolled through a tall wire fence – lunar alloy, spun fine – and drove on to a low regolith-covered dome. A fabric tunnel snaked out to meet the bus, like the walkway from an airport terminal, and it docked on the hull with a delicate clunk. When the door opened a uniformed UN soldier stood there, backed up by armed troops, ready to process them.

As she passed through the hatchway, Maura smelled burning metal, where the hull had been exposed to space, and a hint of wood smoke: oxidizing Moondust. The exotic reality of the Moon, intruding around this dull Cold War-type bureaucracy and pass-checking.

None of the bus's passengers – not even Bill Tybee – got past that first checkpoint. None save Maura.

The walkway was translucent, a tunnel between black sky and glowing ground. Craning her neck, Maura peered through the fabric walls and glimpsed Never-Never Land itself. It was a dome, shaded silver-grey. Hints of green inside. Something moving, like a swaying tree trunk. Good God, it was a *neck*.

Just before the entry to the complex, the aide paused and pointed. 'The dome itself is polarized. It turns opaque and transparent by turns, to simulate an Earth-like day–night cycle. And during the long night there are lights to achieve the same effect. See? There are banks of electric floods on gantries, like a sports stadium.' The aide's hair was blonde, eyes blue, classic Nordic type. Minnesota? But her accent was neutral.

Maura said, 'Did I see a giraffe in there?'

The girl laughed. 'Maybe. That's what we think it is.'

'Don't you know?'

'I only have clearance to violet level.'

'How long have you been up here?'

'Two years, with breaks.'

'Aren't you curious?'

'We're not paid to be curious, ma'am.' Then the professional mask slipped a little. 'Actually, no. Never-Never is just a tent full of those little Blue-ass monsters. What is there to be curious about? Anyhow you have blue clearance, right?'

'Yes.'

'I guess you'll see for yourself, whatever you want.'

At the other end of the walkway was another airlock, another security check, where Maura said goodbye to the aide, whose sole purpose seemed to have been to escort Maura all of twenty yards of this quarter-million-mile journey.

The processing here took another hour. Her pass and other credentials were checked several times over, she was body-searched twice, and passed through an X-ray machine and metal detector and other scanners she didn't recognize. Finally she was asked to strip, and she stood, alone, under a shower that turned hot and cold and stank of some antiseptic agent. She was distantly pleased that she didn't sag quite as much as at home. Then there was a pulse of light, a sharp pain. She was left with a fine ash on her exposed skin.

After that she was given a fresh set of clothes, underwear and a coverall. The coverall had no pockets, just a transparent pouch on the outside where she was allowed to carry her blue pass and passport, handkerchief, other small items.

She was led along one last translucent corridor – one last glimpse of the Moon – and then, escorted by two more soldiers (there must be dozens here, she thought, racking up one hell of an expense) she passed through the curving wall of Never-Never Land itself.

And then there was grass under the soft slippers on her feet, a dome that glowed blue-black over her head, scored by a great diffuse shadow, a shadow cast by Tycho's rim mountains.

There were a few stands of bushes, and a single giant tree, low and squat. The air was cool, crisp, fresh, and it smelled of green, growing things, of cut summer lawns. Green grass, growing on the Moon. Who'd have thought she'd live to see this?

A girl was standing before her: aged maybe sixteen, slender, willowy, barefoot, dressed in a smock of simple orange fabric, a bright blue circle stitched to the breast. Her face wasn't pretty, Maura thought, but it was calm, composed, self-possessed. Centred. She was missing a tooth in her lower jaw.

It was Anna. And she had wings.

'It's nice to see you again, Ms Della,' said Anna gravely.

'Call me Maura. You remember me, then.'

'You were always a friend to us.'

Maura sighed. 'Child, I tried to have you killed.'

'You did your duty. There are many worse people in the world than you, Maura Della. Why don't you take your shoes off?'

Maura smiled. 'Why don't I?' She kicked off the slippers and walked forward on the grass. It was cool and moist under her feet. The blades felt oddly stiff, but she knew that was an artefact of the low gravity.

Anna folded her wings and jumped into the air: just bent her legs and leaped up through ten feet or more. She seemed to hover for a long heartbeat. Then she unfolded her wings and flapped – Maura felt a great downrush of the cool, low-pressure, crystal-sharp air – and Anna shot into the domed sky.

Maura glanced at the two soldiers behind her. One of them, a bull-powerful blond man, was watching the girl's body with narrow, hard eyes.

Anna swept in for a neat landing, slowing with a couple of running steps, thin legs flashing.

Maura applauded slowly. 'I'd like to try that.'

Anna held the wings out. 'It's not as easy as it looks. You have to flap hard enough to support one-sixth of your Earth weight.' She eyed Maura. 'Imagine a nine-pound dumbbell in each hand, holding them out from your body . . . Maybe you should take an air car for today. It's kind of easier.'

Maura turned to her escort questioningly.

The blond soldier spoke. 'We can't go any further into the interior, ma'am. But you're authorized. At your own risk.' He sounded as if he was middle European, German maybe. He pointed upwards. Maura saw a football-sized surveillance robot, small and complex and glittering with lenses, gliding noiselessly through the air. 'Just shout and we'll get you out.'

'Thank you.'

Maura let the girl lead her to a small fenced-off area where three cars sat, parked roughly on the grass. Maura picked one and, with the simulacrum of youthful exhilaration granted her by lunar G, she vaulted neatly over the door into the driver's seat.

The car was just a white box of metal and ceramic, open, with a joystick and a small control panel. It had Boeing markings, and simple instructions marked in big block capitals. The car wasn't wheeled; instead there was a turbofan in a pod at each corner. Maura quickly learned how to use the joystick to make the pods swivel this way and that.

And when she fired up the engine – noiseless, powered by clean-burning hydrogen – the car shot straight up into the air. At a touch of the joystick, it tipped and squirted back and forth, like something out of *The Jetsons*.

Anna jumped into the air and circled higher. When she passed out of Tycho's shadow into sunlight, her wings seemed to burst into flame. Then she turned and streaked towards the heart of the dome.

Maura followed more cautiously, skimming a few feet above the grass.

Never-Never Land was maybe the size of a football field. It seemed to be mostly grassed over, but here and there ponds glinted, blue as swimming pools. She could see small robot gardeners trundling cautiously over the grass, clipping and digging.

Low mounds protruded from the grass. One of them had an open door, bright artificial light streaming out. Maybe the children slept in there, to keep down their hours of exposure to the Moon's high radiation levels.

At the very centre of the dome was an area fenced-off by a tall glass wall. Maura knew that not even her blue pass would get her through that perimeter; for within was the artefact – transport, bubble, whatever – that the children had constructed in Nevada to protect them from the nuke and carry them here.

Even now, no adult had the faintest idea how it worked.

Anna flew towards the dome's single giant tree.

It looked like an oak to Maura, but its trunk had to be twenty feet across, and each of its branches, broad and sturdy, was no less than three or four feet thick. But the tree looked somehow stunted, constrained to grow broad and flat rather than tall; if it had remained in proportion it might, she supposed, have reached five or six hundred feet, busting out of this stadium-sized dome.

Anna glided to a branch and settled there gracefully, folding her wings behind her. Maura killed her engine and, with a soft creak, the air car settled into place in a crook of the branch.

Maura saw some of the other children, seemingly far below. There were two groups, each of four or five kids each; the oldest of them looked around ten. After five years on the Moon, they looked skinny, graceful. One group was playing what looked like a tag game, chasing with great loping strides and somersaults and spectacular lunar leaps. Maura could hear them laughing, the sound drifting up to her like the ripple of water.

The other group seemed more solemn. They were moving around each other, but in a series of patterns, each of which they would hold for a fraction of a second of stillness, and then move on to the next. They seemed to be talking, or maybe singing, but Maura couldn't make out any words.

'Anna, where are the Tybee children? Tom and Billie –'

Anna pointed.

The Tybees were part of the solemn party below. Maura recognized Tom, ten years old now, his face round and set and serious. At his waist he had his electronic Heart – battered, dirty, probably non-functioning, a gift from his long-lost mother. She wondered which one of the younger kids was Billie.

Once she had promised to his father that she would protect Tom. It was a promise that had brought her all this way. And yet, what protection could she offer him? What could she ever have given him?

'Can you tell me what they are doing down there?'

'They're working. It's what your people call –'

'Multiplexing. Yes, I know. What are they talking about?'

Anna's face worked. 'They are considering constraints on the ultimate manifold.'

Maura suspected that she was going to struggle with the rest of this conversation.

'The manifold of what?'

'Universes. It is of course a truism that all logically possible universes must exist. The universe, *this* universe, is described – umm, that's the wrong word – by a formal system. Mathematics. A system of mathematics.'

Maura frowned. 'You mean a Theory of Everything?'

Anna waved a hand, as if that was utterly trivial, and her beautiful wings rustled. 'But there are many formal systems. Some of them are less rich, some more. But each formal system, logically consistent internally, describes a possible universe, which therefore exists.'

Maura tried to follow that. 'Give me an example of a formal system.'

'The rules of geometry. I mean, Euclid's geometry.'

'High school stuff.'

Anna looked at her with reproof. 'I never went to high school, Maura.'

'I'm sorry.'

'Some of these universes, as described by the formal systems, are rich enough to support self-aware substructures. Life. Intelligence. And some of the universes *aren't* rich enough. A universe described by Euclidean geometry probably isn't, for example. Therefore it can't be observed. What the group down there is trying to establish is whether a universe which cannot be observed, though it exists, may be said to have a different category of existence . . .' Anna glanced at Maura. 'Do you understand?'

'Not a damn word.'

Anna smiled.

Maura could see firefly robots hovering over the heads of the children, peering down, recording everything they did and said. There might be a rich treasure of knowledge and wisdom being conjured up in the dance of those slim forms, but the world's massed experts couldn't begin to decode it. IBM had quoted development times in decades just to construct a translation software suite.

The children had, it seemed, evolved their own language from elements of their native spoken languages, mixed with gestures, dance and music. It was a complex, multilevel communication channel, with many streams of information multiplexed together. Linguists believed it was a true language, with a unifying grammar. But it transcended human languages in the richness of its structure, the speed and compression of its data transmission, the fact that it was analogue – the angle of an arm or head held *just so* seemed to make an immense difference to meaning – and its rate of evolution, sometimes changing daily.

And besides, there seemed to be some features that could not be translated into English, even in principle. Such as new tenses. There was one based on palindromic constructions, symmetric in time, that seemed to be designed to describe situations with looping causality, or even causality violation.

Grammar for a time traveller.

Some theorists were saying that the orderly linear perception of time, of neat cause and effect, enjoyed by humans was an artefact of a limited consciousness: like the way the brain could 'construct' an image of a face from a few lines on a page. Perhaps the children could experience time on a deeper level: nonlinearly, even acausally.

And the farthest-out theorists wondered if their minds were somehow linked, permanently, by the neutrino ocean that filled the universe. As if Feynman radio technology was allowing some higher strata of consciousness and self-awareness to operate here.

The various strategies that had been tried to keep a handle on the children had yet to pay off. The Trojan Horse kids – like little Billie Tybee, below – seemed to have melted into the strange community here without a backward glance. The Trojan Horses had been heavily indoctrinated with a basic common grammar and quantification rules, in the hope that they would at least continue to talk comprehensibly to the outside world. But even that had failed. They just didn't have the patience or inclination to translate their thoughts into baby-talk for their parents.

The only Blue who would regularly talk to those outside was Anna, five or six years older than any of the rest. And the specialist observers believed that – though Anna was the de facto leader of the children here – she herself was too old, her grammatical sense frozen too early, to have become fully immersed in the complex interchanges that dominated the lives of the rest of the children.

And besides, Anna was hardly a useful ambassador. Adults had damaged her too much.

. . . A section of oak tree trunk seemed to split away, bending stiffly, and a thin, distorted face turned and peered up at Maura.

Maura nearly jumped out of her seat. 'Oh, my good gosh.'

Anna laughed.

The giraffe stepped out of the shade of the tree. The yellow and black mottled markings on its body had made it almost invisible to Maura, startling for such a huge animal. The giraffe loped easily forward, fine-chiselled head dipping gently, the lunar gravity making no apparent difference to its stately progress. Now two more animals followed the first, another adult and a baby, its neck stubby by comparison.

Anna said, 'There are little NASA robot dung beetles that come out at night and roll away their droppings. They're really funny.'

'Why are the giraffes here?'

Anna shrugged. 'We asked for them. Somebody saw one in a picture book once.' Maura watched the giraffes recede, loping easily in the wash of sunlight and crater-wall shadow, their bodies and motion utterly strange, unlike the body plans of any creature she had seen. A real extreme of evolution, she thought.

Just like these damn kids.

Anna's eyes, grey as Moondust, were grave, serious. 'Maura, why are *you* here?'

'You deserve the truth,' Maura said.

'Yes, we do.' Anna looked up at Earth, fat and full, its roundness slightly distorted by the fabric of the dome. 'We see the lights sometimes, on the night side.'

'What do you think they are?'

Anna shrugged. 'Cities burning.'

Maura sighed. 'Have you studied history, Anna?'

'Yes. The information is limited, the interpretations partial. But it is interesting.'

'Then you'll know there have been times like this before. The religious wars during the Reformation, for instance. Protestants against Catholics. The Catholics believed that only their priests controlled access to the afterlife. So anybody who tried to deny their powers threatened, not just life, but even the afterlife. And the Protestants believed the Catholic priests were false, and would therefore deny *their* followers access to the afterlife. If you look at it from the protagonists' point of view, they were reasonable wars to fight, because they were over the afterlife itself.'

'Are the wars now religious?'

'In a sense. But they are about the future. There are different groups who believe they have the right to control the future of mankind – which, for the first time in our history, has come into our thinking as a tangible thing, an asset, something to be fought over. And that's what they are fighting for.'

'What you mean is they are fighting over the children. Blue children, like me, and what they think we can offer.'

'Yes,' said Maura.

'They are wrong,' Anna said carefully. 'All of them.'

'Here's the bottom line,' Maura said. 'I'm not sure how much longer, umm, wise heads are going to prevail. Even in the US.'

Anna listened, her eyes soft. 'How long?'

'I don't know,' said Maura honestly. 'Months at the most, I would think. Then they will come for you.'

Anna said, 'It will be enough.'

'*For what?*'

Anna wouldn't reply.

Frustrated, Maura snapped, 'You frighten people, Anna. Christ, you frighten me. Sitting here on the Moon with your plans and your incomprehensible science. We detected the artefact in the lunar mantle . . .'

It had been picked up by seismometry. A lump of highly compressed matter – possibly quark matter – the size of a mountain. It was right under this dome. Nobody had any idea how it got there, or what it was for.

Maura glared at Anna. 'Are we right to be frightened?'

'Yes,' Anna said gently, and Maura was chilled.

'Why won't you tell us what you're doing?'

'We are trying. We are telling you what you can understand.'

'Are we going to be able to stop you?'

Anna reached out and grabbed Maura's hand, squeezed it. The girl's skin was soft, warm. 'I'm sorry.'

Then, without warning, Anna tipped forward, falling out of the tree, and spread her wings. She soared away, sailing across the distorted face of Earth, and out of Maura's view.

When Maura got back to the tractor, Bill was waiting for her. He affected a lack of interest. But, as the bus crawled its painful way back to the NASA base, he hung on every word she had to tell him about conditions inside the dome, and about the children, and what she had glimpsed of Tom and little Billie.

The sun had set over the rim walls of Tycho, but the walls were lit by the eerie blue glow of Earthlight. The sun would linger for a whole day, just beneath the carved horizon, so languid was the Moon's time cycle. There was no air, of course, so there were no sunset colours; but there was nevertheless a glow at the horizon, pale white fingers bright enough to dim the stars: she was seeing the light of the sun's atmosphere, and the zodiacal light, the glimmer of dust and debris in the plane of the Solar System. It was calm, unchanging, unbearably still, austere, a glacier of light.

She found Bill Tybee weeping.

He let her hold him, like mother with child. It was remarkably comforting, this trace of human warmth against the giant still cold of the Moon.

Reid Malenfant:

His suit radio receiver was designed only for short distances. Nevertheless he tuned around the frequency bands.

Nothing. But that meant little.

If he couldn't hear anybody else, maybe they could hear him. The backpack had a powerful emergency beacon. He decided that was a good investment of their remaining power. He separated it from the pack, jammed it into Cruithne soil and started it up.

Then he shook out the bubble shelter, zipped himself and Emma into it and inflated it. Once more it was a welcome relief to huddle with Emma's warmth.

He took a careful look at Emma's damaged leg. Much of the flesh seemed to have been destroyed by its exposure to the vacuum. But at the fringe of the damaged area there was discoloration, green and purple, and a stench of rot, of sickly flowers. He drenched the bad flesh in an antiseptic cream he found in the backpack, until the place smelled like a hospital ward. But at least that stink of corruption was drowned.

And she didn't seem to be in any pain. Maybe all this would be over, one way or the other, before they got to that point.

He sacrificed a little more of their power on warming up some water. He mixed up orange juice in it, and they savoured the tepid drink. They ate more of the backpack's stores, dried banana and what seemed to be yoghurt. They used scraps of cloth torn from their micrometeorite garments to improvise facecloths, and then he opened up their suits and gently washed Emma's armpits and crotch and neck. Malenfant took their filled urine bags and dumped their contents into the military backpack's water recycler, and he filled up their suit reservoirs with fresh water. Almost routine, almost domestic.

He was, he realized, on some bizarre level, content.

And then the shit hit the fan.

'. . . Malenfant.'

He turned. She was holding his personal med kit. With her gloved hands, she had pulled out a blister pack of fat red pills. And a silver lapel ribbon. It was his med-alert.

Oh, he thought. Oh, shit. There goes the Secret.

*   *   *

'Tumour-busters. Right?' She let the stuff go; it drifted slowly to the floor. Her face was a yellow mask overlaid with Big Bang sunburn; her eyes were sunk in dark craters. 'You're a cancer victim.'

'It's manageable. It's nothing –'

'You never told me, Malenfant. How long?'

He shook his head. 'I don't want to talk about this.'

'This is *why*. Isn't it? This is why you washed out of NASA. And it's why you pushed me away. Oh, you asshole.' She held out her arms.

He pulled himself over to her, held her shoulders, then dipped his head. He felt her stroke his bare scalp. 'I couldn't tell you.'

'Why not? What did you think I'd do, run away?'

'No. If I thought that I'd have told you immediately. I thought you'd stay. Care for me. Sacrifice yourself.'

'And you couldn't stand that. Oh, Malenfant. And the affair, that damn Heather –'

'The cancer wasn't going to kill me, Emma. But it screwed up my life. I couldn't have kids, I couldn't reach space . . . I didn't want it to screw your life too – *ow*.'

She'd slapped him. Her face was twisted into a scowl. She slapped him again, hard enough to sting, and pushed at his chest. She was weak, but she was pushing them apart. 'What right did you have to mess with my head like that?' And she aimed more slaps at him.

He lifted his hands, let her dismally feeble blows rain on his arms. 'I did it for you.'

'You control freak. And then, even after you engineer a divorce, for Christ's sake, you still can't let me go. You recruit me into your company, you even drag me into interplanetary space.'

'I know. I know, I know. I'm fucked up. I'm sorry. I wanted to let you go. But I couldn't bear it. I could never let go. But I tried. I didn't want to wreck your life.'

'My God, Malenfant.' Now her eyes were wet. 'What do you think you *did*? What do you think life is *for*?'

'Emma –'

'Get out. Leave me alone, you cripple.' And she turned her face to the wall.

He stayed, watching her, for long minutes. Then he closed up his suit.

He found remnants of human presence on Cruithne: footprints, scuff marks, even hand prints. There were pitons stuck in the regolith, dangling lengths of tether, a few abandoned scraps of kit, film cartridges and polystyrene formers and lengths of cable. There were a few fresh, deep craters that looked as if they might have been dug by the bullets of troopers' guns.

A few yards from the portal itself he found the battery of instruments which, a million years ago, Cornelius Taine had set up to monitor the artefact: cameras, spectrometers, Geiger counters, other stuff Malenfant had never been able to name, let alone understand. The instruments were still in their rough circle, centred on the portal. But they were uniformly smashed, lenses broken, casings cracked open, cabling and circuit boards ripped out. The regolith here was much disturbed. It was obvious somebody had deliberately done this, taken the time and effort to wreck the instruments. Tybee J., maybe, while she prepared to chase them into the portal.

He picked up a busted-open camera. There was a fine layer of regolith over the exposed workings. The gold foil insulating blanket was blackened, cracked and peeling, and the paintwork on exposed metal was flaking away. He ran his gloved finger under a plastic-coated cable that stuck out of the interior. The discoloured plastic just crumbled away.

He wondered how long an exposure to vacuum, the sun's raw ultraviolet and the hard radiation of space you'd need to do this much damage. Years, maybe. There was no guarantee that their subjective time during their jaunt across the manifold universes had to match up with the time elapsed here.

Anyhow it sure looked as if nobody had been back here since they had left in such a hurry. He felt his heart sink at the thought.

He placed the camera back where he had found it, and let it resume its slow, erosive weathering.

Taking up the familiar routine of moving around the asteroid – piton, tether, glide, always at least two anchors to the regolith – he glided over Cruithne's claustrophobic, close-curved horizon, pressing on, further and further.

There was little left of the O'Neill, or the troop carrier: just scattered wreckage, crumpled and charred, a few new blue-rimmed craters punched into Cruithne's patient hide. He supposed most of the debris created by the various attacks had been thrown off into space. He rummaged through the remains of the ships and the hab shelters. What wasn't smashed and vacuum-dried was crumbling from sunlight and cosmic irradiation. Still, maybe there was something he could use here.

He came across a firefly, inert, half dug into the regolith. He tried to haul it out, but it was dead, its power indicator panel black.

He found only one body.

It was a trooper, a young man – not much more than a boy, really, wadded into the shadow of a crater. He wasn't in a suit. His body was twisted, bones broken, and his skin, freeze-dried in the vacuum, was like scorched, brittle paper. His chest cavity was cracked open, presumably by the explosion that had taken out the troop carrier. His heart, stomach and other organs seemed to have desiccated, and the cavity in his body gaped wide, empty, somehow larger than Malenfant had expected.

Maybe Tybee had taken the time to bury her other fallen companions, Malenfant thought. Or maybe this was the only body that had finished up here, and the rest, burned, broken and shattered, were somewhere out there in a dispersing shell of debris.

And meanwhile, Cruithne spun on. How strange, he thought, that Cruithne had waited out five billion years in cold silence – and then endured a few months of frenetic activity, as life from Earth, bags of water and blood and flesh, had come here and built their enigmatic structures, fought and blown everything apart, and departed – leaving Cruithne alone again, with a few new craters and a scattering of shattered structures, at the centre of a dispersing cloud of glittering rubble.

That, and the enigmatic blue circle put there by the downstreamers.

He passed into Cruithne's long shadow.

The stars wheeled over his head, the familiar constellations of his boyhood, but crowded now with the dense stars of deep space. At last, at the heart of the sparse constellation of Cygnus, he found a bright blue star. He gazed into that watery light, savouring photons that had bounced off Earth's seas and clouds just seconds before entering his eyes. It was the closest he would ever come, he supposed, to touching home again.

He thought of the lifeless corridors he had travelled, the long, painful gestation of physics and fire, birth and collapse, that had finally, it seemed, evolved to *this*: a universe of carbon and supernovae and black holes and life, and that beautiful blue spark. But Earth was an island of light and life surrounded by abysses.

In the shelter, he found Emma dying.

*   *   *

398

He did what he could. He massaged her limp hands, trying to keep the blood pumping, and upped the oxygen concentration in the air. He pulled a lightweight silver-foil emergency blanket around her, did everything he could think of to keep her body from deciding this was the end. But her decline, rapid, seemed irreversible.

Her fingertips had turned dead white, the skin pasty and lifeless, even bluish.

Not yet, not yet. How can it end here? It's *wrong* . . .

The sun was a ball of light that glared through the fabric, its glow soaking into the warp and weft of the fabric. Malenfant watched as it edged across the dome of the tent. Cruithne was turning patiently, just as it always had.

But the air in here was growing stale. The carbon dioxide scrubbers and other expendables built into the mil-spec backpack were presumably reaching the end of their design lifetimes; the pack wouldn't be able to sustain this habitat much longer.

She woke up. Her eyes turned, and her gaze settled on his face, and she smiled, which warmed his heart. He fed her sips of water. 'Try to take it easy.'

'It isn't so bad,' she whispered.

'Bullshit.'

'Really. I don't hurt. Not much, anyhow.'

'You want some more dope?'

'Save it, Malenfant. You might need it. Anyhow I'd prefer a shot of tequila.'

He told her about the radio beacon. 'Somebody will be coming.'

'Oh, bull, Malenfant,' she said gently. 'Nobody's going to come. It wasn't meant to end like that, a cavalry charge from over the hill. Not for *us*. Don't you know that yet?' She gripped his hand. Her touch was like a child's. 'This is all we have, Malenfant. You and me. We've no future or past, because we don't have kids, nobody who might carry on the story. Just bubbles, adrift in time. Here, shimmering, gone.' She seemed to be crying.

'I'm sorry,' he said.

'Never apologize,' she whispered. 'We've come a long way together, haven't we? All those universes without life. And the downstream. Life slowly crushed out of existence . . . You need stars and supernovae, to make black holes, to make more universes. Fine. You need those things to make life too. But is that how come we're here? Are we just a byproduct – are minds just something that happens to rise out of the blind thrashings of matter?'

'I don't know. Try to take it easy –'

'But it doesn't *feel* like that, Malenfant. Does it? I feel like I'm the centre of everything. I can feel time, flowing deep inside me. I'm not a kind of froth on the surface of the universe. I *am* the universe.'

'I'm listening,' he said, wiping her mouth.

'Oh, horseshit,' she hissed softly. 'You never did listen to anybody. If you had you wouldn't have fucked up our entire relationship, from beginning to end.'

'Emma –'

'Maybe the children know,' she said. 'The new children. Michael, wherever he is now. *You* know . . .'

She drifted between sleeping and waking. He soaked a cloth in water and moistened her lips when he could. When she was asleep he infused her with more morphine. There was nothing he could do but watch, as her body shut itself down. He had never seen anybody die this way before, up close, peacefully. She actually seemed to be getting more comfortable as the end got closer, as if there were mechanisms to comfort her.

She licked her lips. 'You know, I guess we couldn't manage to live together, but at least we got to die together. I wouldn't have missed it for the world, Malenfant. For *all* the worlds . . . And wear your damn ribbon. It's a med-alert. They gave it to you for a reason.'

'I will.'

'You really are an asshole, Malenfant. You were so busy saving the world, saving *me*, you never thought about yourself . . .' She opened her eyes, and smiled. But her eyes were unfocused. Her hand fluttered, and he took it.

'What is it?'

'I saw a light,' she whispered. 'Like the phoenixes. The light of creation, all around everything. And I could smell the high desert. Isn't that strange?'

'Yes. Yes, that is strange.'

'And I think . . .'

But she was asleep again.

Her breathing changed. It became a gurgle, like a snore, intermittent, deep, very fluid. Her mouth was open, her skin sallow, her face very still.

She stirred once more. She smiled. But, he knew, it was not for him.

*   *   *

He assembled Emma's suit around her, her helmet and gold visor and gloves and boots. When he was done she looked as if she was sleeping.

He washed his face, drank some water, even managed to eat a little. He recharged his reservoirs and suited up.

He collapsed the shelter. Since it was the last time he would be using it, he folded it up neatly and stowed it away in trooper Tybee's backpack.

Then he prepared his tethers and pitons, and carried Emma around the curve of Cruithne, to the crater where he had found the body of the anonymous soldier. The only sound was his own breathing, the only motion the patient wheeling of the stars and sun and Earth in Cruithne's splendid sky.

He laid Emma down beside the trooper. She was so light in Cruithne's toy gravity her body barely made an indentation in the soft regolith.

It was easy to bury the two bodies. He just kicked over the crater wall, loosely shovelled dirt forward with his gloved hands, allowed it to settle over them.

He seemed aware of every detail of the world: the grittiness of the regolith he had spilled on the bodies, the slow tracking of the shadows, the ticks and whirrs of the mechanisms of his suit – the meaningless texture of this, the latest of a parade of meaningless universes.

He ought to say something. He had for Cornelius and Tybee J., after all, and they had died in a much stranger place than this, much further from home. But he had no words.

He left her there.

For the last time he worked his way around Cruithne, and stood, tethered, before the portal.

He had searched Tybee's backpack and he had found a grenade: a simple sleek thing, easily small enough to fit into a glove, with a pull-ring fat enough for a spacesuited finger. Ten second timer, he guessed. He cradled the grenade now, clutching it to his belly.

He had no doubt it would work.

Cruithne turned. Shadows fled towards him, and he was plunged into darkness. He heard pumps clatter and whirr in his backpack as his battered suit prepared to fight the cold. He waited until Earth was high above the portal, blue planet over blue artefact.

He pulled the grenade's ring. *Ten, nine, eight.*

He started his languid microgravity jump in good time. He

401

would enter the portal head first, hands clutched to his chest, over the grenade. The complex, ancient ground of Cruithne slid beneath him.

Then the portal was all around him. He grinned fiercely. Made it, by God. End of story.

Two, one.

There was a blue flash, an instant of searing pain –

Maura Della:

... And, on the Moon, it took just six more months for it all to fall apart.

The scrap of paper had been brought here, all the way to the Moon, by a burly looking Marine. He looked as if he had been ordered to drag Maura out of here by her hair if necessary.

She fingered the document suspiciously. It was written, by hand, on what looked like authentic White House notepaper, and signed by the President himself. But she had a lot of trouble with any text that contained phrases like 'US Constitution as amended' and 'emergency powers'.

Maura Della was ordered to return to Earth – specifically, to submit herself to a Washington court within a couple of weeks. They wanted her to denounce the future. To deny that the information Reid Malenfant gleaned from his Feynman radio came from the future. To deny that the Blue kids were influenced by information from the future.

Of course it wouldn't be true. But America was run by a government now that had been elected, essentially, on a platform of removing all this stuff, this *madness*, from public life.

It was impossible. But they were having a damn good try. An obvious method was to treat it all as a conspiracy by the people who had been close to it all. People like Maura.

But such orders were easy to hand out in executive offices in Washington; this was the *Moon*, and after three days in space – presumably without proper training or orientation – this poor grunt was green as a lettuce leaf and looked as if he could barely stand up, here in the cold antiseptic light of the NASA base.

Meanwhile she had heard other rumours that the Witnesses – as they were called – were being recalled for fresh 'trials', whether or not they had already recanted as required. And this time, it was said, when the Witnesses walked into custody, they were not coming out again.

She was still a citizen of the United States. She had always regarded it as her duty to uphold and submit to her country's laws, whatever she thought of their philosophical basis. Maybe she should pack up her bag and go home with the goon Marine, and submit herself, like Galileo, like Jesus. Maybe it would be an example that might even do some good.

But Maura Della never had been good at turning the other cheek.

She wasn't without allies, even here. After six months on the Moon she had gotten to know most of the military types, NASA astronauts and staffers who manned this cramped little base. There was a bunker mentality. At first she'd been the outsider. But she'd taken her turns with the chores, like hand-cleaning the hydroponics feed lines. And she had brought them handfuls of fresh-cut grass from Never-Never Land, its green springtime scent making the unimaginative metallic confinement of this base a little more bearable.

All this bridge-building had been quite deliberate, of course. And now it wouldn't be hard for her to get a little protection and assistance, enough to deflect this goon for a couple of hours.

The question was, what to do with those hours.

Never-Never Land, she thought. Anna and the children. That's where I must go.

Working on automatic, she reached for a bag, started to make mental lists of what she should take. Then, deliberately, she put the bag aside. Just go, Maura, while – if – you still have the chance.

She stepped out of her cupboard-sized personal quarters and headed through the complex towards the bus docking port.

Bill Tybee was there, looking lost, hurt, frightened, fingering his silver med-alert pin. He was carrying a light transparent briefcase which contained a set of big chunky plastic toys. For Bill, this had begun as just another working day. 'Maura? What's going on? They won't let me on the bus.'

'Take it easy,' she told Bill. 'We'll sort this out . . .'

There was a military officer, a woman, blocking the way to the bus. She had her weapon exposed, and her hand lay on its stock. She looked young and scared and uncertain. It took Maura five minutes of patient negotiation, a mixture of reassurance and veiled threats, to get them both past the officer and onto the bus.

Maura and Bill were alone here in this autonomous Moon bus. As the minutes wore away to the bus's appointed departure time they sat on a bench and held hands in silence.

Maura could think of any number of ways they could be stopped. But they weren't. Maybe, for once, the frustrating layers of security here were working in her favour. When things went wrong fast, like this, nobody knew what the hell was going on, because nobody knew who they were supposed to be able to talk to.

And in the meantime her own need to reach the children grew to an overwhelming obsession. That was the centre of things, and that surely was where her duty – her deepest duty, embedded deep in whatever morality she had left – must lie now.

Maybe this is how Bill Tybee, a parent, feels all the time, she thought. She felt a prickle of envy.

At last the bus doors slid closed. Maura waited for the soft clunk of the docking tunnel disconnecting from the hull of the bus, and then came the jolt as the bus pulled away and drove itself off through the Moon's marshmallow gravity.

The sun was high, and unfiltered light, harsh and static, flooded down into the complex canyons and crevasses of the brutally folded surface of Tycho.

Bill was shaking, sweat clustering on his forehead in great low-G beads. She got up and brought him a plastic cup of water. Slowly he calmed down. For now they were safe. You couldn't mount a car chase through this ancient, hazardous maze of canyons. Besides, the military presence on the Moon remained small; she doubted the commanders would risk any kind of surface operation to intercept them en route to Never-Never Land.

Anyhow there was no need. All that was necessary was to wait until Maura and Bill arrived at Never-Never Land and take them out then; there was, after all, no other place to go.

Well, she would deal with that eventuality when it came.

Bill pointed upwards. 'Look.'

A star was crossing the sky with ponderous slowness. It seemed to be sparkling, pulsing with light with slow regularity. It was, of course, artificial: a satellite, slowly rotating, new, bigger than anything she had seen before. She had absolutely no idea what its purpose might be.

She found herself shivering, and she clutched Bill's arm.

Strange lights in the sky, she thought. Scary. Even if we put them there.

Especially if we put them there.

It proved easier, oddly, to get into Never-Never Land than to get out of the NASA base. The troopers here seemed to be operating under radio silence. And besides, as Maura herself was quick to point out, once they were inside Never-Never Land they were effectively under house arrest anyhow. What were they going to do, climb out of a window?

So she was admitted. Bill had to wait in the bus.

At first glance nothing had changed here. The dome glowed its daytime sky blue, sun and Earth hung there like lanterns, and the grass was a livid green, almost shocking to the senses after the grey of the Moon. But nevertheless Maura sensed there was something wrong. The air seemed chill, and she saw the leaves of the fat, squat oak tree rustle. From somewhere there came an odd cry, perhaps human, perhaps animal.

At the airlock's inner door was the bulky blond German trooper whom Maura had come to know during her visits here, and to dislike intensely. He was fingering the revolver at his waist. Anna stood before him, talking earnestly. Her wings were on the ground behind her. There were no other children in sight.

Anna hurried to Maura. 'You have to help me. I'm trying to make him understand.'

Maura held Anna's arms. 'What do we have to understand?'

'What is to come.'

Maura's skin prickled.

Maura glanced at the trooper. He was staring at Anna. *Leering*, Maura thought uneasily, leering without speaking.

Anna led her away, deeper into the dome across the grass, talking intently. It came out of Anna in broken fragments, scraps of speech. Occasionally the girl would lapse into metalanguage: shards of song, a few clumsy dance steps. 'The arrow of time,' she said. 'Inner time. Do you understand? This is the key. If you close your eyes you feel time. You feel yourself enduring. Time is essential to awareness, where space is not, and so is more fundamental. The flow of time, events happening, the future coming into existence.'

'Yes.'

'But you don't *understand* time. Your scientists use time as a co-ordinate, a label. You even have theories which are time-symmetric,

405

which work whether you run them forward or back in time.' The girl actually laughed at that.

'And that's wrong?'

'Of course it's wrong. It is trivially wrong. There is a severe discrepancy between your theories and what you feel is the reality of the world. And that is telling you, *should* be telling you, something quite fundamental about the physics that *actually* underlies your conscious processes.'

'All right. Tell me about the arrow of time.'

Anna danced, whirled, her dress lifting; and Maura was uncomfortably aware of the soldier's eyes. 'There are an infinite number of possible universes in the manifold,' Anna said. 'Of those only a subset – nevertheless infinite itself – are capable of supporting self-aware substructures. And those universes are characterized by a flow of time, which is created by unfolding cosmic structure. Gravity is the key.'

Maura was getting lost again. '. . . Gravity?'

'A universe with gravity is driven from smoothness to clumpiness because of gravitational collapse. And the arrow of time comes from this flow of matter and energy, from the gravitational arrangement of the universe at its beginning, to the equilibrium state at its end. Life depends on a flow of energy and information, to be dammed and used. So the arrow of time, like perception itself, is intimately linked to the structure of the universe.'

'Go on.'

Anna was still talking, still dancing. 'But structure and change are not restricted to a single universe. *They span the manifold of evolving universes.* And so, therefore, does life. Do you see?'

'. . . No.'

'When this universe was spawned from the previous generation, it went through a series of phases. That is, the vacuum did.' Anna was watching her, seeking signs of understanding. 'The vacuum is a complex thing. Space can be bent by gravity, but it resists with a strength far stronger than steel. The vacuum is a sea of energy, of virtual particles which pop in and out of existence.'

'All right,' Maura said, struggling to keep up.

'But it is possible for the vacuum to take different phases. Think of water. Liquid water may achieve a higher energy phase – it may flash to steam – or it may seek a lower energy phase –'

'By freezing, forming ice.'

'Yes. Systems lose energy, tend to seek the lowest energy state.'

'I understand. And so the vacuum –'

'After the Big Bang the vacuum itself descended through a series of energy states. This is the most primitive unfolding of all, the source of the time river, the source of life and mind.'

'Until it settled on the lowest, umm, energy state. Which is our vacuum. Right?'

Anna frowned. '*No.* Our vacuum is only metastable. It is not in the lowest level, not even now. This began in the Big Bang and continues now. But it needs, umm, help.'

'Help? What kind of help?'

The girl grabbed her hands. 'You must see what this means. *The evolution of the vacuum is a flow of information.* But this is a flow which spans the manifold itself, and is therefore fundamental.' Anna's eyes searched Maura's. 'Life spans the manifold. The vacuum metastability makes you what you are. This is the reason for what we are doing. And this is what you must tell them.'

'Who?'

'The people.' She waved a hand at the soldier, vaguely in the direction of Earth. 'Make them understand this.'

'What for?'

'Consolation.'

'My God, Anna –'

And then, it seemed, time ran out for them all.

It was as if a cloud had passed over the sun.

Anna licked a finger and raised her hand. 'There's no breeze,' she said. 'They turned the systems off.'

Maura looked up. The dome had darkened. She could see the sun, just, a diffuse distorted disc, shedding no meaningful light. Perhaps the polarization had been switched to its night setting.

Artificial lights sparked, flooding the dome with a cold fluorescent glow, a deadness that contrasted powerfully with the living green warmth of a moment ago.

The German trooper touched Maura's elbow. She heard the insect whisper of a speaker in his ear. 'We have to get you out of here, ma'am.' He was pulling at her, firmly but gently, separating her from Anna; Maura, bewildered, let it happen.

And Maura saw how his fat fingers had wrapped around the girl's upper arm. Anna wriggled, obviously in pain. But the trooper was holding the girl's fragile body against his battle dress.

Ugly suspicions coalesced inside Maura; a subplot was reaching its resolution here. 'Let her go.'

The trooper grinned. He was tapping at a pad on his chest, perhaps calling for backup. 'Ma'am, this is nothing to do with you. The bus will be waiting outside to take you back.'

'I'm not going to let you harm her.'

He just stared at her, holding the girl effortlessly despite her squirming.

Maura braced herself, cupped her hand, and slapped the side of his head as hard as she could.

'Ow . . . shit, *Gott* –' He pressed his hand to his damaged ear and let the girl go.

'Run, Anna!'

The girl was already fleeing over the darkened, grey-green grass, toward the centre of the dome. Maura saw a giraffe, terrified, loping across the miniature veldt.

'Ma'am.'

She turned. The German was standing before her. His fist drove into her stomach.

The pain slammed into her, doubling her over. She felt as if her intestines had been crushed against her spine, and perhaps they had. She wrapped her arms around her belly and tipped onto the grass, falling with lunar slowness.

But Anna had gotten away.

Now a klaxon started to sound, loud, insistent, a brutal braying, filling the dome with its clamour. Whatever was coming must be close.

She could see the German. He looked after Anna. 'Shit, shit,' he said, frustrated.

He walked up to Maura. She saw a flash of leather and combat green. Her right knee exploded in pain, and she howled.

Then he ran off, towards the exit.

Her world was pain now, nothing but that. She was suspended between twin poles of it, at her stomach and her shattered knee, as if a lance had been passed through her body. She was unable to move. She even had to control her own breathing; if she disturbed the position of her body by as much as an inch the pain magnified, never to diminish again.

The klaxon seemed to be growing louder. And lights were pulsing across the dome roof now, great alternating bands of black and white that rushed towards the exits. The light patterns were neat, clean, almost beautiful. Their message was unmistakable, but Maura knew she could not move.

She closed her eyes, longing for the oblivion of unconsciousness. But it didn't come.

Some Galileo you would have made, Maura.

The light seemed to be fading, even the pain – if not dwindling – then at least growing more remote, diminished by distance.

She looked within, and sensed time flowing, as it always had: the blossoming of multiple universes reflected in her own soul. Well, soon the flow of time would stop, for her. How would it *feel*?

. . . But now there was something new. Hands, small hands, at her shoulders and knees and feet and head. She tried to focus her eyes. A face swam before her. Anna's? She tried to speak, to protest. But she failed.

Then they were lifting her – as children would, clumsily – and her knee erupted in white-hot agony.

She was being carried across the veldt. This was still the Moon, and the low gravity was making it easy for the children to carry her quickly. But even so, every jolt sent new rivers of metallic pain coursing through her leg and belly.

She looked up at the dome. It had turned transparent now, and there was a glaring sun, a blue marble Earth over her.

They came to a glass fence. One section of it had been shattered, and the children hurried through. She was inside the central compound, the forbidden area, where the children's bubble of spacetime had rested for five years.

And now she was approaching a wall of silver, that sparkled, elusive.

She tipped up her head. Something else in the sky beyond the dome. Beams of light, radiating from a complex, drifting point. The beams were red, blue, yellow, green, rainbow colours, a rotating umbrella. Laser beams? They must already have kicked up debris, she thought: ground their way into Tycho, filled the vacuum with vaporized rock, making the beams themselves visible.

The beams were approaching the dome, rotating like an H.G. Wells Martian tripod.

Now she was being pushed into something that gently resisted, like a thick, viscous liquid. She looked down. Her legs were disappearing into the silver wall, now her waist, arms.

There was a glare of complex light, a sound of tearing, a ferocious wind that ripped over her face. The air was sucked out of her lungs. The dome had been breached. Seconds left –

There was a flash of electric blue, an instant of searing pain.

Reid Malenfant:

. . . found himself falling.

It was just a couple of feet, but he landed on his belly, and his helmet slammed against the ground. He tasted copper. Maybe he'd bitten his lip.

He'd fallen hard. His faceplate was badly scuffed, and he had trouble seeing out.

He pushed at the surface under him, expecting to find himself floating upwards, defying the feeble tug of Cruithne's gravity. He could barely raise his upper body. He was *heavy* here.

And where was here?

The ground was purple. It had a furry texture. It was obvious this wasn't the coal-dust regolith of Cruithne. Christ, it looked like carpet.

'No.' His own voice sounded loud in his head. 'No, no. I don't want this.' He fumbled at his chest, probing at his ribs through the layers of the suit. There was no feeling of pain. 'I just set off a damn grenade in my face. I don't *want* this.' It was true. He had been reconciled. It was done. This surreal coda was not welcome.

He shut his eyes, and lay flat on the floor, the ridiculous carpet. But the world didn't go away; he could still hear the whirring of the faithful little machines of his backpack, the pumping of blood in his ears, his own reluctant breath; and he could feel, deep within himself, the slow pulse of time, the river bearing him endlessly downstream.

He was still alive, still embedded in the universe, whether he liked it or not.

Emma, I'm sorry.

He started to feel ridiculous. Suppose there were a bunch of medics (or orderlies or guards or inmates) standing around laughing at the asshole who was trying to bury himself in the carpet? Angry, embarrassed, he opened his eyes and pushed himself upright to a sitting position. He glanced around. He got a brief impression of a room, shadowy bulks that must be furniture. There was nobody here, laughing or otherwise.

He stayed there unmoving. He, and Cornelius and Emma, had not been too scrupulous in maintaining their zero G exercise routines. If he really was back on Earth he could expect to fall straight back over as the blood drained from his head and his weakened heart struggled to keep up. But he felt, essentially, okay.

So maybe he had been back for a while, months even. But he didn't remember any of it. The last thing he remembered was the portal and the grenade. How could he have survived? And, if this was a hospital, why the pressure suit?

He found himself staring at a wall, a few inches from his face. There was a notice stuck there. He leaned forward and squinted to read it. It was written out in clumsy block capitals.

ABOUT THE GRAVITY. THEY MADE SOME ADJUSTMENTS TO YOUR SORRY ASS SO YOU DON'T PASS OUT AND SO FORTH. IT SEEMED THE SIMPLEST WAY.

It was in his own hand.

He growled, exasperated, and reached out for the notice with a gloved hand – a glove still stained dark with Cruithne dust – and ripped the notice off the wall. It had been stuck there with tape. On the back was another message, again in his own hand.

GO WITH THE FLOW, MALENFANT.

He crumpled up the paper and threw it aside.

For a few heartbeats he just sat there. He ran his gloved hand over the carpet, leaving a grimy streak. Seemed like good quality, a thick pile.

Impulsively he reached up and cracked the seal of his helmet. As the seal broke there was the softest hiss of equalizing pressure. Not a vacuum, then. The air seemed neither warm nor cold, a neutral temperature. He held his breath. His heart beat a little faster – after all, if the atmosphere wasn't exactly right he was about to *die*, probably painfully, and despite his determination to do just that he was afraid – but he gripped his helmet and pushed it up.

The enclosed, magnified noises of the helmet were replaced by a remote, deeper hum. Air conditioning?

He gasped, releasing the last of his suit air, and dragged in a lungful of whatever filled this room.

Well, he didn't start gagging or choking and his lungs didn't hurt. That didn't mean there wasn't something else, something colourless and odourless like carbon monoxide lingering here to kill him, but there wasn't anything he could do about that.

At least he could see clearly now.

He was in what looked like a small hotel room: a single bed, a table and chair, a TV on a wall bracket, a little corridor with a bathroom and a wardrobe, a door. He could see into the bathroom. There was sanitary tape on the toilet, fluorescent light panels in the ceiling.

It wasn't the kind of place he'd choose to stay. But it looked clean, and at least it didn't look like a prison cell.

He got to his feet. He felt a little stiff, and his suit was heavy in the full gravity. He walked to the door, wrapped his gloved hand around the handle, and twisted. It felt like he was dragging at a concrete wall.

There was an in-case-of-emergency notice stuck on the door in front of his nose. ONE STEP AT A TIME, MALENFANT. YOU OBVIOUSLY AREN'T IN A REAL HOTEL ROOM, AND THIS IS NOT EARTH. BUT YOU ALREADY KNOW THAT.

. . . And of course that was true. After all, he *had* jumped into a time-hopping, universe-breaching alien portal with a grenade clutched to his gut; it wasn't your conventional way of checking in. Anyhow he thought he knew what must have happened to him.

'I don't think I'm me,' he said aloud. 'I think I'm some kind of reconstruction in a giant computer in the far downstream. Tell me I'm wrong.' He scanned down the notice.

SOMETHING LIKE THAT, IF YOU MUST KNOW. ALL WILL BE REVEALED. IN THE MEANTIME, CHILL OUT, HAVE A DRINK, TAKE A SHOWER.

'A shower?'

There was one more line on the notice.

MALENFANT, IF ANYBODY CAN TELL YOU THIS IT'S ME. YOU STINK, BUDDY.

Malenfant stalked back into the bedroom, leaving more dusty boot prints, and sat on the bed, which creaked under the combined weight of himself and the suit. He said, 'On.' The TV didn't respond.

He looked at his gloved hand, its gritty texture. His hand wasn't real. None of this was. He was completely powerless. He could be turned off, changed, distorted, reprogrammed, whatever the hell they wanted, whoever *they* were.

He tried to lie back on the bed, but his spacesuit backpack was in the way.

'Jesus Christ,' he said to himself. 'What a mess.'

He didn't want this. He didn't want any of it. He ought to be dead, or grieving for Emma, in that order. He had seen enough. He looked around the room, hoping for another notice, a couple of lines from himself to himself, telling him what to do, how to feel. But there was nothing.

What would he tell himself, if he had the chance?

Get a grip. Don't worry about what you can't change. In the meantime take the shower.

With a sigh, he started to peel off his suit, his boots and gloves first, then his zips. He dumped the suit in the middle of the floor. Cruithne dust and flakes of charred fabric – scorched by multiple Big Bangs, for God's sake – fell to the bright purple carpet.

When he got down to his skinsuit, life got a lot more unpleasant. The stink of his own body, exposed, hit him like a smack in the mouth. He had been living in the suit, after all, for days. In places the suit stuck to him, and when he tried to peel it away he found himself pulling the skin off blisters and half-healed friction rubs. In a couple of places he found oedema patches and busted blood vessels.

He picked up the pieces of the battered, grimy suit, folded them up and crammed them into the cupboard. He brushed at the bedspread, but he only succeeded in grinding Cruithne dust deeper into the fabric.

He gave up and went to the shower.

It turned out to be a power jet. When it first hit his damaged skin it hurt, but he stuck with it, bathing the wounds gently. He just ran the spray for a while, and dark dust ran out of his hair and skin and down the plug. He kept the water running until it ran off him clear, except for traces of crimson blood from his broken skin. Even so he still had Cruithne dirt buried under his fingernails and worked deep into his fingertips; he suspected it would be a long time, if ever, before he was rid of the stuff.

Then he used shampoo and soap, stuff that came in bottles and wrappers and boxes in a little wicker basket. There was no manufacturers' logo, no hotel title.

There was no bathroom cabinet in here, no place he could see where there might be a resupply of his cancer drugs. Well, maybe he wasn't going to be here long enough for that to matter.

The shower actually felt good. He was feeling pleasure.

. . . *Emma.*

He tried to explore his feelings, tried to find regret, a sense of loss. And failed. And now here he was washing his damn hair.

If they did reconstruct you, Malenfant, they didn't take time to put in a soul.

When he came out of the shower, wrapped in a fat white bathrobe (no monogram or label), the dusty mess he had left on the carpet had vanished. Not only that, a shirt and slacks, socks and slip-on leather shoes had been laid out, nice and fresh. Neat touch, he thought; that much unreality he could stand.

He went around the room. The mini bar turned out to be tucked under a desk near the TV bracket. The desk held a writing pad and pencils. There was no heading on the paper. The mini bar wasn't locked, which was *definitely* a touch of unreality, and the bottles and cans and packets, while looking authentic enough, weren't labelled either.

He pulled out what looked like a miniature of whisky, broke the seal, threw the liquor into his mouth straight from the bottle. The heat hit the back of his throat. He may be one computer simulation sucking on another, but that felt authentic enough, and the spreading of the warmth through his chest and head was welcome.

He reached for another bottle, then thought better of it. Maybe now wasn't the time to get smashed.

If it was even possible. If *they*, whoever had reconstructed him, permitted it. He wondered if they would let him hurt himself. What if he busted one of the bottles, and started to saw at a wrist? Or –

There was a knock at the door. It made him jump, and he dropped his miniature. He got up, checked his robe was closed around him (why, Malenfant? – like your mother, they have surely seen it all before) and he padded across the carpet. The bristles were sharp under his cleaned feet. He grasped the door handle. This time, of course, the door opened easily.

There was a corridor beyond, but it was somehow blurred, as if he couldn't see it properly. 'Imperfectly simulated,' he muttered.

Something like that. A Seattle accent.

'. . . Yow.' He looked down.

It was Michael.

The boy was just standing there, hands at his sides. He was wearing a gold-orange jump-suit with a blue circle at his breast, just like in those damn Schools.

'You're Michael,' he said.

Yes. The boy looked fresh-scrubbed, healthy, his eyes bright, even happy. Eerily, the voice coming out of his mouth was that of the old softscreen simulation, the nasal Seattle matron, slightly distorted, like an airport announcer's.

'What I mean,' Malenfant said, 'is that you're a simulacrum of Michael. A program running inside some hideous end-of-time God-type computer.'

The boy looked puzzled.

Malenfant leaned out into the corridor. He couldn't see further than a few feet in either direction, though he couldn't figure out why. The same purple carpet lay on the floor. There were no other doors. 'What if I run off down this corridor?'

I don't know.

'Will they have to create more of this virtual stuff? Will the room disappear?'

Try it if you want.

Malenfant thought about it, sighed. 'Ah, the hell with it. You'd better come in.'

Michael looked around the room, for all the world like any curious kid, and he jumped on the bed and bounced up and down. Malenfant shut the door. Then, immediately, he tried it again. Naturally it had melted into seamless wall again, and wouldn't open.

'The TV doesn't work,' Malenfant said.

Michael shrugged. He was toying with the empty whisky bottle.

Malenfant said, 'You want something from the mini bar?'

Michael thought for a long time, as if the choice was the most important he had ever made. *Peanuts*, he said, in his eerie middle-aged voice.

'Plain or roasted?'

What have you got?

'Jesus Christ.' Malenfant got on his hands and knees and rummaged through the bar. He dug out a couple of foil packets. He tossed one to the boy. Michael's turned out to be plain nuts, Malenfant's roasted. Michael pointed to the roasted, so they swapped over.

Malenfant threw a nut into his mouth. 'Too much salt,' he said.

Michael shrugged. *These are okay.*

'This is kind of a cliché, you know,' Malenfant said. 'The virtual-reality hotel room.'

You had to get out of that spacesuit.

'True enough. So,' said Malenfant. 'Here we are. Where the hell?

. . . No, forget that. We're programs running on a huge computer at the end of time. Right?'

No. Yes. This is, umm, a substrate.

'A substrate?' Malenfant snapped his fingers. 'I knew it. The lossless processors we saw in the far downstream. The dreaming computer.'

Michael frowned. *But you are Malenfant.*

'The same person I was before?'

Of course. Which other?

'But I can't be. *That* Malenfant blew himself to bits. I can believe the portal stored information about me, sent it to the far future, and here I am reconstructed in this –' he waved a hand '– this virtual reality Bates motel. But I'm not *me*.'

Michael looked puzzled. *You are you. I am me. Information is the most important thing. There was a German called Leibniz.*

'The philosopher? Never heard of him.'

Entities which cannot be distinguished by any means whatsoever, even in principle, at any time in the past, present and future have to be considered identical. This is called the Identity of Indiscernibles. It really is you, Malenfant, just as it feels.

Malenfant stared at him. All this was delivered in that ridiculous scratchy middle-aged woman's voice. The illusion of kid-hood seemed suddenly thin, Malenfant thought, and he wondered, with some dread, what arrays of shadowy minds lay behind this boy, feeding him, perhaps controlling him . . .

Can I finish your peanuts?

'Have them. So how did *you* get here?'

All Michael would say was: *Differently.*

Malenfant got up, prowled around the room. There were curtains on the wall. When he pulled them back there were no windows.

'Who did this, Michael? Who brought me back?'

The downstreamers. The dreamers. The boy frowned again. *The people in the lossless-processing substrate –*

'What am I supposed to do?'

Whatever you want. You must only, umm, exist. The information that defines you was stored by the portal, and therefore is part of the substrate.

Malenfant frowned. 'You're telling me I don't have some kind of mission? That the decadent beings of the far future don't need my primitive instincts to save them?'

I don't understand –

416

'Never mind.' Malenfant looked down at his hand, flexed it, turned it over: a monkey paw transmitted to the end of time, a perfect copy . . . No, if Michael was right, *this really was his hand*, as if he'd been teleported here. 'I can live on here? Like this? How long for? No human of my era lived beyond a hundred and some years. So when I reach two hundred, three hundred . . .'

Your brain can store around a quadrillion bits. That corresponds to a thousand years of life. After that –

'I stop being me.'

You could be enhanced. There would be continuity. Growth.

'But I wouldn't be *me*.'

You aren't big enough to think the thoughts you would become capable of.

Malenfant hesitated. 'Is that what happened to you?'

I have lived a long time.

'Longer than a thousand years?'

Michael smiled.

'And so, you aren't Michael any more.' Of course not. How could he be? 'Don't you regret that?'

Michael shrugged. *My people, in Zambia, believed that we, on Earth, are the dead. Left behind by the true living, who have passed through their graves.*

'And that's what you believe?'

The boy I used to be was partial. Very damaged. He was a husk I gladly discarded. He studied Malenfant, and Malenfant thought there was a trace of accusation in his eyes, accusation over crimes long gone, buried in the glare of the Big Bang afterglow. He said, reasonably gently, *A thousand years isn't so bad, Malenfant.*

'It's more than I deserve . . .' He glared at the boy. 'If you can do all this – *bring Emma back*.'

I can't. I mean, they can't. They don't have the information.

'Emma passed through the portals. There must be records.'

But she *would only be, umm, a simulation. The identity principle only works if the information is perfect. And because of the explosion as you went through –*

Malenfant held his head in his hands. 'Now,' he said, '*now* it hits me. If I'd known I could have saved her. Emma, I'm sorry. Somehow I managed to kill you twice over . . .'

You sound like you think it's your fault.

'People around me tend to die, Michael. Cornelius. Emma. You, unless you count *this* as living on.'

417

The kid was nodding. *I understand.*

'You're just a kid,' Malenfant snapped. 'I don't care how augmented you are. You *can't* understand. If I hadn't screwed up her life, if I'd left her on Earth –'

Would you have wanted that?

'Yes. No.' We wouldn't have made love, floating between planets. She wouldn't have followed me across universes. She wouldn't have learned the truth, about the cancer, about us. I'd have lost – well, everything. My life would have remained meaningless, like your damn downstreamers. '*But she wouldn't have died*. All I had to do was push her away, in that scramble at Mojave . . .'

Then make it so, Michael murmured.

'What?'

Michael held his hand again. *Malenfant, the universe has many values. There is no one single path. Do you understand? The future can't be determined. Nor can the past. Therefore we are free to choose . . .*

Malenfant spoke slowly, carefully. 'What you're telling me is that I could change the past. I could spare Emma.' The thought electrified him. 'But I'm no downstreamer.'

You are now, said the Michael-thing.

I pushed her away before, when I learned about the cancer, and it didn't do a damn bit of good. And if I lost her, I'd lose everything. I was ready to die.

But you would spare her, Malenfant. Give her years of life, maybe. Let go.

Michael was watching him, wide-eyed, chewing nuts. *There is something else*, Michael said. *The eschatos.*

'The what?'

The end of things.

'The Carter catastrophe. My God . . .'

We could go back. Become part of it. If you wish.

'I don't understand any of this, Michael.'

You will.

What the hell are you doing, Malenfant? If you reject this you're throwing away immortality. A thousand years of life, recognizable human life, followed by – what? Transcendence?

But, if I lose myself, I'll lose Emma. And that, surely, would be the final disrespect.

You always were decisive, Malenfant. If there was ever a time to make a choice it's now.

418

Malenfant closed his eyes. 'Let's do it,' he said.

You're sure?

'Hell, no. Let's do it anyhow.'

The boy pulled him towards the door.

Malenfant's heart was thumping. 'You mean *now?*'

Will your decision be different later?

Malenfant took a deep sigh. 'Do I need to dress?'

Malenfant went to the bathroom. He washed his face, had a leak, a dump. He had time to be impressed by the faithfulness of the mysterious processes which had restored him here, which had even, presumably, reconstructed the contents of his stomach, after his last meal.

He looked at himself in the mirror, studied a face that he had known all his life. The last time for everything, even for the simple things. Here, in his body, in this place, he was still himself. But what was he about to become? He'd built up his courage to blow himself to bits once today already, and his reward had been *this*, this Alice in Wonderland bullshit. Could he go through with it again?

Of course, if he chickened out, it would have to be in front of Michael, and the weird entities who were watching through him.

Malenfant grinned fiercely. To hell with it. He checked his teeth for bits of peanut, then went back to the room.

Michael was wearing his kid-sized pressure suit now, and he had laid out Malenfant's suit on the bed, beside the unused shirt and slacks. The components of the suit – skinsuit and outer garment and thermal garment and gloves and helmet and boots – looked unearthly, out of place in this mundane environment. And yet, Malenfant thought, the suit was actually the most normal thing about the whole damn room.

'Are we going to need suits?'

If we go like this. If you'd rather –

'Hell, no.' Malenfant suited up quickly.

Michael came to him with a pen he'd taken from the desk. *You have some notes to write.*

'What notes? Oh. Okay.' Malenfant sighed, and bent stiffly in his suit. 'What if I make a mistake? . . . Never mind.'

He wrote out the notes hastily, and stuck them where he thought they ought to be. And if he got it wrong, let some other bastard sort it out.

He put on his gloves and helmet, and he walked to the door with

Michael. When they got there he closed up his own suit and sealed Michael's, and ran quick diagnostic checks on the kid's systems.

They turned and faced the door. Michael reached up and, clumsily, pulled it open.

The corridor was gone. A blue-ring portal floated there, framing darkness.

'Is this going to hurt?'

No more than usual.

'Great. Michael . . . I saw the future. But what was it *like*?'

Michael paused. *Huge. Primal. Beyond control. New minds emerged in great pulses.*

'Like Africa,' said Malenfant. 'We always thought the future would be like America. Clean and empty and waiting to be shaped. I always thought that way. But our past was Africa. Dark and deep. And that's how the future was.'

Yes, Michael said.

Malenfant braced himself and faced the portal. 'Visors down,' he said.

Michael lowered his gold visor, hiding his face. Malenfant saw the portal's blue ring reflected in his visor. Then Michael held up his hand, like a son reaching for his father. Malenfant took the hand. The child's fingers were buried in his own begrimed glove.

They stepped forward. There was a blue flash, an instant of agonizing pain –

. . . and Malenfant was floating in space. The instant transition to zero gravity was a shock, like falling off a cliff, and he had to swallow a few times to keep his peanuts down.

He was surrounded by patient stars: above, below, all around him, childhood constellations augmented by the rich still lights of deep space. There was a single splinter of brilliance below him. The sun? It was a point source that cast strong, sharp shadows over their suits.

He was still holding Michael's hand.

Michael said, *Are you okay?* His Seattle whine was a radio crackle. *If you become uncomfortable –*

'I'll be okay. What are we looking at, Michael? The sun?'

Yes. We're out of the plane of the ecliptic. That is, somewhere above the sun's north pole. We're about five astronomical units out. Five times Earth's orbit, about as far as Jupiter is from the sun. Forty-three minutes at light speed. What do you want to see?

'Earth.'

Then look. Michael pointed to a nondescript part of the sky.

Malenfant sighted along his arm, and saw a star, a spark that might have been pale blue, a lesser light beside it.

. . . And suddenly there was Earth, swimming before him, oceans and deserts and clouds and ice, just as it had always been. Sparks of light circled it, and drifted on its seas. Ships, people, cities.

He felt a lump knot in his throat. 'Oh, my,' he said.

We are two hundred years into the future, roughly. Our future.

'The Carter catastrophe date. So Cornelius's prediction was right. He would have been pleased . . .'

Malenfant. There is little time. If you want to make your change, to reach back. It must be now.

He drifted in space, letting his suit starfish, thinking of Emma.

He whispered, 'How do I do it?'

Just tell me what you want.

'Will I remember?'

Consciousness spans the manifold.

I don't know if I have the strength, he thought.

'She'll forget me. Won't she, Michael?'

I'm just a kid, he said. *How would I know?*

Your call, Malenfant. Keep her, or give her back her life.

'Do it,' he whispered.

. . . And the universe pivoted around him, the lines of possibility swirling, knitting new patterns of truth and dream, and he clutched at the boy.

Emma Stoney:

. . . Death always fascinated me. Ever since the death of my father, I suppose. I was just a kid. The endless slow rituals of funerals and mourning, the morbid business of moving the bodies around, boxing them and dressing them. It was as if we humans were seeking some control of the horrible arbitrariness, a cushion against the blunt finality of it.

But that finality came, for me, when my father's corpse was at last laid into the ground, and stopped moving, I realized, for *ever*. I remember I wanted to clamber into the grave and dig it up and somehow re-animate him a little longer. But even at age eight I knew that was impossible.

All of the ceremonial stuff focuses on the needs of the living. But at the heart of every funeral there is the central mystery: that a sentient, conscious being has ceased to exist. It is a brutal reality our culture simply refuses to face – the reality of death for the dying.

And the reality of my life is this, Maura: that if I had got on that rocketship with Malenfant, if I'd gone with him to the asteroid, I'd be dead now, as he is dead.

But I didn't go. I miss him, Maura. Of course. Every minute of every day. I miss his laugh, the way he tasted of the high desert, even the way he pulled my life around. But he's gone.

Anyhow, that's why I'll take the job. The Moon, you say?

Maura Della:

And for Maura – who had never been to the Moon, and now never would – the Moon hung in the Washington sky as it always had, the scar of the failed attack invisible to the naked eye. She kept a NASA feed running in her office, compiled from Hubble and lunar satellite cameras, images of the unmarked bubble artefact there on the Tycho surface.

After all, if things had been just a little different, Maura Della might have been up there when the shit hit the fan. Caught in the crossfire herself, rather than her envoy.

But as the incident on the Moon receded into the past, life went on. The panic subsides even as the data burns, she thought. Cruithne, even the Moon, are after all just lumps of rock a long way away.

Maura tried to concentrate on her work.

Here was a self-justifying report from the Lawrence Livermore Laboratory on the exotic weapons technology they called FELs, free electron lasers, into which a goodly portion of the federal budget had been sunk, and which had been deployed, to spectacular failure, on the Moon. The basis of a FEL was a cyclotron, a closed ring which could be used to accelerate electrons. Although it was impossible for the electrons to exceed the speed of light there was no limit, it seemed, to the energy that could be piled into them. And that unlimited energy was the big advantage of FEL technology over conventional laser technology, like chemical. The report writers noted with jaunty technocrat-type confidence that a FEL should have been an ideal sword for fighting a war in a vacuum: in Earth orbit, or on the Moon.

But it had failed. The FEL had burned the lunar base and the Never-Never Land dome to the ground. But it hadn't so much as scratched the droplet of twisted space, or whatever it was, which sheltered the children – and presumably continued to do so, even now, sitting like a drop of mercury amid the rubble of the Tycho battlefield.

All bullshit. The FEL was just another magic sword, in a long line of such swords, technical solutions that were supposed to make the world better and safer and which, of course, always failed.

Without finishing the report she consigned it to her incinerator.

Here was an extraordinary hand-written memo from a colleague relaying rumours Maura had already heard, about the President himself. Whittacker always had a grim religious bent, Maura knew. It had been part of his qualification for election, it seemed, in these fractured times. Now he was sunk in an apocalyptic depression from which – so it was said – teams of e-therapists and human analysts were struggling to lift him. That a man with his finger on the nuclear trigger should believe that the world was inevitably doomed – that life wasn't worth living, that it may as well be concluded now – was, well, worrying. One beneficial side-effect of the Bonfire strictures, oddly, was that you could rely on confidentiality rather more than in the past, so that information and speculation like this gained a wider currency . . .

There was a soft knock on the door. Bonfire cops. She hastily incinerated the note and let them in.

They came every hour, roughly, at irregular times. This time she had to endure a recording-gear sweep. It was brisk, thorough, humourless.

It was all part of the Bonfire, a massive national – indeed international – exercise in paper-shredding and data-trashing. Maura was allowed to keep no records beyond a calendar day. Everything had to be hand-written and incinerated after use; not even carbon copies were permitted. Federal records – anything to do with Bootstrap, the Blues, the Carter phenomena – were being burned or wiped.

Even beyond the bounds of the federal government, tapes and paper archives relating to the various incidents were being impounded and destroyed. Data mining routines, legal and illegal, were being sent out to trash computer records.

Of course there were standalone machines that couldn't be reached by any of these means. But even these were being dealt with. For instance there were ways to monitor the operation of computers within buildings, using water pipes as giant antennae. There were even outlandish Star Wars-type proposals coming out of the military, such as to drench the planet in magnetic-media-wiping particle beams.

All of this was incidentally doing a hell of a lot of damage to the economy, making the day the Dow Jones bust through 100,000 – blowing up all the computer index stores in the process – seem like a picnic.

The objective was simple, however. It was to remove *all* records of the Nevada Blue centre, of the nuclear cleansing there, of Cruithne, of the battle on the Moon.

The physical evidence would linger for decades. But it was essential that no record remain to contradict the official cover stories concocted by the FBI: the big lie about the rogue Army officer, the piece of hostage-taking terrorism in Nevada whose attempted resolution had gone horribly wrong, the drastic accidental explosion which had wrecked NASA's (purely scientific) Moon base, and so on.

Of course even if every record was expunged, the truth would still exist, in the heads and hearts of those involved. And so everybody with any significant knowledge – especially those, herself included, who had actually seen the Nevada centre and had witnessed the failed 'cleansing' operation – was under special scrutiny. There had been the public trials at which they had been forced to deny the truth of Carter, Cruithne, the Blues, all the rest. Even after that she was searched on entering and leaving the building, and she knew she was under heavy and constant surveillance.

But still, as long as the memories existed, how could it be certain that not one of them, for the rest of their lives, would betray the great lie? Maura, depressed, could imagine an FBI lab somewhere even now cooking up a grisly high-tech mind cleansing method, whose respect for the subject would be a lot less important than its efficacy. And there was always the simplest way of all: the bullet in the back of the head . . .

There were, in fact, rumours of suicides already. People dying for what they knew, what they remembered.

The Bonfire had two goals. The first was simply crowd control. The extreme reactions to Malenfant's wild broadcasts of future visions and time-paradox messages and doom-soon predictions had made authorities, all around the planet, wary of how to handle such information from now on. Bluntly, it didn't matter if the world was coming to an end a week on Tuesday; for now, somebody had to keep sweeping the streets. So Malenfant's information was being diminished, ridiculed, faked up to look like clumsy hoaxes. In the end – the e-psychologists promised – anybody who clung to the bad news from the future would start to look like a Cassandra: doomed to know the future, but powerless to do anything about it.

Not everybody was going to be fooled by all this. But that wasn't the real point. Bonfire's true purpose was to fool the future. It was essential that the balance of evidence bequeathed to future historians was not sufficient to *prove* that the people of twenty-first century America had gone to war with their children.

Despite the personal difficulty, the infringement of various rights, Maura supported this huge project. This was, after all, a matter of national security. More than that, in fact: it was essential to the future of the species itself.

The US government seemed to have fallen into a war with indefinable superbeings of the future. The only weapon at its disposal was the control of the information to be passed to future generations. And the government was pursuing that project with all the resources it could command – attempting to blindside the downstreamers before they were even born.

The battle wasn't completely impossible. There were precedents in history, some academics were pointing out. Almost of all history was a carefully constructed mythology, for use as propaganda or nation-building. The writers of the Gospels had spun out the unpromising story of a Nazarene carpenter-preacher into an instrument to shape the souls of mankind, all the way to and beyond the present day. Shouldn't the modern US government, with all the techniques and understanding at its disposal, be able to do infinitely better yet?

But Maura had a premonition, deep and dark, that it was a war the present couldn't win. The artefact on Cruithne, now in irradiated quarantine, and especially the spacetime bubble on the Moon, were *there*: real, undeniable. And so, in the end, was the truth.

The cops left her.

There was one more report on her desk. She skimmed it briefly, held it out to the incinerator.

Then she put it back on her desk, picked up her phone, and called Dan Ystebo.

'News from the Trojans,' she told him. 'One of NASA's satellites has picked up anomalous radiation. Strongly red-shifted.' She read out details, numbers.

My God. You know what this means?

'Tell me.'

The squid are leaving, Maura . . . He talked, fast and at length, about what had become of his enhanced cephalopods. *I guess he doesn't get the chance too often,* Maura thought sadly.

. . . We know they've spread out through the cloud of Trojans. We can only guess how many of them there are right now. The best estimate is in excess of a hundred billion. And it may be they are all cooperating. A single giant school. Do you know why the numbers are significant? A hundred billion seems to be a threshold . . . It takes a hundred billion atoms to organize to form a cell. It takes a hundred billion cells to form a brain. And maybe a hundred billion cephalopod minds, out in the Trojans, just light-minutes apart, have become something –

'Transcendent.'

Yes. We can't even guess what it must be like, what they're capable of now. Any more than a single neurone could anticipate what a human mind is capable of. Space is for the cephalopods, Maura. It never was meant for us.

His voice, his bizarre speculation, was a noise from the past for Maura. *It's all receding,* she thought. She sighed. 'I think it no longer makes a difference one way or the other, Dan. And you ought to be careful who you discuss this with.'

. . . Yes.

'Where are you working now?'

Brazzaville. I got a job in the dome here. Biosphere reclamation.

'Rewarding.'

I guess. Life goes on . . . Those redshift numbers. The cephalopods must be leaving at close to lightspeed.

'Where do you think they are going?'

Maybe that isn't the point, Maura. Maybe the point is what they are trying to flee.

At the end of the day she sat quietly at her desk, studying the Washington skyline. She snapped off the noise filters, so the chants and banners of the protesters outside became apparent.

There was still much to do. The immediate future, regardless of Carter, was as dangerous as it had ever been. And the temptation many people seemed to feel to sacrifice their freedom to stern utopians who promised to order that future for them was growing stronger.

Maura, with a sinking heart, thought the loss of significant freedom might be impossible to avoid. But she could strive, as she always had, to minimize the harm.

Or maybe that was a fight too far for her.

If she left Washington now she wouldn't be missed, she realized. She had few friends. Friendship was fragile here, and easily corroded. Not married, no partner, no children. Was she lonely, then?

Well, perhaps.

For a long time she had been, simply, so *busy*, even before this Malenfant business had blown up to consume her life, that she sensed she had forgotten who she was. She sometimes wondered what had kept her here for so long. Were her precious values – formed in a place and time far away from here – just a cover for deeper needs? Was there some deeper inadequacy within, a dissatisfaction she had wrestled to submerge with relentless activity, all these years?

If that was so, perhaps now, when she was left stranded by age and isolation, she would have to face herself for the first time.

She looked out her window, and there was the Moon in the daylit sky. Beneath her the planet turned; sun and Moon and stars continued to wheel through the sky. She felt lifted out of herself, transcending her small concerns, as if she was a mouse running around some grand, incomprehensible clockwork.

There was a knock on the door.

Maura despatched the NASA report to the incinerator, and let in the cops once more.

Emma Stoney:

. . . fell into grey light.

Watch the Moon, Malenfant. Watch the Moon. It's starting –

For a moment, a brief, painful moment, she thought she was with Malenfant – where? Cruithne?

But she had never been to Cruithne, never left Earth before this jaunt to the Moon to inspect Never-Never Land on Maura's behalf. And Malenfant, of course, was long dead, killed when the troopers stormed Cruithne.

And the Blue children of the Moon were all around her, clutching her hands and clothes, lifting her.

She started to remember. The German blue helmet, his assault on her. The escape into the children's electric-blue spacetime anomaly wall.

She looked around for whoever it was who had called out, but couldn't see him.

They lowered her carefully – onto what? some kind of smooth floor – and then the children started to move away, spreading out.

She was lying on a plain, featureless, perfectly flat. The air was hot, humid, a little stale. Too hot, in fact, making her restless, irritable.

There was nothing before her: no electric-blue wall, no far side to this unreality bubble, which should have been just a couple of yards away. She reached out a hand, half-expecting it to disappear through some invisible reality interface. But it didn't.

She pushed herself upright. The pain was, briefly, as blackly unendurable as before, and she lay where she was, longing for unconsciousness. But it didn't come. And the pain, somehow, started to recede, like a tide imperceptibly turning.

The children were scattering over the plain. The greyness and lack of contrast washed out the colours of the children's skin and clothes and made them look ill. They seemed to be receding from her, remarkably quickly, perspective diminishing them to tiny running figures. Maybe this place was bigger than it looked.

The sky was an elusive greyness, blank and featureless. There was no sense of distance – no sign of stars, of sun or Earth or orbiting spacecraft, no clouds. The light was shadowless, sourceless.

As they moved further away from her the children seemed to grey out completely, fading to black, as if there was something wrong with the light. There was nothing beyond the children, no fences or buildings, all the way to the horizon. Except there was no horizon. The floor simply merged into the remote greyness of the sky. It was like being inside a huge glass bulb.

Maybe this whole damn thing is some kind of near-death experience, she thought. An illusion.

But it didn't feel like it. And her restless brain kept analysing, observing.

There were little piles of gear: bright primary-colour plastic toys, what looked like heaps of bedding or clothes, food packets and water bottles. There was one more substantial structure, a shack-like assemblage of wires and cables and bits of metal. A Tinkerbell cage, a quark nugget trap. But there was no order, no logic to the layout. Stuff just seemed to have been dumped where it was last used. If it wasn't for the sheer size of the place, it would be a pig pen.

But then she was looking at this place through adult eyes. It was just a kids' playroom, writ large.

Somebody spoke. The words were muffled.

She turned. There was Anna, standing solemnly, her hands at her sides, regarding her. The girl seemed greyed out, like the other children.

Emma tried to shout. 'I can't hear you!' There was a dull deadness to the sound, like an anechoic booth.

Anna began to run towards her. She seemed to approach remarkably quickly, growing in perspective with every lunar-hop stride, the colours washing back into her clothes and hair. In a few seconds she was at Emma's side.

'Sorry,' she said. 'I just asked if you wanted a drink.' She held out a clear plastic carton containing a gloopy orange liquid.

Emma's throat was, now she thought about it, rapidly growing dry in this sticky heat. 'Thanks.' She took the drink, pulled off a foil tab, and sucked the liquid out of the carton. It was a fruit juice mix, sticky and heavily sweet.

'How do you feel?' Anna asked.

She looked down at her shattered leg. The pain had diminished so steeply the limb no longer seemed to be a part of her, as if she was studying some broken piece of machinery. 'Not better, exactly,' she said. 'But –'

'The pain can't reach you,' Anna said gravely. 'But it is still there. You should be careful.' She was studying Emma. 'Do you know who you are?'

Emma frowned. 'I'm Emma Stoney.'

'Do you know why you're here?'

Strange questions, like a doctor's. Go with the flow, Emma. 'I'm with the UN. I report to Maura Della. I've been working with the Blues, with you, since Malenfant pushed me away in the Mojave to go fly his spaceship, and Bootstrap was broken up, and Malenfant died in space . . .' She had been fixing things, righting some of the wrongs Malenfant left behind. Everything, of course, defined by her relationship to Malenfant, even though the man had been dead five years. 'Maura sent me here.'

You married a spaceman, Maura had said to Emma. *Now's your*

429

chance to do the Buck Rogers stuff yourself. If not for you I'd go myself. But I'm too old to fly . . .

And so she had come to the Moon. And now – this.

Anna folded her thin legs with an enviable ease and sat squat-legged with her. 'That's right,' she said solemnly.

'What do you mean?'

'It doesn't matter now.'

Emma stroked the floor. The surface was smooth, seamless, warm, and it gave a little, like rubber. Like the floor of a playpen, or maybe an insane asylum, she thought sourly. She eyed Anna. 'This place is strange,' she said. 'Distances are funny. It was like I was watching you through a fisheye lens.'

Anna frowned. 'What's a fisheye lens?'

'Never mind.'

'Of course distances are funny,' Anna said. 'Everything here is folded up.' She waved a hand at the blank plain, the neon-tube sky. 'How else could we fit all of this into that little bubble you saw?'

'Are we still on the Moon?'

'Oh, yes. Or rather we are still *connected* to the Moon. Actually the geometry here is hyperbolic. An infinite volume contained within a finite circumference.' Anna reached up, her fingers flexing towards the horizon. 'The walls are infinitely far away, and six feet away, at the same time. Minutes pass in here, while two centuries pass on the outside.' She was watching Emma sympathetically.

Well, it didn't matter whether Emma understood or not. It was just that this place, it seemed, was to be the end of the road, for the children, for herself. Whatever happened from now on, there was no going back: back to the world she had grown up in, with its comfortable furniture of sky and clouds and leather armchairs and other adults and, for Christ's sake, coffee – one last cup of coffee, instead of this sickly orange syrup . . . She felt she would give her soul for that. Better yet, one last tequila sunrise.

Two centuries, Anna had said.

Anna's eyes were empty, watchful. She knows the significance, Emma thought. It's real; it's happening; that's why we're here.

I've been fast-forwarded in time, to Carter Day.

Fear clutched her heart.

Now the children were coming back. Some of them carried toys – dolls, even a toy gun. One boy came pedalling on a small plastic bicycle, adapted for the Moon with fat mesh wheels.

'This has been a good place to cycle,' Anna said dreamily. 'Of course that's why we built it this way.'

'You built a toy universe so you could ride your bikes?'

She grinned at Emma. 'If you were ten years old and could build a universe, what would you do?'

Emma frowned. 'It's been a long time since I was ten.' And, she realized, at some point I forgot how it is to be a kid. How very sad.

As the children neared they loomed, unnaturally quickly, and the grey flatness washed out of them. Emma could smell them, their hot, moist little bodies, a playground smell, comforting here in this bright grey-white light-bulb unreality. Billie Tybee, seven years old, reached out a hand. Emma took it. The small hand was warm, perfect in hers.

Anna stood up.

'Is it time?'

Anna said, 'Soon.'

Emma began to struggle to her feet. 'Then let's get it over.'

'Oh,' said Anna, 'it isn't waiting for *us*.'

Little Billie Tybee was still clutching her hand. Emma relaxed her grip, trying to release her, but the little girl held on. So Emma limped forward awkwardly, helped by the older children, leaning to hold hands with Billie.

Emma looked back the way they had come. She tried to remember the place she had arrived here, the location of the invisible gateway back to her own familiar universe. Surely if there was any way out of here it would be from there. But the surface was as smooth and featureless as bare skin.

She sighed. Forget it, Emma. Where you came from isn't important any more. Where you're going to, however, is.

She found herself shaking.

Was not knowing, not understanding, making this experience so much harder to bear? But if she did know – if the kids were dragging her towards some folded-spacetime equivalent of an electric chair, if she knew every detail of how her life was going to end – would that be any easier?

The party resumed its slow hike across the featureless plain. Piles of kipple, clothes and toys and food packets, seemed to swim around them, the distances melting and merging in this folded place.

They were slowly nearing the one substantial structure on the plain, the shack-like structure of metal and wire she had noticed earlier. It was indeed a Tinkerbell trap: an electromagnetic cage made of junkyard garbage, capable of containing a chunk of quark matter. Like the prototypes, she could see how this cage had been made by the hands of children, a thing of lengths of wire and metal and bits of plastic clumsily twisted together.

But however crude its construction the cage evidently worked, for there was a Tinkerbell in there, a hovering point of light. It seemed to be following a complex path, darting back and forth, slowing as it reached maybe six inches from the centre of the motion, then slipping back. Emma tried to pick out a periodicity in the motion. Perhaps there were many oscillations here, overlaying each other in three-dimensional space.

The children slowed, broke up as they reached the cage. Anna and the others lowered Emma carefully to the floor; though littered with scraps of wire, the floor was as featureless and unpleasantly warm here as where she had first emerged. Billie Tybee sat on the floor beside her now, cuddling up close.

One little boy walked around the back of the cage, and Emma heard a gentle splashing, glimpsed a thin stream of yellowish liquid.

Anna squatted on her haunches. She asked Emma, 'Are you still okay?'

'So you built another Tinkerbell cage. More quark matter?'

'Oh, no. Not yet. That stuff isn't quark matter. Can't you tell? . . . I don't suppose you can.'

'Then what?'

'It's yolk,' Anna said. 'Yolk, from an egg star.'

'A what?'

Billie sighed with all the seriousness a seven-year-old could muster. 'She means,' she said, pronouncing the words carefully, 'a neutron star.'

'But it's *like* an egg,' Anna said. 'The collapsed remains of a supernova. Solid outside and a lot of funny liquids churning around on the inside.'

'And that's what this stuff is? This Tinkerbell? A droplet of neutron star matter?'

'Only a billion tons or so,' Anna said. 'Originally material from the Moon.'

'Tell me what you want with it.'

'We don't want *it*,' Billie said seriously, and she wiped her nose on Emma's sleeve.

Anna said, 'What we want is what it will become. The degenerate matter is, umm, a fuse. In a moment a fragment of true quark matter will arrive.'

'From where?' Emma asked.

But Anna didn't answer that. She said, 'When the nucleus of quark matter enters the fuse, it will quickly develop an equilibrium strangeness content via weak interactions, and free neutrons will be absorbed as there is no Coulomb barrier –'

'Anna, my dear, I don't understand a damn word.'

'The fuse will turn into quark matter very rapidly, all of it.'

Emma remembered a briefing Dan Ystebo had prepared for Maura. A neutron star flashing to quark matter. Half its mass being converted to energy in a few seconds. Explosions so vigorous they could be observed from another galaxy.

'In fact,' the girl said with an element of pride, 'the degenerate matter droplet has been shaped so that its collapse will be concentrated. At the very centre of the droplet, in a space smaller than a proton, we will reach higher energy densities even than at the hearts of collapsing neutron stars. Higher energy densities than can form anywhere, naturally. Densities that need intelligence, design, to occur.'

'Jesus. *Why*, Anna? What are you trying to do? Blow up the Moon?'

'Oh, no,' said Anna, a little impatiently. 'Not *just* that. The point is not the amount of energy that's released here, but the precision of its application.'

'Which is why,' Emma said with growing dread, 'you are calling this thing a fuse. You're intending to use this to trigger something else. Something much bigger. Aren't you?'

Anna smiled happily. '*Now* you're starting to understand,' she said brightly.

Seven-year-old Billie turned her sweet, round face up to Emma. She said carefully, 'Vacuum collapse. Are you afraid?'

Emma swallowed. 'Yes. Yes, I am, Billie. But I don't know what I'm afraid of.' Now Emma saw the kid's lower lip was wobbling. Emma bent, painfully, and leaned towards Billie. 'Tell you what,' she said. 'It's okay to cry. But I'll try not to if you try not to. What do you think?'

And then – suddenly, without warning or fanfare – it began.

Reid Malenfant:

Here was Malenfant, drifting in space.

He remembered how he had grabbed Emma, coaxed her, forced her onto the *O'Neill* to be with him. And he remembered how he had pushed her away, protected her with lies, left her on Earth.

He remembered how he had made love to her in the darkness and silence of space. And he remembered how he had started awake, weightless and disoriented, looking for her, and she had not been there, never had been there.

He remembered how she had come with him on his strange journey through the manifold of universes. And he remembered how he had journeyed alone, lost, frightened, incomplete.

He remembered how she had learned the truth about him at last. He remembered how she had died in his arms. He remembered how much he had missed her, longed to have her back, to *tell* her.

He remembered how he wanted it all: his relationship with Emma, to spare her pain, his glorious future vision. And he'd finished with none of it.

The change was done, the timelines rewoven. But, by God, it had cost him.

Malenfant turned his head, refocused his eyes' new zoom feature, and there was the Moon, swimming alongside the Earth as it always had. Beautiful doomed Earth.

'Shit,' he said. 'It's the end of the world. And all I can think about is myself.'

What else is there?

'. . . The downstreamers. Are they gods?'

No. They're just people.

'That's hard to believe.'

But the human race is very old. They would not recognize you.

'Why not?'

Because your time was very strange. Really, it was still part of the Big Bang, the afterglow. Bright.

'What are they like?'

They are diverse. As diverse as you and me. More. But they have one thing in common. These are the people who chose to live on.

'There were others who chose death? Why?'

Because there are problems with the substrate. It is not infinite in size. No computer can exceed the limits set by the Bekenstein Bound.

'The what?'

It's difficult to talk to you when you know nothing.

'Sorry.'

The uncertainty principle, then. You know about that. Because of the uncertainty principle, a given amount of mass and energy can only assume a finite number of quantum states. So the number of different states achievable is bounded above by the number of states achievable by the whole universe, if all its mass and energy were converted to information, which has not occurred. The number is ten to power ten to power one hundred and twenty-three –

'Ten to power ten to power one hundred and twenty-three, huh. And that's the number of possible thoughts, inside this computer. Is that what you're telling me?'

Yes! The substrate is a finite state machine. It can take only a fixed number of states, and it works in discrete time intervals. A finite state machine must, after long enough, enter a periodic state. That is –

'They live the same lives,' said Malenfant. 'Even think the same thoughts. Over and over. My God, what a fate.' Like autism, he thought. '*Why?*'

The kid sighed. *There was no other way for mind to survive the Heat Death.*

The same thoughts over and over, circulating like farts in a space-suit. What a destiny, what an end to all hope, what a culmination to all those universes painfully evolving to the point where they could support life and mind, the uncounted years of struggling to survive in *this* universe . . . What an end, he thought, to my own grandiose projects.

But Cornelius would have loved it. Sanity, control forever, no change. Just an endless cycle of sameness.

Michael was watching him. *You understand.*

'Understand what?'

Why the . . . Feynman project was initiated.

'The portals? The messages upstream?'

There are some who do not believe it was meant to be like this. That life, humanity, had a different purpose.

'You're telling me we have a *purpose*?'

Oh, yes. Humans are the most important sentient creatures who have ever existed, or will ever exist.

That sent a shudder down Malenfant's spine. *God damn it, I waited all my life to hear someone tell me that. And now I have, it terrifies me.*

'So these downstreamers of yours have reached back in time and changed things, created another timeline, in which –'

Michael frowned. *Your language is like noise. But you are more right than wrong. Yes, I can say that. But there are no such things as* timelines. *There is a universal wave function which determines a sheaf of paths –*

'I heard all that before, and didn't understand it then . . . Earth. Do they know what's going to happen?'

People are, umm, at peace, Malenfant. In a way they weren't in your day.

'Even now, as the lights are going out?'

Even now.

'But, no matter how prosperous and contented and understanding they are, they're all going to die. All the people on Earth, and the Moon and Mars and wherever else the hell they got to . . . Tell me about Earth, Michael.'

Michael smiled, and Malenfant heard voices.

AD 2051:

In Britain, and other parts of the European Federal Union, God is dead. Or if not dead, irrelevant.

Believe me, Monsignor, I know. I just got back from a year's assignment in London. Religious practice and belief has genuinely collapsed, on a mass scale.

It's clear that the absorption of the Carter message in some corners of the world has led to a kind of group despair, the feeling that nothing is worth struggling for. In Britain, this is manifesting itself in a denial of any external basis for moral action. Essentially the Brits are redesigning the moral basis of their community. They are appealing to such philosophical doctrines as ethical relativism – weighing moral codes relative to each other and not against any imagined absolute – and emotivism, acting on a gut response to injustices and so forth – and prescriptivism, relying on the announcement of appropriate moral standards based on human authority without appeal to a higher or external source.

That the British state is holding together at all, that it hasn't all lapsed into barbarism or chaos, is probably some kind of tribute to the basic British character. But then, just as the Brits were the first industrial society, so they became, arguably, our first post-industrial culture. Similarly they are comparatively recently post-imperial. Now they seem to be becoming the first truly post-religious nation.

Strange that a country we think of as being staid and old-fashioned should once more be forging the way into an unknown future.

Will the Brits survive? Will they tear each other apart? I find myself hoping they have a chance to grope their way out of this darkness, to find the end of their story, before the curtain falls on us all in a couple of hundred years – assuming it's all gloomily true, of course.

But maybe these are controversial views for a Jesuit. We are all, after all, missionaries.

I'm recommending the Vatican funds further missions, a presence. We have to go in there and talk about God, as well as study this new phenomenon. But how much good it will do – or even what 'good' means in this context – is hard to judge . . .

AD 2079:

You must not be alarmed. You must understand why extreme force was required to quell the unrest in this neighbourhood. Orientation classes like this are provided as a service to help you come to terms with the losses you have suffered, and your long-term injuries.

Unrest is fuelled by nostalgia for an imagined 'better time', when America governed herself, there was economic growth and fast cars and cheap food, and so forth.

But you must *not* be nostalgic. Nostalgia is harmful.

Look at the big picture. Earth has passed through the Malthusian bottleneck. We avoided major war, and more than three billion souls have passed into a better future. The others, on the whole, met their end with dignity, and we salute them.

Today Earth is stable.

We have become a closed-loop economy, a giant spaceship. From the surface of the Earth, raw materials production and energy production have all but disappeared, along with the damage they did – particularly pollution through mining, refining, transportation, combustion, waste disposal. It is important to understand that the amount of key commodities such as metals and glass in circulation at any moment is constant. The only requirement is an input of energy, which is largely provided from the orbiting solar power plants and the quark nugget installations.

Certainly there are costs. The standard of living of some is not as high as it once was. But the standard of living of us *all* is about equivalent to the well-off of Soviet Russia, circa 1970: that is, beyond the dreams of much of mankind for much of our history.

Economic growth is not possible. But growth was always an illusion, bought only by exploiting other people or the Earth's irreplaceable resources or burning up our children's future. Now we are mature.

Consider the indicators the UN uses to measure our wealth and happiness today.

We count more than simple economic facts. We measure the health and education and even the joy of our children. We consider the beauty of our poetry and our art, the strength of our families, the intelligence and integrity of our public debate. In a very real sense we are measuring our courage, wisdom, learning and compassion: everything that makes life worth living. And by every such measure the world is a better place.

You are not as free as your grandfather was to foul up the neighbourhood, or to own three cars. But what would you want with such freedoms?

Some say the UN has become undemocratic. But the control required to run the planet today would be impossible without the powerful central authority wielded by the UN.

What would happen to us without central control?

Remember the lesson of history. Easter Island – remote, cut off – was a close analogy to our present situation, a human population essentially isolated within a finite resource.

The islanders bred until they had destroyed their biosphere. Then, starving, they almost killed each other off in the resulting wars.

So do not mourn freedom. Freedom was an illusion, paid for by the death of others less fortunate. Today you have the freedom to live in peace, and not to starve.

Support us. We will save you from yourself. After all, without us, things would be a lot worse.

And, incidentally, Peacekeepers are not police. They merely reinforce the popular will. There is a difference.

AD *2102*:

. . . But what we call the biosphere – yes, make a note of the word – was left badly depleted before the end. There was a great wave of extinctions which, ultimately, couldn't be stopped. How bad was it? Well, Oona, we don't really know. We didn't even get as far as counting all the species before destroying them. Yes, that's right; a lot of species must have died out before we even knew they were there. Shivery thought, isn't it?

The sea fared a little better than the land. We lost some species, mostly from overfishing and from the dumping of pollutants, and washed-off topsoil in the shallow waters around the coastlines. But today things are fairly stable. In fact there are enhanced cephalopods, squid and octopuses, managing the big undersea farms for us now.

Still, it was a severe extinction, in historical terms. Worse than the one which wiped out the dinosaurs, sixty-five million years ago. Not as bad as the one at the end of the Permian.

Now, of course, we live in a world where evolution has been ended, and the future depends on conscious management by . . .

No, Maisie, I never saw a chimp or a gorilla, so I can't tell you what it would have been like. Now *you* are the only surviving primate species. Anyhow I'm just an e-person. I don't know how it would have *felt* to meet your cousin like that: like you, yet not quite you.

I can make a guess, though.

AD 2147:

So there is fifty years to go before the Carter firework show and the population is increasing, despite all the UN can do to discourage us.

Sure is in my house.

What, you're surprised?

Look, for a long time many people accepted the UN below-replacement-number childbirth guidelines – and a lot even went further, having no kids at all – because they were depressed about the future. That is, they didn't expect there to *be* any future. It seemed unfair, maybe even immoral, to bring kids into a situation like that. After all, you never treated anyone unfairly by leaving them unborn, because they never existed to suffer in the first place. Right?

Well, the world may be heading for the iceberg, but the dead hand of old Darwin is still on the tiller.

What am I talking about? Just this: if *most* people stop breeding, the handful of people who love kids and want to have them – people like me – are, within a generation or two, going to outnumber everyone else. Simple math.

And that's exactly what is happening.

439

Friend, I'm your neighbourhood representative of a new species: *Homo Philoprogenitus*, which means 'lover of many children'. As you can see, or maybe hear.

I pay my UN fines. For me they are worth it. A happiness tax. What's money for?

Sure, if Carter is right, these kids are not going to live to a ripe old age. But it's better for them to have existed and been happy than not existed. What are we here for except to add to the sum total of human happiness-days? Right?

And besides, I plan to be around to usher in Carter Day too. We'll probably have one hell of a party. By then there will be nobody left around but us *H Phils*, and we're a friendly bunch.

You'll be invited. Bring the wife and kids. Oh, they're e-kids? Yes, I know, a comfort. Never worked for me. Bring the dog, then. He's not an e-pooch too, is he? Hey, you still up for poker Tuesday night?

AD 2198:

You have to understand that Christianity has always been built on certain primal mythic elements. Fundamentally there is the Holy Family, in the shape of Father, Mother and Child. And the character of the Child, Jesus, has always been at the forefront of Christian consciousness. As in other myth structures the Child represents renewal – the spring-like rebirth of life after death, here of course standing for the renewal we all hope for in the arms of God, as further symbolized by Christ's resurrection after his own physical death.

But, it seems, we are a generation doomed to live in the end time. We live in a world without hope of renewal: ten more springs, and then the final winter will descend on us all, leaving us without hope.

Where, then, is the relevance of the Christian mythos for us, whom God has abandoned?

The relevance is in the character of Mary, Mother of Jesus.

Mary stood and mourned at the foot of the Cross. Even as her Son gave His life for mankind, so He abandoned His Mother.

So, today, we reject the grandiose and selfish ambitions of the Son, and embrace the grief of Mary, the Mother He abandoned.

For we, too, have been abandoned. We draw strength from Mary's dignity in betrayal. We are no longer Christians. We are Marians.

Let us pray.

AD 2207:

It is the best of times, and the worst of times. Who wrote that?
. . . It does not matter. We have been drawn together by the tragedy;
that is clear. Those of us who have a glimmering of understanding
– who see that even the awesome destruction to come is merely a
stage in the endless evolution of life and mind, as regrettable but
inevitable as the death of an individual, just as the Blues tried to
teach us – are consoled, even if we cannot comprehend it fully. And
we do not condemn the Ocean Children, who have fled into the
bright comfort of mindlessness. The world spins on, full of heroism
and selfishness and despair, just as it always has. The children have
been a comfort, of course. A preliminary perusal of history shows
that, and the happy lack of any Blue births after the Nevada event
. . . I apologize. Even now I am more prepared to analyse history
than to talk about myself, about us! Well. There is no more to say.
We are here together. We choose to end it now, rather than submit
to the arbitrariness of history. Goodbye, my darling, goodbye.

AD 2208:

Where were you on The Night?

If you're reading this, it must be over, and you survived. Right?

As I'm recording this there are twenty-four hours to go.

I can tell you where I'll be. In orbit around the Moon.

For two centuries people have been probing and prodding and
cracking at that damn energy bubble up there. Of course they've
had no success. But that hasn't stopped them trying. And it won't
stop me now, right to the end.

I might even meet my uncle and aunt up there. Tom and Billie
Tybee. My grandfather, Bill Tybee, left me this diary, which he kept
from the day he was first married, and even the gadget, the little
plastic Heart, which taught us all so much about our Blue cousins.
Hell of a guy, my uncle. Lost his wife, lost both kids to the Blue
hysteria, survived a war on the Moon, and still built a life: married
again, more kids – none of them Blue – and died in his bed.

People tell us we're at peace. We're all just waiting, praying if
we choose to, otherwise just turning out the lights. Calm, dignified
acceptance.

Yeah, right.

For me, I mean to go out of this world the way I came in: dragged
out head first, kicking and screaming.

Anyhow this will probably be the last entry. I'm burying the diary in hardcopy a hundred feet down in a disused mine. If it gets to survive anywhere, it will be there.

Godspeed.

Michael:

Watch the Moon, Malenfant. Watch the Moon. It's starting –

Emma Stoney:

A bolt of light streaked vertically down from the grey dome sky above. It headed straight for the degenerate matter, merged with it unerringly.

The children made sounds like it was a firework display. *Ooh. Aah.*

Anna's gaze was fixed on the Tinkerbell nugget in its cage; Emma saw its light sparkling in her clear eyes. And the Tinkerbell was getting brighter.

'How long?'

'A few minutes,' Anna whispered. 'This is what we were born to do. It is what *you* were born for –'

A wave of pain, unexpected, pulsed from Emma's leg, and she gasped.

Billie Tybee pulled away from her, eyes wide.

Emma made an effort to calm down. She deliberately smiled. Billie crept slowly back to her, and Emma laid a hand on her head.

They may be about to kill you. Even so, don't frighten the children. It surely isn't their fault.

'Vacuum decay,' she said to Anna.

'Yes –'

'Will it be quick?'

Anna thought that over. 'More than quick. The effects will spread at lightspeed, transforming everything to the true vacuum state.' She studied Emma. 'Before you know it's happening, it will be over.'

Emma took a deep breath. She didn't understand a word; it was so abstract it wasn't even frightening. *Thank God I'm no smarter,*

442

she thought. 'Okay. How far will it reach? Will it engulf Tycho? The Moon?'

Anna frowned. 'You *don't* understand.'

And the droplet exploded.

Emma flinched.

The cage held. Light flared, a baseball-sized lump, dazzling Emma, bathing the faces of the watching children, as if they were planets turned to this new sun.

Billie was cuddling closer, wrapping her arms around Emma's waist. Emma put her hands on the child's head and bent over her to shelter her. 'It's okay,' she said. 'It's okay to be frightened.'

The light got brighter.

'Nearly, now,' Anna said softly.

'*Why*, Anna? Revenge?'

Anna turned to her. 'You don't understand. You never will. I'm sorry. This isn't destruction. This isn't revenge. This is –'

'What?'

'It's *wonderful*.'

Emma felt heat on her face, a wind, hot air pulsing out of the cage, fleeing the heat of the Tinkerbell.

Now more children came creeping closer to Emma. She reached out her arms and tried to embrace them all. Some of them were weeping. And maybe she was weeping too; it was hard to tell.

At last even Anna came to her, buried her face in Emma's neck.

She thought of Malenfant: Malenfant on Cruithne, defying fate one last time. She might easily have been with him, up there, sharing whatever had become of him. Even at their worst times, the depths of the divorce, she had expected, in her heart, to die with him.

But it hadn't turned out like that, for better or worse.

In the years after Mojave, after Malenfant, Emma had had relationships. She'd even inherited some children, from previous broken relationships. None of her own, though. Maybe this was as close as she had ever come.

But the children around her seemed remote, as if she touched them through a layer of glass. She felt incomplete. Maybe she was spread too thin over the possibilities of reality, she thought.

The light grew brighter, the heat fiercer. The wind was beginning to howl through the loose, shuddering framework of the cage.

The children whimpered and pushed closer to Emma.

There was a blue flare. Through the tangle of the Tinkerbell cage, Emma glimpsed an electric-blue ring, distorted, twisting away. And more of them, a great chain disappearing to infinity, a ribbed funnel of blue light. Sparks flared, shooting out of the blue tunnel, disappearing into the remote grey dome of sky.

They're reaching into the past, Emma thought, wondering. Sending off the quark nuggets that reached the centre in Nevada – even the one that initiated this event. Closed causal loops.

It was always about the children, she realized now. Not us, not Malenfant. All we did was help it along. But this has been their story all along. The children.

The light sculpture was gone, the burst of blue light vanishing like soap bubbles. Then there was only the fierce white glow of the Tinkerbell itself.

'It isn't so much energy,' Anna was murmuring. 'Not so much at all. But all of it concentrated on a single proton mass. *You* could have done this. You built particle accelerators, reached high energies. But you gave up. Besides, you were doing it wrong. You'd have needed an accelerator of galactic dimensions to get to the right energy levels –'

'We weren't trying.' Emma said. 'We didn't know we were supposed to.'

Anna looked up, her eyes wet, her hair billowing around her face. 'That's the tragedy. That you never understood the purpose of your existence.'

Emma forced a smile. 'Guess what? I still don't.'

Anna laughed, and for a moment, a last moment, she was just a kid, a fifteen-year-old girl, half-laughing, half-crying, happy, terrified.

And then the Tinkerbell exploded.

It *wasn't* instantaneous. That was the horror of it.

It washed over her, slicing her through, burning her out of her own skull. She could *feel* the modules of her brain, her mind, wiping clear, collapsing into the new vacuum beyond the light.

Until there was only the deep, old part of her brain left, the animal cowering in the dark.

Malenfant!

And the light broke through.

Reid Malenfant:

The brighter areas – the older terrain, the highlands of the near side and much of the far side – looked much as they had always done, tracing out the face of the Man in the Moon. But the seas of grey lunar dust, Imbrium and Procellarum and Tranquillity, seemed to be imploding. Even from here he could see cracks spreading in the lava seas, sections of crust cracking, tipping, sliding inwards. The Moon was two thousand miles across; given that, the speed of the process he was watching – and the scale of it, hundred-mile slabs of lunar crust crumbling in seconds – was impressive.

The Moon had companions in this moment of convulsion, he saw: bright sparks that orbited slowly, like fireflies. Ships from Earth. He sensed they were helpless.

It's beginning, murmured Michael, in his Seattle-tinged middle-aged voice.

'What is?'

The Moon is being collapsed to a new form. Quark matter. The weaker areas of the crust, the areas crushed by the ancient basin-forming impacts, are imploding first. Michael hesitated. *Do you understand? The Moon will become, briefly, a single giant nucleon, an extended sac of quarks at nuclear density which –*

'Who is doing this?'

The children, of course.

'Why, for Christ's sake?'

It is the fulfilment of mankind. Of the cosmos . . . Ah.

Now the Moon's ancient, cratered highlands were starting to crumble too. Malenfant felt a stab of regret as the Moon's bony geography collapsed into dust and light. Five billion years of stillness, Malenfant thought, ending in a few heartbeats. And we thought those Apollo footprints would last a million years.

Now a light started to shine out of the heart of the Moon, out of the eyes and mouth of the Man, as if something was burning there. He could actually see shafts of light cast through lunar dust, as if the Moon was a Halloween lantern hanging in a murky room.

And – with startling suddenness, in utter silence – the Moon imploded, shattered, burst into an expanding cloud of dust and rubble.

445

The orbiting ships were immediately overwhelmed. So, Malenfant thought, people are already dying.

The cloud began to disperse, spreading out along the Moon's orbit. Maybe, given time, it would form a new ring around the Earth, Malenfant thought. And there would be spectacular meteor showers on the Earth, skies that would burn like a salute to the death of the Moon.

But now the dispersing debris revealed a point of dazzling white light, difficult to look into even with Malenfant's mysteriously enhanced vision. The dying Moon had birthed a new star, a terrible, brilliant companion to the sun.

Just seconds now, murmured Michael, staring.

Malenfant glanced at the boy's face. The quality of light had become strange, sharper. 'Michael, what is *that* going to do to the Earth? The heat it's putting out will surely play hell with the climate. And –'

You're asking the wrong questions again, Malenfant. There will be no time for that. The quark nugget is only a tool.

'A tool to do what?'

To create a pulse of high energy density.

Malenfant longed to understand. '*How* high?'

Would the numbers mean anything to you? The most energetic particles are cosmic rays: iron nuclei fleeing the explosions of stars, moving close to the speed of light. If an apple falls from a tree to the ground, the energy it gathers is shared over its billions of billions of atoms. The most energetic cosmic rays have comparable energy focused on a single nucleus. If two such nuclei were to impact head-on the energy released would be two orders of magnitude higher again. It is believed that no such event has happened in the history of the universe.

'And the children –'

Are seeking to create an event six orders of magnitude higher even than that. There are no natural processes which could produce such a thing. This is the first time there has been a mechanism – a mind, us – to deliver such gigantic energies. In this universe or any of those preceding it.

Malenfant frowned. 'Are you saying *this* is our purpose? The purpose of man, of life, is to produce a single, unnaturally huge energy pulse, this one thing? That's *all*?'

The purpose is not the act. It is the consequence of the act.

The light in the Moon wreckage grew brighter. It flared, electric blue, and then white.

446

And the point burst, became an expanding bubble of light, pink-grey, ballooning into space. In a heartbeat it had overwhelmed the debris cloud. Malenfant glimpsed its glare in the oceans of Earth, like a terrifying new sun born out of Earth's lost companion.

But it took only a second for the bubble to grow monstrously large, fifty or sixty times the size of Earth, dwarfing the planet.

The wall of light swept across Earth, devouring it. And Earth was gone.

Malenfant grunted, the breath forced out of him. He felt as if he had been punched.

As suddenly, as quickly as that, it was over.

The bubble was growing, larger and brighter every second, a cancer that seemed to be sucking energy out of spacetime itself, and Malenfant saw its light washing over Michael's face, his round childish eyes. It was huge, startling, already dwarfing the points of light that populated the universe.

Michael said, *The interface is growing at near lightspeed. It took a little more than a second to cover the Moon's orbit to reach Earth, just a twenty-fifth of a second to cover Earth itself. After five seconds it was as large as the sun. Lightspeed is fast, Malenfant. Now we have seven or eight minutes before the wave reaches the sun. The inner planets, Venus and Mercury, will be covered before that.*

The ballooning bubble wasn't a perfect sphere, Malenfant saw absently. It was becoming blistered, growing irregularly, as if diseased. Its surface glowed pink-white and it was speckled, as if illuminated by laser light. The stars seemed to be shifting around the swelling edge, their position sliding, turning briefly to arcs of light before the shell obscured them – gravitational lensing, perhaps, as the shell distorted spacetime itself.

. . . *Earth gone*, just like that, in a fraction of a second, as if it was no more substantial than a match stalk caught in a firestorm. *Earth*, all of its billions of years of geology and life, core and mantle and oceans and drifting continents, evolution and climate: all of it gone, as if it never existed, its story over.

And the people. Billions dead, their stories summarily ended. The species already extinct, unless anybody had managed to get away to the outer planets, the stars.

He felt numb, unable to believe it. Shouldn't he have *felt* it, the brief cries of those billions of souls, caught in the middle of their lives, arguing or laughing or crying, giving birth or dying, making love or war?

Michael was watching him, as if trying to gauge his reaction. *They would have seen nothing. An instant of glowing sky, a moment of pain –*

'Michael, what's inside the bubble? What happened to Earth when it passed the barrier?'

Different physical laws. Anything of our universe that survived the unreality pulse itself would immediately decay into new forms. Physics, chemistry as we know it could not proceed.

But even this new regime, the regime of changed matter, would not persist. The energy density in there is intense, the gravity field it generates very strong. In microseconds after the nucleation – even before the bubble expanded beyond the Moon itself, when the bubble was only a mile across – a gravitational collapse started.

'Like a Big Crunch.'

Yes. But none of the slow collapse and compression you witnessed in the precursor universes, Malenfant. Immediate. This is the true vacuum, Malenfant, the final state of the universe . . .

When the universe was born, erupting out of its Big Bang, it went through a series of phase changes, the vacuum collapsing to new, more stable forms. And with each change, with the decay of each false vacuum, energy was released. Those monstrous energy pulses fuelled the initial expansion of the universe.

At last the phase changes ceased, and the universe stabilized.

But the stability it reached was false.

I was told a story of a princess who is imprisoned on top of a perfect crystal sphere. There are no iron bars to hold her there, yet she is trapped, at the sphere's highest point. As long as she stays there, at the point of maximum symmetry, she is safe. But if she steps aside in any direction, she will slip and fall. So it is with the universe. Maximum symmetry is unstable.

'But now the children have disturbed that symmetry.'

Yes. Their high energy event allowed quantum tunnelling to a state of true vacuum . . . Ah. There was a burst of light on the edge of the expanding bubble. Venus, I think . . .

The unreality wall approached the sun. The bubble was now sixteen light-minutes across, two hundred million miles wide, dwarfing the sun. But the star seemed unperturbed, even as the great hull raced towards it.

Lightspeed, Malenfant, whispered Michael. *If you were standing*

448

on the surface of the sun, you would still see stars and Earth and Moon, the last photons reflected by the planet before its destruction. The wall arrives with the light itself . . .

The wall blew across the sun, a tornado engulfing a brightly-lit farmhouse. But the sun, a million miles across, was no mere mote of rock and water and life, like Earth. The wall took three, four, five seconds, to overwhelm the sun's glowing mass. Right to the end the surviving sector of the sun kept its spherical shape, kept shining, emitting photons generated by a fusion core that had vanished into unreality seconds before.

Still, it took just heartbeats.

When the sun was gone it grew darker. A final nightfall, Malenfant thought.

And now there was only the sphere of unreality, growing ferociously and unevenly, sparkling, clumpy blisters bursting from its sides, stars curdling around its edge. Soon, he realized, it would become a wall, blanketing the universe.

There will be little to see for a while, Michael said. *It will sweep across Mars, the asteroid belt.*

'Cruithne?'

Gone already. Then, in half an hour, it will reach us.

The bubble continued to swell visibly, its light glaring.

'It's never going to stop,' Malenfant whispered. 'It will consume the Solar System, the stars –'

This isn't some local phenomenon, Malenfant. This is a fundamental change in the structure of the universe. It will never stop. It will sweep on, growing at lightspeed, a runaway feedback fuelled by the collapse of the vacuum itself. The Galaxy will be gone in a hundred thousand years, Andromeda, the nearest large galaxy, in a couple of million years. It will take time, but eventually –

'The future has gone,' Malenfant said. 'My God. That's what this means, isn't it? *The downstream can't happen now.* All of it is gone. The colonization of the Galaxy, the settlement of the universe, the long, patient fight against entropy . . .' That immense future had been cut off to die, like a tree chopped through at the root. '*Why, Michael?* Why have the children done this? Burned the house down, destroyed the future –'

Because it was the wrong future. Michael looked around the sky. He pointed to the lumpy, spreading edge of the unreality bubble. *There. Can you see that? It's already starting . . .*

'What is?'

The budding . . . The growth of the true vacuum region is not even. There will be pockets of the false vacuum – remnants of our universe – isolated by the spreading true vacuum. The fragments of false vacuum will collapse. Like –

'Like black holes.' And in that instant, Malenfant understood. 'That's what this is for. This is just a better way of making black holes, and budding off new universes. Better than stars, even.'

Much better. Much. The black holes created as the vacuum decay proceeds will overwhelm by many orders of magnitude the mere billion billion that our universe might have created through its stars and galaxy cores.

'And the long slow evolution of the universes, the branching tree of cosmoses –'

We have changed everything, Malenfant. Mind has assumed responsibility for the evolution of the cosmos. There will be many daughter universes – universes too many to count, universes exotic beyond our imagining – and many, many of them will harbour life and mind.

'. . . But we were the first.'

Now he understood. *This* was the purpose. Not the long survival of mankind into a dismal future of decay and shadows, the final retreat into the lossless substrate, where nothing ever changed or grew. The purpose of humankind – the first intelligence of all – had been to reshape the universe, in order to bud others and create a storm of mind.

We got it wrong, he thought. By striving for a meaningless eternity, humans denied true infinity. But we reached back, back in time, back to the far upstream, and spoke to our last children – the maligned Blues – and we put it right.

This is what it meant to be alone in the universe, to be the first. We had all of infinite time and space in our hands. We had ultimate responsibility. And we discharged it.

We were parents of the universe, not its children.

Michael said softly, *Isn't this why you came to Cruithne, Malenfant? To discover purpose?*

'I never understood. Not until now.'

Nevertheless you were a catalyst.

Malenfant found he was bleakly exhilarated. 'Life is no accident,' he said. 'No second-order effect, no marginal creation. *We* – small, insignificant creatures scurrying over our fragile planet, lost in the Galaxy – we *were*, after all, the centre of the universe.'

It was, in its extraordinary way, an affirmation of all he had ever believed. 'Hah,' he barked. 'Copernicus, blow it out your ass!'

... Malenfant? I think I'm scared.

Malenfant pulled the boy to him, wrapped his arms around this complex creature, the ten-year-old boy, the superbeing stranded here from a vanished future.

'Will they remember us? The children. In the new universes.'

Oh, yes, Michael said, and he smiled. He waved a hand at the bubble. *This couldn't have happened without mind. Without intelligence. Who knows? They might be able to reconstruct what we were like, how we lived our lives.*

'I hope they forgive us,' Malenfant whispered.

Sheena 47:

It was the hour.

Sheena 47 prowled through the heart of the lens-ship. On every hierarchical level mind-shoals formed, merged, fragmented, combining restlessly, shimmers of group consciousness that pulsed through the trillion-strong cephalopod community, as sunlight glimmers on water. The great shoals had abandoned their song-dreams of Earth, of the deep past, and sang instead of the huge deep future which lay ahead.

The diamond machines – transformed asteroid hulks – had worked without fault. Now the starbow arced around the lens-ship, complete and beautiful, the universe relativity-compressed to a rainbow that shone on the rippling water.

The helium-3 store, laboriously mined from the great cloud ocean of Jupiter, was all but exhausted. Sheena 47 paid a final farewell to the brave communities who had colonized those pink seas and delivered the fuel for the exodus. Those cousins had stayed behind and would soon be overwhelmed by the anomaly, but they had gone to non-existence proudly.

Now was the time. Excitement crossed the great cephalopod communities in waves, and they crowded to the huge lenticular walls to see.

And, just as they were designed to, the magnetic arms of the ramscoop opened, like the arms of a giant cephalopod itself. The intangible limbs sparkled as thin matter was hauled into its maw, to be compressed and collapsed and burned.

It was working. The lens-ship was cut loose at last of the System which had birthed it. Now its ocean was the thin, rich interstellar medium which drifted between the stars. The fuel was limitless, and the cephalopods could run forever . . .

Well, not forever, Sheena 47 knew. The great ship could approach but never exceed lightspeed; slowly, inexorably, the unreality tide must outrun the lens and wash over them all.

But, so stretched was time by their great speed, that moment was many, many generations away.

She felt a stab of regret for humanity: the flawed creatures who had given mind to the cephalopods, and who had now, it seemed, been consumed by the fire. But the cephalopods were young, hungry for time, and for them, the future was not done yet.

The ramscoop was working perfectly. The future was long and assured. The great hierarchies of mind collapsed as the cephalopods gave themselves over to a joyous riot of celebration, of talk and love and war and hunting: *Court me. Court me. See my weapons! I am strong and fierce. Stay away! Stay away! She is mine! . . .*

The city of water and light, pursued by unreality, fled into the darkness of the far downstream.

Reid Malenfant:

The bubble of glowing, laser-speckle light was looming now, a wall that cut across the universe, plummeting toward them at lightspeed. It could have been a mile away or ten million. Malenfant could feel nothing: no heat, no cold, no tug of the anomaly's monstrous gravity. Maybe he was already falling into its maw.

He wondered how long there was left. Then he put the thought aside. No more countdowns, Malenfant.

. . . *Malenfant. There's something I didn't tell you.*

'What?'

We might survive. We might get caught in one of the false-vacuum black holes. We are here, but not here, Malenfant. The information that comprises us might be preserved during –

'Where would we be? One of the new universes?'

I don't know.

'What would it be like?'

Different.

'I think I'd like that. Maybe this is just the beginning. Hold on, now –'

The unreal light grew blinding. He pressed Michael's face to his own belly, so the boy couldn't see what was coming. Malenfant grinned fiercely.

AFTERWORD

I owe Kent Joosten of the Johnson Space Center, NASA, even more gratitude than usual for his contribution to the cephalopod sections. Thanks also to Eric Brown and Simon Bradshaw for reading manuscript drafts.

* The idea that squid and other cephalopods may be intelligent is real. A recent reference is *New Scientist* of 7 June 1997; *Cephalopod Behaviour* by R.T. Hanlon and J.B. Messenger (Cambridge University Press, 1996) was a valuable source.

* The riches available to us from the asteroids and other extra-terrestrial resources, and plans to exploit those riches, are real. A good recent survey is *Mining the Sky* by John S. Lewis (Addison Wesley, 1996).

* The probabilistic Doomsday prediction called here the 'Carter catastrophe' is real. It has been well expressed by John Leslie in *The End of the World* (Routledge, 1996).

* The 'Feynman radio' idea of using advanced electromagnetic waves to pick up messages from the future is real. This has actually been attempted, for example by I. Schmidt and R. Newman (*Bulletin of the American Physical Society,* vol. 25 p. 581, 1979). And the extension of the idea to quantum mechanics (the 'transactional interpretation') is real. See John Cramer, *Reviews of Modern Physics,* vol. 58 p. 647, 1986.

* Cruithne, Earth's 'second Moon', is real. Its peculiar properties were reported in *Nature* vol. 387 p. 685, 1997.

* The 'quark nugget' idea of collapsed matter, with its potentially disastrous implications, is real. It was proposed by Edward Witten in 'Cosmic Separation of Phases', *Physical Review D*, vol. 30 p. 272, 1984.

* The physics of the possible far future drawn here is real. A classic reference is 'Time Without End: Physics and Biology in an Open Universe', Freeman Dyson, *Review of Modern Physics*, vol. 51 p. 447, 1979.

* The idea that our universe is one of an evolutionary family is real. A recent variant of the theory has been developed by Lee Smolin in his book *The Life of the Cosmos* (Oxford University Press, 1997).

* The notion of vacuum decay is real. It was explored by Piet Hut and Martin Rees in 'How Stable Is Our Vacuum?', *Nature*, vol. 302 p. 508, 1983.

The rest is fiction.

STEPHEN BAXTER
Great Missenden
February 1999